S0-ADP-735

DISCARD

ALSO BY BRIAN TOBIN:
THE RANSOM

THE

MISSING
PERSON

THE
MISSING PERSON

Brian Tobin

St. Martin's Press New York

mys
TOBIN
22

FOR VICTORIA

This novel is a work of fiction. Names, characters, places, and incidents are either the product of the author's imagination or used fictitiously. Any resemblance to actual events, locales, or persons, living or dead, is entirely coincidental.

THE MISSING PERSON. Copyright © 1994 by Brian Tobin. All rights reserved. Printed in the United States of America. No part of this book may be used or reproduced in any manner whatsoever without written permission except in the case of brief quotations embodied in critical articles or reviews. For information, address St. Martin's Press, 175 Fifth Avenue, New York, N.Y. 10010.

Design by Basha Zapatka

Library of Congress Cataloging-in-Publication Data

Tobin, Brian.
    The missing person / Brian Tobin.
        p.   cm.
    "A Thomas Dunne book."
    ISBN 0-312-11028-6 (hardcover)
    1. Missing persons—United States—Fiction.   I. Title.
PS3570.O288M57   1994
813'.54—dc20   94-1111
                                                                     CIP

First Edition: July 1994
10 9 8 7 6 5 4 3 2 1

PART ONE

1973

ONE

"HAVE YOU SEEN JANINE?"

Mrs. Smith was standing in the doorway of the apartment. In addition to the usual expression of rebuke, a smudge of dirt marred the forehead of her perfectly made-up face. Willy felt a twinge of malicious pleasure at seeing the usually polished Amanda looking foolish.

"Isn't she home?" Willy asked.

"I wouldn't be here if she were. You haven't seen her?"

She was glancing over his shoulder as if expecting to see Janine hiding in the corner.

Willy couldn't take his eyes from the dark gray smudge on her forehead. Amanda Smith was a remarkably good-looking woman, and it was obviously from her that Janine derived her own beauty.

Janine's mother faced him imperiously, waiting to be asked in.

"I haven't seen Janine," Willy said. "Maybe she ran into bad weather and stopped off somewhere. She could have decided to stay another day."

"I called the State Troopers' Barracks. The weather and roads are fine. She should have been home hours ago, even if she started late."

"Did you try calling her at school?"

Amanda sighed as though Willy's simplemindedness was too much to bear. "Of course I did. There was no answer."

Amanda Smith was going to be a pain in the ass as usual. Janine had probably been fooling around, reminiscing, having a good time. Perhaps she got a little high and decided to stay another night at Colgate. And now her mother was ready to call out the cavalry.

"May I use your phone? I want to call Howard. Maybe she's home by now."

Willy opened the door and let Mrs. Smith into the apartment. She strode through the kitchen, making a point of giving the two dirty dishes in the sink a disapproving look, and followed Willy into the dim living room. Derek and the Dominoes was playing on the stereo; the top of a Monopoly box holding half an ounce of marijuana rested on one of the speakers. Janine used the box top to sift out stems and seeds before rolling a joint. The disapproval did not leave Mrs. Smith's face, even though Willy didn't think she had noticed the pot.

Amanda picked up the phone, dialed, and held the receiver a few inches from her face as though afraid of infection.

For what he thought must be the thousandth time, Willy said to himself, "God, you're such an asshole!"

"Any word from her?" Janine's mother asked. She frowned, then barked, "Oh for God's sake, Howard, no I don't think that's a good idea."

Willy could picture Howard Smith by the phone in their spotless kitchen, stoically enduring his wife's browbeating.

"Now stay off the phone, I don't want you tying up the line," Mrs. Smith said.

What an asshole. That's a thousand and one. Amanda was talking to Howard as she would to a ten-year-old—a backward ten-year-old. Which was the way she usually spoke to Willy. Howard Smith had a Ph.D. in Mathematics; he worked for IBM in East Fishkill where he was a project manager or head systems analyst or one of those terms that meant big shot at IBM, and here was his wife explaining the obvious to him.

Howard Smith had married Amanda Smith a year, or as Janine always said, fifty-two weeks and four days after Janine's real father had died of leukemia. Though they were not related, both of Amanda's husbands' names were Smith. This minor coincidence had been a source of endless interest in Beacon, and just about every wag in town had noted that Amanda would not have to pack away her monogrammed linens and embossed stationary. In addition, Howard's middle initial was K, and Janine's father's full name, which everybody knew because it had hung on a shingle in front of his law office, had been Edward Sullivan Smith.

First, Ed Sullivan and now Howard K. Smith, the names of two television personalities. Even at the time, when he was fourteen and listening to adults gossiping, Willy had thought it incredibly moronic how people stretched to make a very tenuous connection between their names as if it betokened some weird meaning. That was Beacon for you.

Mrs. Smith hung up the phone and looked at the furniture in the living room with haughty disdain. She was incredible. Until a month ago, most of the furniture—the overstuffed couch and chair, the coffee table and lamp—had been in Amanda's basement. It had been her own living room furniture until she had redecorated four or five years ago. Now, of course, the couch would be deemed something slightly unsavory.

Amanda turned her gaze toward the window and her expression softened. The light from the street lamp outside, filtered through the bare tree branches, cast shadows on her face. She really was a beautiful woman, and Willy could see that Amanda was sincerely worried about Janine. Then in the next instant, the withering mien returned. Abruptly, she marched back into the kitchen.

"If you hear from Janine or if she drops by, call me immediately," Mrs. Smith commanded.

Hoping to annoy her, Willy ripped a sheet of paper towel from a roll and handed it to her. "Here, you've got some dirt on your forehead."

Annoying Mrs. Smith was one of the few ways he could enjoy himself when he was around her. As soon as he and Janine were married, in five weeks, he intended to start calling her Mom. That should drive her out of her mind. It would amuse Janine as well.

Mrs. Smith again gave the withering look. Could she give him any other kind? "That's not dirt, it's ashes. Today's Ash Wednesday."

Willy opened the door. "I'll call you the minute I hear from Janine."

The phone jarred him awake the next morning a little after six. Willy crawled up from the mattress on the floor, stepped over all the boxes they hadn't unpacked yet, and stumbled down the hall into the kitchen. It was freezing. With a hoarse voice, he answered the phone which, on the end of a twenty-foot cord, rested on the table.

"Have you heard from Janine?" he heard Mrs. Smith ask. Amanda considered anyone not up at dawn to be morally bankrupt, so she would think nothing of calling while it was still murky. It was one of her many irritating traits. But now, Willy heard real concern and fright in her voice.

"No," Willy murmured, beginning to feel uneasy. He had not been unduly concerned last night. Janine had told him she would get back from school Wednesday or Thursday. Earache had dropped by with some hashish and a six-pack an hour after Amanda left, and they had stayed up watching a dubbed movie about a masked, crime-fighting, Mexican wrestler named Samson.

"Do you have the number where Janine was staying?"

"I thought you called already."

Amanda sounded defensive. "It's Janine's fault."

"What are you talking about?" Willy was getting angry: it was six o'clock in the goddamn morning, he was cold, and Amanda was scaring him.

With prodding, she told Willy about her mistake, or rather the confusion that was "entirely Janine's fault." Amanda had been calling Janine's old number at school. But that number had been disconnected and just this week assigned to a new party. She had discovered this two hours ago when she woke the irate man.

"It doesn't make sense. All of Janine's roommates are still in school, why would they change their number?"

"Janine had a private line. I think they all do."

"She did?" Amanda cried, making sure Willy knew she was aghast at such extravagance.

Amanda paused, then said, "I'm going to call the police."

Janine would be incensed if her mother embarrassed her by calling the police. "No, wait. Before you bring in the cops, let me call Colgate first."

"I tried phoning a little while ago. No one will be in until nine."

Mrs. Smith had probably called the administration office. No, she had probably called the university president. "Hello, this is Mrs. Amanda Smith," as if someone might care. "Where is my daughter?" Right, like the dean of students was going to say he saw her at the Rathskeller last night, don't worry.

"No, I mean some of Janine's friends," Willy said. "I'll phone back in a few hours."

"I'm not going to wait a few hours." The fear in her voice was chilling. This wasn't just a case of Amanda being difficult. "I'm very frightened. Something isn't right. Please call *now*."

Her tone was pleading, heartfelt. Willy had never heard Amanda sounding so fragile, or so sincere.

"I'll try now. You'll hear back from me in ten minutes."

Willy knew the area code for Colgate. He had phoned Janine just about every week for the two-and-a-half years she had gone to school. Janine had quit at the end of last semester, midway through her junior year. Willy dialed the area code and the number for information.

About a week ago, Janine had told him she had to go to Colgate for a make-up exam. They had been in Zep's and he was a little high, or maybe it was the way she said it, but Willy had at first wondered what going back to school had to do with lipstick and mascara.

Janine had laughed. "Not makeup, I have to make up an exam I missed. Art history."

"Why bother? You quit school."

"Yeah, but one day I may want to transfer to Vassar or New Paultz, or someplace around here. I took the course for a semester, I might as well get credit for it. Besides, it will be fun seeing everybody again."

Janine had left Sunday morning, even though her exam wasn't until Tuesday. Most of her friends were still at school, and she thought she might do a little studying for the test. It would be a lark, a vacation. And, it wasn't as though any compelling reasons existed for her to rush back to Beacon. She wasn't working, the wedding was still five weeks off; not that Janine was going to spend a lot of time choosing a wedding gown or borrowing something blue.

The directory assistance operator came on the line. Willy asked for the number for Laura MacLean.

"I'm letting Amanda get me as crazy as she is," thought Willy as he dialed the phone. Laura, Janine's former roommate at Colgate, was really going to appreciate being awakened at this hour.

Janine would certainly be staying with Laura. She and Laura had been roommates as freshmen, then they and two other friends had rented a house that everyone called Disgraceland. Willy had visited the house countless times. It had four small bedrooms, one for each woman, and even when everyone had a boyfriend over, there was still plenty of space on the couches in the living room. Willy remembered waking up one snowy morning after a party and finding that twelve people, some sleeping, some passed out, had spent the night.

Willy almost hung up when there was no answer on the fifth ring. This was asinine, disturbing people because Mrs. Smith was paranoid. The phone rang a sixth time and a seventh, then Willy heard a husky, sleepy voice say hello.

"Laura, this is Willy Buchanan. I'm sorry to wake you." He was now annoyed at himself as well: he had allowed Mrs. Smith to pressure him into this absurd situation. "Is Janine there?"

"Janine?"

"She was supposed to come home yesterday and she didn't. Her mother is causing an uproar."

"I don't understand. Janine quit school. She doesn't live here anymore." Laura sounded half asleep.

"I know, but she went up to Colgate for an exam. Isn't she staying with you?"

There was silence, and then Laura said, "No."

"But, you've seen her?" Willy asked.

"I haven't seen Janine since before Christmas. She didn't tell me she was coming up," Laura said in a hurt tone.

Willy again felt a chill. Even if Janine had found someplace else to sleep, she would have gone by to see Laura and all of her other friends at the house. That was the main reason for Janine's trip back to school; the make-up exam had been secondary, an excuse to go.

Laura was suddenly very alert. "What is going on?"

Willy explained about the exam. Janine had said it was art history, he was certain of that. He couldn't remember if she had specifically said she would stay at Disgraceland or not. "Where else might Janine have stayed?" Willy asked.

Laura hesitated before saying, "I don't know."

Willy could feel his heart pounding. There had to be a reasonable explanation. He had misunderstood Janine, or perhaps she had had a falling out with Laura.

"Willy, you're scaring me."

"I think I'm scaring myself."

"Listen, I'll start calling people up here. And I'll get in touch with Janine's art history professor, maybe he'll know something. Give me your phone number, I'll get back to you as soon as I hear anything."

Willy gave Laura his number and said good-bye. Dialing another number, he noticed he was shivering.

"Maybe you should call the police," Willy said when Mrs. Smith answered the phone.

From where he knelt on the roof of the Castronova house, Willy could see both the wide expanse of the Hudson River to the west, and the mountain from which the city had taken its name, Mount Beacon, to the east. During the Revolutionary War, beacon fires had been lit atop the mountain to signal George Washington's troops across the river in Newburgh as well as West Point, five or six miles to the south. Now, an electric beacon cast a forlorn beam from a radio/television transmitting station.

In addition to the trails from a small ski lodge, a railroad track climbing to the summit disfigured the face of the mountain. This railroad, a rinky-dink tourist attraction grandly called the "World's Steepest Incline Railroad" also laid claim to being one of the "Seven Modern Engineering Wonders of the World." It was more commonly referred to as "the trolley" by most in town. A large, stucco, vaguely Mediterranean-looking building known as the Casino, improbably stood at the crest near the end of the railroad tracks.

Willy was hammering the last shingle of the row when he saw the police cruiser coming up the street. The car stopped; Emil Deshayes got out and sauntered toward the white clapboard frame house. He was sporting a wispy mustache now.

"How are you doing, Willy?" Emil called up. "Can I talk with you a second?"

Willy drove in the last nail. Climbing down the ladder, he tried to find a meaning in Emil's expression. Surely, if Emil had something grim to report, he wouldn't have that goofy smile on his face. Jimmy Guido, Willy's boss, stared down from the scaffolding, probably thankful that Emil Deshayes was not there looking for him. Willy hadn't mentioned anything about Janine when he had shown up late for work.

"Mrs. Smith called us about Janine. She made out a missing person's report. She said you'd be here."

Willy nodded, feeling a sense of relief. Emil wasn't bringing bad news about Janine.

"She still hasn't come home?" Willy asked.

"No, I was hoping you had heard from her."

For hours, Willy had been expecting Janine to drive up and yell, "Did you hear what my mother did? I'm on the FBI's Ten Most Wanted List. She's such an asshole!"

There had to be a reasonable explanation. Willy had been repeating that to himself all day.

After having awakened a lot of Janine's friends, Laura had called from Colgate at eight o'clock that morning. No one had seen or heard from Janine since she quit school. Laura had talked to the art history professor. He had not scheduled any make-up examinations for Janine or for anyone else. In fact, Janine had taken the regular final exam and had received a B for the course.

There had to be an explanation.

"Mrs. Smith said that Janine was supposed to return by Tuesday night," Emil said.

Willy was about to correct Emil, but stopped himself. Somehow, from a movie or a book, he knew that a person could not be reported missing for twenty-four hours. Amanda must have said Tuesday night so that she could make out the missing persons report.

"So, you haven't seen or heard from Janine," Emil remarked, looking up at Willy who stood a half head taller.

"No, not since she called me on the phone. Monday night about ten."

"She called you from Colgate?"

Willy shrugged. "That's what I thought. Now . . ."

"When was the last time you saw her?"

"Sunday morning about five or six." Janine had spent most of the night at the apartment. Then, for the sake of a pretense that she and her mother kept up, she had gone home.

He and Janine had rented the apartment, the second floor of a two-story duplex, just a few weeks ago. They had painted it and lugged in Amanda's old furniture. Janine had moved in some of her belongings. Unpacked boxes were still strewn about. Mrs. Smith had been insistent that no daughter of hers was going to live with Willy out of wedlock—she was less than thrilled at the prospect of her daughter living with Willy *in* wedlock—and Janine, curiously, had gone along with her mother's wishes.

"Janine is something of a free spirit. I'm sure she'll show up," Emil said pleasantly.

Willy had known Emil since grade school. Emil had flunked the second grade, or was "left behind" as the teachers called it, and had to repeat it with Willy's class. All through those years at South Avenue School, Emil had seemed a quiet, unassuming kid. Though they had spent seven years together in the same classrooms, Willy had very few recollections of him. Once, while reading aloud in class, Emil had mistakenly said, "Sarah lungered over her pancakes" instead of reading what was in the text, "Sarah lingered over her pancakes." Willy vaguely remembered that Emil had worn what was probably his favorite sweater every day for about a month until Kyle McGwire had brought it loudly to everyone's attention. Then Emil had stopped wearing the sweater. That was all he could recall of Emil until their senior year in high school.

Then one day in the cafeteria, Willy had happened to sit down beside Emil. They hadn't said a word to one another in years, and Willy had intended to eat his lunch quickly and skip fifth period. But to Willy's surprise, Emil had started to talk about football, and Willy, to his further surprise, found himself arguing about the Dallas Cowboys, a team he didn't care about one way or another. Somehow the argument became heated; Emil sort of flicked a french fry at him, and the next thing Willy knew, he had tackled Emil to the floor and was smearing a piece of pie all over his face. Willy had been astonished at how easily Emil's slight resistance was overcome, how easy it had been to throw him to the floor. But he had also been abashed at having put humiliation on Emil's face along with the bloodlike cherry mess.

People had rushed over to break up the fight, not that Willy needed restraining. Friends started to crow on his behalf, making fun of the ridiculous figure of Emil on the ground, but all Willy wanted was to act as if it had never happened. He wanted to apologize, but Emil had slunk out of the cafeteria, and everything returned to normal within minutes. Emil had not shown up in home room the next day.

For a while after that scuffle, an ill-defined animosity existed between them. They would avoid each other's gaze in the hallway. After months of studiously ignoring the other, they found themselves at the same chemistry lab table. They had performed the experiment, passing sodium and test tubes back and forth, and speaking only of milliliters and ccs, and then their animosity slowly devolved into a casual dislike.

Now, Emil was standing in front of him, smiling blandly and making pleasantries as though the little altercation had never happened.

"You guys are getting married pretty soon, aren't you?"

"Yes, in April."

"I'm supposed to ask some questions, they're a little personal, so don't take them the wrong way, okay?"

Willy suddenly wanted to apologize for that high school tussle, but instead said, "I won't. Ask anything you want."

"Uh, did you and Janine have a fight?"

"No, we get along fine. It was nothing like that."

"Was she depressed?"

"Not at all. She was excited about going back to visit her old friends. She seemed happy the last time I saw her."

"Was Janine having trouble at home? Arguing with her parents?"

"No more than usual. No, everything was fine."

"Okay, like I said, she'll probably show up soon."

As Emil walked back to the police cruiser, the gun and holster flapped awkwardly against his thigh. Willy watched the police car drive away.

Jimmy Guido called down from the scaffold, "What the hell is going on?"

Good question. There had to be an explanation.

Amanda opened the front door as Willy climbed the slate steps that led to the elevated front yard. The house was brick, painted white, with black shutters and ivy tastefully climbing up one side. It seemed every light in the house was on. A snippet of an old song—"leave a light burning in the window for me"—drifted into his thoughts. Amanda had a hopeful, expectant look.

"She still isn't home?" Willy asked.

"No, come on in." Amanda's tone was subdued and gentle.

After Emil had left, he and Jimmy had worked for another couple of hours. Or more precisely, Willy had worked on the roof and Jimmy had finished off a six-pack of Rheingold while he supposedly straightened up the debris and old shingles in Mr. Castronova's yard. Then Willy had gone back to the apartment and called Laura at Colgate.

Laura had spent the whole day talking to anyone who, even remotely, might have seen Janine. No one had. No make-up exams had been scheduled this week in any of the departments.

When Laura had hung up, Willy just sat in the living room, letting the sense of dread he had been holding at bay all day sweep over him. Everything in the room seemed ominous, fraught with a terrible, inexplicable meaning. Then, not knowing what else to do, he had gone over to the Smiths.

Willy followed Amanda into the kitchen where Howard Smith was speaking on the phone.

"She's twenty years old, blond, five foot six, one hundred and fifteen pounds. She's a very pretty young woman."

Howard was leaning against the blue-tiled counter, gesturing with his free hand. A map of New York State was spread out on the kitchen table. The route between Beacon and Hamilton, where Colgate University was located, had been traced in magic marker.

"Okay, thank you," Howard said. "What's the name of the hospital in your town? All right, thanks again."

Howard hung up and looked at Amanda. "They're going to check the hospital and a motel near the thruway."

Willy shook hands with Howard. The Smiths had been calling every police department and sheriff's office between Beacon and Colgate. Beside the phone was a legal pad with an orderly list of phone numbers, separated by area codes. Howard had neatly crossed out about half of the numbers on the list.

Janine had always made fun of Howard's precision, his orderliness, and, in fact, almost everything else about him. Unfairly, Willy thought. Janine made Howard out to be a pointy-headed Tom Swift with a slide rule. Willy found him to be an open, friendly, literate man. Howard played the piano, mostly bluesy jazz; he skied and played golf; he was well-read. Most important, he had a sly sense of humor that helped diffuse the uproar that constantly erupted between Janine and her mother. The only character flaw that Howard had, as far as Willy could determine, was the emotional blind spot or sexual need that allowed him to live with Amanda. Janine, however, just couldn't give him a break.

Amanda poured Willy a cup of coffee he hadn't asked for, then sat down opposite him at the table. She seemed to be on the verge of tears. It was shocking; Willy was so used to her being the Dragon Lady that it made him uncomfortable to see this more vulnerable side of her.

They both listened as Howard made phone calls. Willy would announce the next number on the list, then cross it off when Howard had finished. Howard would briefly and concisely explain to whoever answered the phone, some bored deputy working the night shift probably, that his stepdaughter was missing. There was no stammering, or fumbling for words, just Howard's voice, patient and articulate. Within fifteen minutes, he had phoned all but one number on the list.

As Willy read aloud the last phone number, the doorbell rang. Amanda started at the noise, then bolted for the front door.

Willy followed down the hall and saw Emil Deshayes standing in the doorway, speaking in a low tone to Amanda. Emil's wispy mustache looked more like a shadow in the dim light, but he had the same easy expression. He couldn't be bringing bad news, Willy thought.

Emil glanced over Amanda's shoulder at Willy and said, "We still haven't heard from Janine."

Willy could hear a sigh of relief come from Howard who was standing behind him.

They all went into the living room. Emil looked uneasy, fidgeting in the chintz-covered armchair. He gave Willy a smile that seemed apologetic.

"I just want to go over a few things," Emil said. "Janine left Sunday morning about nine. She said she was going to Colgate University, in Hamilton, New York, to take a test and visit friends. On Monday night, she called Willy and talked for a while. She was supposed to come back Tuesday night. Is that correct?"

"Yes," Amanda said quickly, before anyone else could contradict her about Janine coming home Tuesday instead of Wednesday.

Emil turned to Willy. "What time did she call you Monday night?"

"About ten o'clock," Willy said.

"She said she was calling from Colgate?"

"Yes. No . . . Maybe, I just took it for granted." Emil's Bulldog Drummond manner was beginning to irritate Willy. Christ, he was the kid who had once read that Sarah lungered over her pancakes.

Emil must have sensed Willy's vexation because he again gave that apologetic look.

"Do you know specifically where Janine was calling from?"

Willy remembered the phone call. He could hear the jukebox blaring and the whoops, laughter, and din of people in the background. He had thought, It sounds like a wild night at Hickey's. Janine had only spoken for a few minutes when the operator came on the line to ask for more money. Cutting the conversation short, Janine's last words to him had been, "I love you."

"She called from a bar. I had assumed it was a place in Hamilton called Hickey's."

"This was around ten o'clock?"

"Yes. A few minutes before." After hanging up, Willy had turned on the television. The credits to the movie on Channel Five were rolling. It had been a western starring Kirk Douglas and Anthony Quinn.

Emil took out a notebook and turned to the top page. With his wispy mustache and baby face, the holstered gun too big for his thigh and bunched up on the cushion, he looked like a kid playing grownup.

"On Monday night, you received a long distance phone call that lasted from 9:51 to 9:57. It was placed from a pay phone in a bar called Johnny White's. That's in New Orleans."

TWO

"NEW ORLEANS?" Amanda's confusion quickly gave way to anger.

Emil squirmed in his seat. "We checked the phone records. The call definitely came from New Orleans."

Amanda directed her ire toward Willy. "What is going on?"

Willy shook his head, perplexed.

"Are you covering for Janine?" Amanda spat out.

He returned her accusatory glare. "If Janine had asked me, I would have lied to you. But she didn't. She told me she was going to school."

"This might be good news," Emil ventured, then presented a conciliatory grin in response to Amanda's wrath. "It might explain why Janine hasn't returned. Tuesday was Mardi Gras. New Orleans is bedlam this time of year. Hotels and airlines are all filled. If Janine missed her return flight, or maybe she was flying standby and didn't have her return flight booked, she could be stranded down there for days."

Howard was about to say something, but his wife's expression stopped him.

"To be on the safe side," Emil continued, "we've contacted the New Orleans Police Department and forwarded the missing persons report. But, who knows? Janine could be on a plane back to New York right now."

"We're very appreciative of what the police department has done," Amanda said in the same tone a judge would use to condemn a prisoner. And then her expression made it clear that Emil was dismissed.

Amanda shifted her eyes to Willy. He was dismissed, too.

As Willy and Emil ambled down the front walk in silence, the light sconces on either side of the front door went out. Emil started to get into the police car, but stopped.

"Does Janine have any friends in New Orleans?"

"I don't think so."

Emil slid into the front seat of the police car. "Janine will probably show up real soon. But, if she doesn't, Lonnie Kroll and I will drop by your place tomorrow morning about ten. Will you be there?"

Willy nodded.

"We're actually going to come into your house, and I will be with Lonnie, so you might want to . . . straighten up."

Willy smiled, "Okay." He knew Emil wasn't worried about his housekeeping. Emil was telling him to make sure no pot or hash pipes were lying around. Or else Lonnie would wind up arresting him.

"I'll see you tomorrow," Willy said. He got into his fifteen-year-old Chevrolet panel truck and drove away.

On the way back to the apartment, Willy nearly went through a red light on Verplanck Avenue. He could understand Janine lying to Amanda, but she had lied to him as well.

At home, though he knew what he would see, Willy checked the *TV Guide*. On Monday night, the night the phone records indicated he had received a call from New Orleans, was the listing: *Last Train from Gun Hill (1959) A marshal seeks vengeance for the brutal murder of his Indian wife. Kirk Douglas, Anthony Quinn, Carolyn Jones.* The movie had ended at ten o'clock.

He had talked to Janine on the phone, then turned on the television and saw the credits to that movie.

"I'm having a good time," Janine had said. She had had to shout over the noise in the background, a roar that, now on reflection, had been much too raucous for a college bar at ten o'clock on a midsemester Monday night.

He had started to ask about everyone at Disgraceland, but Janine had interrupted, wanting to discuss the apartment. Willy had finished removing wallpaper from the bathroom. Janine's questions had seemed innocent at the time, but now? Had she been evasive, steering the conversation away from school?

Willy had been chattering about wallpaper and spackle while all around Janine a bacchanalia reigned. Shrieks of laughter had come over the phone line. Music had blasted. Willy couldn't stop himself from imagining pagan, orgiastic revelry.

But then, right before saying good-bye, Janine had said, "I love you."

* * *

The first time Willy became aware of Janine was on a hot August night at Memorial Field. A summer league basketball game had just finished, but the lights were still on above the asphalt court that doubled as a skating rink in the winter. A group of girls he knew were standing across the court and among them was Janine. Willy saw Janine standing beneath the light, which shimmered on her hair and gave it an aura. The sight of her caused a physical reaction. Her beauty startled him, his heart actually raced. He remembered thinking that those sappy poems were true, hearts really did go pitter-patter. His mouth literally gaped open—she *was* breathtakingly beautiful.

Crossing the asphalt, Willy began talking with his former girlfriend, Kim Mooney. He barely heard what Kim was saying. Willy couldn't stop looking at Janine. Her hair had the soft sheen of a baby's, and her long legs were very tan. He could see the outline of Janine's nipples poking though the old-fashioned rayon print dress that she wore. Much later he learned that Janine had taken off her bra in her backyard after leaving the house and hid it in her purse because Amanda would not have let her out without one.

She was Teddy Smith's sister, he found out. Willy played baseball with Teddy, first in Babe Ruth League and then for Beacon High. In Willy's freshman year of high school, when Teddy and Janine's father died, the entire baseball team had gone to the funeral, so Willy must have seen Janine then. How had he not noticed her?

A few weeks after that night at Memorial Field, on the first day of school, he saw Janine again. Willy's had been the last class to enter Beacon High as freshmen. The previous year, the ninth grade had been shifted to the middle school, Rombout, so Janine's class had entered as sophomores. Willy spied Janine in the halls of Beacon High and couldn't stop himself from turning and staring at her as she glided gracefully down the corridor.

Others noticed Janine as well. One day when he was hanging out in front of the Yankee Clipper Diner, the topic of reincarnation had improbably come up. Earache Kehler had offered that he would like to come back as Janine Smith's panties.

Another afternoon, Willy was at Kim Mooney's house with a few others, and Patty Chisolm started to read aloud from *Seventeen* magazine. The gist of the article, which had a title something like "What's Your Desirability Quotient," was that people were assigned points for personal attributes, such as beauty, intelligence, wit, social status, and that people tended to date those who had an equal number of points or "desirability quotient."

" 'So, even if you are not the prettiest girl in school' " Patty Chisolm read, " 'don't give up hope.' Are you listening Kim, there's still hope. 'You may still catch the class hunk' Ohhh. And if you catch the class hunk, you might catch something else."

They began to assign points to kids they knew from Beacon High. Denny Quinn, with inch-thick Coke bottle glasses and learning disabilities, was deemed to be two-hundred-and-fifty pound, unwashed, Therese Ivarone's dream date.

"Teens can be so cruel," Earache said.

Earache's desirability quotient was figured. It was decided that he should be dating Denny Quinn as well.

After a while, someone said, "Janine Smith."

Willy felt himself redden and was embarrassed to realize that he wanted the others to say that he, Willy Buchanan, was the perfect one for Janine Smith.

"Janine?" Patty asked. "That's an easy one. Eric Boyd."

Everyone else concurred. Eric Boyd was the golden boy of Beacon High; handsome, the best athlete. He was like a cliche from *Seventeen* magazine: the one they referred to when they wrote, "class hunk." Even though Willy had not yet formally met Janine, hadn't said a word to her, he felt pangs of jealousy.

He felt those same pangs of jealousy weeks later when he saw Janine walking down Verplanck Avenue holding hands with Eric Boyd. And mingled with jealousy was anger. That ludicrous article in *Seventeen* had been right.

Willy called Jimmy Guido and told him he wasn't coming to work.

"Yeah, I don't think I'm going to work, either. It looks like snow. Besides, I'm too hung over."

During the long sleepless night, Willy had almost convinced himself that some huge misunderstanding had occurred. Then, Amanda had phoned, desperation in her voice, and asked if Janine had shown up.

Now the more he thought about Emil's theory of Janine being stranded in New Orleans, the less convinced he was. If Janine had lied about going to Mardi Gras, and apparently she had, and then found herself stuck in New Orleans, she would have called. She would have said her exam had been postponed, or her car broke down, or she was having such a good time she was staying an extra few days at Colgate. Janine would do something. Otherwise, she would have to know that her lie would be discovered.

Despite all of Emil's reassuring words, Janine was still missing.

Emil and Lonnie Kroll arrived a little after ten. Willy had heeded Emil's advice: the pot was now in the bottom drawer of the bureau.

Lonnie sat down on a kitchen chair which creaked beneath his bulk. He was wearing a polyester suit with wide lapels that sported an American flag pin, and a clip-on tie. His hair was cut short in a flat top, but his sideburns reached below his ears.

Lonnie was a moron: a figure of ridicule in Beacon, and among most of the Beacon Police Department as well. After spending almost twenty years as a patrolman—a record for the Beacon Police—and after also setting a record for failing advancement exams, Lonnie had finally become a detective by dint of his seniority alone.

One summer night, when Willy was about eleven, he and his brother, Michael, who was four years older, had been riding their bikes down a grassy knoll in the Methodist cemetery onto North Walnut Street. Lonnie Kroll, who was still a patrolman then, had stopped his police car and called up to them.

"Hey, get down from there."

Willy had been about to dismount his bike and walk it down the little hill, when he heard his brother say, "Fuck you, Lonnie."

Willy had been stunned. He couldn't believe Michael had told Lonnie to fuck off. And then to Willy's further amazement, Michael had thrust his bike down the knoll and raced off. Not knowing what else to do, Willy followed him. With a squeal of tires, Lonnie took off after them.

It must have presented a sight: A patrol car with its cherry top flashers ablaze in the twilight, chasing two children on bicycles. At the end of the block, Michael called over his shoulder, "I'll see you later," and veered off onto Church Street. I'll see you later? Willy had thought, When? When we get out of reform school? To Willy's immense relief, Lonnie followed Michael down Church Street. Willy pedaled furiously home and hid his bicycle beneath the porch. Moments later, Michael threw his bike over the back fence, hopped the fence, and smiled triumphantly. He told Willy of his getaway, barreling down driveways and across backyards, making it sound like Steve McQueen fleeing the Nazis in *The Great Escape*.

Lonnie had not been able to catch them—two misbehaving children. Now he was investigating Janine's disappearance.

"So, your girlfriend is missing?" Lonnie asked.

Willy nodded.

"You and your girlfriend been getting along?" Lonnie had a crafty look on his face. It was embarrassing.

"Yes, we have."

"No fights?"

"No."

"Hell, I find that hard to believe."

"I guess it is farfetched that two people who just got engaged would like each other and be compatible."

"Your girlfriend—"

"Her name is Janine."

Lonnie gave what he must have thought was a hard, steely glare. "Janine lied to you, though, didn't she?"

"Fuck you, Lonnie." Through his anger came the realization that those were the same words his brother, Michael, had said to Lonnie all those years ago.

Lonnie was outraged. "Who the hell do you think you're talking to?"

"You don't really want me to answer that."

Emil stepped forward. "Hey, hey. Let's all calm down." He looked between the two. "We all want Janine to come home."

Lonnie snorted and leaned back in the chair.

"Let's go over everything you told me, Willy."

Willy told them what he knew. It was futile speaking to Lonnie, who appeared to be vacant or bored or stupid. It was probably all three.

"Where were you the early part of this week?" Lonnie asked.

He should have expected something like this from Lonnie. Still, it came as a surprise.

"I was here in Beacon."

"Did anybody see you?"

Willy looked past Lonnie at Emil. Emil just shook his head in disgust.

"Yeah, Jimmy Guido saw me. I work with him."

"On Sunday, too?"

"No, I didn't work on Sunday."

"Did anyone see you on Sunday?"

"Yes. Janine."

"Yeah, but you said she left early in the morning. Did anybody see you after she left?"

On Sunday, Willy told them, he had slept in until ten. Then he had worked on the apartment. About six, he had gone out and run five miles on the Asylum Road. He didn't remember seeing anyone while running, though cars had passed by. Of course he had been bundled up in a hooded sweatshirt, scarf, and knit cap. And the Asylum Road was poorly-lit. He had spent the rest of the night at home reading.

"So, no one saw you," Lonnie said in a tone he no doubt thought trenchant.

Willy felt two conflicting urges. He wanted to laugh. Lonnie was such an idiot and this situation, this interrogation of the suspect, as Lonnie must think of it, was so absurd. His other urge was to grab the cast iron skillet from the stove and smash it over Lonnie's skinhead and scream, "Go find Janine, you asshole!"

Instead, he said, "No, I guess not."

Lonnie heaved himself up from the kitchen chair and glowered at Willy.

"We'll be in touch."

Willy opened the front door for them. Emil made a sign behind Lonnie's back that Willy didn't understand. As Willy watched them descend the steps to the first floor, he expected Lonnie to turn and say, "Don't leave town."

As they reached the ground floor front door, Willy thought, Now he'll turn.

Lonnie opened the front door. He turned and looked up at Willy. "Don't leave town."

Emil returned about an hour later and apologized.

"Lonnie's such a fool. He's an embarrassment. Don't worry, I want you to know that he won't be handling this case. Ron Antone told me personally to make sure that he doesn't screw up." Ron Antone was the chief of police. "Lonnie is nominally a detective, I mean that's Civil Service and we're stuck with him. But all he'll be allowed to do is insult people and make an ass of himself. Sam Pittman and I are going to take care of the investigation. And, we're not taking it lightly."

"No? What are you doing?"

Emil hesitated, then said, "I was going to tell you this earlier, but . . ." he shook his head and said, "Lonnie," as if that was all the explanation needed. "Janine had a round trip flight to New Orleans booked on American Airlines. She flew down on Sunday out of La Guardia at 11:15 A.M. She was supposed to return Wednesday afternoon. The return ticket was never used."

Willy wondered if he would ever hear good news again. Janine really was missing. This wasn't a misunderstanding, or a lark.

"We've informed the New Orleans police, we're going over the Smiths' phone records right now. Beyond that . . . I don't know what to tell you."

"Thanks, Emil."

"Did Janine ever mention Mardi Gras to you? Even in passing?"

"Not that I remember."

"Could you imagine Janine going to Mardi Gras by herself? It just seems to me that it wouldn't be much fun going there by yourself."

21

I would have gone there with Janine, Willy thought. "No, it doesn't make sense."

"And you don't know of any friends in New Orleans."

"No. Maybe someone from school."

"Is there anyone at Colgate you could call and ask?"

He phoned Disgraceland. Laura had just come in from class. She said she had been beside herself with worry.

"Did Janine have any friends up there who came from New Orleans?" Willy asked.

After a long pause, Laura said, "Yes. Susie Conover. You remember her, don't you?"

"Sure." Willy experienced a rush of relief, then felt ashamed when he realized it was because Janine's New Orleans friend was not a man.

"She's not around, is she?"

"No, she graduated last year. She's back living in New Orleans."

Laura didn't have Susie Conover's New Orleans number, but said the student loan office or the alumni association should. They hung up.

"Do you know Susie Conover?" Emil asked.

"Yes. She's nice. I didn't know she was from New Orleans. She doesn't have a Southern accent."

"Nothing will probably come of it, but I'm going to track down this Susie Conover. I'll keep in touch. If you think of anything else, anything at all, call me."

When Emil left, Willy allowed feelings of hope to rush over him. Janine was visiting an old school friend in New Orleans. That had to be it. Emil would find Susie, and Janine would be with her drinking coffee and gossiping. Sure, it didn't make sense that Janine hadn't called, but she would be able to explain it. She was alive.

Willy shocked himself with that thought. Janine was alive. For the last few days, something evil, threatening, had been flitting about in his thoughts, trying to surface, but Willy had always forced it back. By asserting Janine was alive, he had let the unthinkable fear, that Janine was dead, surface.

He realized he was pacing up and down the hallway. Willy turned on the television and tried to watch it, but he couldn't sit still. So, he went into the bedroom, stepped over the unpacked boxes, and put on his running clothes and shoes.

Outside the duplex, he stretched, then ran the quarter mile past single-family houses and through streets lined with maple, oak, and elm to the Asylum Road. The Asylum Road started at Verplanck Avenue and wound through playgrounds and open fields toward the prison— the Mattawan State Hospital for the Criminally Insane. This was

22

Willy's favorite route to run in Beacon. The road had little traffic, and a sidewalk paralleled the road for over a mile, so that he didn't have to worry about uneven footing or being crowded off the shoulder of the road by cars.

Willy ran hard up the Asylum Road, trying to bring on an exhaustion that might quell the turmoil in his mind for a little while. The road edged along Hammond Field, which was deserted now, buried under a covering of snow. As a child, playing at Hammond Field, he would sometimes see trucks full of inmates on their way to work in the fields of the prison farm. Invariably, someone would start to sing, "Chock Full of Nuts is the heavenly coffee." Or, the Patsy Cline song, "Crazy."

Also located in town was an exclusive private sanitarium, a former estate set off in an Arcadian parklike isolation. Kids in Beacon liked to joke that insanity was the main industry in the city.

The "Mad Bomber," a man who became famous for exploding bombs throughout New York City in the early 1950s because of a grudge against a utility company, was imprisoned at Mattawan. When Willy was a child, the "Mad Bomber" had come to represent the boogie man, lurking in the cemetery, or about to escape from Mattawan and on his way to get you. Insanity, unspeakable and depraved, lay in wait nearby. It didn't take much for evil to be set loose.

Willy turned onto a bend in the road, and the red brick, nineteenth-century prison came into view. Though running faster than usual, he increased his pace up the long incline. A wind blew over the open field, kicking up a fine mist of powdery snow.

At the deserted guard shack, Willy turned and ran back down Asylum Road. The wind was at his back now, and he sped down the grade. With feet pounding on the cement, he pumped his arms and legs wildly, lengthening his stride. His chest heaved with the exertion, his sides cramped, but still he ran furiously, until all he could think of was the pain screaming from his legs and sides.

Finally, his body stopped running. He leaned over gasping for breath. Blood pulsed in his head, and the cold air burned as he breathed it in greedily. He wiped away the sweat and tears from his face, then bellowed in pain. The roar echoed across the empty field. He shouted out again.

Janine had gone out with Eric Boyd for most of her sophomore year. Willy would see them together in the halls of Beacon High, or at parties. Occasionally, Janine would show up at games that Eric played in—football, basketball, and baseball, take your pick. At one baseball game, Willy was on first base, having bunted on, when Eric hit a game-winning home run. As Willy rounded third base, he saw Janine in the bleachers. She was the only one who was not wildly cheering. He felt a rush of elation.

Late that spring, Willy heard from his former girlfriend Kim, that Janine had broken up with Eric. Kim had looked astonished when Willy laughed and said, "Great."

A few weeks later, he ran into Janine. Willy could still remember everything about that night, a balmy Wednesday near the end of May. School was off the next day because of a teachers' meeting. Baseball season had just ended. Willy had gone out with Earache and Andy Brascia to have a few beers. They were all underage, so going out to have a few beers had meant a trip to Carrie's Corner Store.

Carrie's Corner Store was a Mom and Pop establishment that had been carved out of the ground floor of an old frame house. Carrie wasn't too particular about I.D. or the age of those buying beer. Willy had once joked about a typical order at Carrie's Corner Store. "I'll have five cents worth of licorice, two wax lips, a jawbreaker, and oh yeah, a six-pack of Schlitz."

Willy had been buying beer there for over a year. The first time, he had gone into Carrie's while his friends waited outside, and put five quarts of beer on the counter. Carrie, who was a diminutive woman with dyed black hair and cat's eye glasses, had asked, "Can I see your I.D., honey?" It seemed that Carrie was incapable of speaking a sentence without including a term of endearment.

Willy had shown her his brother's expired license. Michael was four years older than Willy, two inches shorter, and had brown eyes as opposed to Willy's green. Carrie had looked at the license and smiled. "Anything else, dear?"

An hour later, Willy had returned to the corner store to buy five more quarts of beer. Carrie's husband, a gruff, gray-haired man who had never called anyone dear in his entire life, had asked to see Willy's license. Carrie, who was helping another customer, had glanced over at Willy and said, "He's all right, hon, I've checked him." Willy had been buying beer there ever since. Most of his friends had had similar experiences. Kim claimed she bought beer using her mother's Blue Cross card as identification. She also maintained that Carrie had once called her "sweetie," "love," "honey," and "dear," in the same sentence.

Willy, Andy, and Earache had just left Carrie's Corner Store and were walking down the dark side street, drinking cans of Rolling Rock when they encountered Janine, Diane Niedzialkowski, and Kim. Beacon's nighttime attractions being what they were, it was not unusual to see other groups of kids drinking in the streets. On his way to Carrie's, Willy had seen four guys he knew slightly who went to Saint Patrick's, the Catholic high school in Newburgh, weaving down the street, chugging quarts of Colt 45. Janine and the others had just finished their last cans of beer and were headed back to Carrie's for more.

"You're drinking?" Kim scolded in mock dismay. "Aren't you guys supposed to be in training?"

"We are. We're training to become bald, potbellied, middle-aged boors," Willy replied. He heard Janine laugh. He handed one of the three six-packs he had bought to Kim. "Care to join our sad decline?"

Janine took a can from Kim and said, "I can already feel everything beginning to sag."

Spread out six across, they sauntered down the dark residential streets. Janine was talking with Andy Brascia all the way to the left; Willy was on the far right. His mind raced for a way to sidle up next to Janine without seeming obvious. He barely heard what Earache and Diane were saying.

They left the streets and went into Hammond Field. Kim's cousin, Mickey, and some of his friends were already in the park, drinking. So were the guys from Saint Pat's that they had bumped into earlier. One of them, a redheaded kid who they called Tubbs, was on his hands and knees, dry-heaving.

"That makes a lovely picture, doesn't it?" Kim said.

" 'The Garden of Earthly Delights,' " Willy murmured, more to himself than to the others. Janine had looked at him with a bemused smile.

"He's having too much fun," Earache said. "I can remember seeing you in that same position, Kim."

"No way. I was much more ladylike puking."

"Who said anything about puking?"

They had sat on the bleachers near the football field and drank until the beer ran out. Willy had not been able to figure out a way to strike up a conversation with Janine. When they left the park, Willy assumed that they were heading back to Carrie's for more beer. At Verplanck Avenue, though, Janine and Kim stopped.

"We're going to drop by play rehearsal," Kim said.

The Beacon High drama class was rehearsing *Arsenic and Old Lace.* Kim wanted to stop by, it later turned out, because she was smitten with Paul Barich, who was doing the lights for the play. Janine wanted to see her brother, Teddy, who was in the cast, perform.

On impulse, Willy said, "I'll go with you."

The others decided to go to Carrie's. As Kim, Janine, and Willy turned to leave, Willy thought he saw Andy and Earache smirking at him. He suddenly realized he didn't care what they or anyone, except Janine, thought.

On the way, Janine teased Kim about Paul Barich. The high school was dark and appeared deserted. The iron picket fence in back was locked. Beacon High had been built of yellow brick in the 1920s on the side of a slope so that the school's height varied from two to four stories.

One of the side doors was unlocked. Kim, Janine, and Willy entered and headed toward the auditorium where full dress rehearsal was in progress. Their footsteps reverberated in the deserted, locker-lined hallways.

"We're not really supposed to be here, so keep it down," Kim said. She spotted Paul Barich, who smiled and put a finger to his lips to quiet them.

Janine turned to Willy and said, "I want to see Teddy make a fool of himself. Let's go up to the balcony."

Though he knew Janine had suggested the balcony so that Kim could talk to Paul Barich in private, he still couldn't believe his luck. He was going to be alone with Janine.

Willy followed as she raced up the stairwell and down the corridor to the balcony. They slouched into seats in the front row.

Teddy Smith was on stage with Patty Chisolm who was made up to be one of the elderly aunts.

"Look at Teddy!" Janine said with delight. "And look at Patty. Is she supposed to be old? She looks like somebody dumped a bag of flour over her head."

They watched the rehearsal. Patty was wooden on stage, but Teddy was a surprisingly graceful farceur, delivering his lines with such ease that they both had to suppress laughter in the balcony. Willy saw the pride and happiness in Janine's face, and he felt like standing and giving Teddy an ovation.

The scene ended. Mr. Richler, the drama teacher, was yelling at Patty Chisolm.

"Teddy is good. You can see he is having a lot of fun," Willy said.

"You can tell?" Janine continued to stare at her brother. "Teddy has been trying not to let on how much he enjoys it. He doesn't want everyone to know what a big ham he is."

"I once played the same role."

Janine was intrigued. "You did? Where?"

"When I was a kid, my family used to vacation on the Finger Lakes.

We would rent a cabin, and my aunt and uncle and four cousins would have the cabin next door. Every year, my aunt would bring ten copies of a play in case of bad weather. If it rained, we would all gather on a screened-in porch and perform the play. Not really perform, we'd read it with a lot of flourish. It probably sounds sappy, but it was a lot of fun. One year, we did *Arsenic and Old Lace*."

"Well, well, well. You're not just another Beacon lunkhead jock."

"Are you sure? I thought I was."

The door opened behind them and Earache, Andy, and Diane entered the balcony. Willy thought he heard Janine swear under her breath, and he felt a flush of excitement—could it be that Janine was annoyed because she was having a good time with him and didn't want the others to intrude?

Earache let go of the door and it closed with a loud bang. Andy started to laugh, but as he turned a bottle fell from the paper bag he carried. The beer exploded on the floor.

"God, what's next?" Janine murmured. "Bells and whistles?"

Mr. Richler bellowed angrily from the proscenium, "What's going on up there?"

"Kiss my ass," Andy yelled, then raced out the door. Earache and Diane followed, snickering.

"I guess the show's over," Janine said and bolted out of her seat. Willy ran out of the balcony after her.

The others had turned a corner of the second floor hallway, but their screams and shrieks and laughter seemed to echo throughout the school. "How drunk could those guys get?" Janine wondered. "They were only gone an hour."

Suddenly the uproar became louder, and Earache, Andy, and Diane raced back around the corner toward them.

"Richler!" Earache cried, gasping and laughing.

They turned and ran. At the end of the hallway, Janine veered to the right instead of heading down the stairs. Though he thought it would probably mean getting caught, Willy followed her.

A classroom door that Janine tried was locked, but a janitor's closet opened. "Come on," Janine whispered. They crowded in beside the utility sink and closed the door behind them.

Willy could hear her breathing, and then the sound of suppressed laughter.

"Don't think about how badly you have to pee," Willy said softly. Janine laughed again.

The image of the children's party game, Post Office, came into his mind. He was alone with Janine Smith in the dark, so close he could feel the warmth of her body. "I couldn't have planned this better if I had tried," he spoke aloud.

It was too dark to see, but Willy sensed Janine's puzzled reaction. They both heard someone outside in the corridor.

"Shh."

Footsteps pounded past the broom closet and slowly faded away. Janine cautiously opened the door, then tugged at his arm. "Come on." Her touch on his sleeve thrilled Willy.

They darted down the stairwell and out the side exit. A block away, they caught up with Andy, Earache, and Diane.

It seemed that none of them could stop laughing. Willy felt so exuberant and thrilled that when Earache and Andy suggested going for more beer, he agreed.

"I have to go home," Janine said. "I'll see you guys later. It was a wonderful night at the theater."

Diane had to leave as well and said she'd walk with Janine. Willy watched them stroll down Kent Street until they disappeared into the darkness.

Willy went to see both performances of *Arsenic and Old Lace* that weekend. He spent most of the first act Friday and Saturday night searching the audience for Janine's blond hair. It turned out that Janine was sick and never got to see her brother's acting debut.

Willy rang the doorbell to the Smith house.

He had trotted, stumbled, and walked back to his apartment from the Asylum Road, feeling numb. Then, sitting on the tile floor of the shower, Willy had let the hot water spray over him. He didn't know how long he had stayed there.

Howard answered the door. "Amanda's taking a nap," he said quietly.

They went into the den where flames were blazing in the fireplace. "I thought you might be Teddy. He's coming home."

Teddy was taking the train up from New York City where he was in his first year of law school at Fordham University. He had not heard from his sister in over a month.

"Emil told you about the airline ticket?" Willy inquired. "And that Janine may have been visiting a friend of hers, Susie Conover, in New Orleans?"

Howard nodded.

"None of this makes sense," Howard said. "What is it that people always say in situations like this? That it's like a nightmare? It's much worse than that."

Howard stared into the fire. "I just keep hoping . . . I don't even dare hope too much. Instead, I make these little bargains with myself, or with God, I suppose. I'll hope that Janine is angry with us. Or even having second thoughts about marriage." He glanced at Willy. "That way, she's not missing, she's just staying away for a little while. That way, there can be a happy resolution."

The phone rang. Howard started and rushed into the kitchen. Willy followed him.

"Hello," Howard's voice quavered. He listened a moment, then continued, "I'm Janine's stepfather."

Willy saw Howard's face pale. The sound of hurtling footsteps came from the staircase, then Amanda raced into the kitchen, wild-eyed, her face still creased by the lines of a pillow.

"Yes, we think she was in New Orleans," Howard said, and then, "You saw her?"

Howard listened on the phone. "Oh my God."

Amanda let out a muffled cry. Willy reached out to her because he thought she might collapse, but she steadied herself on the counter.

"Janine is missing," Howard exclaimed into the phone. "We haven't heard from her since Monday night. We've made out a missing persons report. Didn't the New Orleans Police contact you?"

"Howard!" Amanda cried out. "Howard, please, what is it?"

"Yes, I understand. I'll call the police up here," Howard said and slowly hung up the phone. He gave Amanda a bewildered look. "That was Susie Conover's parents. Their daughter is missing, too."

THREE

WILLY WAS STARING OUT the window when he saw Teddy loping up the dark street. Teddy had a distinctive, energetic gait, almost a prance. On more than one occasion, he or Janine had spotted Teddy blocks away, or in a crowd, just by his walk. Teddy glanced at the police car parked in front of the house, then hopped up the steps to the front walk in two bounds. He gave a wave of sorts to Willy in the window, raising the overnight bag he carried.

Teddy entered the house. His mother rushed into his arms. As he hugged Amanda, he gave Howard an inquisitive glance. Howard looked bewildered and shook his head.

Emil and Lonnie were also in the living room. Though only this morning Lonnie and Willy had almost come to blows, Lonnie now smiled at Teddy, a smile open and sincere.

Teddy brought that out in people: He was likable; people were drawn to him. In high school, though other players were better athletes, Teddy had been captain of the baseball team. Still friendly with every one of his former girlfriends, he had even been a member of the wedding at his college sweetheart's marriage. He was clearly the family favorite, though Janine never seemed to resent it. Indeed, she was very close to her brother.

Teddy gently stroked Amanda's back, and it seemed that she was the child and he the parent.

"Janine will come back. She'll come back," Teddy murmured.

Lonnie told Emil to "catch Teddy up on what we know." Emil

somberly repeated all the information he had discovered from the New Orleans Police.

Mr. and Mrs. Peter Conover of Metarie, Louisiana had reported their daughter, Susan, missing this morning. The parents had not heard from their daughter since Monday. Susie had not shown up for work at the advertising agency where she was a copywriter, but it *was* the day after Mardi Gras, so no one was unduly alarmed at first. By that evening, however, when Susie had still not called the office, her co-workers had tried phoning her home and then her parents. They had not been able to get in touch with the Conovers until Thursday morning.

Susie Conover's parents, meanwhile, had started getting nervous by Wednesday evening. They had been trying to reach their daughter on the phone because she had missed a planned dinner. When her co-workers finally contacted the Conovers, Peter Conover left his own office and let himself into his daughter's apartment in the French Quarter. Susie was not there, and her car was missing from the courtyard parking space she had a block away. The Conovers had spent a sleepless night, the father having gone over to his daughter's place several times to check, then they reported her missing Friday morning at dawn.

Janine had in fact visited Susie Conover. Susie's mother, Anne, had seen and talked with Janine on Sunday evening. It had been a light-hearted conversation, and both young women had been looking forward to the festivities. Anne Conover was sure it was Janine: they had met once before when she and her husband had visited their daughter at Colgate. In addition, Susie had told her mother at least a month ago that Janine was coming down for Mardi Gras.

"What have you been able to do?" Teddy asked.

"We're working hard on this," Lonnie replied. "Don't worry."

Right, Willy thought, as if Lonnie being on the case wasn't cause to wake up screaming in the middle of the night.

Emil said, "The most important thing we've discovered is that Janine went to New Orleans, not to Colgate. Now, I'm afraid we're not going to be of much use to you."

Lonnie bristled in the wingback chair and flashed a dark look Emil's way.

"There's not much for us to investigate here. Janine apparently disappeared in New Orleans. She was seen there, but did not use her return ticket. No physical evidence is here for us to examine. There's no crime scene, if in fact a crime has been committed. It's now up to the New Orleans Police. We'll help them in any way, but . . ."

"Call in the FBI," Amanda demanded.

"We can't," Emil answered. "To anyone's knowledge, no federal crime has been committed. A woman . . . two women are missing. That's not the jurisdiction of the FBI."

"But they must have been kidnapped."

"There's been no ransom demand, no evidence of foul play yet. As far as the FBI is concerned, it's just a disappearance. And even if later evidence does suggest foul play, it still won't be the jurisdiction of the FBI unless it's a federal offense, which in this case means a kidnapping for profit."

"Isn't there anything we can do at all?" Teddy implored.

Lonnie said from the wingback chair, "I'm going to do everything in my power to see that she's found."

Before Willy could say that didn't include a whole fucking lot, Teddy nodded and said, "I'm sure we can depend on you."

Emil said, "With your permission, we would like to go through Janine's room."

They all went up the stairs. Janine's bedroom reflected more of Amanda's taste than Janine's. The wallpaper was a rosy pink with tiny flowers, and a white bedspread with pink and blue needlepoint flowers covered the single bed. A framed print of a Degas ballerina hung on the wall. As far as Willy knew, the only change Janine had made in Amanda's decoration was to replace a frilly lamp on the blond wood bedside table with a plain, goose-neck light that was better for reading. Willy remembered Janine once saying she didn't care what the room looked like because she couldn't wait to leave.

They stood uncomfortably in the bedroom, as if afraid of violating a trust. Except for Lonnie, who began pawing through the top drawer of the bureau. Did he have a clue? What did he expect to find? A smoking gun? Bloodstained clothes?

Emil timidly opened the closet door. "Is there anything here, a favorite article of clothing or something, that Janine would have brought with her if she had intended on staying away for a long period of time?"

Willy recalled kids making fun of Emil in grade school for wearing a red sweater every day for a month.

Amanda said, "She would want to take that blazer. She wouldn't leave that." Willy saw the blue wool jacket. He had seen Janine wear it once, a year ago on Thanksgiving, when they had eaten at his parents' house. Janine rarely wore clothes that formal; it had been a present from Amanda.

Willy pointed at a man's beige cashmere sweater resting on the closet shelf. "Janine loves that sweater." It had belonged to Janine's father, who had been a tall, athletic man before disease had wasted him, so that the sweater hung loose and baggy on her. She wore it often, lounging around home or studying at school, but her fondness for the sweater was not only because of its softness and beautiful construction. It had been her father's, and Willy would sometimes see Janine absentmind-edly stroking the wool, the feel of which seemed to comfort her.

Amanda quietly agreed. "Yes, she would have taken that sweater."

Emil sat at the blond-wood vanity with the round mirror and opened a hammered silver box. Most of Janine's jewelry was still there. If Janine had planned on disappearing, Willy thought, she would have taken the jewelry with her.

Amanda inspected the bathroom and reported that Janine had not even taken her toothbrush. She had taken a small travel toothbrush instead. "Janine meant to return, it's absurd to think otherwise," Amanda said.

"We're just trying to be thorough. I'm sure you'd want us to investi-gate every angle, no matter how remote."

"That's not really good news, is it?" Teddy noted.

Lonnie screwed up his face, a show that he was getting ready to ponder hard and long on the question. Emil saved him the trouble by saying, "No it isn't."

"There's still a chance your daughter is alive," Lonnie said.

Willy heard Amanda gasp, then a startled silence came over the room. Lonnie had expressed in his blunt, unthinking way what they all had tried to suppress—that every minute Janine was missing it grew less likely that she was alive.

Emil flushed with discomfort, then peered angrily at Lonnie. "I suppose we're done in here," he said and left the bedroom.

Downstairs, Lonnie said good-bye and was already out the door when Emil asked for some other recent photos of Janine to send down to the New Orleans police. Howard had them ready, along with a written description and Janine's personal data.

Willy left right after Emil and Lonnie and drove back to the duplex. Inside the apartment, he took a bottle of tequila from the kitchen cabinet and rolled himself a joint. Eight hours later, he woke up sick and shivering on the living room floor. He noticed, when he went racing into the bathroom, that he had tears on his cheeks.

The summer before his senior year in high school, Willy worked for Pileggi Paving and Asphalt. It had rained for most of June, so that when the weather finally cleared and turned hot, Pileggi was overwhelmed with jobs and had two, sometimes three crews working.

Pileggi himself had shown up at the job site that morning—the Beacon Federal Bank was replacing its cracked and uneven sidewalks. Pileggi set up the dayglow traffic cones on Main Street and inspected the work already completed—half of the old sidewalk had been jack-hammered—and then left Willy alone to go to another job.

By ten o'clock in the morning, the temperature was already over ninety degrees. Local businessman Gene Wolff and Carl, the sundries store owner, commiserated with Willy at having to work while it was so goddamn hot. Willy wrestled the heavy jackhammer, his legs wide and arms shaking, as the old sidewalk was chipped away.

Then, peering toward the mountains through the shimmer of heat on Main Street, he saw Janine approach, driving her mother's car. Willy barely had time to make the wish, when it came true: Janine stopped at a meter in front of the bank.

As Janine strolled toward the bank, Willy turned off the compressor and said hello.

"You look hot," Janine said.

"Hot? You mean hot, as in sexy, hot-looking?"

"No. I mean hot, as in sweaty, smelly, dank."

"Oh."

She smiled at him flirtatiously, at least Willy hoped it was flirtation, and went into the bank.

Willy finished the front sidewalk. Though work still had to be done around the side of the building, Willy began shoveling, just moving dirt back and forth near the door. He didn't want to risk missing Janine when she left the bank.

Finally, Janine came out.

"It's still hot out," Willy remarked and thought it wasn't the cleverest thing he had ever said.

"It sure is, that's why I'm going to Sylvan Lake." She gave him a teasing look. "Cold, wet, refreshing Sylvan Lake."

Willy smiled, "I wish I was going there." And then he surprised himself by adding, "With you."

Janine raised her eyebrows.

Willy could feel his heart racing as he blurted out, "I'd love to be going anywhere with you."

"It's too bad you have to work."

"Why is that?"

"Because I'd ask you to come to the lake with me."

Willy threw down his shovel, picked up his T-shirt, and sauntered toward Janine's car. "Let's go."

Driving away from the bank, Willy looked back out the car's rear window at the truck and compressor and jackhammer and hand tools. "How long do you think it will take for all that to get stolen?"

"Aren't you going to get fired for this?"

"Jesus, I would certainly think so. I mean you just can't leave tools lying around and a gaping hole in the middle of Main Street."

"Why are you doing this?"

"To be with you," Willy had replied. He kept himself from saying, "I would do anything to be with you."

On the way to the lake, Willy barely took notice of the lush, green woods, the small hamlets with old stone Dutch Reformed churches, the lonely houses built by the county highway, the gas stations and aluminum buildings, the open fields. He watched Janine behind the wheel of her mother's large Chrysler Imperial, so correct, turning the steering wheel hand-over-hand just as she had been taught in Driver's Ed., and the act of driving seemed such a marvel, something wondrous. They talked effortlessly, and when Janine would laugh at something Willy had said, pleasure surged through him.

At the toll shack at the entrance to the lake, Janine let Willy pay the admission, and it dawned on him that this was a date. He was on a date with Janine Smith!

Janine drove the Imperial toward the front of the unpaved parking lot, beneath the shade of a maple tree. Willy took off his work boots and threw them in the trunk of the car. The cut-off dungarees he had worn to work were what he normally swam in, so there had been no need to go home and pick up a swim suit.

The beach at Sylvan Lake was a grassy area between a cinder-block refreshment stand and a thin strand of sand that descended into the water. Janine stopped ten yards from the sand, undid the top button of her cut-off jeans, and lowered the zipper. She eased the jeans from her hips, let them drop to the grass, then stepped out of them. Her navy blue T-shirt seemed to soar over her head as she took it off. Her actions seemed so intimate, so sensual. She was wearing a pale rose bikini underneath her clothes. Willy was riveted by the beauty of her body.

An old patchwork quilt came out of Janine's straw beach bag and was billowed onto the grass. The quilt had tattered in places, and a faded bloodstain in the center had not quite washed out. Janine spread her beach towel over the stain and sat down. Willy lay on his side beside her.

She began to spread suntan lotion over her body. Willy watched as her hands rubbed the oil up her legs, and inside her thighs. Willy caught a quick glimpse of a lone hair peeking out of her bikini bottom. She stroked the lotion up her arms and down between her breasts.

Janine said, "Now is the time, in your dreams, that I say, 'Could you help me rub this on?' "

Willy let out an exaggerated sigh.

She smiled, then tossed him the bottle of oil and turned her back to him. "Could you help me rub this on?"

Willy squeezed some of the oil into a warm puddle in his palm. Smoothing the lotion into the center of Janine's back, he gently massaged it over her skin, under the strap of her top, and along her sides. His hands seemed to tingle, and his mind wavered between a yearning ache for her and a delirious joy. As he finished, he wasn't sure, but he thought she might have quivered slightly.

They lounged on the quilt, swam in the lake, talked. Everything about the day seemed extraordinary—the green-hued water of the lake, the crystalline sunlight, even the music playing from the tinny speakers at the refreshment stand. When Janine gave Willy her towel to dry himself, he could smell her suntan lotion and the faint sweet scent of her, and he wanted to hug the towel to himself. Later in the afternoon, Janine fell asleep on the quilt. Willy lay beside her, listening to her soft breathing. Once she stirred, and her arm just barely brushed his own. Willy felt a transcendent happiness wash over him.

They left Sylvan Lake, and Janine dropped Willy off at home. As he entered the kitchen where his parents and brother were eating cold chicken and salads because of the heat, the expression on his father's face told him that Pileggi had called. Before his father could start yelling, Willy dumbfounded him by saying, "It was worth it. It was the best thing I've ever done in my life."

He called her on the telephone. Amanda answered and said Janine couldn't come to the phone, they were eating. Should she have Janine call him back?

"No, just say it's Willy Buchanan. Tell her I got fired."

He heard Amanda repeat the message. As Amanda said good-bye and hung up, Willy could hear Janine's gleeful laughter in the background.

Janine went to the New Jersey shore the next day. She stayed almost a month. About two weeks after he was fired, he received a postcard from Janine. Cryptographers trying to break the Japanese code before Pearl Harbor did not work as hard as Willy did trying to decipher hidden meanings in Janine's message.

Dear Willy, the card had read. She had written *Dear*. Didn't that mean she liked him?

Greetings from the shore. I don't want to make the beach sound too tempting: some more power tools might wind up strewn all over Main Street. And haven't I already brought enough misery and heartache into your life? Not to mention your résumé. See you soon.—Janine.

Willy read and reread the card. Janine was coming back and she wanted to see him. See you soon, she had written, see you soon.

FOUR

"YEAH, WE HAVE IT. A light blue '66 Mustang. GGZ 966," the voice with the Bronx accent said over the phone, "We've checked it out. Everything looks fine."

"Thanks for getting back to me," said Emil. "I appreciate it."

"No problem. It's nice to get a request where we don't find a body in the trunk."

Emil had been surprised to receive the call from the Port Authority Police at La Guardia Airport so quickly. He had made the request to search the airport parking lots for Janine's car less than eight hours ago and assumed they would give the search a low priority, maybe get around to it in a few days. But then the call came in for "Detective Deshayes." Thank God he had picked up the call himself. He could just imagine the fit Lonnie would have had with that "Detective Deshayes."

Outwardly, Lonnie had made a show of being unhappy when Emil was assigned to assist in the investigation of Janine Smith's disappearance. But, Emil thought, Lonnie must be secretly relieved to have someone guiding him. Because it was obvious that he hadn't the faintest idea what to do in this fairly straightforward investigation. Working with Lonnie was like living a constant good cop, bad cop routine. No, make that good cop, bonehead cop routine. And working as a cop in Beacon was hard enough.

People seemed to think of cops as stupid, lazy, or, lately, fascist. In a city as small as Beacon—just twelve thousand inhabitants—you couldn't help but know all the police, just as you knew the town drunks and the town idiot. Emil would walk into a bar, off-duty, just wanting to get a beer on a hot summer night, and the patrons would look at him warily, as if he were a stern parent come home too early. Or people, made uncomfortable by the uniform, would utter vague, insincere, right-wing bromides to him about law and order.

He looked around the bullpen area of the police station. Emil had figured it out a while ago that he was going to be chief of police before he was forty. The Beacon Police Department had grown old. In his nearly four years as a cop, twelve policemen had retired or quit. That meant that at age twenty-three Emil was now senior to nearly a third of the force. Every one of his superiors, the sergeants, the detectives, the chief, was over the age of forty-five. The promotions, retirements, and seniority of officers could be charted out, and indeed Emil had done just that. Sam Pittman would succeed Ron Antone as chief, and Emil would succeed Sam.

Janine's car had been found at La Guardia. That had been expected, and was just one of those leads you followed to be thorough. The discovery supported the other evidence. Janine had gone on a little fling to New Orleans and didn't want her parents or boyfriend to know. Emil had uncovered that much. He had informed the New Orleans Police and had passed along the pictures and the description. His involvement in the case was probably now at an end. Emil was surprised how depressed this prospect left him.

Living in Beacon was strange. It seemed everybody in town knew you, or thought they knew you. And too often you were defined by things that had happened while you were growing up. If you had flunked second grade, you were considered a dullard for the rest of your life. People's estimation of you was based on how well you had played basketball during recess fifteen years ago, or if you had failed to make Pop Warner League. Your social status, if such a thing existed in a dump like Beacon, was frozen at high school.

Emil remembered a party which, as it turned out, had been his last ditch attempt at breaking into the cliquish social life of Beacon High. He had overheard kids at school talking about a party down at the river. It had sounded like a huge bash, with a keg and a hundred people in the darkness. He would go there, he had thought, and be protected by the anonymity of the crowd and . . . Emil felt himself shudder with embarrassment as he recalled what he had hoped would happen. He would have a few beers; Eric Boyd or Andy Brascia or Willy Buchanan would joke around with him; he'd meet a girl, not Janine Smith or Cheryl Melton, you know, not a goddess, but someone like Patty

Chisolm or Diane Niedzialkowski who would . . . God, what could he have been thinking? That his life would turn into some fantasy from a Teen Romance comic book? That he would be *popular*? *Perky, peppy* Emil Deshayes, homecoming king. Jesus Christ.

That Friday night, he had gone to the river. To get to the party, Emil had to drive alongside the railroad tracks half a mile, so that people saw his distinctive Plymouth Barracuda coming for minutes. A keg stood by the bonfire, all right, but only twenty or so kids were staring at who was coming into their midst. Not one of those staring eyes belonged to someone who was even remotely his friend.

His first thought had been to turn the car around and leave. But everybody knew his Barracuda, and it would take two or three passes to turn the car in the other direction. He couldn't just say he had happened by—why would he come down the deserted dead-end dirt road by himself? To whack off?

He got out of his car and nodded. Everyone's eyes were still on him. No one spoke. Emil wanted to run away into the woods and never set foot in school again. Kyle McGwire's smirking face loomed in front of him. Seemingly compelled to aid in his own downfall, he approached Kyle. Emil's words rushed out in a slurred garble. "Areyougettingmoneycollectthekeg?" it must have come out. He had wanted to know if he had to chip in money to help pay for the keg.

McGwire's evil face had sneered. "Emil, you got the engraved invitation? What the fuck are you doing here?"

Emil had actually prayed. "Please, God, just let me leave. Just let me get far away from here." He heard some snickers beyond the bonfire and saw McGwire's grin. It was so unfair. People weren't invited to parties in Beacon. There wasn't a fucking guest list.

"I asked Emil to drop by," Emil heard someone say. It was Janine Smith! Jesus Christ, it was Janine Smith, someone he had never spoken to! Emil was shocked that she even knew his name. She was looking at Kyle McGwire. "I didn't realize you were Pearl Mesta, the hostess with the mostest, or I would have cleared it with you." Laughter rang out, louder this time, and it wasn't directed at Emil.

McGwire laughed and said, "Hey, I'm joking."

Emil laughed too, a sheepish moronic laugh, no doubt, and hoping to disappear, skulked off to the keg. His hand shook as he poured a beer. Then he had leaned against the hood of his Barracuda near the edge of the party. Maybe, he prayed, everyone would just ignore him. Then, Janine sidled up and sat on the hood beside him.

He wanted to thank her for her kindness, but couldn't make himself speak. And he was terrified of what she would say now. Emil didn't think he could bear her condescension. *God, Kyle McGwire is such an asshole,* she would say, or *I can't bear cruelty to others,* or *I didn't do that for you, it was the principle.* If she said something like that, he would just turn from her and walk down the train tracks until he met a locomotive.

"The heat from the engine feels nice and warm on my heinie," Janine had said.

Emil laughed, startled. It was so unexpected. Heinie? And then he felt an absurd pride, because it was his car providing the warmth.

"Anyplace else, if you hear of a party, you want to wear your nicest clothes. In Beacon, you wear your warmest."

Emil nodded in agreement, as if he had the same dilemma.

They talked for fifteen minutes, or rather Janine talked and Emil, thrilled and tongue-tied, managed only to nod and laugh knowingly and say, "yeah," "that's right," and "uh huh." Then Patty Chisolm came over. She gave Emil a perfunctory smile and said to Janine, "I've got to pee like a racehorse." She and Janine went off down the rocky river bank, out of sight. When they returned, they proceeded to the keg. Before Janine finished pouring her beer, five or six others joined her, and then it seemed that they edged Janine away from him toward the warmth of the bonfire. An amber glow was cast over Janine by the flames which appeared both inviting and threatening. He longed to join them, but sat immobile on the hood of his car.

Emil forced himself to stay at the party for an acceptable amount of time so that it wouldn't seem quite so obvious that he was fleeing in embarrassment. And then he fled in embarrassment.

He had to make a five-point turn to reverse the car on the narrow road. Making the turn, the Barracuda stalled, of course, and then he nearly flooded the engine. Finally he drove back down the dirt road. As he left, he heard loud guffaws of laughter. Immensely relieved to be away from the party, Emil almost didn't mind that the laughter was probably at his expense. On the way home, he slammed the steering wheel with his fists and screamed at himself, "You asshole, you pathetic, little asshole."

After that night, he hadn't exactly adored Janine from afar, wasn't her devoted puppy, had no delusions of a romance or dreams of kissing her in the moonlight. Yet Emil felt affection and tenderness toward her. He wished her well, rooted for her as a fan cheers for the quarterback. She would see him in the halls and nod or say hello, and one time when they both happened to be skipping sixth period, racing down the stairs toward the exit, she had laughed and said, "Aren't you supposed to be in class?" before veering off in the other direction.

When Janine started to go out with Willy Buchanan, Emil was not jealous, or not very much, but rather, was happy for her. It seemed fitting that she should be going out with someone like Willy, who was witty, handsome, athletic. Willy had always been pleasant to him, but, Emil had managed to blow that, too. He had allowed himself to think that since they both had this . . . attraction to Janine that, well, they were friends. Emil shuddered again, as he recollected that appalling day in the lunchroom, when he had been so nervous and couldn't stop himself from babbling like a fool about football and then . . .

Emil took two deep breaths and tried to think of other things. Why was he berating himself about all this ancient history? Hell, next he'd be bringing up the time he had wet his pants in kindergarten.

He exhaled slowly. Willy probably never thought about that fight, if you could call Emil's getting his ass slammed to the floor and pie smeared all over his face a fight. These last few days, Willy had been friendly, even grateful for all that Emil was doing.

And Janine? Janine was probably dead. Soon, someone in New Orleans would notice a sickly-sweet smell coming from a motel room, or a child at play would run horrified from a dumpster. And Emil could do absolutely nothing about it.

He had never thanked Janine for that night. Emil had written a letter, but had torn it up. Not because he would be embarrassed to send it, but because she would be embarrassed to receive it. During long, boring Geometry classes, however, he fantasized ways to repay her. He would save her from a demented rapist; he would be the first to come upon a car wreck and have to give her mouth-to-mouth resuscitation. Lurid, absurd daydreams, usually featuring a torn blouse, that stopped just short of Emil battling a black-clad villain and untying Janine from the tracks seconds before a train crushed her.

And now when Janine was really in danger? Where was Emil, the intrepid, the rescuer?

The New Orleans Police Department telexed the Background Information Form, requesting additional information about Janine, the next day. The request, no doubt, was precipitated more by Susan Conover's disappearance than Janine's; pressure was probably being brought to bear on the New Orleans Police by the Conover family. At the least, Emil thought, the form indicated that the Missing Persons Bureau in New Orleans was taking Janine's case seriously.

After speaking with Willy Buchanan and Amanda Smith on the phone, Emil started to fill out the Background Information Form. Janine Ann Smith, born May 14, 1952, in Beacon, New York; her telephone number; her mother's house on West Willow Street as her permanent address; another at Colgate as her previous address. Time at permanent address: twenty years.

Emil began to fill out the Personal Description. *Height: Five foot six. Weight: one hundred and fifteen pounds. Build:* Emil almost wrote phenomenal. He could remember seeing Janine in a bikini at Sylvan Lake. Thinking back, he had an image of himself staring at her body, his eyes telescoping out of his head like a lecherous, zoot-suited Big Bad Wolf in Looney Tune cartoons. Emil was torn between writing very fit or athletic and had finally settled on *slim.*

Eyes: Blue. Hair: Blond. Race: Caucasian. Complexion: Honeyed? Like peaches and cream? He wrote *fair, clear.*

Scars or Tattoos: None. Deformities: None. Unusual Mannerism (stammer, facial tic, etc.): None. No space was set aside where he could communicate that, out of a room of a hundred people, you would notice Janine, or to write: Look for an amazingly beautiful woman.

Emil continued. Janine had never been arrested, or fingerprinted for employment. She had never been in the armed forces. She belonged to no unions or organizations. She had worked, summers only, as a waitress and behind the counter at a dry cleaners. He jotted down her driver's license and social security numbers, knowing that none of this information was going to be of any use if Janine's body had been thrown into the Mississippi River.

When he came to the financial history section, Emil wrote down her credit card number and the numbers to her checking and savings accounts. Amanda had mentioned that Janine had almost seventy-thousand dollars in savings. Emil already knew about this money, however, not because of any investigation on his part, but rather because he lived in Beacon.

Emil recalled when Janine's father was dying. One Sunday in church, he was shocked when he saw Mr. Smith, gaunt and with most of his hair gone. Afterward, at home, his mother and aunt discussed his appearance. "He has . . . cancer." His mother had said the word "cancer" furtively, in a whisper, though only the family sat in the kitchen. Later, after Ed Smith had died, his mother and aunt had discussed the will, noting that the kids had received most of the money. That conversation, down to exact dollar figures, had probably been repeated in half the homes in town. Certainly almost everybody in Beacon High had known that Teddy Smith and his little sister had sixty-thousand dollars each in a trust fund.

Now, with interest, the sum was almost seventy-thousand dollars. No money had been withdrawn from the account. And though it was being held in trust until she turned twenty-five, surely if Janine had planned on disappearing, she would have found a way to take some of that money with her.

Family Data: Emil copied down the Smiths' names, maiden name, ages, and relationship to Janine. He included aunts and uncles from both Edward's and Amanda's families, as well as Howard Smith's. None of this information was likely to be of any use. Yet, just listing the names was comforting and gave Emil the sense that he was actually doing something to help find Janine.

Church Membership: Emil wrote down, *Catholic, St. John's Church, Beacon, New York,* as Amanda had told him, even though Willy had said that Janine hadn't been to church, except for Midnight Mass on Christmas Eve, for years.

Hobbies, Activities, Interests: Emil wrote down *reading, movies, dance, art,* hoping that it didn't make Janine sound like a vacuous Playboy centerfold or a beauty pageant contestant.

When was Subject last heard from? Emil gave the date of the Monday night phone call to Willy and noted that it was from the bar in New Orleans.

What has been done to locate this person? Emil, finally giving in to his feelings, wrote, *Not enough.*

FIVE

THE HEADLINE OF THE *Beacon-Newburgh Evening News* read: AREA WOMAN MISSING. The story went on to say that Janine Smith, daughter of Howard and Amanda Smith of Beacon, had disappeared. She had not returned from a trip to New Orleans to visit friends and attend Mardi Gras. A friend she was visiting had been reported missing as well. The Beacon Police were investigating in conjunction with the New Orleans Police Department. No mention was made of Janine's lies about going to Colgate, or of Willy.

Willy sat at the counter of Carl's and read the article three times. The story seemed not quite real, about someone else, not Janine.

It was Saturday afternoon, Janine had been missing now for—three days? Just three days? It seemed so much longer, weeks, months.

"Any word of Janine?" Carl asked, a self-conscious expression on his face as he refilled the coffee cup. When Willy had slipped in, Carl had given him a solemn nod instead of yelling, "Here's another gutter-snipe," or "You're late, all the other deadbeats are gone." He had placed a cup of coffee in front of Willy, as he had been doing since Willy was a boy, and then had gone down to the end of the counter.

"No, we haven't heard anything."

Carl shook his head. "This is unbelievable."

Willy had waited until two o'clock to come to Carl's. His friends, Earache Kehler, Terry Pritchard, Andy Brascia would have left by then. They would have heard about Janine, so the usual conversation about hangovers and the misadventures of the previous night would have been dispensed with. Willy had felt strange coming here. It was as if he should be in mourning, and he felt he was casting a funereal pall. Scott Donleavy's father and Alan Chopus, who were sitting at a table by the paperback book rack, were speaking in hushed tones.

Most of the regulars, including Willy, ran a tab for the week and paid Carl on Saturdays. But Carl had not handed Willy his tab as he normally would have.

Willy gazed across the counter. By the cash register, a cardboard display contained plastic disks with teeth that were supposedly used for combing hair. The Ease of a Brush, the Convenience of a Comb! was emblazoned over the picture of a man who looked like a 1920s matinee idol. A few months ago, Janine had been with Willy at the counter. She had teasingly questioned Carl about the dusty display.

"Carl, do you sell a lot of those?"

Everyone at the counter had laughed. Carl sold a weird hodgepodge of items at his store, which was stocked, it appeared, by whim. You could buy a zipper, but not thread, cough medicine and aspirin, but no Kleenex. "You see the sign out front," he would say, "it says Sundries and that's what I sell, Sundries."

"Yeah," Carl had answered Janine. "I sell them all the time."

"I've been coming here for five years, and that same picture of Rudolph Valentino, or whoever he is, and those same brushes were there back then."

"I sell them all the time. As a matter of fact . . ." Carl had taken out a magic marker and added, MARKED DOWN, below the matinee idol's face.

Janine had counted the brushes.

"I'm going to come back after twenty years, and you'll still have those same eight brushes."

Willy counted the brushes. Eight still hung on the display.

Willy asked for his weekly tab, paid it, and left. He drove by the Smith house but didn't stop. He went instead to his parents and ate dinner there. His Mom and Dad tried to be upbeat, but during dessert his mother rushed from the table, sobbing. Willy followed her, hoping to comfort her, but he couldn't think of any soothing words.

"I'm all right, everything is going to be fine. I'm just so upset," his mother said, then started to cry again.

He left around nine and went back to the apartment. A note from Earache was taped to the inner door: "If you need anything, give me a call." It's what people wrote in sympathy cards, Willy thought.

Last night, Emil had gone through Janine's closet, seeking some clue to her disappearance. It had seemed foolish to Willy then. Though skeptical that he would discover anything, Willy began to search through the apartment with about as much understanding of what he was looking for as Lonnie had yesterday in Janine's room.

Willy opened the bedroom closet. Except for a new white terry cloth robe and a paint-splattered work outfit, all of Janine's clothes were still at the Smiths. He took the robe from the hanger and inspected the pockets. They were empty.

In the bathroom, Janine kept a toothbrush, a hairbrush, Tampax, perfume. That was it. She was going to bring the rest of her makeup and toiletries after the wedding.

The boxes that had yet to be unpacked were scattered all over the apartment, but most were in the spare bedroom. Willy separated the boxes, piling the ones he had brought against one wall. He began sorting through Janine's.

The first box contained pots and pans. Aware of the foolishness of his behavior, he took out every pan and inspected it. It came as no surprise that the ten-inch saucepan gave no clue to where Janine had gone. The next box was books. Saul Bellow, Carson McCullers, Kurt Vonnegut, Henry Miller, Margaret Mitchell. He fanned every book, to make sure nothing was hidden in the pages. Willa Cather, Germaine Greer, Sylvia Plath, Joan Didion, J.D. Salinger, Vladimir Nabokov.

Bed linens were neatly folded inside another carton. He shook out every sheet and pillow case.

Another box held more books, textbooks from school: biology, poetry anthologies, Sartre, art history. Beneath were about fifteen bound composition books with black and white covers. Willy opened the top notebook and saw jottings about Heidegger in Janine's neat handwriting. He leafed through the pages. "Important: paper must be handed in before midterm," Janine had printed in large block letters on the top of one page.

The next notebook was for a biology class, the one below that in the pile was for Modern British Fiction. Willy fanned the dozen or so remaining notebooks. Nothing fell out.

Record albums, many of them duplicates of Willy's own records, overflowed another box. They would have two copies of the Beatles' *White Album* and *Abbey Road*, two of *Are You Experienced?*, two Sam and Daves. Double copies of Crosby, Stills & Nash, the Grateful Dead, *Eat a Peach*, *Tommy*, *Sticky Fingers*, Wilson Pickett, and Joni Mitchell.

A jar full of loose change sat beside a tennis racket in another box. A manila envelope was stuffed with warranties, guarantees, sales slips, instruction booklets. A five-dollar bill fell out of a Beacon High Yearbook. A long-forgotten, crumbly joint and what looked like two yellowed hits of blotter acid were hidden in a small fake jade case.

Willy opened a large cookie tin. It contained hundreds of photos. Pictures of Janine as a little girl, squealing with delight as her father lifted her high in the air. A skinny four-year-old Janine at the beach, and a rounder thirteen-year-old Janine at the same beach, this time wearing a top to her bathing suit. Snapshots of Teddy and Janine unwrapping presents.

Willy picked up a picture of himself with Janine. His hair was longer, and he had his arm around Janine's shoulder. She looked impossibly beautiful and happy.

Janine had come back from the New Jersey shore very tan.

On the night she was to return, Willy had gone past Janine's house three different times. Finally, resigning himself to another day without seeing her, he had decided to go down to Main Street to hang out with his no-account friends.

Then, walking down Main Street, he had spotted the Smith car, piled high with vacation luggage, driving toward home. Janine, who was in the back seat with Teddy, noticed him and waved. Willy immediately turned around.

Two blocks from the Smith house, he saw her sauntering toward him on West Willow Street.

"I'm back."

"Good," Willy said. "Now I won't have to drive by your house six times a day and stare longingly at your bedroom window."

Janine gave Willy a quizzical glance.

"Where are you going?"

"I was going to drop by Patty's," Janine replied. "Then maybe to the movies."

"I was going to the movies, myself."

"You were?"

Willy nodded.

"What's playing?"

"I haven't the faintest idea."

"*The Thomas Crown Affair*," Janine said. "With Steve McQueen."

"Right, Steve McQueen, former Olympic swimmer, the guy who plays Tarzan. He's my favorite actor."

They had reached the end of the block. The way to the Beacon Theater was to the left; the way to Patty Chisolm's was to the right.

"Would you like to go to the movies with me?" asked Willy.

Janine hesitated, then said, "You're going to have to buy me popcorn."

On the way, Janine told Willy about the shore. She had had a wonderful time, the month had gone by in a whir. The time Janine was away had seemed interminable to Willy.

"Were your parents mad at you for getting fired from your job?" Janine wondered.

"It was the best thing that happened to my father all summer. He decided that since I was part of the hard-core unemployed, I might as well paint the house this year instead of him." Willy twisted his paint-flecked arm and held it up in front of her. "Do you like the color? My father does. He told me so the other day as he was lying in the hammock."

Janine laughed, and all the hours in the hot sun scraping paint chips suddenly seemed worth it.

Willy and Janine arrived at the Beacon Theater twenty minutes before the start of the show. They sat and talked in the air-conditioned darkness, and Willy would have been happy if the projector never rolled. Finally, the United Artists logo appeared on the screen.

During the picture, Willy was more aware of Janine—her shifting in her seat, the crossing and uncrossing of her legs, the moments when their arms or thighs would briefly touch—than of what was happening up on the screen.

When the movie let out, they headed back to Janine's house through dark streets, moving from one pool of light spilled from a streetlamp to another. Occasionally a car would drive by, or they would see a cigarette burning or hear murmuring from a front porch, but for the most part, it seemed as though just the two of them wandered over a private domain. Their voices and laughter carried in the darkness, so Janine huddled close, brushing his shoulder with her own as she spoke about a party down at the shore.

They came, at last, to Janine's house.

"I forgot to ask. Did you like the movie?"

"It was all right," Janine answered. "Though I liked it more tonight than when I saw it three nights ago down at the shore."

Willy leaned down and kissed her and was surprised and overjoyed when she returned his kiss passionately.

Janine stood back and looked up at him. Willy thought he discerned the same exhilaration he was feeling in her eyes. Before climbing the slate steps and going into the house, she said, "I had fun."

The next night, Willy had to play in an American Legion baseball game. In the top of the sixth inning, trotting out to his position at second base, he saw Janine arrive and sit in the bleachers. Willy knew that Janine couldn't care less about baseball; she had come to see him. That inning, Willy made an error, his first in over nine games.

After the last out, Willy joined Janine who was sitting alone on the top row of the bleachers.

"You screwed up that play."

"I intended to throw the ball five feet over the first baseman's head." Willy smiled. "Actually, I had a loss of concentration."

"Did it have anything to do with my showing up?"

Willy nodded.

"Good," Janine said. "Did it cost you the game?"

"No."

"Would it have mattered if it had?"

"No."

"I think you're getting your priorities straight."

An hour later, Willy, still wearing his baseball uniform, and Janine were on the couch in the family room in the basement of the Smith house. Willy, deliriously happy, had his mouth to Janine's breasts, flicking her nipples with his tongue.

After that, with nothing really said between them about it, they had started to go out. Willy would dumbfound himself by thinking, "I'm Janine's boyfriend. She is my girlfriend. We are going steady."

It was incredible, he thought, that something he had dreamt about could actually come true.

SIX

A WEEK WENT BY. Every morning, Willy would think, Today's the day that we will hear something. He no longer thought he would hear from Janine, just that he would hear of her. Instead, there was only a fearful silence.

Teddy went back to school the next weekend. Nothing was being accomplished by his remaining in Beacon. He wasn't helping Janine or even Amanda. Howard returned to his job at IBM the following Monday. He couldn't think of anything else to do.

Willy worked for Jimmy Guido as he always had—day-to-day depending on the jobs, weather, and the extent of Jimmy's hangovers. He toiled mindlessly, sometimes looking with amazement at a roof half covered with shingles, two or three hours of labor he was not aware of doing. Every day, Willy would call or drop by the Smith house. He and Amanda had come to a truce of sorts. They both were too numb to continue their bickering.

Time was passing, and still no news of Janine came.

Janine's credit card bill arrived in the mail. At first, Amanda had stared at Janine's name in the glassine window of the envelope and had wanted to cry. Then, she opened the bill mechanically. Janine owed close to seven hundred dollars. Normally, Amanda would have been peeved at Janine for letting her debt get so high, but now it seemed so unimportant. The terrible thought that this was the last expense she would ever have to pay for Janine had just entered her mind, when she noticed an item on the statement.

Five dollars and forty cents had been charged at a New Orleans gas station on Wednesday, March 7, the day after Janine had disappeared.

Emil was angry at himself.

This morning, Emil had placed yet another phone call to Dave Grischuck, a security officer for the company who had issued Janine Smith a credit card. As usual, Emil had been put on hold: Grischuck clearly felt that Emil's calls were a nuisance.

At the beginning of the investigation, just about the first thing Emil had done was to contact the credit card company. It was standard procedure. One of the best ways to track missing persons, especially those who wanted to vanish, was by checking on the financial ties that entangled almost everyone. It was surprising how many people who disappeared on their own continued to use their social security numbers or checking accounts or credit cards.

In that first call, Emil had explained about Janine's disappearance. Dave Grischuck had promised to contact the Beacon Police should any activity occur on Janine's card. Emil had phoned Grischuck the next day, and then the next to see if any charges had been credited overnight. Grischuck had testily assured Emil that he would be contacted immediately, that there was no need to call daily. Emil had taken him at his word. Against his better judgment, he had not bothered Grischuck again. Until this morning. When finally put through, Emil had heard, "I was just about to call you."

Startled, Emil had replied, "There's been activity on Janine's card?"

"Yes. After you say she disappeared. On the seventh, the tenth, the eleventh, and the fifteenth."

"The seventh? The tenth?" Emil couldn't keep the outrage out of his voice. "You were supposed to call me the moment anything arrived. You promised me—"

"We only received the first charges three days ago. It often takes a while for us to get them."

"Three days ago! Do you know how long that is in an investigation? Why didn't you call us then?"

"I've been away from the office since the beginning of the week," Grischuck said in an unconvincing voice.

Emil was enraged at both Grischuck and himself. Aware that his daily calls to check on Janine's account had annoyed Grischuck, he had let his irritated tone cow him. He had not wanted to displease.

"Those are all the charges?"

"There may be other transactions as well that haven't been posted yet. Retailers vary."

"How close is Janine to her credit limit?"

"The account is over, way over. The credit limit is only seven hundred and fifty dollars. Right now, it's almost at two thousand. But, that's typical for stolen cards. I'll cancel it immediately."

"Wait a minute," Emil must have yelled, because Sam Pittman stuck his head out of a cubicle and stared. "This is our only lead. You can't cancel that card."

"It's way over the limit."

"Listen, I guarantee that the family will pay the bill. And if the family doesn't, the Beacon Police Department will. Don't cancel the card."

Emil had no authority to make either of those promises. As strapped as the Beacon Police Department was for funds, the chief would not be likely to fork out thousands of dollars if the Smith family refused to pay. Would Grischuck be aware of that?

"Well, we're on computer. It will automatically flag the card."

"A woman's life may be at stake. I can't tell you how important this is. I'm sure if you want to, you can see to it that Janine's account remains open. You have to do this."

Emil heard silence, then Grischuck's reluctant answer. "All right, I'll see what I can do."

Grischuck was going to see what he could do, Emil knew, and then would cancel the card. *I did everything possible*, he would whine afterward.

Emil couldn't give him that opening. "What's the exact current balance of Janine's account? A check will be in the mail today."

Grischuck gave him the amount. Arrangements were made to get copies of the credit card slips to both the New Orleans and Beacon police departments, and Grischuck pledged once again to alert both police forces immediately if any more charges arrived.

After the call, Emil stood, sat down, and then stood again. He tried to bridle his feelings of rash optimism. The person using the credit card probably was not Janine. The spending pattern, over a thousand dollars in five days, indicated a stolen credit card. Still, it was possible that Janine, for whatever reason, wanted to disappear and was using the card herself. Or she might be under duress. If someone other than Janine was charging on the card, that person's capture might lead the police to Janine, or help resolve what had happened to her.

When Emil phoned Amanda, he was amazed to learn that she already knew about one of the credit card charges. Incredibly, she was holding the bill in her hand and had been about to call the Beacon Police.

"There are other charges beside the one on the bill?" Amanda asked.

Emil was thankful that he could rattle off all the information he had received from Grischuck. Amanda, if not impressed, at least seemed persuaded that Emil and the Beacon Police Department were doing a competent job. Emil was not as sure. If he had not chosen this morning to contact Grischuck again, he would not have seemed the assiduous police officer that Amanda supposed.

He should have had this information days ago. They might have been able to follow the trail of credit card receipts more closely. Certainly, the memories of store clerks and gas station attendants would be fresher. What were the odds that the person who pumped five dollars worth of gas in New Orleans, someone who had probably run off credit card slips for hundreds of people in the interim, would remember anything about the person who had charged that tankful of gasoline?

Amanda said she was going immediately to the post office to mail the check special delivery to the credit card company. She thanked Emil for all his work.

Copies of Janine's credit card slips arrived at the Beacon Police station that evening just as Grischuck had promised.

Emil called Detective Huey Oliver of the New Orleans Police Missing Persons squad for the second time that day. The earlier call had been to inform New Orleans of the credit card activity.

Huey Oliver recognized his voice. "Emil, how are you doing? We got the copies."

This was about the twentieth time they had spoken. In the beginning, Oliver had been a bit abrupt on the phone. It wasn't that he was disagreeable, or failed to treat Emil with professional courtesy. His tone simply stated that Janine's disappearance was not going to be a high priority of the New Orleans Police. Emil had understood. Like most other big city police forces, the New Orleans Police were under-staffed and overburdened with cases. With Missing Persons, where most of the cases ended with bickering spouses or hungry, disillu-sioned, runaway teenagers returning on their own, the workload was especially onerous.

In addition to the crushing number of cases, usually not much could be done to trace a missing person. Detectives could check hospitals, jails, or morgues. They could list the person with a national registry of missing persons or runaways. There was rarely a crime scene to investigate. Quite often there wasn't a crime—it wasn't against the law to run away from an abusive husband, or to die with no identification. Little money was available for detectives to traipse around the country. Usually missing persons were found when they were arrested on other charges, or died, or applied for some social service like Welfare.

So Emil had not been particularly surprised by Oliver's initial tone. Nonetheless, he had phoned Oliver four times in those first two days, hoping that his insistence would keep the New Orleans cops from filing Janine's case and forgetting about it.

Susan Conover's disappearance had changed Oliver's attitude. Two women were missing now, one of whom belonged to a well-connected New Orleans family. Susan Conover's father had worked in the New Orleans District Attorney's Office before going into private practice. Emil had been heartened by this new diligence. Lately, though, Oliver had been calling and telexing Emil nearly every day. Suddenly, Janine and Susan Conover's case had acquired an importance and urgency that the Conovers' connections did not explain.

"Have you had a chance to look over the credit slips?" Emil asked.

"Yeah. Seems like a stolen card to me. Look at those signatures. I'm not a handwriting expert, but those later ones aren't even close."

Grischuck had telexed copies of all of Janine's credit card slips from the beginning of the last billing period. The earlier charges were from the Beacon area—a travel agency in Poughkeepsie had issued a ticket to New Orleans almost a month before Janine left. All these slips bore Janine's neat, rounded signature. The other charges, starting from the tenth of March, were all signed in the same hurried, slovenly hand that was obviously not Janine's.

"And they're from all over the goddamn country which isn't going to make our work any easier," Oliver added.

Emil scrutinized the copies. Louisiana, Texas, New Mexico. Charges for gas, food, men's clothing, sporting goods, jewelry. He picked up the slip, dated the seventh, for the gas station in New Orleans.

"What about this slip for Mighty Mobil?" Emil asked.

"Yeah, I'm going over there in a few minutes and question them. Did you notice the tag number on the slip? That was a bit of luck, a lot of the time, they never write that down. That's Susan Conover's license plate number. Her car is still missing, by the way."

"What about the signature?"

On the slip for five dollars and forty cents worth of gas, a fat, rounded J and an S, similar to how Janine made those letters, were followed by scrawls. Perhaps, Emil conjectured, Janine had written it in a hurry, or when upset, or under duress.

"Or it could be a very bad forgery," Oliver said. "We've sent it out for a handwriting analysis. They might be able to tell."

Emil had an apprehensive feeling. "Handwriting analysis! For a Missing Person's case? You guys are going full out, aren't you?"

"Yeah, I guess."

"Why do I get the feeling that something is going on that you're not telling me?"

Oliver hesitated, then said, "I haven't been holding out on you, but . . ."

"But?"

"We're hoping there is no connection, but we might have something. Three weeks ago a twenty-four-year-old female Caucasian, Francine Heer, was reported missing. Her body was found in a bayou, thirty miles away, a couple of days before Mardi Gras. She had been stabbed, strangled, sexually molested. The case is high-profile down here, and Homicide has next to nothing to work on. I mean they are desperate. The press and television glommed onto the story right from the start, and they don't got shit. So, they're sort of interested in Janine Smith and Susie Conover."

"What are the similarities?" Emil said.

"Nothing that really stands up and bites you in the ass, and that's why I haven't mentioned this to you before. The Heer woman and Susan Conover both lived in the same section of town. All three of the women fall into the same age group. All three had been seen in bars shortly before they disappeared. We think Francine Heer either met her killer in a bar, or was followed from one. See, there is nothing concrete, but it's enough that we're looking at it."

Though Emil had been preparing himself for bad news for weeks, Oliver's words jarred him. "It all sounds a little vague," he said as his mind raced to find some other explanation for the similarities.

"Yeah, you're right, it is. I'll leave it up to you if you want to tell the Smith family any of this. We haven't mentioned anything to the Conovers, though. There just isn't any purpose yet, and they're already pretty upset as it is."

Emil suddenly felt very tired. "Is there anything else you're working on?"

"A lab-tech team examined Susie Conover's apartment. I'll send you the complete report the minute we get it back. It doesn't look too promising, though. Conover's father has been in and out of the apartment numerous times since the disappearance.

"And get this, on Saturday, the day after he reported her missing, Conover went over to his daughter's place to see if she had returned.

He opens the door, hears a woman's voice humming along with the radio, and rushes into the kitchen with his arms wide open to hug his daughter. This woman he's never seen before lets out a scream. It's Susan Conover's cleaning woman, and he nearly scares the poor woman to death. The cleaning lady has her own key and has just spent four hours scrubbing and vacuuming and wiping and making this a completely worthless crime scene—that is if the apartment was a crime scene.

"According to the tech guys, this woman is like the best maid in New Orleans. You could eat off the floors after she's done with her cleaning. She couldn't be like the woman who does my place, right? Not only that, but this supermaid, in addition to probably wiping out every latent in the place, also picks this day to empty out the vacuum cleaner bag, so we can't even go through that for hair and fibers. She couldn't have done a better job of screwing up the crime scene if she were the perpetrator."

"Did she have any information?"

"No, she goes to the apartment every other Saturday. She usually lets herself in, though Susan Conover occasionally would be home when she arrived. The only thing out of the ordinary was that Conover normally left twenty dollars on the kitchen table for the cleaning lady, and this time there wasn't any money. Of course, that makes sense. Conover had already been missing for days by then."

"Was there any sign of Janine Smith?"

"Her suitcase was in the living room, but you knew that. The lab-tech guys are going over it now. I'll let you know what comes back."

"Thanks."

Oliver must have heard the discouragement in Emil's voice. "Hey, man, keep the faith. Something's gonna give."

That's what I'm afraid of, Emil thought.

Huey Oliver called the next day and told Emil that handwriting analysis had been inconclusive. The signature on the copy of the gas station credit card slip was little more than a scribble. Even though Janine's other signatures were neatly legible, it was possible that she could have made the scrawl hurriedly, or while terrified, or drunk—it was Mardi Gras after all. Equally possible, and more likely in Oliver's mind, was that someone else had made that scratching. Oliver had telephoned Grischuck and asked that the original credit receipt be sealed in a plastic bag and sent to New Orleans. The handwriting expert might be better able to determine a forgery working with the original, though it wasn't likely.

Oliver had gone to the Mighty Mobil station, a huge sprawling place with over twenty-five pumps near the interstate. Most of the pumps were self-serve, although an attendant made change and pumped gas in the lone full-service island. Though nearly midnight, the place was busy, and the attendant was barely managing to keep up with the steady flow of cars. Oliver watched the attendant work until he had a credit card purchase. The attendant *did* write down the license plate number, but he barely glanced at the driver when he gave him the receipt to sign.

The night manager, who was also the cashier, was sitting behind a pane of bullet-proof glass in the narrow booth. He remembered nothing about the credit card slip, but the initials on the receipt were those of Aundray Perkins, who was the same attendant Oliver had just been observing.

Perkins, a tall thin man with a billowy Afro, couldn't remember anything about the credit card purchase either. Indeed, when Oliver asked, he couldn't recall the name of the customer who had just charged his gas.

"Man, do you know how many of those things I run off a night?" Perkins had said. It was Oliver's experience that most cashiers and service people rarely looked at anything beyond the expiration date of a credit card.

Oliver had asked about Susan Conover's car.

"A gray Pinto? Are you kidding me? Man, if you want me to remember anything you got to give me more than that. Was there a dent, was it burning a lot of oil? That's like asking me if any guys with dark hair been in here."

Oliver had finally shown Aundray photos of both Janine and Susan Conover. He couldn't recollect seeing either one. "That's not to say, they weren't in here. But you can see how busy I am. Could you remember someone you saw two weeks ago for a minute at night though a car window?"

The lab results were equally unenlightening. Conover's apartment had been spotless. Susie's fingerprints were on file—she had once been bonded for a summer job as a bank teller—but very few of her prints were found in her own apartment, a testimonial, Oliver supposed, to the quality of the cleaning woman's work. In addition to Susie's latents, two other sets of fingerprints belonging to Mr. Conover and the cleaning lady were discovered. Surprisingly, since Janine had stayed there for at least two days, no other prints were uncovered.

Similarly, Mr. Conover and the maid accounted for most of the hairs found. Two long blond hairs were on the couch. They were compared to hairs from a brush in Janine's overnight bag and were ascertained to be a match.

Janine's overnight bag had been examined closely. It was made of a heavy tan canvas that didn't yield any fingerprints.

The bed was made. Some stains were on Susie's mattress, but they were consistent with everyday use by a sexually active woman with normal body functions.

No signs of forced entry were uncovered. And nothing seemed to be missing from the apartment except for the purses of the young women.

Susie Conover's car was gone, however. Mr. Conover had been adamant that Susie would not have driven her car on Mardi Gras day. Oliver believed him. With the streets jammed with drunken revelers and parades and good times, one just didn't drive to Mardi Gras. You hit the street and partied.

Given these facts, the New Orleans police had worked out a scenario. Susie and Janine had gone out to Mardi Gras. They had met or been followed by the wrong person or persons. Before they had a chance to return to the apartment, they had gone in Susie's car, either willingly or unwillingly, with the person or persons unknown.

As a theory, it couldn't get much vaguer, but it was all they had.

SEVEN

EMIL HANDED WILLY THE TELEX with the list of the contents of Janine's suitcase that was found in Susie Conover's apartment. Each item was recorded individually: one underpants, white; one underpants, white, with lace trim; one pair of jeans. Emil had called Willy, asking that they meet at Amanda's house. He wanted them all to go over the list; they might be able to ascertain what Janine was wearing when she disappeared. Possibly, something which should be on the inventory was missing—a distinctive piece of jewelry, perhaps—and might be traced.

Willy asked about other articles of clothing that were cataloged under a subheading marked IN PLASTIC BAG.

"The plastic bag was inside the suitcase," Emil said. "We're assuming that Janine used it as a laundry bag, and that the clothes inside were those she had already worn. As far as we can tell, two changes of clothing are in the dirty laundry—the clothes she wore Sunday and Monday—which leads us to believe that Janine did not come back to Susan Conover's apartment after leaving Tuesday, Mardi Gras day."

They were going through Janine's dirty laundry—literally. Willy glanced back at the piece of paper. One pair of cotton socks, white; one wool sweater, dark blue; one Estee Lauder eye makeup compact with brush; one lipstick; one green plastic travel toothbrush with case, one American Express traveler's check, twenty-five-dollar denomination.

Lately, Willy had tried to find refuge in the least horrifying of all the lurid possible explanations for Janine's disappearance. Against logic, he had clung to the theory that a confused or manic Janine had impulsively gone off with Susie Conover on some sort of spree. This list, however, dashed that feeble hope. Janine would not have gallivanted off wearing just the clothes on her back.

He read down the sheet of paper. One travel-size tube Crest toothpaste; one bottle Norell perfume; one Ortho-Novum plastic compact containing twelve pills (sixteen missing).

Willy felt a flash of jealousy. Janine had brought birth-control pills with her to Mardi Gras. Dark suspicions began to form in his mind, but Willy drove them back. The presence of the contraceptives in Janine's suitcase did not mean that she had intended to have an affair while in New Orleans. The pills had to be taken daily regardless of her intentions; that is how they worked. In the next moment, Willy felt cheapened, disloyal. Just weeks ago, he would not have doubted her.

"Janine's engagement ring isn't listed here," Willy said.

"Wouldn't she be wearing it? Isn't that something she wouldn't take off?" Emil asked.

Willy stared at the inventory again. One white blouse with blue trim at collar. The description sounded so impersonal, so objective. He knew that shirt, could almost feel the crinkly fabric and see the rounded collar with the light and dark blue embroidery. It reminded Willy of a child's blouse, and Janine had looked wonderful in it.

"What about her shoes?" Howard queried. "We should be able to figure out what shoes she brought with her."

They all went upstairs to Janine's bedroom. Willy had brought a box containing the few clothes—the bathrobe, the old pants and shirt used for painting—Janine had left at the apartment. He spread those out on her bed, then he, Amanda, and Howard began to go through the closet. It was finally Howard who noticed that a pale yellow sweater and a pair of black flats were not in the house nor on the police list.

"I don't see the dress with the little flowers," Willy said after a while.

Amanda looked at him inquisitively, and in response, Willy continued, "It's real loose; she used to put it on over her head," then fell silent.

"The shift with a floral pattern."

As Amanda gave Emil a detailed description of the dress, sweater, and shoes, Willy sat down on the bed. The spread with its pink and blue needlepoint flowers was the same one that had covered the bed when he and Janine had been in high school. Years ago, Janine had flung the bedspread so that it floated across the vanity's mirror and remained propped up like a Halloween ghost observing them on the bed as they first made love.

* * *

In Willy's senior year in high school, he and Janine went together to parties, to the movies, to dances. One day, Patty Chisolm asked Willy, "Are you and Janine going to Diane's party?" That question had thrilled Willy and had filled him with such joy that he couldn't answer for a moment. Other people thought of him and Janine as a couple; they validated and confirmed what he felt. He and Janine were in love.

That year, drugs hit Beacon. It seemed that when people skipped class, it was to go get high. Kids would drive up to the foot of Mount Beacon and smoke hash from homemade pipes made of cardboard toothpaste packages and tinfoil, or would go over to Kim Mooney's house during sixth period and smoke joints and watch "The Little Rascals." On Friday nights, instead of buying beer, those going to Carrie's Corner Store were likely to be picking up raspberry swirl ice cream and pepperoni, Oreos and pork rinds, all sorts of unlikely combinations of snack foods to satisfy their "munchies"—Willy could remember a very stoned Earache once eating an onion as if it were an apple.

One night, at the uppermost part of the Mountain View cemetery that clung to the side of a hill, he and Janine sat on the hood of Willy's father's Buick, smoking grass and looking down on the lights, or as Janine had said, "the light" of Beacon. Janine had been eating a container of yogurt bought at Carrie's and spilled some down the front of her dungarees. Chuckling at her clumsiness, she was about to dab at the fly of her jeans with a Kleenex, when she turned to Willy and said, "Take care of that for me, will you?" She handed him the Kleenex.

Willy took the tissue, but then, standing before her, he leaned over, put his face in her lap, and licked away the sweet, berry yogurt. He licked again at the denim, and Janine had reclined on the hood of the car. She moaned and pressed his face to her lap, but stopped Willy as he went to unbutton the fly of her jeans.

Other nights in the finished basement of the Smith house, he and Janine would start to watch television, but would wind up on the floor, groping at one another. Occasionally, to make Willy laugh, Janine looked up as if she had heard something interesting on the television which played loudly to allay the suspicions of Amanda who was in the living room above. They would tantalize one another—Janine rubbing his erection through the barrier of his clothes; Willy stroking back and forth at her crotch with his thigh, Janine's legs clasped around his—but within boundaries that seemed increasingly absurd to them both.

One rainy Sunday afternoon, Janine called Willy and asked him to drop by her house. When Janine answered the door, the Beatles' *White Album* was playing much more loudly than Amanda would have permitted on the elaborate stereo system that Howard had built. Amanda and Howard had gone into the city to see a Broadway show; Teddy was away for his freshman year at Williams.

"We're all alone?" Willy came up behind Janine and encircled her with his arms. He kissed the back of her neck and felt her shiver slightly.

Janine went to the stereo and, smiling enigmatically, turned off the music. Then she came back to Willy, put her hand to his lips, and said, "Shh."

She unbuttoned his denim work shirt. Willy started to embrace her, but she stopped him when he went to help her take off the shirt. Janine tossed it on the floor and pulled off his undershirt.

The touch of Janine's fingers stroking his chest overpowered Willy. He took in Janine's face, not quite believing what was happening. Again she gave that mysterious smile.

He let her undo the top of his jeans and pull the zipper down, her hand brushing lightly against his erection. Slowly, she pulled his pants and underpants down. His hard-on sprang into view.

Janine grasped it as if shaking hands and said, "At last we meet."

Willy kicked off his shoes and stepped out of the clothes at his feet. He took off his socks and stood naked in the middle of the living room.

Janine said, "I just want to look at you a moment."

She peered deep into his eyes, then Willy saw her gaze roam over his body, down his chest, down his stomach. Something in her unabashed expression, a curiosity, a desire, exhilarated Willy.

Janine came forward and reached out. Her hand followed the path her eyes had, gently touching, teasing.

Then her hands came back up to his face. She kissed him passionately. Willy put his arms around her, tentatively at first, and hugged her. His naked body pressed against hers, and he could feel her skirt and blouse against his skin.

Taking his hand, Janine led him out of the living room, up the stairs, and into her bedroom. They kissed again, then Janine stepped back and slowly undressed. Her blouse flew over her head. Her bra hooked in the front; she took it off and revealed her breasts. Willy was sure his mouth gaped. The rest of her clothes came off in one motion. Willy stared at her, awestruck.

"You are so beautiful."

Janine reached back and sent the bedspread flying across the room. It draped itself on the vanity, knocking over a picture frame.

She embraced Willy. Feeling her warm naked body against his own, he trembled. They lay down on the bed.

Later, Janine spread her hands across his middle, then guided him into her.

With every moment, it seemed, Willy experienced some new emotion. He was absolutely astounded to be inside Janine, so overcome with joy that he thought he might cry, and throughout, he felt desire and pleasure. Every little move of Janine's body, her expression, her appetite roused him.

After a while, Janine turned him over on his back and slowly rocked back and forth. Willy put his hands to her cheeks, caressed them, and kissed Janine again. "I love you so much," he thought. He kissed her neck, and Janine leaned forward and pressed her breasts to his face. Willy could feel the slick wetness of her as she thrust down on him.

Janine exhaled in quick gasps, then she moaned loudly, rubbing against him, and moaned again and again until she collapsed. They lay still, and Willy was overjoyed, grateful that he had been able to provide Janine with this pleasure. He felt a bit of relief and a pride which, even at that moment, he realized was silly and strutting.

Janine stirred and rolled them over again so that she was on her back. She wrapped her legs around his back, and as Willy began to move, her breath came again in short spurts. Willy couldn't get close enough to Janine, no matter how tightly he held her, and then came the exquisite pleasure. Through his gasps, he heard Janine moan again.

They stayed in bed all afternoon. After it turned dark, Janine dozed in his arms, her head resting lightly on his chest. Though Willy had had sex with Kim Mooney, and with another girl named Nancy, who he had met at Lake George, Willy felt as though he had finally lost his virginity. He wondered if Janine, who had slept with Eric Boyd when she was going out with him, also felt the same way. It was strange, he thought, that people sometimes referred to this moment in life as a "loss of innocence." Far from being a loss, it was closer to the opposite. It was like entering a state of grace.

From his desk at the Beacon Police station, Emil called David Grischuck and found out that forty dollars worth of Mexican food and margaritas had been charged with Janine's credit card at a restaurant in Taos, New Mexico. The charge was only two days old.

"It's the forged signature on the slip," Grischuck said. "It looks like the same woman."

They now knew a little more about who was using Janine's credit card. Huey Oliver had communicated with all ten of the people who had accepted the Visa card. Eight of the ten could not remember their transactions. The two others, a waitress and a shoe salesman, did recollect the woman who had used Janine's card, and Oliver had flown to Texas and New Mexico to interview them. The matronly waitress described the suspect as around twenty-five, thin, pretty, with short dark hair. She was accompanied by a man the waitress described as "very good-looking, though his hair was too long." The dark-haired woman had left her a generous tip.

The shoe salesman had depicted the suspect in similar terms, though, no doubt thinking the New Orleans Police were vitally interested in what he found attractive in women, he had added that the dark-haired woman "was pretty, but not my type." Both the waitress and the salesman, when shown photos, stated that the dark-haired woman was not Janine Smith or Susan Conover. An Identikit drawing had been made of the suspect. Thousands of young women resembled it.

"The restaurant did not call in to verify the card?" Emil asked.

"No."

Anti-fraud and -theft systems existed in the credit card company's security. Whenever a purchase was made, merchants could call and find out if the card was overdrawn or stolen. However, many smaller businesses didn't bother checking. With overdrawn accounts, vendors were instructed to seize the card and destroy it. A twenty-five-dollar reward was given to salespeople as an incentive to do so. With stolen cards, the credit company had the ability to call local police and to have the thief arrested at the store. The sale would go ahead as if nothing were amiss, and the salesclerk would be unaware of the fraud until the police arrived. That is what Emil was hoping would happen with whoever was using Janine's card. Grischuck had agreed to contact Emil whenever any credit activity occurred.

"The account is over its limit again. And that's just with charges we're aware of. Who know's what's in the mail, or what is being charged today."

"I'll have the family send you another check."

Emil hung up the phone and leaned back in his chair. This investigation had been particularly frustrating. He seemed so far removed from everything. The crime had been committed in New Orleans; a dark-haired woman was forging Janine's name on credit card slips throughout the Southwest; he was dealing with people—Huey Oliver in Louisiana and Grischuck in New Jersey—who were just disembodied voices on the phone. Yet Emil was tentatively allowing himself to feel optimism. If only the dark-haired woman kept using Janine's card. She would be caught eventually. One clerk calling and verifying a sale would be all that it would take.

* * *

The next day, Emil dialed Grischuck's number again. A woman's voice came on the line. Emil identified himself.

"Just a moment," he heard, then a few seconds later, the same woman's voice came back and said with some embarrassment, "Mr. Grischuck is not in today. May I help you?"

Emil felt an inchoate fear sweep over him. He explained why he was calling.

"Just a minute, please, while I check," the woman said and put him on hold.

A Muzak version of *Eleanor Rigby* played over the phone line. *No,* Emil thought, *don't say what I'm afraid you're about to say.*

The Muzak stopped abruptly. "Officer Deshayes? That account is delinquent. The card for Janine Smith has been rescinded."

Emil forced himself to keep a steady voice. If he started to scream at this woman, she would hang up. "You've closed the account? Grischuck promised me that wouldn't happen. He swore to me."

"I'm sure it wasn't Mr. Grischuck's doing. The computer probably flagged the card after it went past its limit. It's programmed to do that automatically."

"There was no reason for closing the account. A payment was sent in, you cashed it." Emil could feel his anger rising. He had to get a grip on himself. "You can reopen the account, can't you? What if the family posts a cash bond to cover future charges?"

"No, I'm afraid that's not possible. We have a very strict policy with overdrawn accounts."

"That account is not overdrawn. The family has been making all payments. Grischuck agreed to raise the credit limit."

"The account's limit is only seven hundred and fifty . . ." The woman paused. Emil could almost see Grischuck cowering by the phone, gesturing to her. Moments later he heard, "The account was not overdrawn. But the card was stolen."

"We're aware that the card is stolen. So there's no problem, right?"

The woman on the phone stuttered, confused and upset, "I don't know. I'm not familiar with this account. All I can tell you is that the account has been closed."

"Listen, I know it's not your fault." Emil exhaled slowly. "Two women are missing. These credit card slips are the only lead we have to work on. Surely, something can be done, so when Janine Smith's card is used again—"

"There is no card," the woman interrupted.

"What do you mean?"

She sighed in exasperation. "I told you, Janine Smith's credit card has been rescinded. Rescinded, cut up, taken away! A store employee in Taos, New Mexico refused to return the card to the person who tried to use it. They cut it into pieces and sent it to us. There is no card."

It was Grischuck, Emil knew, who had ordered the card seized. The procedure that was supposed to be used, the course Grischuck had agreed to, was that of a stolen card, not an overdrawn one. No doubt, when the verification request came in, the local police had been contacted. Grischuck, however, had also put in place the automatic confiscation directive. Afraid that his bank, which made millions by charging what used to be considered usurious rates, might be stuck for a few hundred dollars, he had destroyed their only lead. It didn't matter that two women's lives might be at stake. Business was business.

Emil spoke softly into the phone. "I'd like you to give a message to Mr. Grischuck. Tell him he's scum. Tell him he's a spineless weasel. I know he's putting you up to this. He's not even man enough to talk to me over the phone. Well, you tell him if we later find out that this jeopardized Janine Smith in any way, I'm coming looking for him. He'll wish he was never—"

The line went dead. Emil slammed the phone down, then picked it up and slammed it again. Sam Pittman, who was had just come into the station, looked at him strangely.

Emil was given an even stranger look by Sam when, a few minutes later, after posing as an official of Chase Manhattan Bank, he heard Grischuck's voice on the telephone.

"Hi, this is Dave Grischuck."

"You can get cancer, you motherfucker," Emil screamed into the phone. "You scumbag, you fucking worthless lowlife piece of shit."

Emil continued to yell obscenities into the phone even after the phone went dead.

Sam Pittman shook his head.

EIGHT

THE TWENTY-FIVE DOLLARS FROM the Visa company was going to help. Jennifer had only been working at the store that sold Indian jewelry and artifacts to tourists for three weeks. She had arrived in Taos a few months ago, liked it, and was hoping to stay for a while. The mountains, the air, the sunlight, everything about the place was phenomenal, everything, that is, except her job here at the store. She had only planned on working until something better came along, waitressing maybe, or a not-too-demanding housekeeping job for some of the rich hippies or artists in town. After spending three weeks of unsurpassed tedium, however, with a boredom so intense that no matter how much pot she smoked it never abated, Jennifer knew she was going to quit. Any day now, she was going to receive the twenty-five-dollar reward for slicing up the overdrawn credit card, and then she was out of here.

When the cop from New Orleans came into the store, it freaked her a little. After all, she had some pot and a peyote button in her purse, but all he wanted was to talk about the credit card. Had Jennifer ever seen the woman before? Could she describe her? Was she with anyone?

She recalled the incident. The woman who had tried to use the Visa card was Jennifer's age and pretty. What had first attracted Jennifer's notice was the woman's hair, which was cut short with bangs and looked wonderful. Jennifer had been thinking of cutting her own hair the exact same way. The woman's hair was also dyed jet black. Normally, Jennifer hated dyed black hair, which reminded her of cheap-looking girls from factory towns, or all-girl singing groups from the early 1960s. This woman, though, carried it off and made it look like some avant-garde fashion statement.

The guy she was with was handsome. He had striking eyes, and Jennifer had wondered, were they really that amazingly blue, or was she a lot more stoned than she had thought? An old, inch-long scar ran along the depression between his lower lip and chin, and Jennifer had the slightest inclination to reach out and touch it. That scar, Jennifer thought, had probably helped him get laid.

The man had browsed in the back of the store, while the woman had come up to the jewelry display case. She wanted to buy some silver and turquoise bracelets. Though the store's sign said, Indian jewelry, all the bracelets had Hecho in Mexico etched on the inside band. The three she chose were ones that Jennifer would have picked for herself. They were also the most expensive.

The woman gave Jennifer her credit card to pay for the purchase. Following the store's procedure, which she had just learned, Jennifer checked the expiration date and asked to see the woman's driver's license. It was from New York, which was nothing out of the ordinary since most of the store's customers were tourists, and the name on the license, Janine Smith, matched that on the credit card. Jennifer had not bothered to look at the physical description on the license. She worked in a store not a carnival; she wasn't about to guess people's ages, heights, and weights. Then the message had come back over the credit card verification system to seize the card.

Jennifer had been embarrassed for the woman. She had taken a liking to her and had been tempted to ignore the system's command and just hand back the Visa card. Still, twenty-five dollars *was* the equivalent of a long mind-numbing day working in the store. The woman did not seem at all perturbed when Jennifer told her the bad news.

"The nerve of those people," she had joked, "they actually expect you to pay the bill."

She had given the bracelets one last, longing look, sighed, and left the store. The man had departed with her, but not before giving Jennifer a flirtatious sly smile.

When the Taos police arrived in the store ten minutes later, the couple were long gone. Jennifer had been astounded—not because the credit card was stolen, but because the tedium of the job had finally been interrupted.

The New Orleans detective took the descriptions of the man and woman, and went over her story again. Then he showed her pictures of two young women. Neither of them was the person who had tried to buy the silver and turquoise bracelets. The detective pointed to one of the pictures again, the woman with the beautiful face and blond hair, and asked Jennifer to imagine her with dyed hair.

"She isn't the one who came into the store," Jennifer said. "I'm positive."

He handed her a police drawing of a woman. Jennifer almost said that the Shroud of Turin looked more like a human face than this drawing, but instead she said, "Yeah, that looks a little bit like the customer."

Finally, reluctantly, the detective left.

Willy nearly didn't go to college. He applied at four universities without giving much thought to the process and did not bother to visit two of the schools, including Rutgers, where he eventually went. To his and his father's surprise, he was accepted at all four. He chose to go to Rutgers, which was not the best of the four schools, for only one reason. It was close enough to return home to Beacon—and Janine—on weekends.

Until the very day his parents drove him to the campus, Willy toyed with the idea of staying in Beacon, getting an apartment, and finding a job. He imagined the freedom and privacy he and Janine would have, daydreamed a life for them that was as close to being married as he dared hope. Finally, it had been Janine who persuaded him to go to school.

"We don't want to get stuck in Beacon for the rest of our lives. You don't want to wind up like most of the morons in this town."

That first semester, Willy made up his schedule with one concern. He took only the classes that would allow him to have Fridays off. Four days after he had gone away to school, and then on all but three weekends that academic year, Willy hitchhiked home to be with Janine. On one of the other weekends, Janine snuck down and stayed with him.

Janine had told Amanda she was going camping with Diane and instead had arrived at Rutgers early Friday evening. That weekend had been full. First, a Sly and the Family Stone concert, then parties, and much of the time had been spent in bed. It had been the small things, waking up in the morning together, eating breakfast, taking a nap, that had given Willy an inkling of what life with Janine might be like.

Janine applied early and was accepted at Colgate, which was in the process of going co-ed. Willy had hoped she would join him at Rutgers; he envisioned them sharing an apartment. Her decision to go to Colgate, however, was firm. Against the advice of her guidance counselor at Beacon High, Janine didn't even apply to any other schools.

Her father had graduated from Colgate, and she remembered going up with him to Homecoming and Alumni weekends as a girl, so that the words *college* or *university* always brought images of its granite buildings and bucolic campus. She went off to Hamilton, New York, the next September and did not return to Beacon until the following Thanksgiving.

That year, because hitchhiking to Colgate, which was far removed from major highways and where it seemed to snow constantly from October to April, took eight or nine hours, Willy was able to visit Janine only every second or third weekend. In Willy's freshman year, their separation had not seemed so pronounced. Because of his long weekends and semester breaks, as well as Rutgers's shorter school year, which was further curtailed by the killings at Kent State that closed universities across the country, they had spent more time together than apart. The next year, however, Janine's first at college, the loneliness that Willy felt was intense. He knew exactly what he desired in life. He wanted to be with Janine, and he wanted a job that could give him some sense of satisfaction. Willy didn't see how going to school would help him achieve either goal. At the end of his second year, he dropped out of Rutgers.

Willy moved into a trailer on the outskirts of Beacon with Earache and Andy Brascia, and began working for Jimmy Guido. He bought a panel truck in order to visit Janine at school. For the next year and a half until Janine also quit school, Willy would drive up to Colgate whenever he could.

Those visits to Disgraceland seemed to Willy the only time he was truly alive. He realized that he enjoyed the best features of going to school—parties, weekends, concerts—without any of the drawbacks— tests, term papers, having to plow through *Marius the Epicurean*. Yet it wasn't the social life that cheered him—he was happy just to read while Janine studied.

The weeks between visits, no matter what else he did, were just waiting periods.

Like a child anticipating Christmas, Willy had longed for the day when Janine would be done with school. Then, four months ago, Christmas had finally arrived.

Willy was putting two six-packs of Rolling Rock on the counter of Carrie's Corner Store when he noticed the headline of the *New York Daily News*.

"Will that be all, honey?" Carrie asked.

Willy added the newspaper to the beer.

He waited until he had uncapped his first beer at the kitchen table of the apartment before folding open the paper. SEX SLAVE FREED the headline screamed. The story went on to tell the account of a woman who had been missing for over three years. She had been held captive in the back of a converted school bus by a man who had made the woman, according to the paper's overheated prose, his "sex slave."

He sipped the beer and read the story again. It seemed so unbelievably lurid. Willy scrutinized the picture of the kidnapper. The man's appearance added to the sensationalism of the story; he *looked* like a maniac, with a dark, Rasputin-like beard and wild strange eyes.

The newspaper report seemed so implausible, but then, Janine's disappearing was implausible, preposterous.

What had happened to Janine?

Willy began writing down possible answers to that question on a legal pad. Randomly scrawling whatever came to mind, he made out a list. Then, irrationally, as if able to bring order to the chaos, he began copying and rearranging the list into a neat page of block letters.

Willy forced himself to write MURDERED on the top line. It was the most logical explanation, he thought, then his mind reeled. Janine and Susie Conover were dead, their bodies buried or hidden! That this should be a most logical explanation was stupefying. Where was the reason in horrible violence, in a man with unfathomable, twisted compulsions coming out of a dark alley, or jimmying open a bedroom window?

Willy meticulously printed AMNESIA, then shook his head in disgust. He knew that real cases of clinical amnesia were so rare as to make the chances of that happening infinitesimal. "Amnesia" was almost always something else: hysteria, stress, a pretense to avoid responsibilities, or an excuse given, after the fact, to explain unacceptable behavior. And for two women to have experienced this extremely rare phenomenon simultaneously was scarcely conceivable.

KIDNAPPING was placed on the list, then Willy added subheadings. If Janine had been kidnapped for profit, why then had no ransom demand come in? And he put down SEXUAL SLAVE and WHITE SLAVERY though he knew they seemed absurd. Yet hadn't he just read about a case that also seemed incredible and ridiculous?

JANINE WANTED TO DISAPPEAR he wrote near the bottom of the page. Willy couldn't believe that Janine was in such misery that she would leave without a trace. Even if the unthinkable had happened, and she was no longer in love with him, wouldn't he have sensed that her life was so unbearable as to make her disappear?

Had Janine been under a lot of stress? In the last few months, she quit school, became engaged, and was getting ready to marry and move in with Willy. Had she wanted some time for herself? Had events seemed to spin out of her control? Though Janine had sometimes seemed quiet and preoccupied since coming home from school, they had still laughed, talked, gone out, made love.

He looked at the neat list, but already other explanations came to mind. Janine could be in a morgue somewhere, listed as Jane Doe. Or incapacitated in some hospital. Or in the throes of a mental break-down. Or the captive of a religious cult. Why not? Was that any more ludicrous than being held prisoner as a sex slave in a converted school bus? What could be more incredible than Janine having vanished?

Willy looked out the kitchen window. Snow was beginning to fall. He crumpled up the sheet of paper.

Last Christmas Eve it had snowed. For a number of years, Christmas had become increasingly mundane for Willy, an anticlimax unable to live up to the fantasies of greeting cards and movies. This past Christmas, however, had been different. It had seemed magical.

Janine had taken Willy to her church for Midnight Mass. After the service, as they mingled outside Saint John's with friends—Earache, improbably wearing a double-breasted suit, Andy Brascia, and those home from school: Patty Chisolm, Terry Pritchard, Kim Mooney with her new boyfriend—it had started to snow. People had *oohed* and *ahed*.

As he and Janine ambled back toward her house, the snow gave the dark streets qualities that, if not quite Currier and Ives, were charming and pristine. Willy felt his heart racing as he touched the small box in his overcoat pocket. Inside was an engagement ring.

From the first time they had made love, years ago, Willy had wanted to ask Janine to marry him. At first, he had restrained himself, partly because marriage had seemed such a starry-eyed, unattainable pros-pect. They were only in high school; they still lived at home. And then college with its demands and forced separations had held him back. Those were not the only reasons why Willy had not proposed. He knew instinctively that Janine did not want to become trapped into life too young. She had dreams of adventure and experience.

Janine had come home from Colgate four days earlier, excited, jumpy. Though she was waiting until after Christmas to tell Amanda, she confided to him that she had quit school.

"Life has officially started," Janine had said.

Willy had been overjoyed. And a little frightened.

He bought the engagement ring the next day. Similar to one that Janine had once admired in a store window, he had long ago memorized her ring size.

The snowfall was captivating, so they took the long way to Janine's house. After a few blocks, they saw and heard Christmas carolers, people just leaving a party who held amber candles that glowed through the snow. The notes of "O Come All Ye Faithful" carried sweetly through the air. Willy could not recall hearing carolers in town before—this was Beacon, after all, not Charles Dickens's London. Normally his reaction to them probably would have been cynical or sarcastic, but he gave himself up to the beauty of the moment. He sensed that Janine had done so as well.

"Tidings of joy," she murmured.

This would be the perfect time, he thought, to propose. The snow, the candle-lit carolers, the tranquility were so close to perfect as to seem art-directed.

He stopped and turned to her, but was unable to make himself speak. Janine had leaned up and kissed him, then they had continued strolling down the street.

Amanda, Howard, Teddy and his latest girlfriend, Sarah, were already home from Midnight Mass. Following family tradition, they gathered in the living room, opened a bottle of champagne—when Janine had been younger, they had drunk sparkling cider out of Amanda's Lalique crystal— and exchanged presents. All the petty family tensions were forgotten, or at least called off for the holidays. Amanda was genial, joking and laughing with Janine and Teddy. When Howard presented Janine with some ruby and diamond earrings, she seemed genuinely grateful and went over to give him a kiss on the cheek. Howard beamed.

Gazing at the proud smile on Howard's face, Willy remembered Janine's eighteenth birthday. At the small family party, Howard had startled Janine by giving her the keys to an old MG convertible. Howard had spent six months painstakingly restoring the car. Janine had handed back the keys and said firmly, "Thanks, Howard, but I couldn't possibly accept this."

Howard, blinking back incomprehension, had stood holding the keys. Seeing how she had hurt him, Janine stammered, "I love the car, but it snows so much at Colgate, and you spent all that time working on the car. You should keep it for yourself."

Howard had nodded, speechless. Janine had stumbled on for a while, trying to undo the pain inflicted, though also making it clear that she was adamant about not taking the MG from Howard.

This Christmas Eve, however, all that seemed forgotten as Janine held the ruby and diamond studs to her ears.

The next day, Willy and Janine went first to his parents' house. On their way over, Willy again patted the engagement ring in his pocket, but again balked. He knew that if Janine refused, he would be devastated.

Willy's parents' house was full of people. For the first time in years, his grandmother, cousins, and aunts and uncles were there as well as his brother, Michael, who had just arrived from Boston with his wife, Betsy, and their one-year-old daughter, Molly. Molly had fine spiky light brown hair that stood straight up and when she had first spied Willy, she had smiled broadly, revealing three little teeth, and then had laughed with delight. Later, Willy saw Janine holding Molly in her lap by the fire, playing with her, and again it seemed that everything about the day was perfect.

They ate lightly at the big Christmas dinner because they were to go back to the Smith house for another Christmas meal with all of her relatives. At the table, his uncles and grandmother had wittily gone over familiar family tales, and Janine had laughed often.

They decided to walk back to Janine's. After a few blocks, a light dusting of snow began to fall again. Of course it's snowing, Willy thought, how could it be otherwise? This Christmas is perfect.

Willy remembered once as a boy he had been goaded by his brother to leap off a high dive. Indeed, Michael had threatened to kick his ass if he didn't. Rooted on the edge of the high board, Willy gaped at the water that seemed so far away, certain that he could never hurl himself from such a height. Then, before he realized what he had done, he was flying through the air toward the blue water of the swimming pool.

As the snow gently swirled, Willy stopped and turned toward Janine. He took out the small box that contained the ring and opened it. Anxiously, he searched her face, hoping to discover what she was thinking. Snowflakes hit and melted against the gold and diamonds of the ring. "Will you marry me?"

Janine looked tenderly at him and said, "Yes."

NINE

TEDDY DIDN'T NOTICE THE broken window pane at first. He had taken the train up from New York City, then walked to the house from the station. Howard wasn't home from work yet, and his mother had left a note stating that she had gone grocery shopping. He had gone into the living room and was about to turn on the stereo when he heard a flapping sound coming from the kitchen.

He saw the muslin curtain wave and felt a draft of cold air when he went into the kitchen. Then he spotted the shards of glass on the counter, and the open, shattered window. The muslin flapped again in the breeze. Teddy stayed very still. All he could hear was the rustling of the curtain. The note from his mother said she had gone to the market to pick up a few things for supper, which led him to believe that the window had probably been smashed within the hour. Possibly within the last few minutes.

The number for the Beacon Police was on a sticker attached to the side of the kitchen's wall phone. Teddy dialed the number, then gave his name and address and said, "I think someone has broken into my home. He might still be in the house."

"Are you able to leave?"

"Yes."

"Then get out of there, right now. An officer will be there shortly."

Teddy hung up the phone. He had entered through the front door, then walked or glanced throughout most of the first floor. If an intruder was still in the house, he could be upstairs or in the basement.

Or in a closet, he thought, stepping hurriedly back from the pantry door.

Suddenly, a rumbling seemed to vibrate throughout the house. Startled and confused by it, Teddy grabbed a wine bottle from a rack on the counter and held it as a club. The rumbling continued loudly, sounding now as if it came from the basement, then stopped as quickly as it had begun. At that moment Teddy realized what it was. Howard had recently installed an automatic door opener for the garage, which was at the end of the sloping driveway beneath the house, beneath the floorboards on which Teddy was standing. This was the first time he had been indoors, rather than in a car, when it was used. Amanda had just arrived back from shopping. She would be coming through the garage and finished basement and up the stairs to the kitchen.

If the intruder was still in the house, he might be in the basement.

Teddy swore under his breath, then slamming open the door to the cellar, barreled down the stairs, ready to lunge at any shadowy figure. He noticed he was making a low growling noise, his teeth bared, the bottle of wine raised. Nobody was in the finished family room. He flung open the door leading to the garage.

Amanda started to smile, but then blanched. "What?"

"Let's go outside." He gently guided her toward the side door.

"What's the matter?"

"There's been a break-in. The thief may still be inside. The cops are on their way."

Teddy picked up an old baseball bat on the way out.

Standing on the walk outside their house, holding the bat, Teddy felt faintly ridiculous. And then, as he explained to Amanda what he had seen, he began to doubt that the house had been burgled. Couldn't he have misinterpreted what he had observed? What if a squirrel or a crow had crashed through the window, or perhaps the kids next door had a slingshot or a BB gun?

A police cruiser came up the street with its lights out. It stopped and Ray Abdarian, an older cop with a weight lifter's body, slid out of the car.

"Do you know if anyone is still in the house?" Abdarian whispered.

"I don't know," Teddy said and recounted what had happened.

Abdarian listened silently, then went to the front door. Before entering, he drew his revolver. A few minutes later, he called them into the house.

"Whoever it was is gone," Abdarian said as they sidled past him into the hallway.

Another police cruiser stopped in front of the house. Teddy saw Emil Deshayes and Sam Pittman get out.

The Bureau of Criminal Investigation forensics team that Sam Pittman had called in from the State Police packed up their equipment and left. It would later turn out that no fingerprints other than the family's nor much other evidence except for a footprint in the ground outside the broken kitchen window had been found.

Nothing had been stolen on the ground floor of the Smith house. The sterling silver tea service and flatware, the television, the stereo, the liquor in the cabinet, the crystal had not been touched.

Upstairs, a quart jar of silver dimes, a short-lived enthusiasm from Teddy's adolescence, remained in plain sight on top of his desk.

A box on Amanda's dresser had been rifled; all of her jewelry was missing.

Janine's room was in shambles. Drawers had been upended, the glass covering the Degas print had been shattered. All the linens had been torn from the bed, and the mattress and pillows had been slashed repeatedly.

Amanda had followed the policemen into the bedroom in shock. Staring at the destruction, she cried, "Why is this happening to us?" and then ran weeping from the room. Teddy had gone to comfort her.

All the jewelry that had been in Janine's hammered silver box was also missing.

Pittman glanced around the room and said, "Isn't this a bitch? If you're going to rob a place, okay. You need the money, or you're greedy. But, why this shit?"

"Is that how you're figuring it," Emil said. "A burglary?"

"Who knows? Someone breaks into a house and steals a bunch of jewelry? At the very least it's a burglary."

"Why didn't he take any of the valuables from downstairs? Or that jar of coins in the other room? There must be fifty dollars in it."

"Maybe Teddy came in while he was up here, before he got a chance to take anything else. Or maybe he's interested in only what he can conceal on himself—he's on foot and he doesn't want to walk down the street carrying a TV and silver candlesticks."

"And all this . . . vandalism?"

"Could be a kid, some punk. He's going to have some fun before he robs them. He gets a big kick out of it."

Emil could tell by Pittman's tone that he didn't put much credence in this scenario.

"And he just happens to pick the bedroom of the one woman in Beacon who just happens to be missing?"

"Yeah, there is that, isn't there?"

Emil studied the bed. It seemed that a fury had been directed toward the bed that exceeded the simple destruction of vandalism. And then there was the mirror on top of the vanity. Someone had drawn a bright red star next to a crescent moon in lipstick.

Emil nodded toward the mirror and said, "What do you make of that?"

Pittman shook his head. "A signature of some sort? It's the thief's brand or something."

Emil frowned.

"You don't buy that explanation?" Pittman asked. "I'm not real convinced myself. What about this? In the deranged mind of the madman who drew it, it explains how God told him to kill Janine?"

Emil stared at the bright red star and crescent moon, which looked vaguely familiar, a symbol he had seen before. Wasn't it the sign of the Infidels during the Crusades? Or Turkish, maybe?

Was it just the trademark of some self-dramatizing vandal, or was it a message of some kind? And if it was a message, what the hell did it mean?

A neighbor, Mrs. Leonard, had seen a man sitting in a car up the block from the Smith house on the evening of the break-in. It was dusk, and Mrs. Leonard had not been able to describe the suspect except in general terms: a Caucasian male, longish hair, possibly between twenty and thirty years of age.

"Was the car a gray Pinto?" Emil asked.

"No, it was a red car. It looked new. It might have been a Dodge or a Plymouth."

Emil asked if the man was good-looking or had a scar between his lip and his chin. Mrs. Leonard had not seen him well enough to say. "If he walked in the room right now, I wouldn't be able to identify him."

Willy showed up at the Smiths' later that evening. Though Emil did not suspect him, he found out that Willy had been working with Jimmy Guido in Fishkill at the time of the break-in. Willy went up to Janine's bedroom and surveyed the room in stunned silence. The meaning of the lipsticked moon and star on the mirror was a mystery to him as well, though he did say, "It looks like the flag of Turkey."

The BCI forensics team called the next day. The footprint taken outside the kitchen window belonged to a common pair of men's hiking boots, sized ten and a half.

Was the incident at the Smith house just a robbery, or was it connected somehow with Janine's disappearance? Earlier, Emil had bemoaned the difficulty of investigating a crime that had occurred thousands of miles away. Now, something to investigate was right here in his jurisdiction and Emil didn't have the faintest idea what he was going to do.

TEN

WILLY HAD JUST COME IN from running when the phone rang. He had found himself jogging farther and farther every day, so that he was doing eight, nine, ten miles daily. He managed to find solace of a kind, racing through residential streets and deserted roads. Though he was drinking more than ever, he had lost weight, close to ten pounds.

Relief was also to be found in work, and he had picked up a side job painting the interior of a run-down rental house that Carl, the sundries store proprietor, owned. In the past, his haphazard employment schedule with Jimmy Guido had suited Willy perfectly. Some week's paychecks were smaller than other's, but Jimmy paid well, and Willy earned more money than he spent, which was all that had mattered. So, it wasn't the extra money—three of Carl's checks lay uncashed on the dresser—it was the work, the anesthetic numbness it brought on, that Willy sought.

The ringing of the phone, so loud in the still apartment, jarred him. Lately, every time that it rang, Willy had tensed, fearing that it was news, horrible news, about Janine.

Willy picked up the phone after the third ring. "Hello."

There was no answer, though Willy knew by the faint static hiss that the line was open. "Hello," he repeated.

Willy's heart began to pound. He was about to speak when whoever was on the line hung up.

He replaced the receiver. Though the call had probably been a wrong number, Willy couldn't stop his imagination from running wild.

He bolted as the phone rang again. "Hello."

The barely audible hissing sound of an open line was audible. "Hello," Willy said once more.

Probably someone, believing he had misdialed earlier, was now scrutinizing a number that had been jotted down incorrectly. Or, Willy told himself, some children were playing a prank. Willy couldn't bring himself to hang up. "Hello," he repeated tentatively.

The line was disconnected.

Willy stared at the phone for a long time. When he finally went into the bathroom to take a shower, he placed the phone in the hallway and kept the door ajar in case it rang again.

A half hour later when the phone jangled for the third time, Willy picked it up and said hello. After a moment of hearing silence on the line, he ventured, "Janine?"

The line went dead.

A week after the burglary at Janine's, when Willy went to the lumber yard, he tried not to think of the absurdity of what he was doing. He paid for the hardware, the finished one-by-twelves, the one-by-sixes, the molding, the carpenter's glue, and then loaded it all in the back of his truck, next to the miter saw that had been borrowed from Jimmy Guido.

At the apartment, he carried everything from his truck to the spare bedroom. When they had been moving in, Janine had mentioned that the space next to the framed-out closet would be perfect for built-in bookshelves. Willy was going to make those shelves.

He had found a set of plans that would adapt easily to the space in a magazine in the Howland Library. The previous night, he had adjusted the plans to accommodate the spare bedroom, all the time not allowing himself to think of anything else but the task at hand. As Willy began to measure, re-measure, and cut the boards on the saw, however, the overwhelming futility of what he was doing bore down on him. He was building the shelves for someone who would never see them. Janine was not coming back.

He was aware of the pathetic quality of this gesture, its weirdness. His actions signaled a mind that was mildly, maybe severely, disturbed, yet Willy would not stop.

As he worked, he remembered the day they had agreed to rent the apartment. On a cloudy Sunday afternoon, he and Janine had met the landlord. Within the first few minutes of looking around, Willy had decided against renting the place. Although it was in adequate condition and the rent was fair, they had already seen another roomier, better-equipped apartment. After the landlord left, and they stood outside the duplex, he was surprised when Janine said, "Let's rent it."

"I thought you liked the place on North Walnut Street better?"

"I do." Janine responded. "But we would have to sign a lease. We won't have to here."

"But the lease would only be for a year."

"I just don't want to get tied down. I want to be able to take off if we feel like it."

Willy was certain that she had said "if *we* feel like it", not "if *I* feel like it."

A few weeks before this, Willy had started to tell Janine of a notion he was entertaining. Carl had let Willy know about a run-down house a few miles outside Beacon. Little more than a hovel, it had belonged to an elderly woman who left no family when she died. The house was to be sold for unpaid back taxes. Carl would have bought the place himself, but he already owned several rental properties and was overextended. Fixing up the home would involve a lot of work, time, and inconvenience, Carl had warned, but Willy and Janine would be able to buy it for very little money.

As Willy had spoken of the house, he saw the look of alarm and dismay in Janine's eyes and quickly changed the subject. If Janine wanted to keep open as many of their options as she could, he would accede to her wishes. He didn't want to hem her in.

They had rented this apartment. When Janine had mentioned the built-in bookshelves, Willy immediately told her he would build them for her. The roots they established would be as deep as Janine wanted. As long as they were together, he didn't care how or where they lived.

Willy ripped another board on the miter saw. He continued working for the next seven hours until he had finished the carpentry.

The next morning, under the grip of the same demented impulse, he sanded and painted the bookshelves. He waited four days to make sure the paint had completely dried before finishing the last part of his self-imposed covenant with Janine. Willy dragged the boxes of her books into the room and began stacking them. The top two shelves he reserved for hardcover novels, another shelf for paperbacks, another for textbooks, and the lowest for Janine's school notebooks. He arranged the books by author or subject, and felt it was a victory of sorts that he hadn't gone so crazy that he was alphabetizing the books in each group.

I've gone out of my mind, he thought. I've completely lost my senses.

Willy was finishing the bottom shelf when he could restrain himself no longer. Opening one of the notebooks, he gazed longingly at the handwriting.

"*The atria receive blood and pump it into the ventricles,*" he read.

When he had gone away to Rutgers, Willy would eagerly await Janine's letters, and just the sight of his name and address in her neat, measured longhand could fill him with contentment. He stacked the notebook, took another out of the box, and lingered over causes of the Russian Revolution in Janine's hand. Leafing through the book, he came upon a doodle of connecting circles and triangles. It had probably been a mild diversion during a dull dusty lecture. Willy couldn't help himself, he gently kissed it.

I miss you so much, he thought.

Willy started a new stack on the shelf with two of the notebooks. Yielding to his maudlin emotion and wallowing in it, he took another from the box and opened it. What he read electrified him.

There were five diaries. Each notebook with a black and white cover was identical to the other school notebooks and corresponded to a single year from 1968 through 1972. Each diary bore the same legend inside the front cover: "*Do not read the contents of this journal. They are my most intimate thoughts and are not to be read without my permission. To do so would constitute an unforgivable violation of my privacy.*"

Willy studied the inside cover. He had already read two pages of one of the diaries—an account of a visit Willy had made to Colgate a year and a half ago—but that had been before he had seen Janine's warning.

He had also browsed through all of the other notebooks. They contained nothing but summaries of college courses. The last of the journals ended on New Year's Eve, 1972, just four months ago. Willy had not been able to find this year's diary, the one that might conceivably cast some light on what had happened to Janine. It was nowhere in the apartment.

Willy picked up the first diary and scanned the legend on its frontispiece again. Though it sounded a bit melodramatic, Willy knew that Janine was very much in earnest. Should she return and find that he had read her diaries, she would undoubtedly feel violated. And what were the chances, Willy thought, that her musings as a high school girl would help find her now?

When Willy had first read the snippet of her diary, he had been startled. He knew Janine better than anyone else, was confident that he was closer to her, yet he had not been aware that she kept a diary. She had withheld it from him for as long as they had known each other.

Willy turned the page of the first diary. He was going to read the journals; he had known that from the very moment he discovered them.

Turning another page, Willy saw *January 1, 1968* inscribed in Janine's handwriting. He began to read.

PART TWO

1968–1972

FOR DAYS, WILLY READ THE diaries over and over, studying them like a seer examining portents. If asked, he could have quoted with a fair degree of accuracy large sections of the journals from memory.

The first diary began on New Year's Day in the middle of Janine's sophomore year in high school. Willy could tell that Janine was initially feeling her way in the journals, unsure of what she wanted to write. In the first few months, Janine had recorded impressions of movies seen, and books read. She had soon dropped these ruminations. Similarly, she stopped prefacing her entries with Dear Diary almost immediately. She dated her writings for the most part, though occasionally she would separate different entries by merely skipping a line in the notebook. The diaries were not a daily record: days and sometimes weeks would elapse between jottings.

Except for the assassinations of Martin Luther King, Jr., and Robert Kennedy, and her involvement with Vietnam Moratorium protests, little of larger political concerns was mentioned in the journals.

The majority of entries dealt with things Willy and Janine had shared together. Willy had been prepared for Janine's account of events differing from what he remembered. He knew that memory was subjective, ambiguous, unreliable. Yet, Janine's version so often coincided with his own recollections, with few real differences, that at first he was heartened. Didn't this accord confirm how attuned, how compatible, how much in love they were?

Then Willy read other sections. It was these entries that he read over and over again.

1968

January 1

Dear Diary,

It is January First and I am starting a diary. How original! So I guess my New Year's Resolution this year is to be banal and self-absorbed.

Actually, I don't want to write a diary. I don't have the patience or time, nor is my life eventful enough for that. I mean, do I really want to look back one day and read that I had tuna fish for lunch, that I nearly flunked a history exam, that Kim said Diane told her that Patty said . . . Do I really need to record all the minutia of my everyday life? It is boring to me now, why should it be of interest in retrospect in ten years?

I hope this journal doesn't turn out to be "Gidget Goes to Beacon." Rather, I hope it will be like the prose equivalent of an album of snap shots—small moments of time captured.

Jan. 2, 1968

Dear Diary,

Today I had tuna fish for lunch. I flunked my history exam. Kim told me that Diane said that Patty said. . . .

February Ninth

Eric and I went to the Beacon High dance tonight. You could just see all these girls, including Diane Niedzialkowski though she'll deny it, mooning over Eric and giving him lovestruck gazes. He really is gorgeous. And he's all mine . . . Well maybe not all mine. He spent about an hour with his friends—all those lamebrained jocks: Andy Brascia, Terry Quinn, Earache Kehler, Willy Buchanan . . .

March 1, 1968
. . . Eric and I had another stupid fight. I guess he thought I wasn't paying enough attention to him, or paying too much attention to Andy Brascia, or who knows what sin I've committed. So as a result of whatever I did, Eric was real moody and pissy. This is so fucking ridiculous, all these imagined slights, and huffy silences, and whiny protests. I wish he would just lighten up.

March 6, 1968
. . . A minute ago, as I was writing this, Mom came into my room. She told me to "put down your books. Supper is ready."
She has no inkling that I am writing a journal. No one has.
Will the actual process of how I write this journal seem juvenile to me one day? I sit in my room or in study hall, an open textbook next to this notebook and write. To all appearances, it looks as though I am doing my homework. This notebook is the same as all my others and rests alongside them on my desk, the theory being that the best place to hide something is in plain sight. Will this subterfuge seem melodramatic or self-important? Will I look back and think, No one was really all that interested?

March 11, 1968
I went to see Eric play in a basketball game tonight. Once again he was the peaches, he was the cream, he was the captain of the team: He scored something like twenty-seven points, and Beacon won. And he was sweet after the game. Maybe things are getting better between us.

April 26, 1968
I am no longer a virgin. I just hope I am not a mother-to-be.
This night, which I had always thought would be magical, and full of love, ecstasy, and passion, was instead messy, hurried, depressing, passionless.
My virginity was not something that I prized above life itself. I don't feel dishonored or deflowered by having lost it. While having no intention of saving it for my husband, I did think losing my virginity would be special, with someone I loved. Or at least fun. I guess one of the reasons I'm depressed is that now I'll always have this squalid memory of my first time.

Here are the facts: Eric and I were making out in the back of his father's station wagon. As usual, he was insistent, pestering. After a while—now in retrospect was it a change of tactics?—he calmed down and just seemed to be caring and thoughtful. So that I was lulled into a tenderness for him. Then, slowly, not quite coming to the point of it, he lowered my underpants. And I thought, What the hell.

That's probably what's so disappointing. I didn't think, I've got to have you, or I love you so much, or I want to be as close to you as I can. No, I said to myself, What the hell.

Our lovemaking, and that's an extremely generous interpretation of what happened, was . . . what? A bit painful? Little more than Eric shoving inside me? Clinical? Inept? How can a boy whose body is so beautiful and lithe, whose movements are so fluid, be so clumsy and insensitive when it comes to something so natural?

If I keep writing about this, I'm going to get angry or bitter or burst into tears.

The only way that this evening could be absolutely perfect in its horribleness would be if I wind up pregnant.

Eric didn't bother to call me today, the day after our "Night of Rapture." It's actually kind of funny. No doubt something more important, Eddie Reinhold's going-into-the-army stag party, probably came up. Of course, I probably would have told Mom to say I was out. The last thing I want to do is share sweet little intimacies over the phone with Eric.

May 1, 1968
Eric now expects sex with me every time we go out.

Eric is so stupid, and not just about me. The areas of his ignorance are vast. How can he never have heard of William Faulkner? It's not just that he's never read Faulkner, or finds him boring or difficult, he's never even *heard* of him. Nor has he ever heard of Gauguin. Or Frank Lloyd Wright. Or Martha Graham, or Francois Truffaut, or Ella Fitzgerald. The list goes on and on.

How have I let myself get into this situation? It has to stop.

May 2, 1968
. . . I am definitely not pregnant. Cramps have never felt so good . . .

May 8, 1968
Eric and I had sex again. If anything it was worse than before. It's astounding how uncaring and selfish he can be. The only thing more

astounding is that I let him fuck me. What am I, a doormat? Why don't I just write WELCOME across my chest?

The honeymoon is definitely over.

May 22, 1968
I called up Eric and told him we were breaking up. He whined a bit, but he finally got the message. Under the circumstances, I was as kind as I could be. I said I was unhappy, I didn't think I loved him, we could still be friends. I did NOT say that he was selfish, piggish, insensitive, boring, illiterate, a terrible lover. That showed remarkable restraint, didn't it?

I feel unburdened.

May 29, 1968
Teddy's dress rehearsal for *Arsenic and Old Lace* was tonight. Kim Mooney, Willy Buchanan, and I snuck in and saw most of the first act. My judgement might be a bit biased since Teddy is my brother and I love him dearly, but he was excellent, especially considering this is the first time he's ever done any acting. With training and work, he probably could be in Hollywood or on Broadway. Of course, he'll never act again. He knows exactly what he is going to do with his life: ten years from now he'll be a lawyer with an office on Main Street. He'll be perfectly happy, living in Beacon. Why does that sadden me?

For a change, it was a fun, exciting night. I had planned on only going to the play rehearsal, but Diane wanted to get some beer first, hoping that she would run into exactly who we did run into—Andy Brascia. He was with Earache Kehler and Willy Buchanan. I'm glad they talked me into it.

Willy Buchanan is a lot more interesting than I thought he would be. We wound up standing in a broom closet together . . .

I'm not sure what to make of Willy, but do know this: he's different from how I thought he'd be.

August 2, 1968
Today was great. Today was unbelievable.

Ever since that night of Teddy's play rehearsal, I've had the feeling that Willy Buchanan was attracted to me. Now, I'm sure of it. And, the funny thing is, I think I'm interested in him, too.

Because we are going to the shore tomorrow, Mom wanted me to run some errands for her before going to the lake. Luckily, the bank was left for last.

Driving up to the bank, I saw Willy Buchanan banging up the sidewalk with a jackhammer. He had his shirt off and was sweating, and he looked really good. I had to laugh out loud, though, because his legs were spread wide, and he was wrestling with this huge power tool between his legs. I mean it was so exaggeratedly phallic.

He flirted with me on my way into the bank, and when I left, I teased him by inviting him to go to the lake with me. He threw down all his tools and came with me! Even though he knew he would be fired—and was—he left everything just to be with me! And what was even more startling was how completely ingenuous he was.

"I'd do anything to be with you," he said. No other boy has ever been so open with me. I was dumbfounded. And thrilled. We spent the entire day together at Sylvan Lake and were absolutely at ease with one another.

Willy is very good-looking. He has a wonderful body. A lot of guys, at Sylvan Lake or down the shore, seem so narcissistic about their bodies. They won't exactly pose, but you'll catch them gazing down at their biceps, or running their hands along their chests or arms. Willy seems completely unaware of his body. I was watching from behind while he was sitting on my blanket. His back makes a V from his narrow waist to his shoulders. Every muscle stood out but not in the overdeveloped way a lot of athlete's do. He is graceful, but seems not to be aware that he is—maybe that is part of what being graceful is.

He may not be aware of his own body, but he certainly is aware of mine.

Tonight, he called during dinner just to make me laugh. I think I have something to look forward to after we come back from the shore.

August 3, 1968
We're at the shore at last. I'm writing this on the beach, ten o'clock Saturday morning.

Judy Shiemler just waved to me from the upper deck of her family's house and yelled, "I'll see you in a few minutes."

It feels great to be down here . . .

. . . Judy is really tan and has lost weight. She has also lost her virginity, but is happier about having lost the weight because it was less work. And more satisfying.

Everybody but Tad and Carol Hollenbeck's family are down again this August. Sean Farrell is here; we spent the afternoon together. This may be a very interesting vacation.

Besides the obvious—the sun, the beach, the fun—what I like best about coming to Long Beach Island is the continuity. It's like a long novel that you pick up only during the summer. Every year you read a few chapters, then have to wait another year to continue it. I've known Judy, and Beth Harrimon, and Beverly Savoca, and the Wahlberg twins, and all the others since I was a child. Sean Farrell and I have been prowling around each other since the sixth grade.

Coming down here every summer is like being able to have another, different life . . .

August 4, 1968
Sean Farrell dropped by our blanket today and stayed all afternoon. He usually doesn't get to the beach until the early afternoon. He has taken up golf and has been playing most mornings. He's offered to take me out and teach me how to play.

"Right," I said. "And I suppose you'd have to rub up against my behind and help me swing the club in order to teach me."

"That's part of the game. That's how you score."

He is such a doggy. There's no way I'm going golfing, but Teddy is playing with him tomorrow.

All afternoon long, Beverly Savoca was reading a Harold Robbins novel and would recite aloud whenever she got to a sex scene. That was every five minutes or so.

I wrote a postcard to Willy Buchanan today. Teddy saw the name and address and raised his eyebrows. I've been thinking a lot about Willy, which is strange, since Sean Farrell is also on my mind.

August 10, 1968
Teddy fell asleep yesterday on his side, so now he has this weird sunburn just on the right side of his body. He was pretty funny today on the beach though. He had me and Beverly Savoca cover his sunburnt parts with wet sand. Beverly, who I think has a crush on Teddy, couldn't wait for Teddy to shift or move, because then she got to slather more wet sand all over him . . .

August 23, 1968
Sean and I finally stopped fooling around. Or should I say that Sean and I at long last fooled around.

Tonight was the last night of vacation, so we were all down at the jetty drinking beer. Sean said he'd walk me back to the house.

As we strolled down the beach, Sean took my hand. I was startled, but happily so. As long as we've known each other, and for all the times we've teased and flirted, this was the first overt physical sign of affection between us.

Sean was very sweet and funny. I was hoping that more would

happen than just holding hands. When we came near to the house, Sean stopped and put his arms around me.

"Every five years, I make a pass," he said, then kissed me. Then I kissed him, my tongue probably halfway down his throat, and the next thing I knew, we were laying on the sand. Finally, after all these years.

Sean said, "Did you ever see *From Here to Eternity?*" then laughed at his own joke.

I rolled him over on top of me.

Maybe it's because we've had all those years of teasing, but I was so incredibly aroused. What I felt was not tenderness or soft, dreamy emotions. It was an overpowering desire to fuck him. Luckily, we didn't.

I heard voices—no I wasn't driven to psychosis by lust: two middle-aged couples were heading toward us. We got up and walked hand-in-hand back to the house. Sean kissed me goodnight and told me he'd write. We both laughed at the old joke; we both know that he won't.

Tomorrow we have to go home. So, once again, I'll have to put this great part of my life, this separate existence, on hold for another year . . .

I'm a slut. Twenty-four hours ago, I was writhing beneath Sean Farrell on the beach, ready and hoping to fuck his brains out. In the car on the way home, I kept playing that scene over and over again in my head, fondly and nostalgically recalling My Summer Love. All that was missing were the chords of "Theme From A Summer Place" coming to a crescendo in the background. And then, I'm not in Beacon fifteen minutes, when I go off on a date with Willy Buchanan to a movie that I've already seen. I am crazy. I must think I'm the Scarlett O'Hara of West Willow Street.

What is even crazier is that I had a great time with Willy tonight. I'm really attracted to him.

If they ever hold a Miss Bitch in Heat of 1968 beauty pageant, I'll be the winner hands down.

August 25, 1968

Great fan of the American pastime that I am, I dropped by a baseball game to see Willy Buchanan play. If I hate jocks so much, why is it that I've gone out with three? Willy and I wound up in the basement, making out hot and heavy.

As for the Miss Bitch in Heat of 1968 contest, they can now retire the crown . . .

September 16, 1968
I have a new boyfriend, Willy Buchanan . . .

October 13, 1968
My sexual history:
I have played doctor and nurse with Craig Richter during kindergarten recess.
I have kissed the boys and made them cry. I have also kissed the boys and made me cry.
I have let boys explore under my shirt with their hands and mouths.
I have masturbated. I have masturbated with foreign objects—the most embarrassing of which is a carrot. I have jerked off Eric Boyd. He fumbled around in my pants; if intentions count for anything, then I suppose he has jerked me off.
I have had sexual intercourse with Eric Boyd. I did not love him. I have not had sexual intercourse with Willy. I think I love him.

October 25, 1968
I finally smoked marijuana today. Lorraine Chisolm was home from college and had a baggy full of grass. She, Patty, and I smoked it out of a corncob pipe. We must have looked ridiculous—I felt like Mammy Yokum. It took me a while to get used to inhaling without choking or coughing. I didn't feel a bit different; I wasn't stoned at all, though Lorraine said she was high. Supposedly, it takes a few times. And then, before you know it, you're wearing love beads and handing out flowers to cops.
Willy was jealous when I told him . . .

November 17, 1968
I am truly, madly, with all my heart, passionately in love with Willy Buchanan.
We made love today.
I had finally come to a decision to sleep with Willy. I had planned it. Mom and Howard were away. This was a safe time for me. I was calculating. How then could everything seem spontaneous, so natural and instinctive?
At long last, I know what drives people mad. Willy was a terrific lover; I was a terrific lover.
I am so happy.

1969

January 14, 1969

This is how I finally got The Pill.

Everyone I had asked about how to get a prescription gave me conflicting advice. Patty's sister, Lorraine, told me it was against the law for doctors to prescribe contraceptives to minors without parental consent. Diane thought you didn't need parental consent at Planned Parenthood.

Then I read in the *Times* that prescribing birth control to underage girls was an unclear legal area. No shit. But the article also said that Planned Parenthood was proceeding as though it were legal. So, I screwed up my courage, filled my pockets with change, went to a pay phone, and dialed the Planned Parenthood office in Poughkeepsie.

"Hello—" a voice answered.

"Hi, I've recently been married," I blurted out in a rush of words, "and would like to get birth control, but my husband and I still live with my mother, who is a strict Catholic, so I don't want her to know anything about it."

The woman on the phone gave a startled laugh, I thought on account of my inept lie. But she said, "You don't want to talk to me. I'm the operator. That will be twenty cents more, please."

What a moron I am.

When finally put through to Planned Parenthood, I repeated the ludicrous fairy tale, then set up an appointment.

Today, going in for my visit, I was so nervous that I kept stuttering. On my finger was a two-dollar zircon wedding ring from Grant's. In the waiting room, it occurred to me that I had never simply asked if parental consent, the reason for this stupid charade and the ring turning my finger green, was necessary for minors. Jesus, I'm such a dumbbell sometimes.

Filling out the patient history form, I wrote that I was eighteen and married. I put down my real name and address, however, thinking there might be a problem getting a prescription filled with an alias.

All my lies were probably unnecessary.

A counselor spoke with me briefly, and then it was time for the pelvic exam. Another milestone in my life, right up there with my first steps, my first day in school—my first pelvic exam. Actually, it was neither as embarrassing nor as painful as I thought it would be, although it did involve another first. It was the first time anyone has put his fingers inside me while carrying on a conversation about the weather.

Afterward, a one-hour class was given, and the counselor talked with me again. I'm positive she knew I was lying. Then to my surprise, they gave me a six-month supply of birth-control pills right at the clinic.

So now I'm a modern young woman. A flapper for the 1960s.

January 30, 1969
Today, Daddy would have been forty-five years old. Though I know it's morbid and pointless, I went to his grave this afternoon. Fresh flowers lay by his tombstone, so Mom must have gone there too, probably this morning. At the grave, I tried to think of happy memories of Dad, times we had together, but couldn't stop staring at those exquisite lilies. How elegant, how tasteful. How hypocritical. Instead of fond remembrances, I kept thinking about that one horrible day.

I don't want to write this—but then, hasn't this journal always been about my one day writing this?

I can still remember the sound of Sister Phyllis's droning voice as I stole away from St. John's School after lunch recess that spring day. I was cutting class, which just wasn't done at St. John's, it would have been unthinkable for me to do so under normal circumstances. But these weren't normal circumstances. My father was dying.

Daddy was in Highland Hospital again, undergoing the last, hopeless course of chemotherapy. We all knew that it wasn't helping him. The best time of his day was the early afternoon, when the tide of pain and nausea had ebbed. Probably, my motives were selfish. He might have enough strength to give me comfort, as I visited with the pretense of helping to ease his pain.

I walked the mile to the hospital, making a big deal of the irony of trees budding and life beginning anew as my father lay dying.

Daddy was happy to see me. There had been no chemotherapy that morning. He, and reluctantly his doctor, had agreed to discontinue it. He told me the unexpected good news: he was going to be released that afternoon; he was going home. What was left unsaid, what I wasn't able to admit to myself, was that he was going home to die.

An orderly came in and helped Daddy dress. I had become accustomed to Daddy's baldness and his sunken cheeks, but was stunned by how emaciated his chest and shoulders looked. So he wouldn't see my shock, and so I wouldn't have to look at the horror his body had become, I left to phone Mom to have her drive us home.

Nobody answered. Maybe that is what is so unforgivable. Why wasn't she home? Was that too much to ask?

We called a taxi instead. The orderly wheeled Daddy to the front desk, then I helped him walk the twenty yards to the sidewalk where the cab waited. All my life, I had depended on him, and now he was leaning on me, depending on my strength to help him.

The cab dropped us off at home, then we tottered up the stairs. Neither of us noticed the maroon Oldsmobile parked on the street.

The front door was locked, but I assumed that Mom was nervous with Daddy away. We unlocked the door and entered the hallway. Then we both heard the unmistakable sounds.

Moaning came from upstairs. Low, guttural, insistent. The bedsprings were creaking furiously. I knew what the sounds were, had heard them occasionally before from my parents' bedroom, though usually they were muffled by closed doors. But this time, Mom wasn't pressing a pillow to her mouth so the kids wouldn't hear.

Daddy halted as though struck. That he could look even more sick didn't seem possible, but he stood there shaking, his face drawn.

If I ever did one wise thing in my life, it was then. I said, "Mom's crying. It's because you're sick."

Daddy nodded at me uncomprehendingly. Then he took my hand and walked back out of the house. We stood on the front steps a moment; I had never seen him, or anyone else, look so sad or lost. Finally, he turned to me and said vacantly, "Let's give Mom a little time to herself. Do you want to go to Tcherny's? We'll get some ice cream."

Ice cream? It was as though he had spoken in some foreign language.

It seemed so incongruous, but we nonetheless started off for Tcherny's Corner Store.

Daddy could barely walk. He was drenched in sweat within fifty yards and leaned more and more heavily on me. His breathing was so labored I feared he might have a heart attack before we made it the two blocks to the store.

He gave me some bills from his pants pocket—a ten and two twenties—and told me to get an ice cream cone. For years, it had been a tradition that he would buy Teddy and me ice cream at Tcherny's. It had always seemed such a treat.

From inside the store, I saw Daddy go to a pay telephone. By his bewildered, hurt expression, it was obvious he was calling home. Mr. Tcherny handed me the cone, then looked out the window at Daddy still on the phone. "How's your father doing?"

I almost threw the ice cream back in his face. I wanted to tear everything in the store apart, but instead said, "He's doing better, thanks."

Tcherny smiled kindly, condescendingly, with the knowledge that my father was decaying, was tinged with death.

Leaving the store, I saw Daddy, frail, bald, sick, sitting exhausted on the stoop. I knelt down beside him and started to cry. "I don't want you to die, I don't want you to die."

He reached up with an arm which had once seemed so strong and held me. We rocked gently for a while, the ice cream becoming a puddle on the cement behind us, then after I stopped crying, we started home again.

I thought Daddy was going to die before we reached the house, was certain that he would simply collapse in the gutter and stop breathing. We rested every hundred yards, until finally, mercifully, Mrs. Feldstein stopped to give us a ride the rest of the way.

Howard's maroon Oldsmobile was gone when we climbed the steps into the house. Mom was standing in the front hallway, afraid to approach. They stared at each other, but then they both glanced at me. I wanted to leave my father and go over and slap her face, spit on it, but feeling Daddy's gaze, said, "Hi."

"Hi, honey," Mom ventured, then tentatively came over and took Daddy's other arm. We both helped him upstairs to the crisply-made bed in their room. Daddy went to sit, but it was more like collapsing. He looked up at me and said, "Thanks, honey."

Mom said, "Why don't you go out and play?"

As I fled out the front door, Daddy's words came from upstairs, "At least you changed the sheets. I should be thankful for that."

"Ed—"

"We'll talk about it later."

In less than three weeks, Daddy was dead. When Mom tried to comfort me, her arms open wide, I struck out at her as hard as I could. She stared at me, frightened, miserable, until I left the room. We've never said a word about any of this since that day.

I allowed Daddy to believe that his daughter was still innocent, unaware.

I hate her.

May 9, 1969

Nine of us, Kim, Andy, Earache, Diane, Eric Boyd, Paul Barich, Terry Pritchard, Willy, and I, skipped school yesterday and dropped acid.

Tripping was indescribable. At first it was just waves of pleasure, and everything seemed hilarious. And then I hallucinated a bit. It wasn't at all like *2001* or William Blake. I did hear what sounded like far off wind, and at one point Willy's voice seemed to echo. His face looked so beautiful, beatific. And thankfully, unlike everything I've ever seen on TV, I heard no sitar music . . .

June 5, 1969

When I came home from school this afternoon, Mom was sitting stiffly in the living room. From that alone, even if she didn't have a dour, angry expression, I knew that something was up.

She held up the compact with my birth control pills. She had found them in the jade box where they were hidden.

"What are these pills?" she hissed.

"Heroin."

"Don't get smart with me. I know what they are." And then came the tirade. Had I no pride in myself? How could I cheapen myself? Did I actually think that any boy could respect me now? I was a fool to think Willy had any respect for me, no matter what he might say.

"I'm assuming that it's just Willy?" she said.

"Go to hell."

Mom slapped me across the face. It was the first time she has ever really struck me. Tears from the force of the blow came into my eyes.

"Unlike you," I screamed at her, "one partner is enough for me."

I snatched the compact from her hands and raced up to my room. She didn't follow.

At supper, she glowered at me throughout the entire meal. We didn't say a word. Howard knew something was going on and tried to lessen the tension by rambling on about Teddy, which is usually a neutral subject we all can discuss. But after a few minutes, he shut up and we finished the meal in silence.

Later, Mom came into my room. She seemed defensive and unsure of herself.

"You think you were the only one hurt when your father died, but you weren't. I had every right to marry again. It's not for you to judge me."

She looked at me tentatively, hopefully, trying to ascertain if my comment about two partners was only a reference to her remarriage, not an allusion to her being a faithless lying cheating bitch slut. Or maybe she was trying to shape my remark to something that we could live with.

"You have the right to marry anyone you want. And, my personal life is my own."

She stared at me a moment, seeking some stronger confirmation that I knew nothing of her affair with Howard, or perhaps trying to reassert herself. I returned her stare. Then she left, taking whatever small victories she could.

She is never going to control my life again. I hate her.

June 12, 1969

Phil Ferguson is home from the army and came by to see Teddy. He can't get over how much people in Beacon have changed in the year and a half he's been gone. Two years ago, everybody was so clean-cut and collegiate. Now everyone is a freak, smoking hash and doing acid.

The Summer of Love hit the rest of America two years ago. It figures it's just reaching Beacon, now.

July 14, 1969

A letter from Teddy came in the mail today. He has finished his French classes, and he's off to Barcelona with a friend. Teddy didn't give any details about the friend, so it's probably *une jeune fille*. Depending on how his money lasts, he may stay the rest of the summer. I hope he gets back in time to go to the shore with us.

Regarding the shore: Willy is not coming down the last two weekends as planned. He has to work. I'm not really disappointed. Part of me wants him to come. I want to show him off, have Judy and Beverly and all the others get a good look at my handsome, witty boyfriend. But another part of me is glad he can't make it down. The shore is something that is mine, apart from the two of us. I want to hold on to that.

July 26, 1969

We're back at Long Beach Island again—at least, Howard, Mom, and I are. It seems strange not having Teddy here with us. I miss him, even more than when he first went away to college. Five years ago, all of us, Daddy, Mom, Teddy, and I were here. Now, it's just Mom and me. I doubt Teddy will ever vacation with us at the shore again.

How many more summers will I have at Long Beach Island? Probably not too many, perhaps this is my last. The long novel that I pick up every summer seems to be coming to a close . . .

Apparently golf has lost some of its charm for Sean Farrell. He dropped by early this morning. His first words to me were, "I thought about you all year long." He couldn't quite manage to keep a straight face.

"Oh really," I replied. "I started going out with my boyfriend the night I came back from the shore."

We went down to the beach and were by ourselves for a couple of hours before everyone else slowly dragged their asses out of bed. The Age of Aquarius has reached the shore as well: everybody's doing drugs. Sean's hair is real long, almost to his shoulders, and looks good. I told him about Willy. He pretended to be happy for me, and then spent the next few hours flirting outrageously. He's such a doggy. It's good to see that some things haven't changed.

Sean said that this is definitely his last year at the shore. His parents are moving to Florida. "It probably would have been my last summer here, anyway. I mean, after a while you stop going on vacation with your parents."

Beverly Savoca's parents are talking about selling their beach house and buying a smaller place at Seaside Heights. She may not be back either . . .

July 30, 1969

. . . Last night, Judy, Sean, Beverly, Tad Hollenbeck, and I all did half a hit of mescaline. It was very mild. We went and hung outside the Tide and basically spent the next four hours laughing like imbeciles . . .

August 2, 1969

Sean Farrell came by early again—the fourth time this week. He had breakfast with us. Mom seems to like Sean. Compared to how she feels about Willy, she worships the ground he walks on. If Mom likes Sean, something must be wrong with him.

We went to the beach and again were by ourselves for a couple of hours. Everyone else is so drug-addled that they can't make it to the beach until noon.

August 10, 1969

I just found out that Sean Farrell is leaving Thursday and won't be coming back. He's going to the big three-day concert in White Lake. It figures that the only time he will be anywhere near Beacon is when I'm down at the shore.

Tad Hollenbeck and Beverly Savocca are going as well. I feel let down, cheated even. To me, every day at the shore is precious. With so many leaving, it just won't be the same.

I just realized something. I probably will never see Sean Farrell again after Wednesday night.

August 13, 1969

I made love with Sean Farrell tonight.

Why did I do it? I love Willy.

We were alone in his parent's house. We had smoked a joint and were a little high, but so what? The grass didn't hypnotize me or make me do something against my will.

As we were talking, he put his hand on my thigh and gently began to caress it. I knew it was a prelude to something else, and should have moved it away. But, I didn't. I even thought, "I'm on the Pill, I don't have that to worry about."

I let him kiss me. We took each other's clothes off. We made love.

I love Willy. We have great sex. What could have made me sleep with Sean?

I was so turned on, I felt so much . . . lust. Why?

And now I feel so terrible and ashamed of myself.

I didn't want Sean to go, I didn't want this to be his last year at the shore, I didn't want all this to end.

August 14, 1969

Sean, Tad, and Beverly left this morning for the concert, the Aquarian Exposition. I'm still real confused.

August 15, 1969

The newspapers and television are full of news about the concert at Woodstock. Half a million kids are there, among them Sean. And Tad and Beverly. A lot of drugs and longhairs and partying in the rain. The weather has turned foul here as well. No matter how I tried, I couldn't make the summer last—what a stunning revelation, huh?

I should have gone to Woodstock. With Willy.

September 1, 1969

Willy's folks had gone to his uncle's and we were up in his bedroom, just starting to fool around. Willy had just taken my blouse off, when I couldn't stop myself; I started crying.

I feel so ashamed, so guilty. Why did I sleep with Sean?

At first, Willy was perplexed, afraid that he had done something to offend me. Seeing how sweet and baffled he looked made me cry even harder. He laid down beside me and held me, but didn't say anything, didn't question me. He knows me better than anyone, understands what it takes to comfort me.

Just writing this makes me want to cry.

I couldn't tell him the truth. I love Willy; how could I hurt him that way?

"I'm just so upset that you're going away to school."

Could I be any more disgusting or hypocritical? Availing myself of his love and using it as an excuse to cover my repulsive behavior. I am vile.

Why did I sleep with Sean? How could I have done that to myself and to Willy? What is the matter with me?

September 2, 1969

Watching Mom and Howard out the window in the yard, I saw Howard put his arm around Mom's shoulder. I bristled, as I still sometimes do when there is any form of affection between them.

Then it dawned on me that what I did to Willy is no different from what Mom did to Daddy. Maybe I am worse . . .

September 3, 1969

Willy left for school today. Perhaps it's for the best that I have a few days by myself, apart from him . . .

. . . I miss Willy, which must seem ironic and contradictory. He called today and said he's coming back for the weekend. He senses how upset and depressed I am. I can never tell Willy what happened with Sean. I would rather die than have him find out.

October 11, 1969

As usual, Willy came home for the weekend. It was almost as before: for a while I was able to forget what I had done to him. For the first time since summer vacation, I was able to experience pleasure and tenderness without feeling disgusted at myself.

What a horrible mess I almost made of our lives. But, thank God, I seem to be getting a second chance.

1970

February 5, 1970

Beacon High was not graced by my presence today, though I had absolutely nothing better to do. So many people are away at school—Willy, Patty, Kim, Andy—that this year is just dragging on. Except for weekends with Willy, I just keep marking time.

Seven more months until I get out of this dumpy town.

April 12, 1970

I have just returned from visiting Willy at Rutgers.

Diane picked me up at the train station and dropped me off at home along with the camping gear that was stashed in the trunk of her car all weekend. Mom never suspected a thing.

Willy has some crazy friends at school; I liked all of them. They're bright, funny.

Now I wonder how Willy can leave school every weekend. So much more is happening there than in Beacon. So much more freedom, to do or be what you want, is allowed.

If Willy stayed away for months at a time, it would break my heart, so I should just be grateful. Still, I don't plan to come home every weekend next fall when I finally go away to school.

April 23, 1970

We are not going to Long Beach Island this year. It wasn't exactly unexpected. Howard's family owns a place in Maine, and that's where he had always spent his summers until he married Mom. He only went to New Jersey with us because he didn't want to cause any ruckus with me and Teddy. Especially with me.

Howard and Mom left the decision up to me. "If it really means a lot to you, we'll go back to the shore."

I had hoped for at least one more time at Long Beach Island, for some sort of closure to that part of my life, but it's time for me to stop being a spoiled brat. I told them to go to Maine.

August 28, 1970
Today, as much as it broke my heart to do it, I quit my summer job. Alas, I'll never again count out grubby shirts that smell of b.o. and ask, "Do you want starch?" Four more days until I go away to school. I can't wait.

August 31, 1970
It is now almost three o'clock in the morning—three hours past my curfew—and Willy just dropped me off at home. Mom didn't bother waiting up for me. She must figure I'm going to be on my own in a few hours, so what's the use. Besides, what was she going to do? Ground me for the next four years?

Tonight was, in a sense, the last night of my high school years. I surprised myself by not getting all maudlin—at Zep's, which was filled with all these people getting ready to go away to school, my urge to lead the crowd in a few choruses of "Those Were the Days" was success-fully suppressed.

When Willy and I left Zep's, we drove to the country club. Grabbing a blanket from the trunk of the car, we strolled onto the golf course. The moon was full, very bright, and high in the sky. Out in the middle of all that open space with no one else around for what seemed miles, we spread out the blanket in a sand bunker and lay down.

It was bittersweet. We both just needed to feel close to the other. For a long time to come, Willy and I will be apart more than we are together.

Afterward, we climbed out of the deep sand trap. Naturally I in-sisted, in compliance with correct golf etiquette, that we rake the bunker behind us. We roamed naked across the clipped grass to the pool. Willy gingerly opened the gate, careful not to let it make even a squeak, put his finger to his lips, and said, "Shh." I carefully lowered myself into the surprisingly warm water. Not daring even to swim for fear of the noise, I turned to see Willy on the diving board, springing up and down with thunderous *thwaaangs*. He did a cannonball, landing with a deafening wallop that sent waves of water out of the pool and that set to barking just about every dog in North America. As he surfaced, laughing, I felt so in love with him. I swam to Willy and held him, our bodies feeling slick in the water. I almost said, "I don't want to leave you. I'm not going to school." Luckily, I held my words.

Though it's depressing now, I feel sure that being apart is the right choice for us. However it works out, if Willy and I continue to love one another, or if we drift apart, it will be for the best.

September 1, 1970
Finally, at last, after eighteen years, I am on my own.

Mom and Howard dropped me off a little after noon. We all lugged my stuff up the three flights of steps to the suite I had been assigned. It is my new home: my name was very elegantly scrawled in crayon on a strip of masking tape next to two others.

Thankfully, Mom did not prolong our farewell. She and I hugged and kissed. Her baby was leaving the nest; she seemed about to cry, but didn't. Howard wished me luck with a melancholy joviality, patted my shoulder, and gave me a quick bashful buss on the cheek. Though I didn't want it to, their emotion touched me.

As Howard's car drove away, I felt elated, though I did not kick up my heels or dance a jig. And I did not say, "Thank fucking Christ," at a set of receding taillights as I heard one girl mutter.

Walking around campus, gathering in first impressions is a bit strange. Having come up here with Daddy those times, I thought I would remember much more. So much seems foreign, even unreal, though in just a few short weeks things will probably become familiar and mundane. One boy—he had the shadow of a goatee that he no doubt had started to grow this morning—was sitting under a tree, playing a guitar, and singing softly. He looked as though he expected people to gather around him, nodding their heads beatniklike, and snapping their fingers in hip appreciation at the end of his numbers instead of clapping.

Although I told myself to wait a week or so, I have just written Willy a letter. It's only been eighteen hours, and I miss him already. I didn't dare tell him how much though; if I had, he would certainly have dropped everything and raced up to see me . . .

It seems strange to be sleeping in the same room with two others. Both of my roommates, Laura and Amy, had shared bedrooms with sisters, so maybe it isn't as unusual for them. I think Laura and I might become friends; I'm not as sure about Amy.

September 16, 1970

Willy called. He tried hard to be jolly and encouraging, but it's obvious he misses me. I wanted to invite him up this weekend, but forced myself not to . . .

September 29, 1970

Willy is coming up next week. It's been a month, the longest we have ever been apart. At first, he was hurt and angry that I hadn't arranged for him to visit earlier, but he seems to be coming around. Everything is falling into place nicely. Amy is going home this weekend, probably to attend a Junior League tea or something. Laura will sleep in Becky's suite. We will have the whole place to ourselves. I'm counting the days.

October 4, 1970

Laura is jealous of my handsome boyfriend. Hitchhiking up here took Willy almost ten hours; it only takes five by car. I have to admit I wasn't exactly disconsolate that the trip was so hard, because that means Willy won't be able to come up every weekend. I'm still confident that we have to live our own lives for a while.

There are so many accounts of unhappy middle-aged women who have not had lives of their own. They've gone directly from being someone's daughter to being someone's wife or mother, with no chance to establish their own identity. That is not going to happen to me.

1971

February 5, 1971

I'm never going to another fraternity party as long as I live. Those guys are such ASSHOLES. Tonight, Laura and I managed to stay all of twenty minutes at one before we both left in total disgust.

When we arrived at the party, a good number of the brothers were already to the drunken point of lighting each other's farts. And how festive to see guys staggering around, the rolls of their beer bellies hanging over their belts. Within minutes, someone came up to us and the first words out of his mouth were, "Do you want to go upstairs and fuck?"

Did he actually suppose that this sophisticated technique would work? That anyone would say, "Yes, there's nothing I would rather do than sleep with a drunken, loutish asshole. Which of the soiled crusty beds upstairs is yours?" What an imbecile.

Then, someone I've noticed around campus came sauntering into the house. I think she's a year or two ahead of me and her name is Susie. She has a sexy figure, voluptuous. The instant she came into the room, I knew she was in for trouble.

All those frat boys just leered. It was disgusting, their eyes, almost as one, zoomed in on her impressive chest. Everyone I know, even Mom, has been ogled by men at one time or other, but this was really obscene. One moron started to call out, "Hoot, hoot, hoot," which must have been some sort of reference to hooters, and then a few others took up the cry.

I turned to Laura and said, "I'm leaving."

She nodded, but before we could go, one of the frat assholes, a well-groomed, healthy, attractive, upper middle-class asshole, went up to Susie, put his face between her breasts, and started to make a noise something like, "Brrrrr."

You could tell Susie was embarrassed and shocked. But she did something I never could have. She stepped back, looked at the frat boy, then slapped him. Hard.

All the other frat boys and, amazingly, even some of their girlfriends, who had been hooting and howling with laughter as if this was the most sublime humor, suddenly shut up. The asshole who had been slapped had a stunned, angry expression on his face. It was frightening; he looked as though he were going to punch her.

Susie continued staring at him. After a tense moment, the asshole tried to smile and held up his hands as if to say no harm intended.

As she turned and went out of the house, the frat boys started to guffaw. Someone in the back of the room yelled out, "Get fucked."

Laura and I left right afterward. One guy gave me a patronizing frown as though I were some repressed spoilsport. Out on the street, Susie turned quickly with fright as the door opened behind her, but relaxed when she saw us.

"Are you okay?" I asked.

She waved her hand dismissively. "I'm fine."

"I'd love to get a bomb," Laura said, "and blow that whole fucking house up."

Susie laughed. "And deprive the world of all that alcoholism and sexual panic?"

She gazed back at the house and added, "Do you know what was most pathetic? Those guys thought they were having a wild, raucous party. If they think that kind of back-slapping, sniggering behavior is wild and raucous, they're beyond hope."

If I ever even consider going to another frat party, I hope someone hits me over the head until I come to my senses.

March 8, 1971

The Sweetheart of Fraternity Row—Susie Conover—sat down next to me in the Student Union while I was eating lunch. She has a funny, wicked sense of humor. I like her.

March 20, 1971

. . . afterward, Laura and I bumped into Susie Conover at Hickey's. We played pool, and Susie had me laughing all night long.

April 2, 1971

Susie Conover dropped by the suite with Linda Nowicki. Linda is making up a directory/survival guide for women students and wanted to know if we had any problems. I had no complaints, but Laura did.

Laura told them about her English instructor. He had fondled her ass once during an office visit, and he was always staring at her tits during class and calling her "little girlie" in front of everyone.

Susie and Linda had both had the same instructor, and both had had similar problems.

"This is precisely why we're making up the directory," Linda said. "If you had the information available, you could have saved yourself a lot of grief. Now, the only place where women can get information is the graffiti in the stalls of the women's rest rooms."

"Which is sort of a fitting analogy for what we hope to do," Susie deadpanned. "Though I doubt the art direction will be as good."

May 12, 1971

Our last night of freshman year. We all got drunk and sloppy and sentimental. Teddy is going to pick me up tomorrow morning, I mean this morning, about ten . . . which is in about five hours. Maybe the best course of action is not even bothering to go to sleep . . .

Back in Beacon. Teddy arrived late, thank God, about noon and found me still sleeping. Or comatose, to be more exact. He took one look at me and the room and broke out laughing. He was kind though; he lugged all my stuff down three flights of stairs while I lay prostrate in bed, then got me two cans of Coke. That and four aspirin helped, but not much.

Deciding to stay up was not a brilliant idea; I finally passed out around seven-thirty.

Willy comes home tomorrow. Maybe I will have recovered by then, though I wouldn't count on it.

May 14, 1971

Big news. Willy has quit school. His father is furious; his mother is astonished and so am I. He never told me until today, after the fact, that he was even considering leaving school.

When I went by their house this evening, Mrs. Buchanan took me aside and asked me to try and talk Willy out of his decision. She said, "Both of your futures are going to be affected by this."

Only later did the import of her words sink in. It had nothing to do with the merits of education; it was that without realizing it, I too have come to assume that our futures, Willy's and mine, are bound together.

I'm not sure whether that scares or pleases me . . .

May 16, 1971

Willy is full of surprises this week. In about three hours today, he moved into a trailer, of all things, which Andy and Earache are renting. I've seen it, and it's real low-rent and funky. To think of these three guys who were brought up in middle-class comfort, living in such country-western-by-way-of-Haight-Ashbury circumstances is either funny or enough to make you break out in a cold sweat.

All these sudden changes. I keep expecting Willy to propose to me. If he does, I don't know what I'll say.

September 14, 1971

Linda Nowicki's mimeographed *Women Students' Guide* finally came out. She and Susie dropped by the house with it. Linda was wearing a T-shirt from some oil company that had DIESEL in bold letters across her chest. I guess she does have a sense of humor about herself after all.

The guide is actually quite good. And significant. I admire them both for doing it.

Susie told me some new slang among her radical feminists and lesbian friends. They are using the word, *cunty*, in a complimentary or favorable manner, as in "The ice cream sundae was really cunty," or "Isn't that a cunty sunset?"

October 8, 1971

We threw a great party—sorry, a cunty party—last night at Disgraceland, though the property damage was not up to our usual high standards. Laura got really drunk, and so did Susie Conover. Willy finally got a chance to meet her. I think he liked her.

November 6, 1971

Susie's parents are visiting. Her mother is small and seemingly demure. Susie is so sexpot-looking and wild that you question how they could be mother and daughter. After a while, though, when you hear some of the off-the-wall things that come out of Mrs. Conover's mouth, your wonder vanishes.

Susie was making plans with them about Mardi Gras. Mrs. Conover turned to me and remarked, "Susie has managed to make it back to New Orleans every year for Carnival. Last year, she had to kill me off."

"I had an exam that I couldn't get out of. Mom, very considerate to the end, died suddenly the weekend before."

"What was the exact cause of my death? I hope I wasn't decapitated, or run over by a steam roller or anything too ghastly."

"You drifted peacefully off in your sleep with angels guiding you to your eternal rest."

"Well, that's okay then."

Susie has told me stories about Mardi Gras. It sounds like some serious debauchery. I'd love to go. Susie invited me down to New Orleans with her, but there's no way I can afford it even if I could take the time off from school.

One day I'll make it there.

1972

February 11, 1972

I have to get laid. It's been two weeks since Willy was here, but it seems longer.

It's beginning to show. I had a weird dream involving Susie last night. Cabin fever has definitely set in.

February 23, 1972

David Milne was at Hickey's tonight. He's witty and cute; I probably would be interested in him if I didn't love Willy. We talked for hours, and then at closing time, he asked me to spend the night with him. It wasn't exactly a shock. He's hinted at it before. What did surprise me though was that, for a moment, I almost said yes.

Why? It wasn't horniness—Willy was here only three days ago and as usual we staged a fuckathon. And my feelings for Willy haven't changed. I'm still in love with him; he's still my best friend. David is fun and attractive, but he holds no overpowering allure for me. And though all the attention and compliments are flattering, I don't think I'm stringing David along to boost my ego.

Is the temptation a yearning for freedom? For wildness? For the idea of throwing everything over for passion, rather than the passion itself? I'm not sure, but I am not going to allow myself to do anything. One Sean Farrell in my life was enough.

March 1, 1972
David is still sniffing around . . .

March 25, 1972
I finally met Susie's latest boyfriend, Richie. For a change, he came here instead of having her visit him in Syracuse. Knowing Susie, I should have guessed what Richie would be like.

Richie looks like he just got out of reform school—the T. Rex Juvenile Home for Glam Rockers or something—yet he exudes this weird sexiness. Sex, I imagine, has a lot to do with their relationship.

Richie had brought up some opium. Lighting it up, he said, "I want to try everything at least once in my life." It was difficult to tell if he was being serious or ironic, because he added, "Of course, you don't see me in a hurry to do anything involving red-hot pokers."

The more I think about it, sex is definitely what Susie sees in him.

What I most admire about Susie is her fearlessness. She has this sort of wildness that's appealing. Richie's swaggering flirtation with decadence is pretty much just bravado, even if it may have its peculiar charm. Susie on the other hand, really does want to experience life to its fullest.

March 29, 1972
David spent an entire evening entertaining me, making me laugh, trying desperately to make me. And again came the proposition at the end of the night. Finally, I had to tell him off. He wasn't going to get anywhere with me, I was in love with my boyfriend, etc., etc. I think I managed to cool his ardor without bruising his male ego.

March 31, 1972
According to David Milne, I am an asshole; Susie and I are dykes; and, oh yes, not to slight any other area of female anatomy, I'm a cunt. So much for not bruising his male ego. As Laura said, "He's what makes you reconsider your views on castration."

Although I'm sort of joking about it now, my first reaction was rage. Wanting to strike back, I imagined belittling him in front of all his friends, cutting down this puny weak excuse for a man with my ridicule and wit, slapping his snide face. Then telling Willy what David had said and watching as he beat him to a pulp.

All these pathetic demeaning fantasies depressed and angered me further. Who am I kidding? I would never have the courage to do any of those things. And as for having Willy beat up David . . . I profess such high feminist ideals, yet regress to a weak damsel in distress in the face of an aggressive lout. And that, unaccountably, made me angry at poor Willy as well as myself.

May 9, 1972
I aced my philosophy final. Mom called with news that a summer job at Alouette restaurant is mine if I want it. Though it will be a drag having to work every Friday and Saturday night, I'm in the process of talking myself into entering the glamorous, fast-paced world of waitressing.

July 29, 1972
It's been over a month since last I wrote in here. With good reason— nothing of note has occurred. Though the summer has whizzed by, I seem to be just drifting. I work, Willy and I go out or I drop by and see him at the trailer. Willy is working long hours, too. There is something soothing about our lives this summer. Not much is happening, but we're both reasonably content.
I guess that's the advantage and the curse of life in Beacon.

Mom and Howard are leaving for Maine in a few days. They'll spend all of August there. Teddy will probably join them near the end of the month for a week or so, but I'm not going. I plan on working straight through until it's time to go back to school.
I keep feeling that I should be doing something to make this summer more than a lull before school starts.

September 12, 1972
It seems strange to be back at school and not have Susie Conover here. I miss her already. This place is bad enough; it's going to be especially grim not having Susie to confide in.
At least Willy will be coming up most weekends.

October 14, 1972
I'm bored with school. I have to force myself to go to class. If I feel this way now, what am I going to do when the bad weather comes and we all start getting crazy from cabin fever?
Willy is not able to make it up this weekend because his truck broke

down. To think that I once considered long separations beneficial to our relationship. Now seeing Willy is the one thing I look forward to.

November 22, 1972

I was feeling lonely, so I called up Susie Conover in New Orleans. She's doing well, likes her job, and her life is . . . varied—she told me that in the last month, she's had the worst sex of her life, and the best.

She mentioned Mardi Gras again. I don't care what I have to do, even if fifty term papers are due on that Tuesday, this coming March, I'm going down to New Orleans.

December 10, 1972

I am writing this in the library. Instead of finishing a term paper on the Platonic idealization of love that was due last week, I've been moping around the stacks, reading old *New Yorkers* from 1936. For three hours, I've been gazing at ads for Plymouths that cost $510 and summer homes that are "highly restricted to desirable families," and reading reviews of Jean Harlow movies and WPA concerts.

Dr. Asher has been very understanding. Friday, after class, he reminded me that my term paper was late.

"Are you having any difficulty? It's a straightforward topic. Are you overloaded with work from other courses?"

"No," I replied. "It's not the work load. I just don't want to write that paper."

He looked confused. He likes me.

Lately, when I've gone to the library to work, I've found myself browsing through biographies of famous women that have nothing to do with Plato or Twentieth Century Russian History or Renaissance Painting. Zelda Fitzgerald went to Paris and the South of France, splashed in the Plaza Hotel fountain. Clare Booth Luce appeared on Broadway, wrote plays, entered politics. Time I should have spent studying, I have instead spent reading about George Eliot, Billie Holliday, Anaïs Nin, Katharine Hepburn, Simone de Beauvoir, Georgia O'Keefe. All of them led such full, eventful lives.

What could a biographer possibly find to write about my life—that I've maintained a B average?

I am wasting my time, my life here. Everything academic seems to have become mechanical. Perfunctory study geared toward an artificial goal. A degree is not going to change how I lead the rest of my life, and if it does, I've done something wrong.

December 16, 1972

The Plato term paper is finally done, finished in a fourteen hour flurry along with another ten-page report on Hieronymous Bosch. They are the last term papers I will ever write.

Tuesday will be my final final exam.

December 19, 1972

It's official. I'm a dropout. I have quit school.

Of course, now that I've quit, I'm beginning to wax nostalgic about Colgate and my school years. Already I'm starting to feel sentimental about my little home here at Disgraceland, and about all my friends.

But, luckily, the crushing boredom and irrelevance of school then comes back to me.

So now the rest of my life is in front of me. That is a frightening thought. From this moment on, any dissatisfaction with my life will be of my own doing.

December 21, 1972

Willy is overjoyed that I have quit school. When I told him, he tried not to let his elation show, but finally he started to laugh and said, "You are throwing away your whole future."

Teddy knows as well. He promised not to tell Mom. I'll let her enjoy Christmas before dropping the ton of bricks on her.

December 25, 1972

Willy asked me to marry him. I have loved him since I was sixteen years old. I said yes. This was the best Christmas.

I told Mom that Willy and I are engaged. And that I've quit school. It's a tossup which is more horrifying to her.

December 30, 1972

I'm a little drunk and more than a little depressed. It was a dreary day in old Beacon today. The sky was slate gray, the snow has melted, leaving everything covered with a dirty brown slush. I walked down to the Grand Union this afternoon, and Main Street, never a vibrant colorful Champs Elysee in the best of times, was grimy and squalid-looking. You couldn't walk a block without a rusty, junky, old car splashing you with slush.

Melanie Adams was at the market, looking tired and worn-down. In eighth grade, I wanted to be Melanie Adams. She seemed so glamorous. I wanted to drive my own convertible down Main Street as she did; I wanted a handsome basketball player as a boyfriend; I wanted to have her long straight hair and her clothes and her bosom.

Melanie's baby daughter was fussing in the seat of the shopping cart and her three-year-old boy was racing around the aisles. He's a beautiful child, but his nose was running and his mouth was stained red by something he had taken from a shelf and was eating.

"Travis, put that down now," Melanie called to her son. She was wearing an old ski jacket over a flannel shirt that probably belonged to her husband, and looked weary. Her hair was dirty, her skin chapped and dry.

She got married at just about the same age I am now.

Though we really don't know one another, Melanie smiled and said hello. I smiled back and thought, "That's me in four more years."

Writing this, I know I'm being unfair and probably a snob. Melanie, I'm sure, couldn't care less about my approval, and she certainly doesn't want or need my pity. She may have days when she's playing on a sunny summer lawn with her children, or lying in her husband's arms, when she thinks that she has everything she will ever need in life.

Is living in Beacon, having children, being Willy's wife all I'll ever need in life?

A few days ago, Willy started to talk about buying some shacky house on the outskirts of Beacon. He was enthusiastic about the possibilities of renovation, of making a home for us. I was filled with dread. Willy quickly dropped the subject. He must have imagined that I was dismayed by the prospect of living in a mess of sawdust, old plaster, and exposed pipes.

What is dismaying me?

I've had two real boyfriends; three, I suppose, if you count Sean Farrell. Eric Boyd was never really important to me. Sean was a summer fling. And a huge mistake of which I am ashamed. As for Willy . . . I love Willy. He is sweet, funny, supportive, kind. He's good-looking. We have terrific sex. We almost never fight; we get along so well, it's almost scary. Though it sounds retrograde, and maybe I shouldn't admit it, and certainly wouldn't say it to anyone else but Willy, I depend on him as I have depended on no one else except for my father. I can't imagine marrying anyone but Willy.

Now that we're engaged, however, I guess I should ask if I can imagine marrying anyone at all?

PART THREE

1973

ONE

On the day she was to leave for New Orleans, Janine leaned over and kissed the back of Willy's neck, then got out of bed. It still seemed strange to see that part of his neck; Willy had just recently had his straight sandy brown hair cut short after having it shoulder-length for three years.

He had walked into the apartment two weeks ago with his new short haircut and a sheepish grin. Janine had laughed with surprise. "Did the barber give you a lollipop for being good and not fidgeting in the chair?"

She had tousled his hair. "You look just like the boy I fell in love with."

"I look pimply and horny?"

Janine thought he looked boyish, a Little Leaguer. Gazing down at him now, he even had the hint of a cowlick where his head met the pillow. He didn't seem like a man about to be married. And though she had been lying naked in bed with him, as she had done hundreds of times before, she wasn't sure if she was a woman ready to be married.

Last night had been Saturday, but they had stayed in, not that that was any great loss on a winter night in Beacon. Most of their friends were away at school. With those who still remained in Beacon, there was little else to do except drink or get high. Janine didn't want to do either. She was about to embark on a major debauch; she was going to be fit and rested for it.

They had worked on the apartment for a while. She had stopped around ten, but Willy had continued his meticulous scouring of the hardwood floor that had been beneath the worn wall-to-wall carpet in the second bedroom. Willy had been sly. The appeal of this apartment had been that they could just walk away from it at the end of any month. Willy, however, almost without her realizing it, was in the process of transforming it into something more—their home, a place in which they had an emotional investment. Watching as he worked with such energy and contentment, she felt a surge of love for Willy, but she also felt afraid and disheartened.

She had gone to bed, taken off her clothes, and drifted off to sleep. Awakening when Willy came to bed, she pretended to be much sleepier than she was. They had not made love; she had not wanted to make love with Willy, though she wasn't sure why, and that made her uneasy.

She dressed hurriedly in the cold room, putting on yesterday's clothes which were draped over the rocker. She would just be taking off the clothes again in ten minutes when she went back to bed at home—that is, the house on West Willow Street where she grew up. Willy couldn't quite understand this charade of waking up and leaving in the middle of the night or early in the morning. After all, Janine had lived on her own at school, Willy had spent countless nights with her, and Amanda had to be aware of it. Though they had both dreamed of a time when they could just live together, and now the opportunity had certainly presented itself, Janine let Willy think she was deferring to her mother's wishes, something she had not done for many years. She wasn't quite sure why she did this, either.

When dressed, she bent over and whispered, "I'm going. I'll call you, probably tomorrow from school."

He murmured something, half asleep. Janine kissed him and left.

Main Street was deserted as she drove home. Janine remembered once when she was very young, she and Teddy had slept out in a pup tent in the back yard. In the middle of the night, they had snuck out of the tent and wandered the streets of Beacon. Foraging through neighbor's milk boxes—a milkman still delivered to customers—they searched in vain for chocolate milk. Finally, as dawn broke, they found themselves on Main Street, which she had then considered bustling and frighteningly hurly-burly. It had been deserted, eerily so, as in movies about the aftermath of a nuclear war.

Teddy went out to the middle of the street and lay down. Not one other person or car was in sight along the mile-long stretch of Main Street. Janine, who had just so recently learned to look both ways, and who, after doing so, would fly across a busy street like a soldier dashing through enemy fire, was shocked at Teddy's actions, and then delighted. Imitating her brother, she lay down beside him. They started to sing, and then made loud whoops that echoed. It was as though they were the only people alive in the world. They had remained in the middle of Main Street for five minutes before meandering home.

Janine pulled her Mustang into the driveway. The kitchen clock read ten minutes of five. Her mother had stopped waiting up for her years ago. She no longer made any comment about the hour that Janine returned home. An understanding of sorts had been reached between them.

Her suitcase was already packed and rested on the floor near the foot of the bed. She had not wanted Amanda hovering over her as she packed and asking why, if Janine was going to snowbound Colgate for a test, she was bringing light summer dresses and pumps. Slipping into a nightgown and then between the sheets, it took her a while to get back to sleep. Images of Mardi Gras, how uproarious and riotous it would be, distracted her.

The alarm woke her three hours later. Janine wanted enough time to take a bath, wash her hair, shave her legs, and not have it seem she was rushing to leave by nine o'clock as was necessary in order to make the plane to New Orleans.

In the bath, she shaved her legs. For a short time, she had refrained from doing so and had also stopped using makeup. She had been caught up in the politics of it, but then, letting the hair grow on her legs had seemed so trivial and unimportant. It wasn't going to change the plight of women. Still, she sometimes felt a little twinge of guilt about such vanities, as if she was letting down the cause. Then again, this day was one of many small pangs of guilt.

Howard and Amanda were getting dressed to go to Mass when Janine yelled up to them that she was leaving. Amanda came down the stairs, kissed her cheek, and said, "Be careful on the roads. You'll be home Wednesday?"

"Yes, probably late in the afternoon."

"Then I'll count on you for supper. Have fun, but remember to study."

Amanda had been hopeful when Janine told her she was going back to school to take a make-up examination. She thought it was a sign that Janine might reconsider and enroll again in college, if not Colgate, at least someplace else.

If Amanda had known that Janine was going to Mardi Gras, she would have called it extravagant for someone who wasn't working, or perhaps unseemly for a proper young woman. That would have been the extent of her protests. She certainly couldn't or wouldn't forbid Janine to go.

That wasn't the reason Janine was keeping her trip a secret.

Because of the demand for airline tickets to New Orleans during Mardi Gras, she had had to buy her ticket weeks ago. Since then, Janine had debated whether to tell Willy that she was going. She knew he would want to go with her. How could she tell Willy she didn't want him coming along without hurting him? This trip would be *hers*. Susie was her friend, and they had planned and anticipated going to Mardi Gras together for a long time. Lately, everything had been about *them*: their marriage, their apartment, their future. What was happening to *her*, to the individual, to Janine? She felt overwhelmed, missing.

She hoped that this trip, this spree, was what she needed.

The drive to La Guardia was uneventful. She parked her car in the long-term lot and arrived at the boarding gate with enough time to read half of a *Glamour* magazine, another guilty pleasure.

On the plane, a middle-aged businessman sat down beside her and tried to pick her up. The company he worked for was having a big party, maybe Janine would like to come, or perhaps they could have dinner tonight. He mentioned a restaurant as if it was supposed to mean something to her. Janine was certain that the restaurant would be some expensive tourist place, filled with people from Detroit and New York and Kansas and everywhere but New Orleans. She smiled and said she was busy for all of Mardi Gras.

Janine was wearing the diamond engagement ring that Willy had given her. It still amazed her that men weren't troubled in the least that she was married or engaged, as the ring plainly indicated, and would try to pursue her anyway. Although in this geek's defense, many men didn't even notice a wedding band or engagement ring. Even Willy would occasionally seem surprised when Janine mentioned that someone they had just met was married. "It's not ESP, Willy," she would say. "All you have to do is look at the ring finger."

Hoping the businessman might take the hint, she pointedly took up the *Glamour* and began to read. It was no use, though, he kept prattling on, mostly about himself. She wanted to move, the businessman made her uneasy, but the flight had been sold out and all the seats were occupied. As a last resort, she turned off her light and pretended to nod off.

As she lay with her eyes closed, Janine could feel resentment for the businessman building up. Though, he was probably only a bore, he frightened her a bit as well. Two years ago, on the train trip home from Colgate for Christmas break, she had found herself next to a man much like the one beside her now. That man had begun to rub his leg against hers. Janine had first moved her leg away, and then again, until she was crowded in her seat and he sat with his legs obscenely splayed. Though she was positive that the man's movements were not accidental, it was also the kind of situation where no obvious offense had been committed. She had tried to build up enough outrage and courage to tell the man loudly and firmly to stop touching her, but she could not make herself speak up. Finally, she had gotten up and stood near the back of the railroad car for an hour until another seat became available, the whole time seething with anger at the man and also at herself.

She had never told anyone else about the incident.

The businessman began talking with someone across the aisle, and Janine actually did fall asleep for a short while.

The plane landed with a lurch, the engines throttling in reverse in the way that always made Janine feel something had gone wrong. The businessman, true to form, stood up before the plane had stopped moving and grabbed his bag from the overhead compartment. When he left, he said, "It was real nice talking to you." Janine smiled and wished him a pleasant stay.

Susie was waiting for her at the gate and smiled broadly when she saw Janine. They both laughed as they hugged.

"Welcome to Mardi Gras," Susie said. "Now let's see what kind of mischief we can get into."

TWO

Susie's second-floor apartment on Royal Street in the lower French Quarter did not have wrought-iron balconies as Janine expected, though it did have fifteen-foot high ceilings. The rooms were large with French windows that rose up nearly the entire length of the wall. Susie had decorated the apartment from antique and thrift stores; individually none of the pieces seemed extraordinary, but taken all together, the furniture gave the apartment an exotic, luxurious air.

In Susie's bedroom stood a large bed with a Victorian iron headboard with wide rungs that had been painted rose and white. On a small table draped with an antique French shawl were candles, old framed photographs, and dried flowers, giving it the appearance of a small shrine. Transoms rested atop the doors, ornate moldings extended throughout the apartment, and on the ceiling above the bed, four little plaster cherubs looked down from on high.

One dawn about a month ago, Susie told Janine, she and a boyfriend were lying in bed, joking that their recent exertions must have put a blush on the cherubs' cheeks. One thing had led to another, and Susie had wound up sitting naked on the boyfriend's shoulders, reaching out a broom handle to which she had attached a makeup brush and just barely managing to apply rouge to the angels' fat cheeks.

Those round, rosy-tinted spots, a commemoration to that night's pleasure, could still be discerned faintly.

Janine said, "So this was the one with whom you had the best sex of your life?"

"No, I'm embarrassed to say he wasn't."

"That must have made quite a picture—you sitting on his shoulders."

"That *was* sort of a strange position. Usually, he would be facing the other way."

Janine dropped off her suitcase, and then they rushed uptown on the streetcar to see a parade—Toth. Oak trees made a canopy above St. Charles Avenue. "This parade isn't as raucous as some," Susie told Janine. "Just real nice and friendly." High school girls wearing tasseled white boots and shiny silky little uniforms did the Second Line, a shuffling kind of dance. Janine saw a very tall man holding his small son upside down by his ankle in one hand, a can of beer in the other. The laughing boy seemed delighted to be surveying the parade from his topsy-turvy vantage. Later, they stopped at the St. Charles Tavern. About twenty people—everyone from spry, dapper pensioners, to horny grinding teenagers, to whirling, wild, drunken crazies—were dancing to the great jukebox that played, "Mardi Gras Mumbo," and "Go to the Mardi Gras," and "Carnival Time." Janine could not recall ever having seen people dancing to a jukebox in a bar, and certainly never on a late Sunday afternoon.

They ate dinner at Susie's parents' home. Mrs. Conover urged Susie to eat. "You're going to need your strength, and a coating for your stomach, to go out and do all those things I've warned you against doing."

There was another parade that night, Endymion. It was breathtaking, with wild dancing and the most beautiful costumes and music. Janine and Susie got drinks in go-cups from a bar and stood on the sidewalk, watching the parade. Almost everyone else in the crowd had go-cups as well. After the parade ended, Susie said, "We're going dancing."

The club they went to, Linny's, was cavernous and crowded. In one corner, a group of longhairs were dancing some weird, drug-induced little jig that had nothing to do with the music. Susie nodded toward them.

"Ever since the movie *Easy Rider*, Mardi Gras has been thick with all these freaks and burnt-out hippies. Don't even think about going near a cemetery around now—the place will be mobbed with people tripping and thinking they're Dennis Hopper."

They danced, first with each other, and then with two guys who turned out to be falling-down-drunk. When the band took a break, the two guys realized that they were incapable of conversation and quickly wandered away. Janine went to the rest room.

Returning to the bar, she saw Susie talking with a man. He was tall and quite tan, but what was most striking were his eyes, which were a deep blue that dazzled. Janine was reminded of the poster of Paul Newman that she would sometimes see in college dorms where everything in the picture was black and white except for the vivid blue of the eyes. The features of this man's face were handsome, marred only by an old scar that jagged in the crevice above his chin. Rather than making him look sinister, Janine thought the scar gave him a winsome air. She somehow felt that he hadn't received it from the jagged edge of a broken beer bottle or a knife. He had probably been teasing the family dog or had tripped over the hedge while playing tag.

"This is my friend, Janine," Susie said, "And by the way, my name is Susie."

"Hi."

"And your name is?" Susie continued.

He hesitated, then said, "Um . . . Spencer."

"You weren't sure?" Janine asked. "Is Spencer your first or your last name?"

"It varies," he said and smiled. His teeth were a brilliant white against his tan skin.

Susie gave him a quizzical look. "Where did you get that tan?"

"Jamaica."

"A vacation?"

"No . . . I was living there."

"Was? You're not living there anymore?"

He shrugged, "It depends. If I go back, I'll be living there, but I probably won't go back."

"Is there any reason why you're being so . . ."

"Obtuse?" Spencer suggested.

"Mysterious," replied Susie.

"Yes, I'm trying to intrigue you."

"Well, you're not doing a half-bad job. You're here for Mardi Gras?"

"No, I had to see some people. Imagine my surprise, I come to town and find music and dancing in the streets."

He had arrived in New Orleans last week, he told them, but had extended his stay because he was having such a good time. His name, apparently, was Spencer Lyle. Having gone to and been asked to leave a number of military academies and colleges, he had wandered down to the Caribbean a few years ago as part of a crew hired to sail a sloop to St. Croix. He had sailed on that yacht and then on others. For a while, he and a friend had been partners in a boat that they had chartered to fishermen.

Though he didn't come right out and tell them, slowly it was implied that he smuggled marijuana in from Jamaica. Spencer wasn't in New Orleans for Mardi Gras; he had some "business" to attend to, but since he was here, why not enjoy it?

When the band came back from their break, Spencer danced with Susie. And then with Janine. Spencer moved gracefully, yet with an open eroticism, and, as often happened when dancing with such a partner, Janine remembered a bit of grade school folk wisdom. Once during recess, Janine had heard a group of older girls discussing how to tell if a boy was a good kisser. According to this playground lore, if a boy was a good dancer, he was also good at kissing. This bit of breathless information had remained with her, and though she didn't give it much credence, whenever Janine spotted a man who danced well, she found herself attributing to him other gifts as well, gifts that went a bit further than dreamy, prepubescent kissing.

"Where's your husband?" Spencer asked above the music.

"I'm not married," Janine replied.

He glanced at the ring on Janine's finger. "Where's your fiancé?"

Janine momentarily thought of a lie to tell Spencer: "My fiancé couldn't make it. He had to work." But for some reason she couldn't quite understand, she also wanted to shock him, wanted to shake the unflappable cool and the challenge in his manner. So, she said, "He thinks I'm visiting friends at school."

"You snuck off to Mardi Gras without him?"

Janine didn't think she cared for the term "snuck off," but said, "Yes."

"Hmm. Do I detect trouble in paradise?"

"No."

At the start of the next song, Susie came out onto the packed dance floor and joined them. Janine thought momentarily to go sit down so that Susie, who was obviously interested, could be with Spencer. Then she realized there was no need to leave, that everyone on the dance floor seemed to be dancing as part of a unified swirling boisterous throng.

They stayed until the band stopped playing at two o'clock. Outside Linny's, Spencer flashed his seductive grin and asked, "So, are you guys coming back to my place, or should I come to yours?" His confidence was unnerving, and for a moment Janine actually considered his proposal, but then said to herself, "Hey, wait a minute."

Susie gave Spencer an amused glance, but Janine could see that she was also tempted. She finally said, "Maybe some other time. For now, I'm going to play hard to get."

"Well, I'll be around for a few more days," said Spencer.

"How about that," Susie teased. "So will we. You never know what might happen."

His deep blue eyes gazed right through Janine, and then at Susie. He smiled again and said, "Well, I hope I run into you again. Because, otherwise . . ."

He shrugged good-naturedly and started to walk away from them.

Surprised by his quick exit, Susie called after him as he strode down the sidewalk. "Otherwise, what?"

"Otherwise," Spencer announced over his shoulder, "you won't have any fun at all."

As they strolled back to Royal Street, Janine asked Susie, "Did you want to go with Spencer? I could have found my own way if you did."

Susie put her arm around Janine's shoulder and gave it a squeeze. "He certainly did have his charms, didn't he? Well, there's good sex, and then there's friendship. And you can get the one any old time."

Janine started to laugh, knowing how Susie was going to continue.

"But," Susie said, "it's not very often that you come across great, dig-your-fingernails-into-his-back sex."

THREE

Janine came out of the bathroom, wearing a white terrycloth robe and brushing her hair that was still damp from a shower. Susie was at the table, drinking coffee from an oversized cup that looked more like a bowl and glancing at the morning newspaper.

"It's Mardi Gras," Susie said looking up from the *Times-Picayune*. "Now, the real fun begins. The last two days were just practice."

Yesterday, Monday, they had managed to get into Galatoires, and they had had some of the most exquisite, delicious food Janine had ever eaten. There had been the Proteus parade, then they had gone drinking with some of Susie's friends at Cosimo's, and the Blacksmith Shop, and Molly's, and the Napoleon House, and Johnny White's, where Janine had called Willy from a pay phone.

Hearing his voice on the line, she had almost blurted out, "Willy, I'm in New Orleans with Susie Conover." She knew though, that he would be hurt, and that no matter what she said—she had kept it a secret because she didn't want her mother to know, or she just wanted time for herself—he would realize her lies had been directed at him. So she had allowed the deception to continue.

After they left Johnny White's, Susie wanted to go to Linny's, the club where they had gone dancing the night before.

"Now why would you want to go there," Janine asked teasingly. "You weren't by any chance hoping to bump into someone, were you?"

But Spencer Lyle, to Susie's disappointment, and Janine had to admit her own, had not been at Linny's, so they had called it a night.

Pouring herself a cup of coffee, Janine sat down beside Susie. She took a croissant from a basket on the table and spread marmalade on it. Susie looked over the paper and said, "I hope I'm never murdered by a maniac." She chortled and added, "Oh this is awful."

Janine gave her an inquisitive look.

"This woman's body was found in the bayou, one of those creepy murders. She had been strangled and stabbed—but that's not the bad part. Look, they have a map of her whereabouts on the last night of her life. She was at all these bars, some of them are real dives, and I should know because I've been to them.

"God, imagine how embarrassing. It's not bad enough you get murdered and mutilated and all, but you have the newspapers implying you're a drunken tramp as well. She was at . . . eight bars."

Janine gazed over Susie's shoulder at the newspaper and saw a map of unfamiliar city streets with numbered black circles highlighted. A key beneath the map listed names of cocktail lounges and bars. The police were asking for information from anyone who may have been in the clubs and observed the woman, Francine Heer, who appeared pleasant and pretty if the grainy photo next to the map was any indication.

"I hate to think what kind of map they could draw for me some nights. They don't even call them *watering holes*, or *popular night spots*. Look at the subhead! WOMAN HAD DISAPPEARED AFTER A NIGHT OF BAR HOPPING. Wouldn't you just want that in your obituary?"

"Well, I guess it's better than being murdered at home Saturday night, waiting by the phone."

They finished breakfast. Janine leaned out the open French window to get a feel for the weather and to help determine what to wear. It was a balmy springlike day, with a clear blue sky. She dressed, putting on a floral print shift and a short yellow cotton cardigan, and then watched, rapt, as Susie put on her costume.

Susie belonged to a social club, the Society of Organized Mirth, one of hundreds that existed in New Orleans. The club had no meetings, no dues; it was a large group of friends and friends of friends whose only purpose was to have a party and parade on Mardi Gras. All of the members wore costumes, and the one Susie put on was exotic, fanciful, and beautiful. It was gold lamé and sheer, pink silk, beaded with gold applique and tiny mirrors, and it exposed much of her impressive cleavage. She also wore a pink silk cape and a feathered and bangled headdress that was utterly fantastic. When Janine had agreed to come to Mardi Gras, Susie had offered to make her a costume. Knowing how much time and care Susie and her friends put into creating the outfits, Janine had declined. Now, she wished she had let Susie talk her into it.

Susie smiled and said, "Now we hit the streets running."

They went to a Creole cottage in Marigny where the Society of Organized Mirth had gathered. Almost all of the sixty or seventy people in the house and on the porch were in costume. The Mardi Gras costumes were unlike any Janine had ever seen. They were not those of Halloween or costume parties—no witches, or pirates, or Groucho Marxes. She couldn't decide what they were reminiscent of: the Arabian Nights, a scene from an opera, a liturgy, the court of Louis XV, a wonderful surreal dream. Care and craft had gone into each creation. Silk, lamé, appliques of gold and silver, taffeta, masks, turbans, headdresses, bangles, beads, mirrors, feathers, brocade, rhinestones, powdered wigs.

One man's costume topped with a miter resembled the raiment worn by a pope, but his face was covered by a gold mask; an old boyfriend of Susie's wore a white brocaded cape, pantaloons, shiny gold slippers, and an Amazonian armored breastplate that curved into twin silver cones over his hairy chest; one woman had painted her face the same shade of blue as the satin of her long flowing garment and jewel-encrusted turban. The clothes lent the cottage the air of a phantasmagoria, or a vision.

Scratchy, old-time jazz recordings—King Oliver, Jelly Roll Morton, Louis Armstrong—played loudly. Janine and Susie grabbed teacups of punch that tasted of bourbon. The man who owned the cottage, Henry, planted a sloppy kiss on Janine's cheek when Susie introduced them and put a gold sparkly mask over her eyes. "You're gonna see some traditional Carnival." Then, Janine found herself dancing with Henry, his boyfriend, and Susie, amid all the others.

"It's nine o'clock in the morning," Janine thought, "and I'm at the best party of my life."

Later, a band showed up, trombone, drums, tuba, clarinet, and trumpets. They played "Down by the Riverside," and "You Are My Sunshine," and of course, "Oh, When the Saints Go Marching In." She had never been much of a fan of Dixieland jazz, but Janine felt herself being swept away by the music, intoxicated with it. The party spilled out of the house and porch onto the street. Everyone milled about for a while, laughing, joking, drinking, and then, as if by common consent, they began to parade.

Preceded by two blue angels on roller skates, the wide wings on their back made of blue feathers, and the band playing, "Back O'Town Blues," everyone started up the street. They were going to parade to lower Canal Street to see the Rex parade, Susie told Janine. Dozens of other krewes were doing the same thing at this very moment. Drinking punch in plastic cups or cans of beer, everyone did the shuffling, walking dance up Royal Street.

The streets, exotic with magnolia, palm, jasmine, banana tree, moss, brick and wrought iron, were jammed with people reveling. *Reveling*, that was the only word for it. It was incredible, and it seemed that all rules of everyday behavior had been suspended. Nearly everyone in the streets was drinking. Two women on a second-story porch lifted their blouses and flashed their breasts to the crowd. Something was different, extraordinary, about the day. Sunday and Monday had been fun, but today, Mardi Gras day, was *magic*. This wasn't just a mammoth party. The order of things had been changed. There seemed to be such freedom, license.

Canal Street was very wide and very crowded. They all went out to a meridian in the middle of the street—"the neutral ground" Susie and her friends called it—so that they could view the parade as it went down one side of Canal and returned up the other. Purple, green, and gold seemed to be everywhere: on the floats, banners, costumes, bunting. Along with everyone else, Janine found herself calling out, "Hey Mister," to the costumed figures on the floats who were tossing out throws, beads, and doubloons. It was like being a child again, and Janine was exhilarated when she caught the cheap plastic beads and arrayed them around her neck.

An immense jester's head bobbed down the street. The floats of papier-mache and gold leaf were on wagons supported by ancient, rickety wooden-spoked wheels and were pulled by tractors. Everything seemed to wobble, but it also seemed as if they were supposed to, that it was part of its charming design. A huge marching band, the St. Augustine High School Band, danced by in the same shambling steps. Everyone on the neutral ground began to dance along with them. That she would ever be frolicking to a high school marching band in the middle of the street seemed astonishing, and she laughed out loud. A drink in a go-cup appeared in her hand as if by magic, and then she was reaching into the sky to grab golden doubloons that were raining down on the crowd. The Boeuf float with its cows and masked chefs and pigs levitated by, above the heads of the crowd.

When the Rex parade ended, the Society of Organized Mirth marched to Jackson Square, people ducking into bars occasionally and rejoining the group with fresh drinks in go-cups. Janine was astounded by the sheer mass and extent of this huge party. With the band playing "Down By the Riverside", they all went down to the banks of the

Mississippi where some of the members dipped long poles into the river, then whipped the poles high into the air sprinkling the group with water. It was a baptism, Susie said, the traditional end of the society's yearly meeting. "Y'all are free to go," Susie's friend, Henry, bellowed as the water drizzled down.

Janine turned to Susie in surprise, "You mean it's over?"

Susie laughed. "Oh no. Good Lord, no. You and I are just starting."

They headed toward Bourbon Street on their way to a party. "Ray always has a great bash," Susie explained, "because his place looks down on a bar called Lafitte's in Exile. There's a pageant of drag queens that has to be seen to be believed. Some great costumes. And those guys; we'll never come close to being as pretty as they are."

Bourbon Street was as mobbed as Susie had warned: "It's so crowded you can lose your shoes." It seemed as though they were being carried along with the throng. At Dumaine, a multitude swarmed outside Lafitte's in Exile, and above their heads, Janine could just see the transvestites in elaborate gowns parading down a runway.

Someone shouted out Susie's name from a second-story balcony that was jammed with partiers. They stepped into a doorway and went up the stairs past a couple kissing in drunken passion and through the open front door into the party.

Janine and Susie made their way through the crush of the crowd, most of whom were not in costume. Two kegs of beer stood beside a new plastic garbage can filled with a punch that tasted like a fruity paint thinner.

Susie seemed to know almost everyone at the party. Janine had never before seen so very many people in such a small space. The apartment was one large studio that had been cleared of furniture. A bed had been dismantled and leaned against the wall. The couch, a chair, and a table were piled on top of the ornate claw-foot tub in the spacious bathroom. "That way, it will keep people from peeing in the bathtub, I hope," Ray Bane, the party's host, told Susie and Janine when they found him on the balcony.

The narrow, wrought-iron gallery ran along both sides of the corner apartment and was even more jammed than inside the room. "You don't think the balcony will collapse, do you?" Ray asked. "My land-lord just called up and started screaming that the whole thing was gonna come crashing down." He grabbed a friend in a headlock, "You know Joe, don't you? He just flunked out of the engineering program at Georgia Tech, and he says my landlord is right, it *is* going to col-lapse."

"Way too much weight here, all this structural stress," Joe said drunkenly.

"You notice he's still out here though, don't you? And he did flunk out, so I imagine he doesn't know what the fuck he's talking about." Then Ray recounted how, earlier, news crews from NBC and ABC had paid him a hundred dollars to let them film the female impersonators' beauty pageant from his veranda.

Janine gazed across the street. The drag queens were dazzling. One flamboyantly sashayed down the runway, wearing a costume made mostly of feathers. He stopped momentarily and blew kisses with both hands, his nails painted turquoise, at the crowd on the balcony. Along with the others, Janine cheered him on wildly.

In addition to those wearing the predictable sequins, torpedo bras, and sporting extravagant, padded hips that seemed a parody of feminity, were the others who had turned themselves into unique and magical creatures. One transvestite was a walking *Moulin Rouge*, arrayed in a costume that culminated in a headdress in the shape of a windmill. Another, who had a dark, mysterious beauty, trailed infernal sulfurous smoke as he swayed down the runway, wearing a cape adorned with lighted Fourth of July sparklers. The little sparks must have burned and flicked painfully, but he strode on oblivious, deep in his own fantasy.

When the pageant ended, the crowd on the balcony thinned out. The setting sun streaked the feathery cirrus clouds purple and pink, and the lavishness of the sky seemed to Janine a reflection of the extravagance of the city below.

"Now I know why you never missed a Carnival," Janine said.

"You're glad you came to New Orleans?"

"If I have much more fun, I'm going to spontaneously combust."

"Look at those cute guys." Down below on the street, three men were passing by. Susie took off a handful of plastic necklaces she had caught at the parade and tossed them down to the sidewalk. They jumped up and shoved each other out of the way to catch the throws. Ignoring them when they called out for more, she turned to Janine. "I'm glad you came."

After the sun set, and when the party was winding down—the kegs had run out and someone had upended himself head first into the garbage can containing the punch—Janine and Susie left and hurried to Felix's where they ate shucked oysters. Then they headed back toward Canal Street for the Comus parade, swept along in the ocean of carousing humanity. At St. Charles Street, they managed to find a place within sight of the Boston Club that had the huge letters M.K.C. ablaze in electric lights.

Susie told Janine that the letters stood for the Mistick Krewe of Comus: "In order to be in Comus, you have to be from an old, influential family. So, if you're not inbred and alcoholic, forget it."

On a balcony, a royal court in costume—including little boys dressed as pages—viewed the parade. Down on the street, black men, costumed all in white, twirled flambeaus. The flaming gas cans spinning at the end of the long poles streaked fire in the night. Janine could see the parade reflected in the purple glass front of the Russell Stover Candies building, and it seemed hallucinatory, miragelike. Floats hovered by; a band played, "If Ever I Cease to Love."

The Comus float approached. Comus, standing in front of a cup, the cup of abundance, saluted the Queen, ending the last of the Mardi Gras season parades.

Linny's was mobbed. Within moments of entering the club and wending their way through the raucous crowd, Janine and Susie were dancing. The loud, pulsating, hard-driving rhythm and blues, and the wild, drunken atmosphere made Janine wonder how anyone could just sit and not dance.

As before, everyone on the floor was dancing with everyone else. One moment she was with Susie; then it seemed she was twirling around with a Mardi Gras Indian, wearing an extravagant feathery costume, who had a gold tooth in which a diamond had been set. Next, she and Susie were with three frat boys from Tulane; and once again with each other.

During a break, one of the frat boys handed Janine a beer, saying, "You look thirsty," before disappearing into the crowd. She and Susie passed the cold perspiring bottle back and forth, then returned to the dance floor. Susie was unabashedly sexy when she danced, and Janine saw one man on the floor staring at her with a mixture of lust and awe.

In between numbers, the band tossed throws and doubloons out onto the floor. The bearded guitar player, in response to Janine's and Susie's flirting entreaties, made a game of pretending to fling the throws all over the dance floor while really pitching the little trinkets a few yards to them.

And then, in the middle of a boisterous version of "In the Midnight Hour," Spencer Lyle was dancing between them. Susie beamed with pleasure.

"It's about time you showed up!" Susie yelled above the music.

Spencer took in Susie's costume with showy approbation. "You are a vision."

"You probably say that to all the women."

"No, just the ones dressed in tasteful understatement."

When the song ended, they went to a table and ordered beers from a harried waitress. Spencer gazed about the frenzied room and said, "So, is there some sort of celebration going on?"

"Did you come tonight, hoping that we'd be here?" Susie inquired.

"Nothing could stop me. I had to fight my way inch by inch against a crazed mob. You know how many drunks passed out in the gutter I had to jump over to get here?" He smiled, then added, "Now let me get this right. People do this every year. It's not just because I'm here."

A manic long-haired man bumped backwards into Janine's chair, nearly sitting on her lap. He turned around, about to apologize, but instead, in a fit of exuberance that was probably chemically induced, he said, "Let's dance!"

She followed him out onto the floor. As she danced, Janine would catch glimpses of Susie and Spencer at the table. Progress was being made: they were talking with their heads inches apart, his hand draped loosely around her shoulder. The music seemed to throb right through Janine, and the longhair's high spirits were infectious. She danced the next two songs, occasionally glancing back at the table where she saw laughter, a playful slap to Spencer's arm, and later, a long lingering kiss.

When Janine returned to the table, Susie was telling Spencer that she always made a point of being in by midnight on Mardi Gras night. "That's the tradition, that's when Mardi Gras ends."

"Midnight is just a little while from now."

Susie nodded.

Spencer stood and took both of their hands in such an easy natural motion, that Janine found herself standing along with him.

"Well," said Spencer, "let's not break tradition."

As they left Linny's, Susie took Spencer's arm. His expression softened, and he was about to speak when Susie shrieked with laughter. She rolled up the short sleeve of his shirt and gave a mock gasp. "You really are a sailor. You've even got a tattoo."

Spencer smiled sheepishly. "I was drunk when I got that."

Susie peered up at him sarcastically, "No? Really?"

"The guy's name who did it was Dirty Needle Darren."

"And why did you have that particular one done? Is there any significance? Or are you just bursting with Turkish ethnic pride?"

"No, I thought it looked vaguely hippyish. It was youthful folly."

Susie grabbed his arm and started to turn him around. "Janine, look."

As Spencer spun around, he said, "Tomorrow morning I'm going to do it right. I'm going to have both of your names tattooed over my heart."

Spencer lifted his shirt sleeve. Janine saw a red crescent moon alongside a star on his muscular arm. She laughed and said, "It's a work of art."

"So," Spencer said, "Are we going back to your place?"

PART FOUR

1973

ONE

WILLY REMEMBERED THE BARTENDER from his underage drinking days. He hadn't been in this place, Spinetti's, since he was sixteen. He had never come here with Janine.

For the last three days, he and Jimmy Guido had been working across the river in Newburgh on a Queen Anne-style house with elaborate gables and complicated angles and pitches. Normally when Jimmy started to drink in the late afternoon, though on some days it was the late morning, Willy would just have a Coke or some water. Today, when Willy heard the *psst* of a beer being opened, he had grabbed a can for himself. He had polished off the Budweiser in three gulps and had gone back up on the roof to finish the crown of a small gable.

The beer hadn't helped, though. As he worked, phrases from Janine's journal kept repeating themselves insistently in his mind. *Sean Farrell and I have been prowling around one another . . . Sean Farrell and I made love tonight . . . The question I should ask is if I want to marry.*

The second and third beers hadn't helped either. Willy and Jimmy had finished the job and loaded up the truck.

Driving through Newburgh toward the bridge, they had stopped at a red light near Spinetti's. It was the first bar in which Willy had been served, and for a short while, he and some of his friends had frequented the place. That was years ago; if you weren't under the legal drinking age of eighteen, there was nothing about the bar to recommend it.

Willy had told Jimmy to pull over. Jimmy stopped the truck directly in front of Spinnetti's.

"I'm quitting," Willy said.

Jimmy was not really surprised. "You mean your job?"

"Yeah."

"Yeah, well . . . if you ever want to come back to work, just let me know." Jimmy glanced at Spinetti's. "You want me at least to drive you to Zep's or Mi-Ro's? Someplace in Beacon?"

"No, thanks." Willy slid out of the truck, waved to Jimmy, and entered the bar.

The bartender didn't remember him, of course. And Willy didn't recognize any of the dozen other patrons at the bar. If he had known anyone, Willy would have turned around and gone to the first tavern he happened upon, and if necessary, to another after that, until he found a place where he would be anonymous.

Willy silently sat at the bar and drank beer. The jukebox played Jerry Vale, Paul Anka, even Guy Lombardo, for which he was grateful: none of the songs reminded Willy of Janine.

After an hour or two, the pain began to ease, and Willy realized he was drunk. He waited until the bartender went into the back to fix a meatball sandwich for a customer before attempting to weave his way into the men's room. He didn't want to be cut off yet.

By the third hour, he was able to think about Janine. There was so much he hadn't known about her. Someone named David Milne had bothered her at school. He had spewed forth insults, he had angered and frightened her. Willy seriously considered driving to Colgate this evening. He pictured himself walking into Hickey's, grabbing a pool cue out of the hands of a startled player, and beating David Milne bloody with it.

Janine had told him little about her father's death and nothing of her mother's affair with Howard. He would have understood; he would have done anything in his power to comfort her.

She had been unfaithful, he told himself. She had fucked someone named Sean Farrell. Though he knew she had regretted it, had been ashamed and disgusted with herself, Willy envisaged Janine in bed with this Sean Farrell, moaning with unprecedented ecstasy, laughing at Willy.

He forced himself to listen to the jukebox. What were the lyrics saying? Frank Sinatra wanted to fly to the moon and play among the stars.

Janine had been unfaithful. She had fucked someone else. Willy drank the rest of the beer in one swallow, then felt an urge to throw the bottle into the mirror in front of him.

She wasn't sure if she wanted to marry Willy. Marrying Janine was the one thing of which he was certain.

Even now, he told himself. She had been filled with remorse for having slept with Sean Farrell; she had called herself vile. How could he not forgive her, if indeed it was his place to forgive her? Hadn't she said over and over again in the years since that one mistake that she loved him? If Janine would just repeat those words, that would be all Willy needed.

But Janine was missing. He tried to force another image of Janine, a vision of her dead in a New Orleans alley, from his mind.

He ordered another beer and, adding a five-dollar bill to the pile, then another, each time surprised that the bartender would keep serving him. Then, he noticed a different bartender was opening the beers for him. Had there been a change of shifts?

Glancing around the bar, Willy took in the crowd. All of the people drinking had come into the place after he had. And then he saw that someone was staring at him. Willy recognized the face.

His name was Alka-Seltzer, at least that was what everyone called him. He had suffered an alkaline burn on his right jaw and neck in an industrial accident. Two summers ago, Willy had gone to a bachelor party given for Terry Pritchard's brother, Jeff. Near the end of the night, they had all crossed the river to go, predictably, to a topless joint. Alka-Seltzer had been there with some friends. Words had been exchanged between Terry and Alka-Seltzer, a fight, and then a full-scale brawl erupted, during which Willy and Alka-Seltzer had traded some punches. The cops had been called in, six cars in all, and the fight had been stopped. No one had been arrested.

Willy had considered both the brawl and the bachelor party childish. A month afterward, however, Terry and Andy had been jumped in Newburgh by Alka-Seltzer and some others. They had both been stomped badly, with Terry being rushed to the hospital and having one of his kidneys removed.

Alka-Seltzer continued to glare from the end of the bar where it veered off at a right angle. Willy returned his gaze. Any moment now, Willy thought, Alka-Seltzer would say, "What the fuck are you looking at?" Willy would try to reply something equally cliched, "Not much," if he could keep the words from slurring.

"Fuck this," he thought, picking up the long neck bottle of beer and taking a sip. From that drinking position, Willy cocked his arm and threw the bottle hard down the bar, like the second baseman he used to be, throwing to first. It hit Alka-Seltzer on the forehead before he had time to bring up his hands to block it.

Willy knocked over a stool and then a chair that should have been well out of his path as he bulled his way toward Alka-Seltzer. The bartender yelled something that Willy didn't understand. Alka-Seltzer had been stunned by the bottle, which, surprisingly, had not broken, but he pushed himself away from the bar and came to meet Willy.

Willy grabbed a mug of beer from a table and tossed the contents into Alka-Seltzer's face, temporarily blinding him. He then threw a punch with all his weight behind it, but missed badly. The blow glanced off Alka-Seltzer's shoulder, but the momentum of the punch propelled Willy into him. They both crashed to the floor.

As he grabbed handfuls of Alka-Seltzer's stringy hair and pounded his head on the floor, someone's arm came around Willy's throat in a chokehold. Somebody else was trying to pry Willy's fingers from Alka-Seltzer's hair. He felt a jarring blow on the side of his head— vaguely he knew someone had kicked him—and later he remembered thinking, I am going to get a beating, and not caring. Then, pain seared throughout his head from the second crashing blow, bringing on flashing pinpoints of light before everything went dark.

He came to in the doorway of a shoe store fifty yards down the street from Spinetti's. His head throbbed, but he could see, his arms and legs moved, he had all his teeth, nothing seemed broken. He must not have been beaten after being knocked out; perhaps Alka-Seltzer had not been in any shape to exact his revenge or had been restrained by others in the bar. Some of those customers must have dragged him here.

Willy didn't think he had been unconscious long. He stumbled to his feet, but then had to lean against the plate glass window of the store. Hush Puppies and penny loafers swirled in his vision. The pain and the nausea subsided, and Willy staggered down the sidewalk toward the bridge.

He swayed and weaved for ten minutes until he reached the on-ramp that led to the Beacon-Newburgh bridge. A car drove past, and he stuck out his thumb. It wasn't until an hour later that a beat-up old Studebaker stopped for him; perhaps it would not have taken so long for a ride if Willy had not had to lean over the embankment to vomit periodically. The man who finally picked him up was immediately unhappy that he had, but said nothing until he dropped Willy off at the ramp in Beacon.

"Man, I hope your night doesn't get any worse than it's been," the driver remarked.

From the bridge, it was over a mile to the apartment. Climbing the stairs to his place, he tripped and slammed into a step with his face, cutting the inside of his lip. Unlocking his front door took Willy a long time. Then not bothering to clean up the blood on the back of his head or in his mouth, he went to bed and passed out.

He awoke the next evening at six o'clock.

The following day, Willy collected his pay from Jimmy Guido, cashed two checks from Carl that had been on his bureau for weeks, and closed out his savings account at the Beacon Federal Bank. After going to his landlord and prepaying the next two months' rent, he still had almost fifteen hundred dollars.

He loaded a suitcase, sleeping bag, foam mattress, and cooler into the back of his panel truck, then drove to his parents' house. For exercise, his mother usually walked home from work at lunchtime, so Willy waited on the porch until he saw her striding up the street. As she climbed the steps, he noted the concern in her eyes.

In the kitchen, Willy told his mother that he was going to New Orleans.

"Honey, what can you do that the police haven't done already?"

"I don't know," Willy replied. "I haven't the faintest idea what to do. I probably won't accomplish a thing."

"Willy, I'm worried about you."

"Yeah, I know."

By noon, he was crossing the Beacon-Newburgh bridge. As he drove through Newburgh, he felt the scab on the back of his head. His concussion was almost gone; all he had was a slight headache. He had been lucky in his fight with Alka-Seltzer. He had deserved a beating for what he had done. Shuddering, he remembered his actions. Everyone in the bar must have thought that Willy was insane. Alka-Seltzer hadn't actually done anything to him; possibly he would have stopped with just glaring at Willy. It suddenly occurred to Willy that Alka-Seltzer might not have even remembered him from the first fight on the night of the bachelor party; that ugly stare might be his natural way of viewing the world. Had he been as astounded as everyone else by the unprovoked attack?

Willy thought his mother was right to be worried about her son.

He drove to Scranton, then headed southwest. Near Wilkes-Barre, Willy picked up a hitchhiker, a wizened old man who carried a bundle wrapped in brown paper. Having spent countless hours on the sides of highways, in the dark or in inclement weather, trying to thumb his way to see Janine at Colgate, Willy pretty much had an indiscriminate policy about picking up hitchhikers. Short of an escaped convict wearing striped fatigues and a ball and chain, he stopped for everyone. When Willy picked up the old man and asked where he was going, the old man replied, "It doesn't matter." Then two hours later, miles away from any town or exit, the old man asked to be dropped off.

"This looks like a good place," he said.

Somewhere in Virginia, Willy pulled over in a rest area, bundled himself in his sleeping bag in the back of the truck, and dozed for five or six hours. He was back on the road by three o'clock the next morning.

In Tennessee, he picked up a pair of hitchhikers, two young women who looked to be college students. The two women gave him cautious appraisals as they got in the truck, but then almost immediately took on an attitude of complete trust. Willy wanted to tell them not to be so trusting, to be careful. Unspeakable horror was possible, it could assault them with no warning. But Willy said nothing; they would think him patronizing or frightening or crazy.

The two college students tried briefly to strike up a conversation, one of them even flirting mildly with Willy, then settled in and chatted softly between themselves for the next fifty miles. One of the women offered to drive when she noticed Willy yawning, so he let her. He slept fitfully in the back for a few hours until the women reached their destination. The flirtatious woman playfully blew Willy a kiss and cried, "Bon Voyage," as he drove off.

He ate dinner in a truck stop in Alabama. The bubbly, high school-aged waitress had a Southern accent. She addressed the couple beside him at the counter as "y'all." It was the first time he had heard that expression used naturally in a real conversation and not for comedic, I-wish-I-was-in-the-land-of-cotton effect.

It was nearly midnight when he crossed the bridge over Lake Pontchartrain. He checked into the first cheap-looking motel he found and went to sleep.

He had no idea what he was going to do next.

TWO

Janine's suitcase was still in Susie Conover's apartment. Willy was surprised, having assumed it would be in a police evidence locker. Willy had also expected that the apartment would be sealed off, but Mr. Conover had just used his key, and they had walked into the large, comfortable rooms.

Mr. and Mrs. Conover had been gracious when Willy had shown up unannounced and told them who he was and what he was doing at their front doorstep. Mrs. Conover had hugged him. "You poor thing. We know what you're going through." They had offered to put him up while he stayed in New Orleans. Willy had thanked them, but declined.

Willy ran his hand along the tan canvas of Janine's overnight bag.

"We didn't know what to do with Janine's suitcase," Mr. Conover remarked. "We considered shipping it back to her parents. Somehow, that seemed inappropriate. It's as though . . ." He shrugged and quickly turned away.

It's as though you didn't expect Janine and Susie ever to return, Willy thought.

Willy had brought along one of Janine's journals. He showed it to Mr. Conover. "Janine kept a diary. Have you seen a notebook like this?"

"No, but let's take a look."

Willy had not shown the diaries to Emil and the Beacon Police. He couldn't bear to think of them pawing over pages of Janine's most private thoughts. He had told Emil in a circumscribed way about Sean Farrell, described as "a former boyfriend at the New Jersey shore," and David Milne, "someone from Colgate whose advances had been rebuffed by Janine." Emil had checked out both men, and, as Willy had expected, they had quickly been cleared.

Willy and Mr. Conover searched throughout the apartment. Though Janine had written in one of the journals that the best place to hide something was in plain sight, Willy looked under cushions, behind the stove, beneath a rug. He found traces of where the police had been—the shiny gray residue of fingerprint powder—but no notebook.

Coming across a recent photo of Susie Conover that would photocopy well, Willy asked if he could borrow it. Mr. Conover stared at the picture for a moment, then nodded.

Willy gazed around the airy rooms and tried to picture Janine here. Had she been excited, laughing and joking about Mardi Gras with Susie?

"The police really went through the place," Mr. Conover said. "And they know what they're looking for. I'm sure if any clues were to be found, they would have discovered them." Still, when Willy was finished searching and suggested that they leave, Mr. Conover moved around the rooms, staring, touching objects with a preoccupied air, seemingly unwilling or unable to depart. Willy felt he was imposing on a private sorrow, so he left and waited on the street outside. Conover joined him a little while later, then, shaking hands with Willy, got into his car and drove away.

"What you really need to do is shoot a halftone and produce a camera ready copy." the sympathetic man at the copy place told Willy. "I can't do that. You should go to a printer or litho shop that does off-set."

Willy peered at the sheet of paper with its grainy, barely recognizable black and white pictures and the descriptions of Janine and Susie in untidy block lettering, and agreed with him. The man recommended a place just two blocks away on Claude Avenue.

A woman with curly auburn hair was at the counter of the print shop. She gave Willy's flyer a cursory glance, then took a sheet of paper and began sketching.

"You should give more play to MISSING," the woman said. "And the photos should be more prominent as well." This woman, unlike the man in the copy center, was businesslike and unemotional. From her manner, she could have been discussing a handbill announcing the grand opening of a car wash; it was the aesthetics of the layout that mattered.

The woman finished her rough sketch of how she thought the flyer should look. "Something like that?"

Willy nodded. Twenty minutes later, she showed him the mock-up of the flyer. MISSING blazed across the top of Janine's and Susie's photos and descriptions. All the other information—where and when they had last been seen, the phone numbers and detectives' names of the New Orleans and Beacon police departments—was listed below that. It was much better than what Willy had devised.

"How many do you want?"

Willy wasn't sure. "A thousand?"

The woman looked at him as if for the first time, "You're going to be handing these out pretty freely, I imagine. And the most expensive part is the layout. Running off more copies doesn't cost all that much. I think you should do two thousand."

Willy agreed.

"We should be able to finish them by the end of the day," the woman said.

Willy left. He ate lunch in a restaurant a few doors down the street. From outside, the restaurant had not looked very promising. The food however was extraordinary. He ordered a bowl of red beans and rice— the simplest, least tempting item on the menu—and was amazed at how delicious it tasted. The pleasure he felt eating made him uneasy and guilty. He was not down here for fun. This wasn't a vacation.

At the back of the restaurant stood an old wooden phone booth which had been painted teal to match the color of the tiled walls. Willy made a call to Beacon. Emil was not in the Beacon Police station; it was his day off. He had given Willy his unlisted home phone number at the beginning of the investigation, however. Willy called it.

"Hello."

"Emil? This is Willy Buchanan. I'm in New Orleans."

"Yeah, I heard. What are you doing down there?"

"I'm not sure. That's why I'm calling. What would you do, if you found yourself in my position?"

After a moment, Emil said, "You should talk with the investigator. A guy by the name of Huey Oliver. I'll call and ask him to help you out. This is an active investigation. They may not want to divulge much to you. Don't take this the wrong way, but they might consider you a suspect. On the other hand, they might be happy to see you. Do you have a picture of Janine?"

"Yeah, and of Susie Conover as well. I'm having circulars made up."

"That might help. Let me level with you, Willy. The cops down there are working hard, a lot harder than usual on a case like this, but there is just so much they can do. They probably haven't questioned everyone in the area near Susie Conover's apartment; they haven't gone house-to-house for a five or six block radius. You could do that. You could talk with shopkeepers near her place, go see bartenders in joints where they might have been on Mardi Gras day, staple your flyers on telephone poles."

"What else would you do?"

"I'd talk with all of Susie Conover's friends and with her parents. Ask about old boyfriends, new boyfriends. Was anyone bothering her? Did everything seem normal? Was she seen talking with anyone? Question the people she worked with. Especially talk with the people who saw Janine and Susie on Mardi Gras day. The New Orleans police have a few names. And this is important, if you should find out anything, anything at all, no matter how innocuous it may seem, tell the New Orleans police about it. And me."

"I will. Do you have any information that I'm not aware of?"

There was a pause. "I probably shouldn't do this, but I'm going to send you a copy of Janine's case file. That way, you'll have everything I have. And one more thing. When you talk to Huey Oliver, have him tell you about Francine Heer."

"Who's she?"

"She's a woman who disappeared shortly before Janine and Susie did. She was murdered; they found her body just before Mardi Gras. The New Orleans police think that there might be a connection."

Willy stared at the chrome dial of the telephone. It seemed to swim in his sight.

"I'm sorry, Willy."

Detective Huey Oliver leaned back in his chair and put his feet up on a desk littered with paperwork. "Janine Smith and Susan Conover were last seen on Mardi Gras night about eight-thirty. That was by a group of acquaintances of Miss Conover. Which is not to say they disappeared at that time, only that no one who knew them, that we're aware of, saw them. Numerous other people saw Miss Conover and Janine earlier in the day."

Oliver let Willy take down the names and phone numbers of everyone who had seen Janine or Susie. He made it clear he was only doing so as a professional courtesy to Emil Deshayes and the Beacon Police Department.

"I know that Emil feels a personal stake in this case, him and Janine being close friends and all," Oliver said. Willy could not remember Janine ever mentioning Emil in any context, but made no reply.

Oliver also gave Willy the names of two of Susie's former boy-friends.

"Neither one of them is under suspicion," Oliver said. "Matter of fact, we've talked to them, we've checked their stories, they're clean. You're not going to go nuts, are you, and start accusing people, getting them upset, and making me regret that I helped you?"

"No. I just want to talk with them . . . I don't pretend to know what I'm doing. But maybe, because I know Janine, something they say might have a meaning to me that wouldn't be of any significance to you. It's unlikely that I'll discover anything, but what else can I do?"

Oliver nodded, unconvinced.

"I'm not going to be a problem," Willy continued.

"You've already talked with the Conovers?"

"Yes. We went to Susie's apartment. Janine kept a diary, I thought it might have been there."

"It wasn't?"

"No."

"Well, you probably know that we went through the apartment. We found nothing. Actually, we did find a little bit of reefer and some rolling papers. The Conovers didn't know their daughter used drugs, though I got the impression that it wasn't a big surprise when we asked them about it." Oliver considered Willy a moment. "We didn't bother to explore that angle any. Basically, we don't care that Susie might have smoked a joint once in a while. Were we correct in our thinking? Are drugs something we should explore?"

"No."

"Did Susie or Janine ever sell drugs?"

"No, nothing like that."

"No, I didn't think so. Let me ask you this. How were you and Janine getting along?"

Willy thought about all he had learned from Janine's diaries. He hesitated, then said, "We got along. There hadn't been any fights. But, Janine was having second thoughts about marrying me; she was begin-ning to feel trapped. She didn't want to get swallowed up in a small town. She wasn't sure what she wanted out of life."

"Could she have disappeared of her own volition?"

The image of Janine waving to him and then walking away down a deserted road came into his thoughts, unbidden. He said, "But that wouldn't explain why Susie Conover is missing as well."

Oliver nodded. A moment later he said, "We don't have a lot to work on. Our best lead right now is Susie Conover's car. It's still missing. But sooner or later, it's going to show up. When it does, who knows what we'll find.

"And you know about Janine's credit card. Somebody else was definitely using it. That's not good news, I'm afraid."

"Tell me about Francine Heer."

Oliver sighed. "Francine Heer was a nice young woman who was murdered. We think, but we're not positive, that she met her killer in a bar."

"Emil said you thought there might be a connection."

"Nothing conclusive. Francine Heer was in her early twenties. She was seen in a number of bars and nightclubs on the night she disappeared. No sign of any foul play was discovered at her apartment, which was only a half mile from Miss Conover's. Is there a connection? There are certainly some similarities, the age, general appearance, place of residence, the partying in bars."

"How was Francine Heer killed?"

"Man, this isn't going to do you any good. You don't want to know. I'm not suppose to tell you anyway. It's an ongoing investigation."

"I want to know."

Oliver sighed again. "What the hell, all you'd have to do is look it up in the *Picayune*. And you'd probably do that, wouldn't you? Francine Heer was raped, then strangled and stabbed repeatedly."

Willy was not horrified. He didn't feel anything. He wondered if what he was experiencing was the beginning of clinical shock.

"So if the man who is responsible for Francine Heer's murder," Willy heard himself say, "is connected with . . ."

"We're not ruling anything out."

Ray Bane wore a frayed polo shirt beneath a blue oxford cloth shirt and faded dungarees. Tape circled one of his penny-loafers. His was the first name on the list of people who had seen Janine and Susie on Mardi Gras day.

"Susie and her friend dropped by my party in the middle of the afternoon. Maybe around two, three? I'm not sure when they left, but it was right around dusk."

"Lola" by the Kinks was playing on the stereo. When Bane spoke, his words came out in such a rush that Willy had to concentrate and found himself staring at his lips.

"How did they seem?" Willy asked. "Did you notice anything out of the ordinary?"

"During Mardi Gras, everything is out of the ordinary. That's the point. But, nothing seemed amiss. I've known Susie since we were like eight years old or something. We met in fucking dancing school, if you can believe that. Susie's a crazy, fun girl. And that's exactly how she was that day."

"Neither one of them seemed troubled or worried?"

"No, they were having a good time."

"Were they really drunk or out of it?"

"I know I was. But, no, they seemed fine to me."

"What about Janine? What was your impression of her?"

"Well, I was struck by how attractive she was." He looked at Willy and shrugged. "She seemed friendly, happy, having a good time."

"Did Susie mention what her plans were for the rest of the day?"

"No."

Willy paused, unable to think of anything more to ask.

"Like I said, they stayed a while and then they were gone."

Bane had given the police the names of all the people he could remember who had been at his party. Of these people, about a dozen had spoken with Susie or Janine. Willy met with or telephoned these friends of Susie's to no avail—almost all of their recollections were even fuzzier than Bane's.

Willy also met with a man named Henry and other members of a krewe, the Society of Organized Mirth, but learned only that Janine and Susie had been dancing and drinking and enjoying themselves.

An old family friend of the Conover's had bumped into Susie and a "friend from up north" about eight-thirty P.M. on Canal Street. They had exchanged hellos and then the two women had disappeared into the crowd.

For three days, Willy handed out leaflets. He started near Susie's apartment and went to every house, apartment, and business in a ten-block radius. Near Susie's apartment, many of her neighbors were aware that she was missing. A brief story about the disappearance had been in the *Times-Picayune*. One of the neighbors, a young mother holding a laughing, squiggling boy, had even seen Susie and a "pretty blond woman" walking up the street early on Mardi Gras day. Nothing had seemed out of the ordinary.

Just blocks from the apartment fewer and fewer people knew Susie or had heard of the disappearance. Occasionally someone would recognize Susie's picture. A shopkeeper might point at her picture and say that he knew her; but it would turn out that Susie had come in to have a picture framed five months ago, or that she ordered take-out Chinese food every so often. Another man remembered seeing Susie doing her wash in the laundromat a few times. No one recognized Janine.

For a while, Willy kept bumping into a dejected salesman who was selling brushes and cleansers door to door. Willy wondered if he looked as defeated as the peddler. Like the salesman, Willy too had worked out a pitch to keep people from closing the door in his face.

"Hello, I'm working with the New Orleans Police Department," Willy would say, not exactly lying. Thrusting a flyer into their hands, he would explain about the disappearances, though he did not tell them of his connection to Janine. Invariably, the person holding the flyer would scrutinize the pictures, wanting to be of assistance. Not one of them, however, knew anything that could help find Janine.

At the end of the three days, Willy had given away, or stapled on telephone poles and empty walls, over a thousand of the leaflets. He went back near Susie's apartment a few times on each of the three days until he was sure that he had spoken with everyone in her immediate neighborhood.

He annoyed a few people, elicited compassion from others. Other than that, he accomplished nothing.

The horn players swung back and forth, their instruments casting off glints of light as they played. Most of the musicians were young, with large Afros and dashikis, or with beards and long hair in ponytails. The lead singer was older though, probably close to fifty. His hair was processed, and he wore an iridescent baby-blue suit cut in a style that had gone out of fashion—if it had ever been in fashion—years ago. His face glistened with sweat as he sang about hurting so bad.

Willy wasn't sure how many bars he had been to on this night, but it must have been close to twenty-five. Surprisingly, none of the bartenders or waitresses had been rude or abrupt with him when he told them he didn't want a drink. They had all glanced at the flyer, but not one could remember seeing either Janine or Susie on Mardi Gras night.

The previous evening, Willy had visited the bars where Susie's friends and parents said she regularly liked to go. Some of the patrons and a lot of the help knew Susie. The bartender at Bruno's remembered serving beers to Susie and Janine in go-cups around one o'clock on Mardi Gras afternoon. Susie and Janine had left the bar and gone back out to the street after being served the one beer. As far as the bartender could tell, they were not with anyone else.

The band took a break and left the stage. Willy stood near the waitresses' station, showing the flyer to each woman as she approached with her order. One of the musicians sidled up to the bar; without asking, the bartender gave him a bottle of Dixie. As he left, he looked over Willy's shoulder at the flyer, then stopped.

"Let me see that." The musician took one of the flyers, studied it, and said, "I saw both of them here Mardi Gras night."

Willy was startled. He had been frustrated so long, had resigned himself to hear negative responses, that it amazed him that he might actually learn something.

"What time?"

"It was during the first set, I'd say ten-thirty, eleven."

"You're sure it was these two women? And it was on Mardi Gras night? That was seven weeks ago."

"I'm positive. Everybody in the band was tossing doubloons and throws to the crowd in between songs, like in the parades, and I remember throwing them some. We had a little game going. They knew I was aiming for them and they kept egging me on."

Willy just stood and stared at the man's bushy beard which came down almost to his chest.

"Let's have a seat," the man said. They went over to a table by the wall. Willy introduced himself and found out that the musician's name was Gene.

Gene stared at the flyer again. "I definitely remember these two." He pointed to Janine's picture. "She's really good-looking, right? And what you notice most about her is her hair. It just sort of shines, doesn't it?

"And this chick," he indicated Susie's picture, "this chick has the most unbelievable body you'd ever want to see. She's why I noticed them in the first place. I saw them dancing with each other and I said to myself, 'Whoa.' "

"They were dancing with each other? Were they with anyone else?"

"Well, at first, they were dancing with each other, and I didn't see any boyfriends around, so I thought, Hmm, I'm definitely going to have to go over and say hello during the break. And like I said, I was throwing them doubloons in between songs, and we were fooling around a bit, they'd wave at me and tell me to throw some more, you know, just the usual shit at Mardi Gras.

"But then I noticed that they were with some guy, or maybe they had met him here. I saw them talking, and they all danced a few songs. But it was only one guy, because I still thought I'd go over and talk with them during the break. And I remember thinking that even if one of these girls is with the guy, it didn't matter. They both were pretty hot-looking, though in different ways."

"What did the guy look like?"

"He was all right, I guess. I didn't pay too much attention to him, except I was sort of trying to figure out which of the chicks he was with."

"Did you ever come to a conclusion? Which woman was he with?"

"I never did figure it out, but it was Mardi Gras, you know. It's not like you go up to someone and say, 'May I have the pleasure of this dance?' People just get up and boogie. You wind up dancing with one person, or two, or by yourself. That's the way we play music, and things start to jump. It's not a fucking cotillion."

"The guy they were with. He was handsome? Tall? Short? Anything you can remember at all?"

Gene took a sip of beer and said, "I didn't really pay too much attention to him. He was white. He had straight dark hair, not quite to his shoulders, I guess. He didn't have a beard or a mustache, just clean-shaven."

Willy thought of the description of the man who accompanied the woman using Janine's credit card. "What about his eyes?"

"Well, he had two of them."

"We're they a real bright blue?"

"Man, I couldn't tell you. They might've been, but if they weren't pink or something, I don't think I would have noticed."

"How about a scar right here?" Willy ran his finger on his chin.

"I only saw the guy from the stage, so he might have. And I wasn't really all that interested in him, you know what I mean? I was checking out the ladies dancing. Especially her," he pointed again to Susie's picture on the flyer. "No offense intended, man, but she was a very sexy dancer, very sexy."

"Did you talk to either woman? Or to the guy?"

"No. By the time we took our break, they were gone. Or I think they were. The place was packed. I took a little stroll around the joint, looking for them, but I didn't see them then or for the rest of the night." Anticipating Willy's next question, he continued. "I didn't see them leave. And I don't know if they left alone or with the guy."

Willy continued with his inquiry, but learned nothing else. Then Gene's break was over, and he went back up to the stage.

Willy watched as Gene played the guitar, his fingers a blur. The lead singer approached the microphone stand. He snatched the microphone violently, bent low over it as if in a swoon, and screamed.

THREE

A LARGE MANILA ENVELOPE containing Xeroxed copies of Janine's case file arrived for Willy, general delivery, at the main branch of the New Orleans Post Office.

Willy sat on the floor in a quiet corner of the post office and read the file. He knew most of what it contained already. In the last few days, he had heard most of the details contained in the files restated by the actual witnesses: the Conovers, bartenders, shopkeepers, Susie's friends, former boyfriends, neighbors, and co-workers. Of the people from New Orleans mentioned in the files, Willy had spoken with all but one—Aundray Perkins, the gas station attendant who had accepted Janine's credit card.

With luck, he would meet with Aundray later in the day. Then he would head out and follow the trail of credit card slips that had been left by a man with vivid blue eyes and a woman with dyed jet-black hair.

Aundray Perkins was no longer employed at Mighty Mobil. He was now working behind the counter of an auto parts store. When Willy called on the phone, Aundray sounded harried. They agreed to meet after work.

Willy showed up at the store a little before six and waited outside. As the neon and interior lights went out one by one, Aundray and four others came out the front door that was locked behind them.

"You the guy who called?" Aundray asked as he approached Willy who was leaning against a parked car.

"Yes. Thanks for seeing me. Do you want to go someplace where we can talk?"

"No, right here's fine." He sat on the hood of the car next to Willy. "What I'll be able to tell you won't take more than a minute."

Willy handed him a flyer. "I know you've seen these pictures before, but could you give them another look?"

Aundray gazed at the flyer, then shrugged. "I wish I could help you out, but nothing's happening. Man, I was really busy that night, and you just don't pay attention to a lot of stuff. You just work your ass off."

"It was Mardi Gras, or the morning after. Was that why it was so hectic?"

"That was part of it. But it was crazy most nights."

"Well, do you have any memories at all, since it was Mardi Gras?"

Aundray looked up at the sky and closed his eyes.

"I remember Harry was cashier. Some of the customers were drunk, you could smell the booze on their breath. A few still had costumes on."

"If a really beautiful woman had given you a credit card, would you have noticed? That would be a bit out of the ordinary, wouldn't it?"

"Yeah, I probably would have noticed at the time, but that was a couple months ago. It all sort of blurs after a while."

"When was the last time you saw a really beautiful woman with blond hair?"

"Jeez, I couldn't tell you, it's been a while."

"Do you remember seeing a guy, he's white, good-looking, deep blue eyes, longish straight hair, with a scar right here?" Willy pointed above his chin.

A look of concentration crossed Aundray's face. "That vaguely rings a bell, what you said about the scar. The cop didn't mention anything about a guy with a scar."

Aundray peered down at the ground, as if trying to bring the image he was visualizing into greater focus. "A scar . . . I definitely have a memory of some white guy with a scar on his chin. It's real hazy though. It seems to me he was tan, cause I can picture real white teeth . . . the scar." He shook his head. "Man, I don't know where I even saw him though." He pointed at the auto parts store, "It could have been here."

"Could it have been Mardi Gras night?"

"Who knows? That scar does ring a bell." He looked up suddenly at Willy. "Yeah, it does seem like it was at the gas station. And I seem to remember that someone else was in the car with him, because it's . . ." Aundray sighed, "I'm not sure if what I'm remembering is what I saw, or if I'm letting what you said lead me on. It's like when you wake up sometimes and wonder, 'Did I dream that, or did it really happen?' "

"At this point, I'm willing to listen to anything."

"The scar is what I remember. A tan, and the scar. I can sort of see the guy turning and giving the credit card clipboard to someone in the passenger's seat." Aundray simulated the motions. "He was staring straight ahead, and I was looking at that scar, and then he handed the clipboard back to me. I think that did happen."

"Did you see the other person?"

"No."

"Was it a woman?"

"It seems to me it was. But, maybe I'm saying that because I know you are hoping that's what I'll say."

"Would you be able to recognize the guy with the scar?"

"It's possible, but I don't think so. It was a while ago, and maybe it wasn't even on the night you're asking about. And I'm not really getting a picture of the guy's face, just that he had a scar."

They went over Aundray's recollections for another twenty minutes. Aundray kept repeating that it could all be a mistake, that he might be letting his imagination run away with him. When Willy left, however, he felt more hope than he had since Janine disappeared.

Huey Oliver thanked Aundray Perkins, then watched as he walked out the door marked MISSING PERSONS. Perkins had just spent the last hour going through mug shot books of convicted sexual offenders to no avail. Oliver had also had the computer make a list of felons with scars on their chins. None of their photographs looked familiar to Aundray either.

Aundray had been the second witness to go through the books. The guitar player from Linny's had reluctantly agreed to view the mug shots, but only after Oliver had a little chat with him about civic duty and the laws governing unpaid child support. Gene Chelkas had been unable to identify any of the pictures. Neither Perkins nor Chelkas could add anything to the Identikit drawing.

If it had not been for the efforts of Janine Smith's boyfriend, neither Perkins nor Chelkas would have inspected the mug shots. That Oliver had not questioned Perkins again had been an embarrassing oversight. After having travelled all the way to Texas and New Mexico, and having gone to the trouble of getting a police artist to make a sketch, he had failed to go back to Mighty Mobile and question Aundray again. It happened. He had been working fourteen-hour days, and Aundray's indefinite remembrance added little to what they knew about the disappearance. Still, Oliver had missed it.

He had missed Chelkas as well, though not through carelessness. Oliver did not have the time to go to every bar in New Orleans, and even if he had, he probably would not have been in Linny's at the exact moment when Chelkas was taking his break. That Willy Buchanan had found the musician was simply a stroke of luck; one, unfortunately, that did not seem as if it was going to help them find Susan Conover or Janine Smith.

At five o'clock in the morning, Willy gave up trying to go back to sleep. He showered, then packed his bag, careful not to bring along any of the cockroaches that infested the motel. He stowed his belongings and the nine hundred or so remaining leaflets in the back of his truck.

The sun was rising as he drove out of New Orleans. The traffic on both sides of the highway was light, so Willy thought that it must be a Saturday morning, though he wasn't sure.

The first of the credit card slips began in Texas, just north of Houston, but Willy planned to stop along the way and hand out flyers. All it would take, Willy told himself, would be for one person to recognize Janine's picture, and his nightmare might end.

166

FOUR

JENNIFER BERGER, THE FORMER salesclerk at the Indian jewelry store, lived in a ramshackle house a few miles outside of Taos where six dogs roamed around the beat-up vans and cars parked on the weed-filled front yard. Willy got out of his truck and knocked on the front door.

Since leaving New Orleans six days ago, Willy had handed out the flyer to hundreds of people. He had gone to every establishment where Janine's credit card had been used. A truck stop waitress gave him a description of the man with the scar that was almost word for word the same one she had given in the police report. A salesclerk remembered that the boots bought by the woman with the jet-black hair for the man with the scar were size 10½. No one had seen Janine.

Driving through flat, monotonous, dreary scrub, or toward glorious, breathtaking vistas, Willy had never felt more alone. He yearned for the sound of Janine's voice. He would see the sun setting behind the mountains, or a thunderstorm far away across the plains and think that Janine should be with him to share the experience. With every mile, he became more aware that he would be this lonely for the rest of his life.

A chubby man in his early twenties with wild curly hair held back with a leather headband answered the door to the run-down house.

"Is Jennifer in?" asked Willy.

"She's back in her room, I think," the man replied in a thick Boston accent.

Willy followed the man into the house. The aroma of cooking mixed with the scents of marijuana and patchouli. Jennifer came out of her room, looking stoned. "Yeah?"

"I'd like to talk with you about the incident with the stolen credit card."

"Are you with the police?"

"No, it was my fiancée's credit card."

She had been peering at Willy with a preoccupied anxious air, but then her agitation subsided. "Let's go out on the porch."

Grabbing a heavy sweater, she led him out of the house to a porch that showed signs of water damage. Jennifer sat on an old wooden bench; Willy perched on the top step, leaning against a pillar whose paint had chipped and faded to a washed-out gray. The sun warmed them.

"You're aware that I've already talked with the Taos Sheriff and the New Orleans Police?"

"Yeah."

"Well, what do you want to know?"

Willy considered the question, then shrugged. "Anything you can remember."

"Was . . . Is your fiancée the one with the brown hair or the blonde?"

"The blonde. Janine Smith." He took out a flyer from his jacket pocket and handed it to her.

"She looks nice. I can tell you for certain that the woman who tried to use the credit card was not her. Absolutely not her."

She related all the details of the incident. Willy had read Huey Oliver's report so often that he knew it by heart. He corrected and added to Jennifer's account.

When she was finished, Willy asked, "What was the man with the scar and the blue eyes like?"

"He was cute, a real handsome guy. But more than that, something about his manner and the way he carried himself was appealing. We didn't talk or anything, but you know how you can make judgments about someone at first sight? Well, mine was favorable. But I also have to tell you that as far as my personal life is concerned, my judgment about men hasn't always been so hot. Matter of fact, it's been pretty shitty most of the time."

They again went over the physical portrait of the man: his height, weight, build, the dazzling blue of his eyes, his age, the scar. Jennifer didn't expand on her previous description.

"Did the woman using the card seem coerced? Did you get the feeling that she was being forced to use the credit card against her will?"

"Was she being forced to buy really great jewelry for herself? No, I didn't get that impression at all. Somehow I felt that they were both quite at ease with one another. Like old friends, or they'd been going out for a while.''

Willy stared out across the scraggly yard to the Sangre de Cristo mountains beyond. After having journeyed thousands of miles to be in this strange place, he knew nothing more about Janine's fate than what he had read in the police reports.

Jennifer must have sensed what he was thinking. "I haven't been able to tell you anything, have I?''

Willy shrugged. "You can't tell me what you don't know.'' He sat a few moments more, gazing out at the horizon. Then he rose to his feet.

"If I remember anything," said Jennifer, pointing to the flyer Willy had given her, "I'll call the number.''

"Thanks.''

Willy walked around the house to his truck. He drove onto the highway and headed back toward Taos. This was the last place Janine's credit card had been used. It was the end of the dubious trail he had been following.

After a few miles, he pulled the truck off the side of the highway. He watched the setting sun turn the mountains blood red.

Officer David Lumb of the Houston Police Department reckoned he knew what the gray Pinto with the Louisiana license plates was doing on Collect Avenue. He thought the car might have been on this deserted dark industrial street three weeks ago, the last time he had been on graveyard shift and the last time he had cruised this area. Chances were it had been on the street even longer than that.

The car was covered with black soot, so it had not been moved in a while. Lumb called in the license plate number on the radio. The computer was down, big surprise. The dispatcher told him to try back in an hour.

He turned to his partner. "So did some moron steal it for a gas station robbery, or did the owner want a little insurance money?''

"Robbery,'' his partner guessed. "I'll even go out on a limb and say it was a 7-Eleven.''

"I'll say it was insurance.''

He was referring to an old and not particularly bright ploy by people in financial straits or by owners of lemons. Cars would be left in high-crime areas, often with the keys in the ignition, in the hope they would be stolen or stripped. Once while on patrol, Lumb had even seen a well-dressed, country-club type park his Jaguar on a street in the

Fifth Ward that looked like a war zone, and then wait nervously until his wife picked him up in her own Coupe de Ville.

Lumb and his partner had laughed out loud at the frantic arguments and head-turning when the couple noticed that a police car was following them. As Lumb turned on the flashers, he could almost hear the wife telling her numbnuts husband that she had told him they would never get away with it. Sauntering over to the passenger's side, Lumb had asked to see the man's identification.

"How are you doing tonight? Everything okay?"

"Everything's fine, officer," the man had replied nervously.

"This is a pretty bad area down here. A lot of crime. The reason I mention it is I noticed that you left a sharp-looking Jaguar up the street. You didn't even lock the doors. I believe you might even have left the keys in it. Maybe you should go back and get your car? You wouldn't want it stolen, would you?"

"No, I wouldn't. I'll go back and get it right now."

"I think that would be a good idea. Of course, you probably didn't have anything to worry about. I mean, what kind of lamebrain would steal a Jaguar? They're always breaking down, the electric system is a joke. Your mechanic sees more of your car and your paycheck than you do. Even the idiots who rip off cars are smarter than that."

Lumb had followed the man and his wife as they drove back to the Jaguar and waited until the man was behind the wheel. "I'm going to do you a favor. I have your license number and I'm going to check the hot car sheet every once in a while to make sure it doesn't get stolen. We wouldn't want that, would we?"

Of course, Lumb had not taken down the Jaguar's license number, and thus had never checked it. He wondered if the man had ever rid himself of the car.

Lumb forgot about the gray Pinto until they drove by it again a few hours later. He stopped the patrol car. While Lumb called in the Louisiana plate again, his partner got out, went to the Pinto, and shined his flashlight inside.

"I think you win," he called out to Lumb, "the keys are in the ignition. Jesus, for all that time, and no one grabbed it. It really restores your faith in mankind, doesn't it? Boy, the owner's going to be pissed."

The dispatcher came back on the radio and squawked that the Pinto was reported stolen.

"No shit," Lumb heard his partner say.

But then the dispatcher told them to stay with the car. The Pinto was not to be towed to the impound yard yet, as was usual. Something must be up, because a forensics team would meet them shortly.

"How about that," Lumb said. "This is what you call solid police work."

"Yeah," replied his partner, "we've cracked the case."

Huey Oliver pored over the forensics report from the Houston Police. Susie Conover's gray Pinto had been found on a deserted street. No one was sure how long the car had been on the street, though the report indicated that it was at least a month.

The way the Pinto had been abandoned did not bode well for Susie Conover and Janine Smith. The car had been dropped off apparently with the hope that it would be stolen again or stripped.

Hair and fiber traces had been found in the interior and the trunk of the Pinto, but were inconclusive.

Four different sets of fingerprints had been found on the car. One set belonged to Susie Conover, though those prints had not been as numerous as one would expect. Nor had they been found in the usual places—the steering wheel, the mirrors, the door handles—but rather in out of the way spots—the seat shift knob, the dome light. The Houston forensics technician thought the car had probably been wiped down.

A dark, oil-smeared thumb print near the gas tank matched Aundray Perkins, the gas station attendant who had filled up the car sometime early on the day after Mardi Gras. Perkins had been in the Marine Corps, so they had been able to get his prints from the FBI for comparison.

Two other print fragments on the passenger side of the car were Janine Smith's as far as they could tell. Though Janine Smith had never been fingerprinted, Emil Deshayes had sent down a copy of fragments that were presumed to be hers. What Emil had done early in the investigation was have a crime-tech team go over Janine's bedroom and lift all the prints they could find. Then the Smith family had been printed. By the process of elimination, they had come up with some fingerprints that they were assuming were Janine's. Those matched the fragments found in Susie Conover's Pinto.

That Janine's fingerprints were found in the Pinto did not really tell them anything, though. Oliver knew that Susie had picked Janine up at the airport, so it was to be expected that Janine's fingerprints would be in the car.

A few latent prints had been found near the gas tank that did not match Aundray Perkins's. Oliver was afraid that those prints belonged to another gas station attendant who had filled the tank, either before or after Perkins had. The trip from New Orleans to Houston was three hundred and fifty miles: whoever drove the Pinto would have had to gas up again. Of course, many gas pumps were self-serve, and the print might belong to whoever had stolen the car, but Oliver didn't think he was going to be that lucky.

The last set of prints, a partial thumb, index finger, and part of a palm, had been found in the trunk of the car. They had not been able to identify whose they were. Why the prints had been found in the trunk could be explained in any number of ways. A mechanic might have taken out the spare tire. A redcap might have put a suitcase in the trunk. There was another possibility, though, that Oliver could not get out of his thoughts. Someone could have left the prints when he opened the trunk and put Susie Conover's and Janine Smith's bodies inside.

After leaving Taos, Willy headed south to Santa Fe. He handed out flyers in the shops and galleries, and dropped one off at the local police station. While in Santa Fe, he called Emil back in Beacon and found out that Susie Conover's car had been abandoned in Houston.

"Is that good news?" Willy had asked.

"No, it isn't," Emil had responded.

Willy spent the night in Santa Fe, then drove west without, he realized, any compelling reason for doing so. There were no more waitresses or store clerks for him to interview. The trail of credit slips had ended.

Looking at a map, Willy saw that the nearest big cities were Denver and Albuquerque. Though the trail he was following didn't really have a pattern, generally it had gone west until heading north to Taos. If his quarry had intended to go to Denver, however, they could have headed north much earlier at Amarillo, or could have even gone through Oklahoma and Kansas. So, Willy was figuring that the trail still led westward.

Willy understood his decision to head west was founded on faulty and illogical assumptions. He didn't know that the man with the blue eyes and his companion *had* a destination, and even if they did, nothing said it had to be a large city. Wasn't it just as likely, given their itinerary so far, that there wasn't any destination, that they had been merely wandering around, buying margaritas and jewelry with a credit card whose bill they would never have to pay? If they were rambling about, wouldn't the Petrified Forest, or Monument Valley, or the Grand Canyon be a logical destination?

But Willy had to do something. So he headed west.

FIVE

ROY GOSSELIN DRAPED THE hip waders over his neck like a grotesque scarf and ambled down the dirt road. He could have driven down this road a quarter mile or so, but the rain had just let up and he didn't want to get his mother's clean car all muddy. Besides, it was pleasant to walk into the bayou as he had done so many times growing up.

He hadn't fished down here in close to five years, but then he hadn't been home in almost a year and a half, not since his last vacation. It was funny how he still thought of Villehure as home, even though he hadn't lived here since college. Of course, in the last decade he hadn't lived anywhere for more than two years, so he had not formed any of the attachments that might make him call another place home. No sooner would he rent a furnished apartment and become familiar with Houston, Kuwait City, Galveston, Juneau, and now Long Beach, than he would get another promotion and another transfer. But that was the oil business.

Roy looked in the ditch on the side of the road. On the way back, he would fill his bucket with the crawfish that teemed in the low ground. Once in New York City, he had been in an elegant restaurant on business and saw *spiny lobsters* on the menu at an exorbitant price. Someone at his table had ordered them, and when the dish came, Roy realized that *spiny lobsters* were actually crawfish. He had almost laughed out loud. Seventeen dollars for crawfish? Here in Louisiana, you could buy a bucketful for a buck, that is, if you were too lazy to stop your car on the side of the road and just pick them up.

Further up the road, he noticed a water moccasin slithering into the water. Roy watched it glide away for a moment. In the water, the snake might have looked like a stick to the casual eye. He stepped forward to keep the snake in view when he saw the foot, black and bloated.

The nude body was lying on its side. It was, or had been, a woman, though Roy would not have been able to say if she had been young or old, pretty or plain. Somehow, he thought she had been a white woman, though even that was not obvious. He stared at the corpse, not ten yards away, and was surprised that he did not feel shock, or horror, or revulsion. It was just another object, he told himself, like the decaying log that was next to her.

Roy put his fishing gear down on the road, so he would be able to bring the police to the exact spot, then turned and walked back toward the highway. Again he wondered at his reaction at seeing the body. He knew instinctively that the woman had been murdered or the victim of some other violence—something in the attitude of the body, her nakedness—yet he felt no sympathy. She could have been a possum run over on the street.

The paved highway was just up ahead. Roy tried to humanize the corpse lying back in the swamp. He attempted to give her a face, imagined that she had laughed, had birthday parties, hugged her Mama. Yet something in him wouldn't let Roy make that connection. By the time he reached his mother's green Nova, he gave up trying. It was probably for the best—some sort of defense mechanism—that he couldn't feel anything for that body.

He got into the car, but had only driven a mile when he saw a sheriff's patrolcar approaching. Roy honked the horn, waved frantically, and stopped the Nova. The sheriff's car slowed and came to rest directly across the road from him. As the deputy rolled down his window, Roy crossed the asphalt.

"I just found the body of a woman," Roy Gosselin said, then felt sadness sweep over him.

Chief Medical Examiner Joseph Unger looked at the fingers and was confident that they would be able to get fingerprints from them even though the woman had been in the bayou for a while, maybe two months. Animals, maggots, insects had gotten to the body. The eyes were no longer in their sockets.

If the fingerprints were not on file, they would probably identify the corpse by the dental records. Because of the quality of the dental work, Unger didn't think that this Jane Doe would be a Jane Doe for long.

People who had the money for root canal and orthodontia usually were missed when they disappeared.

Unger turned on the overhead microphone. The recording system had just been installed; he wasn't quite used to it. One of the transcribers was always chiding that he didn't have to yell, just speak in a normal tone of voice. Unger scraped beneath the fingernails, checking to see if the victim had resisted her assailant. She definitely was a victim and there had been an assailant. The multiple stab wounds in her chest were unmistakable.

The body was severely decomposed, but ligature marks were still visible on the wrists and, most notably, around the neck. From blood pooling and lividity, Unger could tell that the victim had been tied up while still alive. And then strangled.

The external examination showed fourteen stab wounds in the chest area which he measured and photographed. The pattern and number of the wounds indicated the assailant had been enraged, or sexual mutilation had been intended—one of the woman's breasts was nearly severed.

Unger removed the breastplate, then took out the organ tree which he placed on the tray over the sink. He charted the path of the stab wounds through the internal organs, then the posterior tissue of the body. The wounds had probably been administered by a right-handed male using an eight-inch knife. The stabbing had occurred after the woman was dead.

Though the body had been exposed for a long time, and the chances of finding anything were slim, he checked the orifices for semen. Fluid samples were taken from the Jane Doe for blood and toxicology tests.

The victim's thorax was lacerated. The woman had been strangled by something elastic, not a pair of hands, and the pressure had been applied equally around her neck. Her attacker had used a noose, or garrote, or something similar. A minute fiber trace was found imbedded in the neck. Unger suspected that when all the tests were in, strangulation would be the cause of death.

The Stryker saw whirred. Unger cut a circle in the top of the crania and levered it open. He drew the scalp forward over the face, then removed the brain for examination.

At the end of the autopsy, an assistant wheeled the body back to the freezer. It would stay there awaiting identification.

The next day, when all the results came back from the lab, Unger made out a report with his conclusions. Semen had been found on a swab taken from the victim's vagina, so it appeared that the Jane Doe had been raped before she had been strangled. After death, she had been stabbed fourteen times.

Coroner's Assistant Arnold Ohlmer looked at the list of Missing Persons that Orleans Parish had sent down. The two that looked the most likely were Susan Conover and Janine Smith. They were the right age, and both had disappeared two months ago, which would correspond with the medical examiner's report that the Jane Doe had been dead for that long.

Ohlmer made out a request that the two women's files be teletyped from New Orleans to the crime lab across the street. He hoped that the two women had been fingerprinted, so that he wouldn't have to dick around requisitioning dental records. That could take days, especially since one of the women was from New York. If he was lucky, either Smith's or Conover's prints would match those of their Jane Doe, and he would be able to clear this case.

The call came from the crime lab at the end of the day. It was a positive identification. The Jane Doe downstairs in the freezer now had a name. It was Susan Conover.

Huey Oliver wiped away two names written in grease pencil from the wall chart. Two cases had been cleared. Susan Conover was now officially in Homicide's jurisdiction. Though Janine Smith's body had not been found, her file was going over to Homicide as well.

The news of Susan Conover's murder hadn't come as a surprise. Oliver had been expecting as much almost from the beginning of the investigation. Everything about the case, the stolen car and credit card, the connection to Francine Heer, indicated that the two women had disappeared as a result of foul play.

So it went. It wasn't the first time that he had sent a Missing Person file to Homicide, and it wasn't going to be the last. Oliver picked up a new case file. A sixteen-year-old runaway from Pensacola was thought to be in New Orleans. A picture of the girl, smiling near a Christmas tree, accompanied the file. Vice might know if she'd been hustling on the street.

He started making phone calls.

The bus full of cadets from the New Orleans Police Academy stopped on the shoulder of the highway not far from where Roy Gosselin had parked his mother's car. On the forty-minute ride to this part of the bayou a few miles from Villehure, the academy instructors had stated again that should anyone find anything that looked like evidence, he was not to pick it up. The lab-tech team that accompanied them, as well as the three homicide detectives, would handle all examinations.

The forty-one cadets spread out in a hundred-yard cordon and slowly began to comb the brush and swamp of the bayou. The instructors had also warned about snakes and gators in bloodcurdling detail, so most eyes were riveted to the ground. The cordon made a slow sweep down the east side of the road for a half mile until it ended. Old cans, spent shotgun casings, and a bicycle tire were found.

The cordon made a slow pivot and began to search the west side of the dirt road. The paranoia about snakes and alligators gave way to vexation at the insects that besieged them. They had to swat almost constantly, but still they felt the mosquitoes nipping at any exposed part of skin.

Halfway on their sweep back to the paved highway, one of the cadets found the sweater. Even though he had been told not to disturb evidence, he stooped over and nearly picked it up with a stick. Stopping himself just in time, the cadet called for the crime tech team.

The forensics technicians examined the muddy ground near the sweater closely, as did the three homicide detectives. The scene was photographed, and then one of the crime techs put the yellow cardigan sweater into a plastic evidence bag. Though it was covered in mud, everyone there knew that the dark brown stains on the front of the sweater were blood.

The cadets searched for two more hours, but found nothing else of note. They trudged back on the bus, wet, tired, and covered with welts from the insects.

The next day, Homicide Detective Vince Romanelli of the New Orleans Police Department got word from the State Troopers' station near Villehure. A month ago, a teenaged boy had found an eight-inch Henckels chef's knife by the side of the paved highway roughly four miles north of where the corpse had been discovered. He had not reported it to the police immediately, but when he heard about the discovery of Susan Conover's body and the subsequent search, he came forward with his find.

The knife was being sent down to New Orleans for forensic examination. Because of the long delay, and the knife's handling by the boy, his father, and several State Troopers, Romanelli didn't think it would reveal much.

The search through the bayou had been extraordinary, and not only because of the academy cadets deployed.

Lots of people turned up dead in New Orleans. People managed to kill off one another in all sorts of moronic or unspeakable ways. Consequently, Romanelli and the others in the Homicide Unit usually were not eager to go forty miles outside their jurisdiction and spend the better part of the day wading through a swamp and getting eaten alive by bugs.

For the past two months, though, Romanelli had been trying to close out one case—Francine Heer.

She had also been found in a bayou, though thirty miles from Villehure. Because Francine Heer had been abducted from New Orleans, Romanelli had been assigned the case. From that very first phone call, Romanelli had known he was in for a nightmare.

It was the worst kind of case for a homicide detective. The body had been found in a swamp, miles from the streets and neighborhoods he knew, miles from his sources and snitches. He had not been present at the crime scene. By the time he picked up the phone and first heard the name Francine Heer, she had already been in a medical examiner's freezer for two days. Unlike most cases, the crime had probably been committed by someone unknown to the young woman. There was no apparent motive; no obvious suspect to investigate.

As he knew it would, the case degenerated from its inauspicious beginning. The *Times-Picayune* and the television stations latched onto the story with ghoulish enthusiasm. That attention, naturally enough, brought pressure from above. Although he remained the primary investigator, others were assigned to "assist" him. At one point, every homicide detective was working on the case, often at cross purposes.

Nothing had turned up. Francine Heer had been out barhopping the night she disappeared. They questioned everyone they could find who had been in or around the clubs. So desperate were they for information, that Romanelli gave the *Times-Picayune* the story about her pub-crawling, hoping that someone from the bars would read it and come forward. The *Picayune* sold a few papers with the titillating story, and Romanelli learned that Francine Heer liked daiquiris and played David Bowie on the jukebox.

With absolutely nothing else to go on, they had gone through the motions with an ex-boyfriend and with a sex offender who lived down the block from Francine Heer, though from the start it was evident neither man had anything to do with her death. Both had been cleared within hours.

Then, Huey Oliver had come over from Missing Persons and told him about Susan Conover and Janine Smith. The similarities had been disturbing. And intriguing. Romanelli had sent a crime lab team over to Susan Conover's apartment, something that was rarely done for a simple Missing Person case. Even that had not worked out, thanks to the maid's Herculean cleaning efforts and the father's tramping in and out of the apartment.

And now, Susan Conover had turned up dead in a bayou. Again the similarities between Conover and Francine Heer were tantalizing. Both had been found naked in a deserted part of the bayou. Both were thought to have been raped while alive, and strangled, and then stabbed postmortem. Both victims were thought to be stabbed by right-handed men because of the power and angles of the blows. They also knew that the killer of both women had blood type O positive; the blood type had been determined by tests done on the semen found in both victim's bodies.

There were differences between the two cases though. Two different knives had been used. Francine Heer's body had been stabbed thirty-one times in the chest and abdomen with a six-inch hunting knife; Susan Conover had been stabbed fourteen times only in the chest with an eight-inch kitchen knife. Conover's wrists had been bound; Francine Heer had not been tied up. Susan Conover had been strangled with a rope or garrote of some kind—they were still analyzing fiber traces found in her neck to ascertain exactly what had been used. Francine Heer's killer had used his hands to strangle her.

Part of Romanelli wanted both women to have been killed by the same man. If there was only one killer, they would have a little more with which to work. Just because inconsistencies existed, that didn't mean one man couldn't have committed both crimes.

It was a fallacy to think that methods used in multiple murders were always consistent. True, some killers murdered in such a way as to appear ritualistic, with every little detail arranged. Quite often, however, particulars of different murders by the same killer varied, sometimes wildly. Part of it was the compulsion of the murderer. A killer might murder a cheerleader, a grandmother, and then a delivery boy. He might bludgeon one victim, and shoot another. Or use an eight-inch Henckels knife because it happened to be near at hand. In the killer's demented logic, his actions were consistent, even though everyone else might think them insane.

If the same killer had not murdered Susan Conover and Francine Heer, then two alternatives came to mind. The first was that two different men with similar homicidal urges had acted in remarkably similar ways within weeks of one another. That was possible, though unlikely. Of course, Romanelli had investigated any number of crimes that had turned out to be possible *and* unlikely. The other alternative was that the murder of Susan Conover was a copycat killing.

On the face of it, the concept of copycat killing was mind-boggling. The pathology that made one person kill in such horrible ways was impenetrable. Then to consider that someone else would want to emulate such perversion—it was incomprehensible. Yet, Romanelli knew, it happened often enough that he couldn't discount it in this case.

Still, out of all the possibilities, Romanelli thought it probable that Susan Conover and Francine Heer had been killed by the same person. Someone right-handed with type O positive blood. That only narrowed it down to about twenty million people.

Now all he had to do was find him.

SIX

Stopping off at gas stations, rest areas, and truck stops, and handing out his leaflets to just about everyone he encountered, Willy took most of the day traveling from Santa Fe to Albuquerque.

In Albuquerque, Willy talked to a sympathetic police detective who promised that a copy of the flyer would be shown at every roll call the next morning. Then, for nine hours, he posted flyers on bulletin boards and telephone poles, and asked shopkeepers, bartenders, students if they had seen Janine or an attractive man with blue eyes and a scar, accompanied by a young woman with short, dyed-black hair.

Near dusk, he came back to his truck. He still had a little over five hundred dollars and about as many leaflets left. Willy drove to the interstate and headed west.

Romanelli sat at his desk and considered the evidence in the Susan Conover case. The eight-inch chef's knife that had been recovered was the weapon used to stab Susan Conover. Though no traces of human blood were found on the knife—it had been immersed in swamp water and the discoverer had even cleaned it before coming forward—it matched exactly the dimensions of her wounds. More important, when Romanelli went back to Susan Conover's apartment, he discovered that it was missing from a matched set of Henckels knives given to her as a housewarming present by her mother.

The fiber traces in her neck had been identified as well. They were silk and matched fibers from a bathrobe in Conover's closet. The robe's belt was missing. So it now looked as if the killer had been inside Susan Conover's apartment. The belt he had strangled her with had come from her bedroom closet and the knife from her kitchen. Had he accompanied Conover and her friend, Janine Smith, to the apartment, or had he been lurking there when they came home?

Where was she murdered? Where were her clothes? She had been wearing an extravagant Mardi Gras costume. That outfit was not found in her closet nor near her body.

The crime tech team had gone over Conover's apartment with Luminol and had found no traces of blood. Some blood was present, however, in the soil near where her body was found in the bayou. Though they couldn't be certain, because of the time elapsed and the wounds being postmortem, forensics thought she had been stabbed there. So, Romanelli wondered, had Susan Conover been alive when she came to the bayou? And what of Janine Smith?

The sweater found by the academy cadet belonged to Janine. She had been seen wearing it on Mardi Gras day, and it had a label from a clothing store in Poughkeepsie, New York. Though the sweater had not been pierced or slashed by the knife, its front was covered with AB positive blood, which was different from Conover's and a fairly uncommon type. It was Janine Smith's blood; according to her medical records, she had been typed AB positive when she had had a tonsillectomy as a little girl. The sweater was not slashed, but it was a cardigan: it could have been draped off her chest when the attacker stabbed her.

Looking at the scant evidence, Romanelli tried to reconstruct the crime. Janine Smith and Susan Conover had been alive on Mardi Gras night; they were seen dancing. Sometime after eleven P.M., they had gone back to Conover's apartment. Either someone they had met at one of the clubs returned to the apartment with them, or someone had approached them on the street and forced them to take him to the apartment. Someone might also have broken into Conover's place before or after they came home.

Francine Heer though, had also been out barhopping, and they knew she had never made it home the night she was killed. So Romanelli was going to figure that Janine Smith and Susan Conover met the killer in one of the bars. If that was the case, at least they had a description of the man—attractive, Caucasian, over six feet tall—that the musician at Linny's had given them.

A knife and the silk belt used to strangle Susan Conover were taken from her apartment. That was the only evidence of criminal activity in the place, thanks to the goddamn maid. The maid had insisted that the apartment was very neat the day she had gone in to clean. Was Susan Conover raped and murdered there in her home? No sign of a struggle was evident, but conceivably the killer could have put a knife to Conover's throat or a gun to her head. Terrified, she might have yielded to him, desperately hoping that he wouldn't kill her if she complied.

What about Janine Smith? The murderer could have incapacitated her, or threatened them both with a gun. Romanelli remembered the ligature on Conover's wrists, and another scenario came to mind. The killer might have bound Susan and attacked and murdered Janine first. Or had he tied up both victims, so that he could assault each one individually? That would explain why Susan Conover had tie marks on her wrists, while Francine Heer had none.

Then the killer had put both bodies in the trunk of Susan Conover's gray Pinto. He had driven to the bayou where he dumped Susan's corpse and attacked it with the knife. If that was the case, though, where was Janine's body? In a another part of the bayou? In a shallow grave?

Romanelli picked up the copy of the credit card slip. How did it fit in? Janine Smith's credit card was used to buy gas for Susan Conover's stolen car. Why would the killer, in a stolen car and with dead bodies in the trunk, use the credit card of a woman to fill up the car? It would be obvious to any gas station attendant, even one making just a cursory inspection of the credit card, that the man wasn't named Janine. If two dead bodies were in the trunk, why stop for gas at all?

Romanelli did some quick arithmetic and came to the conclusion that the Pinto had been nearly empty when it had gone into the gas station, just a few miles from Conover's apartment. The killer had stolen or hijacked her car, then immediately realized he was out of gas. That still didn't explain why he had used Janine's credit card to pay for it. It didn't make sense.

Unless one or both of the women were still alive when the Pinto pulled into the service station. Didn't the attendant, Aundray Perkins, have vague memories of waiting on a man with a scar on his chin? Perkins had also stated that his dim recollections probably were influenced by his desire to tell Janine Smith's boyfriend what he was hoping to hear.

Romanelli studied the handwriting report. It was the analyst's opinion that all of the credit card slips after Mardi Gras, except for the very first one, were forgeries signed by the same person. From eyewitness accounts, a woman with dyed-black hair who was definitely not one of the missing women had signed the rest. But, the analyst had been unsure who had signed the gas station receipt, though he stated it wasn't the woman with black hair.

The signature was just a scrawl. It could have been Janine Smith. The shakiness of the signature could be explained by her terror at having just been kidnapped. The killer could have been in the back seat with a gun, Janine and Susan, terrified, in the front. Janine might have even been trying to alert the gas station attendant that something was horribly wrong. Or the scrawl could have been written by Susan Conover.

What would that imply, Romanelli mused? If Susan Conover had signed the credit card slip, that could mean Janine Smith was already lying dead in the trunk of the car. That would be consistent with the ligature on her wrists. Susan had been tied up while the killer murdered Janine, and then she had been forced to help him dispose of the body. But why would they use Janine's credit card?

What if no one even felt threatened at that point? Perhaps the killer had come up with some ruse to get them to drive out to the bayou. If that were so, however, wouldn't Janine Smith's name be more legible? All of her other signatures were quite neat.

Susan Conover's wrists had been tied up. Partial fingerprints of someone unknown had been found in the trunk of the Pinto. Janine Smith's credit card had been used to fill up the car early on March 10. The gas station attendant had hazy memories, quite possibly biased by his desire to please, of a man with a scar handing the credit card clipboard to someone in the passenger's seat. The Pinto had been abandoned, and probably wiped down for fingerprints, in Houston. No signs of a struggle or a break-in were found in the apartment, though the murder weapons—the knife and silk belt—were taken from there. A musician at Linny's recalled seeing the two women dancing with a good-looking Caucasian male, a description consistent with that given by people who had later accepted Janine Smith's credit card. Susan Conover's body was found nude, but the clothes she was wearing on Mardi Gras day were not in her apartment. Janine Smith's sweater, soaked with her unusual blood type, was found, but she, or her body, was still missing. What series of events could accommodate all these facts?

Romanelli sat for a long time. Finally, and not very happily, he came to some conclusions that he knew were shaky at best.

The killer had met and ingratiated himself with the young women. He had left the bar with them, and had accompanied them or had forced them back to Susan Conover's apartment where he acquired the murder weapons. At some point, the killer and both women had got into the gray Pinto. They had stopped for gas at Mighty Mobil. One of the women had signed Janine's credit card slip. At some point, Susan, and probably Janine, had been tied up. Possibly they had been put in the trunk of the car. The car had been driven to the bayou. There, the assailant had raped and strangled the women. And then attacked them with the knife. The killer had disposed of their bodies in two different spots. Then, he had fled to Houston where he abandoned the Pinto.

That is, unless one of the hundreds of other possibilities had occurred.

Driving up a slight grade, the truck gave a shudder and then stalled. Willy pulled off onto the shoulder of the highway. Opening the hood, he knew immediately that he wasn't going to be able to get the truck running again on his own. If what he suspected was true, that the engine had blown a head gasket, then he wouldn't be getting the truck running at all.

He looked out across the desert. Miles away from any town, all he could see was scrub, cactus, tumbleweed. He wasn't quite sure where he was, but he thought it might be Arizona.

After leaving Albuquerque, he had gone to Gallup, but by then, he had come to question his arbitrary theory that the trail was heading west. He decided that since whoever was using Janine's credit card had gone to Taos, they might also have intended to go to other tourist spots. So for the last few days, he had been wandering on secondary roads throughout Colorado, Utah, and, he thought, Arizona. His new theory had been no less arbitrary, and the results had been no less futile.

The first vehicle that came by, a pickup truck with three Navajo men in the cab, stopped for him. They were going into the nearest town and would bring him along if he gave them a dollar for gas. Willy handed over the dollar and hopped in the back of the pickup.

It took them over an hour to reach their destination: the pickup never got out of second gear. The town had two gas stations, only one of which had a tow truck. The tow truck would not be able to pick up Willy's truck for "a little while."

Willy walked around the town, a collection of about a hundred dreary cinder block houses built directly on concrete slabs, a few hogans near the outskirts, some stores, cafes, bars, and the two service stations. He stopped at all the stores and showed the flyer, then ate a burrito at the cafe. The haggard, redheaded waitress glanced suspiciously at him throughout the meal. When he went back to the gas station an hour later, the tow truck was still not around. No one knew when it would be available, and no one seemed to care one way or another if it was back in a few minutes or in a few hours.

What did the wait matter? Willy thought. He only had four hundred dollars left. If he was correct about the head gasket, it would not be enough money to repair it. Even if the problem should prove to be less serious, he doubted that any of the necessary parts would be available in this godforsaken place.

He waited on the bench outside the service station for another two hours. The wind was beginning to pick up. The sky seemed vast and ever-changing. Huge gray clouds would race across the horizon, casting sudden transforming shadows on the red-brown earth, then disappear.

A tavern down the road had a pay telephone. Willy hadn't talked with either Emil or the New Orleans police in over a week, not since he had heard about Susie's car being recovered in Houston. He had held off calling, hoping superstitiously that by not phoning, he would somehow increase his odds of hearing good news. Dropping coins in the slot, he played in his mind the conversation he wanted to hear. "Willy, it's a miracle! Janine and Susie are all right! It's all been a huge misunderstanding. Janine is here waiting for you, worried about you. She loves you."

The operator came on the line. Apparently he had reached the reservation exchange, not the phone company. The call was going to cost three dollars more than he had expected.

Willy went to the bar. Two customers were silently hunched over their drinks and cigarettes. The heavy middle-aged woman behind the bar had round squat features and her black hair was in braids. She wore a quilted, insulated plaid shirt and gave him change for the phone without comment.

It would be early evening in Beacon, so he called Emil at home. Emil picked up the phone and said hello.

"Emil, this is Willy Buchanan." He paused, as he always did before asking, "Is there any more news about Janine?"

Emil sighed, and Willy felt dread envelop him.

"Willy, it's not good. Susan Conover's body was found a few days ago. She was murdered . . . and raped."

Willy said, "No," but Emil did not hear it. "What about Janine?"

"They haven't found Janine's . . . they haven't found her, yet. They did find Janine's sweater." Emil sighed again, agonized. "It was soaked with her blood. I'm sorry."

Willy stared out across the barroom. The barmaid was gazing out the window, not saying a word and as completely still as the two bleak customers. It was like a grotesque painting. Willy knew he would never forget this tableau, that it was burned indelibly in his consciousness.

"The New Orleans police think it's connected with the murder of Francine Heer." Willy heard Emil say.

Not trusting himself to speak, Willy hung up the phone, then vaguely realized that his action would seem strange to Emil. He crossed the room and sat at the bar.

"I'll have a bourbon. A double."

The stolid bartender poured the drink and placed it in front of Willy. He gulped it down and motioned for her to pour another. It was a ridiculous gesture, and he knew it, though that didn't stop him from downing the second drink in one swallow. The bourbon burned, choking him, bringing tears to his eyes, and nearly coming back up.

The bartender went to the cash register. Willy didn't want to get drunk, and he couldn't bear to stay in the barroom another moment. He left before the bartender could come back with the change.

Gusts of wind blew; small dust devils swirled in the distance. Willy trotted down the main street, then turned and ran down a dirt road. A scraggly, thin mongrel chased him for a few hundred yards, snapping at his feet, but finally gave up. Within minutes he was alone.

He stopped running. "Janine is dead," he said aloud.

I am never going to see Janine again, Willy thought. I will never hear her voice, her laugh. She will never put her head on my shoulder, or . . .

Willy looked around him, stunned. It seemed as though he could have been on the moon. How did it ever happen that he was in this strange place, in the desert, thousands of miles from home? How could Janine be dead?

He clenched his fists, the nails digging into his flesh, but the pain didn't ward off the horror. His breath came in gasps, and he heard the ghastly noise he made. Great sobs racked him, and his body shook.

Willy bent over, then slowly went to his knees. How was he going to live without Janine? Kneeling, he slammed his fists down on his thighs and cried in convulsive whimpers.

The wind buffeted him. He lowered his head to the ground. The deep wail that roared out sounded to Willy like a cry from hell.

PART FIVE

1976

ONE

WILLY NAILED THE LAST piece of maple flooring into place and rose from his kneeling position. A dull pain ached in his back and legs, but he also felt the satisfaction of having done a job well. He still had to stain, sand, and finish the new hardwood floor, but his work had a raw beauty. Carl had urged Willy to tack down some cheap wall-to-wall carpeting directly onto the subfloor here in the den, or better yet, some linoleum. The money saved would be considerable. Willy, though, had disregarded that advice, just as he had ignored Carl's suggestions to cover the water-damaged bedroom wall with cheap, laminated panelling and to replace the falling-down porch with an aluminum awning. Instead, Willy had replastered and rebuilt.

Of course, Willy had accepted much more of Carl's counsel than he had rejected. After all, Carl had been working on old houses and apartments since Willy was a boy. And indeed, it had been Carl who first told him about this home.

It was a bungalow on Church Street that had fallen into disrepair over the years. Its owner, a reclusive, mentally unbalanced, unwashed man who everybody knew as Bigtop, had barely eked out a living on Veterans Administration disability checks and money earned selling balloons and souvenirs at the four or five parades in the area every year. Bigtop had never taken care of his place—it had had broken window panes covered with cardboard, an overgrown yard, and weather-beaten asphalt siding for as long as Willy could remember—

and when Bigtop was hospitalized for the last year of his life, the house's decline accelerated.

When he first viewed the bungalow, Willy had been intrigued. Why most others would be dissuaded from bidding on it at the tax sale was obvious. The roof had leaked badly and evidence of water damage was everywhere. Badly-worn linoleum covered the scarred and rotting hardwood floors that would have to be replaced completely in two of the rooms. It would take days and several dumpster loads just to cart away Bigtop's clutter before work could start on the house itself.

As Carl pointed out, however, the wiring and plumbing were fine, the foundation solid. The roof needed to be replaced, but wasn't Willy a roofer? He would be able to do the job himself at a third of what it would cost anyone else. Carl had outlined a number of other ways in which Willy could fix up Bigtop's house and still make a good profit for himself. More important to Willy was that, beneath the decay and ruin, a beautiful house of exquisite workmanship could just barely be discerned. For reasons he didn't quite understand, the idea of bringing back beauty and order to the house had a powerful attraction. It was the first time in a long while he had felt this strongly about anything.

Willy had been adrift for the last few years and he knew it. Returning to Beacon a year after he left, he had tried to resume some semblance of his old life. Jimmy Guido was delighted to rehire him; he had had trouble finding a helper who didn't mind doing most of the work while Jimmy drank away the afternoon. Willy had also started to work side jobs for Carl again as if he had never left. As before, he sought to lose himself in toil, and often, for weeks at a time, would do nothing but work, eat, run on the Asylum Road, and sleep.

He lived by himself in a sterile studio apartment in a complex a few miles outside Beacon that was furnished with a bed, a cheap dresser, a TV. When he wasn't working, he would occasionally see those of his old friends who still lived in Beacon. Earache would drop by his apartment every so often. Willy, however, had only gone to visit Earache at his place one time—it was the apartment that Willy and Janine had rented just before she had disappeared.

Although when he thought about Janine's disappearance, he used the term *disappearance* rather than *death* or *murder*, Willy had come to terms, in a way, with having to live the rest of his life without her.

On the day Willy found out about Susie Conover's death, he remained sober. He roamed the dusty desert road deep into a canyon, sobbing, talking aloud to himself, screaming. It was nearly ten o'clock at night before he trusted himself to be with other people. When he returned to the town, every store, gas station, and bar was closed. His truck rested on the apron of the service station. Apparently the tow truck had finally shown up and then gone out to retrieve Willy's truck even though he was nowhere in sight.

Willy crawled into a sleeping bag in the back of his truck, but didn't sleep. At dawn, the gas station owner came around and told Willy the expected news. The head gasket was blown; the repairs would cost two hundred dollars more than Willy had and would take at least a week because parts would have to be ordered.

"Do you want to buy my truck the way it is?" Willy asked.

If the station's owner had said he wouldn't pay a dime for it, Willy would have just taken off the license plates and given him the truck. Instead, the man offered to trade for a decrepit 1956 Pontiac that had at least 185,000 or possibly even 285,000 miles on the odometer and no papers.

"I'll even throw in fifty bucks and tank of gas," the man had offered.

It took Willy a few minutes to load all his gear from the truck to the back seat of the Pontiac. It took considerably longer for the mechanic to get the car running, but finally the engine kicked over with a tubercular wheeze. As Willy sat behind the wheel, the man put ten gallons of gas in the tank and sprayed the windshield with a hose. Months of accumulated dust and grit smeared slowly, obliterating everything. The wipers didn't work, of course, so the owner had to use his squeegee to wipe the windows clear.

The out-of-tune engine shook the Pontiac as Willy drove past his truck. It had been the first vehicle he had ever owned, and figured in so many memories, yet he felt no sentimentality, no emotion of any sort in abandoning it. It was just a part of his old life he was jettisoning. He knew that there was yet much more to relinquish.

The highway lay before him. A right turn from the service station's apron led back into the tiny town. Though the town was spread out over less than a half mile, Willy couldn't bear to look upon that forlorn place even once more. He turned left, and that is how he wound up heading toward Phoenix.

The long desolate highway stretched on to the horizon and only rarely was the shimmering pavement interrupted by a speck that grew into an approaching car, truck, or camper. The Pontiac shuddered violently, and the rear end vibrated whenever Willy drove over a certain speed. Most of the exhaust fumes funneled through the interior of the car, so Willy had to keep all the windows open. A case of reclaimed motor oil rattled on the floor of the passenger's side. Every fifty miles or so, Willy would have to stop and put a couple of quarts of oil in the engine. None of the gauges worked, and the speedometer was frozen at thirty-five miles-per-hour.

Surprisingly, the radio played, though few stations could be picked up. Driving over a crest in the highway, a country-western station suddenly came in clearly, and Willy heard a hillbilly voice singing about losing his girl. He listened to the bathetic song a moment, then reared back and slammed his fist into the radio. The song continued— all the hillbilly could do was cry, his girl was never going to return. Willy slammed on the brakes, and the car took about fifty yards more than was safe to stop on the deserted highway. He cocked his leg back and kicked the radio. Bits of the plastic selectors and a chrome knob flew away, still the hillbilly sang. Three more kicks did not shut the singer up. Finally, Willy found a rusty screwdriver in the glove compartment—no doubt it was used to open the trunk. He jabbed the blade through the plastic station display, then through a speaker, and the song ended, midyodel.

At dusk, Willy arrived in Phoenix. He checked into a motel, but as soon as he had put his luggage inside the room the walls seem to crush down on him, and he fled. Willy paced down the busy strip of highway, past motels, fast-food restaurants, gas stations, until he came to a bar.

The bar was crowded—two softball teams had just finished playing. Willy ordered a shot of tequila and a beer. Since hearing of Susie Conover's murder, a moment that had seemed endless, he had resisted the urge to get drunk. He had thought this resolve remarkable. As he now drank down the tequila and felt it burning, he realized that his extraordinary self-control had only lasted twenty-four hours.

Willy sipped the beer. People were laughing all around him. The San Francisco Giants were playing the Houston Astros on the television. A pretty, chubby woman in a baseball jersey put her arm around her boyfriend. Willy swilled down the rest of the beer and left.

Stopping off to buy a case of beer, he returned to the motel. Again the room seemed oppressive. Willy knew if he stayed there, he would do something crazy.

Coming into Phoenix, Willy had noticed a drive-in movie theater not far from the motel, and it was there he finally went. With the case of beer in a cooler on the seat beside him, he sat and drank while a Hell's Angels picture and then a movie about drag racers played. He listened to snippets of dialogue on the raspy speaker and watched images of fights, car crashes, and motorcycles roaring down highways on the huge screen, but would have been unable to say what either movie was about. He drank three of the six-packs and came close to making his mind a blank.

The third feature came on, a movie about student nurses. Within minutes of the start of the picture, one of the nurses was taking a shower, soaping her body in leering close-up. The intent was obviously to titillate, but Willy stared at the actress and felt his heart break. He left the drive-in, parked the Pontiac on the street outside the theater, and drunkenly staggered the quarter mile back to his motel.

In his room, he lay on the bed and drank beer until he passed out.

The next morning, Willy poured three quarts of orange juice, ice, and a pint of vodka into his picnic jug. Then he sat by the motel's pool and drank. The weak drinks, the sun, and the pool's warm water kept him in a mild stupor that wasn't quite intoxication. He forced himself to eat, then walked back to the drive-in with another case of beer and some ice. His car was still parked where he had left it. He drove the hundred yards back into the drive-in. The triple bill had been changed. The new program was two spaghetti westerns from the late 1960s and *Billy Jack*.

Willy parked off by himself near the back of the drive-in's lot, far away from the teeter-totter and swing set where young children in their pajamas played. A middle-aged couple in a car twenty spaces away were eyeing him anxiously. He probably looked like some psychopathic drifter, Willy thought, with his wrecked, unlicensed car, his three-day growth of beard, the case of beer at his side: the kind of person who made the headlines. The kind of man who had killed Susie Conover. And Janine, he forced himself to add.

He lived this way for a week, maybe more. One afternoon, Willy called up Amanda, rambling incoherently, and then hanging up when he started to cry.

One morning he awoke to discover that he had less than fifty dollars in his wallet. He moved out of the motel and checked into another, more squalid one which had a kitchenette and weekly rates. Then he called Earache Kehler in Beacon. Willy didn't know when or if he was going to return to Beacon. He offered to pay Earache to clear out everything from his and Janine's apartment and put it into storage. Earache at first agreed, but then came up with a better idea. Since only inertia kept Earache and Andy in the cold decrepit trailer, why didn't they move into Willy's place instead? When he returned, Willy could have it back.

Willy knew that he would never live in that apartment again, but he agreed to the plan. Earache promised to pack away any personal things that still remained in the apartment.

After hanging up the phone, Willy bought a newspaper and turned to the want ads. Two days later, he was working as a house painter.

The man he worked for had contracted to paint all the homes in one of the new subdivisions that were scarring the desert. The crew Willy was part of would follow the carpenters and drywallers, priming and painting a house in two days. The work was monotonous but curiously soothing. The paint fumes and the huge joints he and the crew's foreman smoked kept Willy light-headed most of the day. After work, he and the foreman, a longhair from Chicago named String-a-ling, would go to a local bar near Willy's motel and drink beer and play pool.

When all of the completed houses were painted, he was laid off. While working, though, he had become acquainted with one of the carpenters who managed to get Willy hired at a nearby subdivision that was just starting up.

Though not a carpenter, within a week Willy was working as a framer on the subdivision. So much construction was going on in the area, with almost no union regulations, that people like Willy, who were handy and had some experience swinging a hammer, were being hired all the time. Willy worked with a crew, putting up the structure of a split-level, three-bedroom house with attached garage, then abandoning it to the finish carpenters and drywallers, hop-scotching down five or six building sites to start erecting another identical house. The summer heat of Phoenix was hellish, often hovering around a hundred and ten degrees, but Willy worked as often as he could and felt lost on his days off.

He had been in Phoenix for six months when his parents flew down to see him. Earlier, when they had spoken on the phone, he could hear the concern in their voices as they asked what in God's name he thought he was doing. Still, Willy was surprised when they showed up at his motel and tried to talk him into returning to Beacon.

His mother had hugged him, looking with bewilderment at his shabby motel room. "How can you live like this?" she had asked.

His father, hoping to strike a conciliatory tone so that Willy would agree to return home, had replied, "It's not so bad. Hell, it's no worse than that trailer he lived in."

Willy took them out to dinner, taking care to project a sane, sensible image, and making it a point to drink iced tea instead of wine with his meal.

"I'm doing fine," Willy said to his parents. "I'm working a lot, I'm staying out of trouble. I'll be okay."

His mother and father had flown back to Beacon two days later, if not quite convinced that Willy was indeed okay, at least reassured that he was not in any imminent danger.

Willy continued to work at the subdivision where new houses popped up like spores. Every morning before the sun rose, he would run five miles. Some nights he came back to his room so exhausted by the work and the heat that he managed to fall asleep immediately. Other nights and on weekends, he went to a local bar where he came to a nodding acquaintance with the bartenders and some of the regular customers.

Unbelievably, the dilapidated Pontiac he drove was never pulled over by the police even though it had no license plates, and it continued to run as long as Willy put a quart of reclaimed motor oil in the engine every other day. What was even more incredible to Willy was that someone stole the car one night. Staring at the empty parking space in the morning, Willy had howled with laughter, his first heartfelt laugh in a long, long time. He didn't bother to report the theft. The car had never been registered in his name, and he figured the thief was being punished enough by having to drive it. Willy replaced the Pontiac with a 1961 Rambler station wagon with a bashed-in passenger's door that cost a hundred dollars.

One Friday night when Willy had been away from Beacon for almost a year, he had gone to the local bar. A woman he had played pool with a few times sat down beside him.

"Let me buy you a drink," she said.

Her name was Emily Breschard. She had soft, dark brown hair and gentle hazel eyes. She had graduated from Arizona State with a degree in music, but was working as a waitress and had just finished a dinner shift.

"You're a waitress? I thought you just liked to wear a black skirt and white blouse all the time," Willy said.

They talked and played pool, and when the bar closed, she turned to him and asked, "Would you like to come home with me?"

Though he had sensed interest on her part, nonetheless he was surprised. He was further surprised when, in his confusion, he heard himself say, "Yes."

They made increasingly nervous small talk on the short ride to her place, an older Spanish-style stucco building. At the arched door to her apartment, Willy nearly said that this was a mistake, he wasn't ready, but he remained silent.

The living room had hardwood floors, tile around the fireplace, and recessed niches in the plaster. Willy found himself admiring the workmanship in the room rather than thinking about what he was doing there.

Emily came back from the kitchen with a bottle of wine and two glasses. She put an album on the stereo and Chet Baker's version of "Do it the Hard Way" came softly from the speakers. She held up the cover to show him the picture of a romantic couple and gave a self-deprecating laugh. Lighting a candle on the coffee table, she said, "I feel like I should be wearing a smoking jacket and an ascot."

She sat down beside him on the sofa. They talked, and when she laughed at something Willy had said, she touched his arm. They looked at one another awkwardly; Emily leaned over and kissed him.

They rolled around on the sofa for a while—*making out* was the term that flashed through Willy's thoughts—then she led him to her bedroom.

They undressed. Willy felt far removed from what was going on, as though not in the room but rather outside observing it. He watched as Emily's clothes came off. She was pretty, but the self-consciousness in her eyes told him that she probably thought she should lose ten pounds, or that her hips were too big or her breasts too small. None of that was true, and Willy wanted to let her know she was attractive. But, watching her, he couldn't stop himself from thinking of Janine and of all the ways she and Emily were different.

They lay atop the flowery pink sheet. Feeling her body in his embrace, Willy couldn't shake the feeling of not being involved in what was happening. Something hard inside him would not dissolve.

That hardness did not extend to other parts of his body. Emily's hand floated down his stomach and between his legs. She moved her hand away in a too-quick, embarrassed motion, then slowly began to knead the back of his neck. After a while, she glided down in the bed. Willy gently took her shoulders and guided her head back to the pillow.

Before Willy could apologize, Emily said, "It's okay. It's not a big deal. Just being here with you is fine."

She rested her head against his chest, and later, fell asleep.

Willy had never been impotent before this night, but he felt no humiliation. He hoped that he hadn't hurt Emily, or made her feel unattractive or insecure, but mostly what he experienced was sadness. A sweet woman was in bed with him, but she was not Janine. Her hair was different from Janine's, and her eyes, her legs, her hips, her mouth, her breasts. Willy felt as if he had betrayed both women.

The next morning, he awoke before Emily. He lay in bed, thinking of the previous night. After a while, he heard her stir, but feigned sleep when she arose and went into the bathroom. Returning to bed, she brought with her a faint minty whiff of toothpaste. And that somehow touched him. She snuggled up beside him and gently kissed his back. It was such a simple, generous, lovely gesture. Willy turned and kissed her. Emily noticed when he became aroused, and smiled at him tentatively.

They made love for a long time. Try as he might, he couldn't stop himself from thinking that he was not with Janine. When Emily came, it was in gasps that, Willy hated himself for noting, were different from Janine's. A while later, she came again. Willy tried to let go, but something inside him refused to budge. As they continued to make love, he could feel Emily becoming excited again, and he was grateful that he was at least able to repay her in this small way for her kindness. Finally, Willy gave up and pretended to have an orgasm with her.

"Oh, God," Emily exclaimed after they had been still for a moment. "Oh my goodness."

Willy rolled over on his stomach. What other form of sexual dysfunction will I have next, he wondered? That a man might fake an orgasm had never even entered his mind until moments ago, when he had actually done it.

"Oh my goodness!" Emily repeated. She gave a big sigh. Her body glistened with sweat, and she wiped her forehead with the pillow. "I feel like we were just in the Olympics."

She continued in that vein, her jokes meant to compliment Willy as well as reassure him. Again, he felt a tenderness for her. She doesn't deserve to get involved with someone as fucked-up as I am, he thought.

Emily had to work the lunch shift, so when Willy left after showering and eating breakfast with her, their parting did not seem forced.

The next time he saw Emily, the following Friday at the bar, she looked defensive and hurt. He could tell that she knew he had been avoiding her for the last week. Willy's heart melted when he saw the pain in her eyes, pain for which he was responsible. Asking her to sit in a booth with him, he explained everything about Janine. Emily listened to him, barely speaking, then rushed from the bar, Willy thought, so that she wouldn't burst into tears in front of him.

That Monday, Willy gave notice at his job, and two weeks after that, he was on a plane heading toward New York.

Willy took some of his hand tools from the house and loaded them into his pickup truck. Jimmy Guido had a big job and needed an extra helper for a few days. Since buying Bigtop's house, he had spent most of his time renovating it, and just occasionally worked for others. But he knew he could use the money.

He had been able to buy Bigtop's house—he still thought of the bungalow as Bigtop's and not his own—for just the back taxes, twenty-seven hundred dollars. He put all his savings, which were considerable due to his almost constant working for the last three years, into the renovation. When his money ran out, he had been obliged to ask his father to co-sign a loan at the bank for him.

Willy studied the front of the house. Despite the new porch and roof, it still looked like a hovel. The inside of the house however, was nearly done, and soon, when he tore off the awful asphalt siding and restored the clapboards that had originally adorned the house, the transformation would be dramatic.

Too dramatic, in Carl's opinion. Carl kept warning that Willy was taking too much care and spending too much money on remodeling. Willy realized he would probably take a small loss on the house, but that didn't seem important. True, he had made some mistakes, and perhaps he was too meticulous in his craftsmanship. Soon, though, there would be something beautiful that he had made that would last for years. Although he would not live in it, he was going to make a home.

TWO

RICHARD FITZHARRIS AWOKE, then turned in his sleeping bag so that the moonlight hit the luminous dial of his wristwatch. For the last few years, he had been awakening earlier and earlier, but this was a bit much. It was only three in the morning. He had hoped that all the fresh air, the hiking along Yosemite's trails, and his lack of a nap would bring on an uninterrupted sleep till dawn.

His wife, Vickie, snored softly in the sleeping bag next to him. He told himself that as one grew older, less sleep was necessary, but if that was the case, why did Vickie manage to sleep until seven every morning? She was as old as he, in fact she was twelve days older. They had both turned seventy-three last July, but she wasn't dozing only four or five hours a night. Then again, he thought, feeling that old familiar pressure, she didn't have a prostate gland.

Fitzharris pulled on a pair of khakis and climbed out of their tent. The rest rooms were a quarter-mile down the trail, but the Great Outdoors was all around him, and wasn't that part of camping? No one was around, except the young hiker, an athletic woman who had pitched her tent down a bit from theirs. He would go off behind some trees and hope there wasn't any poison oak. Otherwise, if he didn't, the young woman would be sure to pick that moment to wiggle out of her own tent.

At first he had resented the young hiker's presence. They had purposely picked this remote campsite, but it was a public park. It wasn't the young woman's fault that Yosemite had become so crowded with tourists. He and Vickie had hiked here since the 1920s, but so what, that didn't give them any extra privileges. Their young neighbor would never know the park as they had. He was way ahead of her in that respect, so he had decided to shut up and live and let live.

He went to an obscured part of the woods, but it was hardly worth the trip. Coming back, he saw a shadow move near the young woman's tent. Fitzharris stopped in embarrassment, thinking at first that she had come out of her tent with the same intention as he. Then, he realized that it was not the young woman squatting by the back of her tent.

The shadow moved again and went to the front flap of the tent. It was definitely a man. Fitzharris felt a constriction around his heart, and he thought he might have another coronary.

The man slipped into the tent, and then Fitzharris heard a muffled sound.

Terror immobilized him. He had always thought of himself as a physical coward. Once as a young man, he and a friend had been accosted by some toughs on the street. He had fled and left his friend alone to be pummeled. Fitzharris had not been in a fight since grade school, and even in those few boyhood fights, he had lost badly.

Perhaps he had misinterpreted what he saw, Fitzharris desperately told himself. Couldn't that man be the young woman's husband or boyfriend? Couldn't that muffled noise be a greeting or a kiss?

He heard another grunt. It seemed urgent, but with the loose morals young people had these days, who could tell what that noise had been?

Fitzharris looked around and spied a fallen branch. I'm only five-feet-four, he told himself, and I only weigh one hundred and thirty pounds. I'm seventy-three years old, and I've already had one heart attack. What good could I do?

He stared at the open tent flap, then quickly reached down and picked up the piece of wood that was no thicker than his wrist. His brittle, pitiable wrist. Fitzharris found himself racing toward the tent, then bursting into it.

The interior of the tent was dark, but Fitzharris could see the shadowy intruder straddling the woman's chest. She was gasping for air, and he saw that the man was choking her. As the man turned toward him, Fitzharris swung the branch and hit him in the forehead. The man's head jerked sideways at a strange angle. The force of the blow must have momentarily loosened the chokehold on the woman's throat, because she screamed loudly. Fitzharris swung the stick again, but the man blocked it with his forearm. And then the man was on top of Fitzharris.

A punch brought a blinding light to his eye; another blow struck his forehead. Instead of hurting Fitzharris, though, the second blow brought a cry of pain from his attacker. The man must have broken one of the bones in his hand. The woman, who had not stopped screaming, jumped on the man's back, and they both tumbled into the side of the tent which collapsed.

The young woman reared back in a defensive position and was kicking, trying to keep her attacker away. The man reached down to his ankle, and a sheath with a knife came into view. Then, Fitzharris threw the first punch of his adult life. It landed between the man's legs. The man roared and rolled over on his side.

"Run!" he screamed at the young woman. At that moment, he felt a raging hatred for her. If it wasn't for her, he wouldn't be here himself, he would be able to flee.

Still screaming, she scurried out of her tent. Fitzharris followed so closely that his head touched the back of her thigh.

As he got to his feet outside the tent, he saw his wife with her mouth agape, staring at him and the young woman. Months later, she would confess that, hearing the young woman's screams and seeing her scramble half-undressed out of her tent with him right behind, Vickie had thought he had tried to attack her.

The young woman raced down the trail, yelling help over and over. Fitzharris waved his hand violently at his wife, who stood motionless, and called to her, "Run!"

A startled expression crossed her face, then she followed the young woman. Fitzharris thought that if he ran, he would have a heart attack. Walking instead and gasping for breath, he wondered if he might have one anyway. Over his shoulder, he saw the man crawling out of the tent.

Fitzharris wanted to cry, but the man turned in the other direction and crashed into the brush. As relief mingled with exhaustion, he saw three men rushing toward him from the campsites below. Weakly, he pointed toward the woods where the man had fled. Then he sat down on the earth and prayed that his heart would stop pounding.

He rested there for a few minutes until those campers from down below carried the inert body of his attacker past him.

In the shower, Willy bent forward at the waist while Martha coasted the bar of soap down his back. The soap flew off from the ramp of his buttocks, like a skier from a jump, but failed to reach its goal, the tile wall at the end of the bathtub.

"Ohh!" Martha cried, "Did you see how close that was?" She leaned forward for Willy's turn.

Willy lathered Martha's back with the soap, then sent it gliding. It took off from her rear and just barely hit the tile.

Martha smirked and said, "You win."

Willy shrugged. "It's all in the technique."

"Well, at least you didn't say it was because I have a bigger ass than you."

Willy had met Martha just three weeks earlier at a party in Poughkeepsie. She was the first person since Janine that he had gone out with more than once—they had gone out three times. Martha was tall, almost six feet, with chestnut hair and brown eyes. After that first night, she told Willy the reason she let him pick her up. "You were the only man without a date at the party who was taller than I am."

The cynicism behind that comment was typical of Martha and, Willy had to admit, a great part of her attraction. Having recently been divorced, she did not have a very high opinion of men, relationships, or romance. She claimed, however, not to have given up on sex.

Of the three women he had slept with in the two years since returning to Beacon, Martha was the first woman he had actively pursued. In the other two drunken encounters, he had wound up in bed almost by accident. Something about Martha's reserve and the defenses she put up around herself gave Willy a sense of security. She had made it clear from the beginning that things were only going to go so far between them. "But don't worry," she had said, "that doesn't mean I won't wear my go-go boots to bed."

After the shower, they dressed and had breakfast. Willy wanted to get back to Bigtop's house. The plaster in the bedroom had cured enough for Willy to paint it. Instead, he suggested a movie. Martha agreed enthusiastically, so Willy forgot about working. It would be good for him just to relax for a day.

They went to see *All the President's Men*. Returning to Martha's apartment in Poughkeepsie, they made supper. Afterward, Willy could tell that Martha did not want him to stay over again, so he kissed her goodby and drove the ten miles back to Beacon.

As he entered his apartment, the phone was ringing. When he picked up the phone he was expecting to hear Martha's voice. Instead, he heard, "Willy, this is Emil Deshayes."

Willy felt the old dread. There was a pause on the line, then Emil said, "They think they may have found the killer."

* * *

"His name is Brian William Hull," Emil said. "He's being held in California right now. So far, the only charge against him is for the attempted murder of a twenty-year-old female camper out in Yosemite National Park."

Willy noticed the sergeant's stripes on Emil's uniform. He, Emil, and Teddy Smith were in Teddy's law office on Main Street. Amanda and Howard were vacationing in Maine, but Teddy had telephoned and told them the news.

"He's been linked to at least eight different homicides across the country. All women in their early twenties, and all of them had been raped, strangled, and stabbed. Most of the victims had been kidnapped first and their bodies found in remote areas. He's also the prime suspect in the disappearance of three other women whose bodies were never found." Emil looked uncomfortable as he added, "That's including Janine. The FBI has been called in, and right now everyone is trying to figure out which is the strongest case against him."

"What's his connection with Janine and Susie Conover?" Willy asked.

"Hull has been drifting all around the country for the last five years. But he always used his own name when he worked. And his van was littered with receipts, some two years old. I don't know what the motherfucker expected. That he could *deduct* his expenses? Anyway, we know for a fact that he was in certain cities when murders with the same M.O. were committed. And also in the van was some women's jewelry. There was a ring with the inscription, To Francine, Love Mommy. It has been positively identified as a ring belonging to Francine Heer."

Emil went on to tell them all that he knew. Hull had preyed on women in tourist settings. He had been at Fort Lauderdale and Daytona Beach during spring break; in resort towns such as Virginia Beach during the summer, and Key West during the winter. Two murders in Yellowstone and Yosemite National Parks had occurred while he was there. And, one year, he had been in New Orleans for Mardi Gras.

Hull had admitted none of the killings. Indeed, he had refused to make any statement at all. But right now, investigators and local homicide detectives were scrambling to connect him to some of their unsolved murders.

Solid evidence linked him to at least eight murders, but Hull may have been responsible for many more. He was not going to be charged immediately with all of the killings.

"Which of the murders will he be charged with?" asked Teddy.

"It looks like he is going to be extradited to Florida. He killed a college student there two years ago. Hull left his fingerprints in her motel room. And he was seen and almost apprehended by a security guard who had been hired to protect the motel against vandalism by the college kids. The guard identified Hull's picture two days ago. It's an almost certain conviction. And in Florida, now with the Supreme Court decision, there's a good chance Hull will get the death penalty. And be executed."

"What about the other murders?" Willy asked.

"They'll have to go case by case. He'll probably be tried for Francine Heer's death, I mean he had her ring, but I doubt he'll be charged with Susie Conover, unless he confesses. There just isn't enough physical evidence or witnesses. As for Janine's case . . . he probably won't be charged at all. I'm sorry, that's just the way it is."

Willy picked up the file that Emil had brought and glanced at it. Brian William Hull. The name sounded innocuous, one you would come across in a yearbook or a professional directory, not in a police report of a mass murderer. Then Willy noticed the description. "He doesn't have blue eyes."

"No," Emil replied.

"What about the scar on his chin?" Willy asked.

"No, he doesn't have that either."

"I don't understand. I thought you were looking for a man with a scar on his chin and blue eyes?"

"We were. For the credit card. It was a lead we were following. And it was just about the only one we had. So naturally we pursued it with a lot of energy. But as happens most of the time, leads don't pan out."

Willy glanced at the description of Hull again. *Eyes: Brown.* "The New Orleans police think Hull killed Susie?"

"Yeah. Of course, two open homicide cases can now be closed so the inclination would be to . . . close them. But I think they're right. I think Hull did it.

"No one has ever positively placed the guy with the scar with either Janine or Susie on Mardi Gras night. Aundray Perkins couldn't really say, and no one at Linny's could identify the man either. Which is noteworthy, because three different people definitely remembered him after they disappeared. We're pretty sure Scarface had Janine's credit card and was running it up. But when did he get the card? Though we were hoping that there was a link between the credit card fraud and Susie's murder, it was never conclusive. The guy could have found Janine's purse, or he could have lifted it from her while she was still alive. Or he could have gotten the credit card from Brian William Hull, or come across it after Hull dumped it.

"We know Hull killed Francine Heer. We've got the physical evidence. With Susie, we have a murder with the same M.O.—sexual assault, strangulation, then post mortem stabbing. We can place Hull in New Orleans on that day. Hull is right-handed and has O negative blood, which, though both are common, matches Susie's killer. I admit it would be a lot neater if Hull had blue eyes and a scar. But things aren't always neat. It's not a dead solid lock, but I'd say Hull is our man."

They sat in silence for a moment. Willy stared out the window and saw cars driving by on Main Street. In her journal, Janine had predicted that Teddy would be a lawyer with an office on Main Street, and it had come to pass. He could almost see Janine in the balcony of the Beacon High auditorium, watching Teddy rehearse *Arsenic and Old Lace*, and then turning to him with that extraordinary smile.

"One thing is certain," said Emil. "This guy Hull will be convicted. If not in Florida, or if not for Janine, then for someone else. The only way this fucker is getting out of jail is in a box."

THREE

THE RAINSTORM WAS SUDDEN. In the few minutes it took to lock up Bigtop's house and drive down Church Street, the sky turned black, then sweeping sheets of rain poured down.

On Main Street, Willy spotted Teddy Smith, sloshing down the sidewalk, his jacket over his head. Willy honked the horn and pulled over to the curb. Teddy hopped into the pickup's cab, slamming the door behind him.

Water dripped from Teddy and made puddles on the seat. "It's raining."

"Let me guess. Your car wouldn't start?" Willy remarked.

"You must be psychic."

A month ago, after an annual softball game of former Beacon High players, Willy had given Teddy a lift when his car, a ten-year-old Volkswagen, wouldn't start. And just last week, on the night Emil had told them about Brian William Hull, Willy had helped push the car two blocks down the street to Tralen's Texaco.

"What's the matter with it now?"

"Who knows?" Teddy replied. "I hope it's something major. I hope the engine has melted down. Because you know what I'll do? I'll take that goddamn car to a junkyard where they have a machine that can crush it to the size of a suitcase. I want to be there when they do it. I'll be grinning from ear to ear. We'll see who has the last laugh."

Willy put his truck into gear and headed up Main Street. "Where would you like me to drop you off?"

"Could you take me to my mother's house? I've got a court appearance in Fishkill tonight. I'm going to have to borrow her car."

The rain came down with such magnitude and force that the windshield appeared to be underwater. Willy had to slow the pickup to a crawl; a running pedestrian on the sidewalk raced past them.

"I'm considering buying Andy Brascia's car," Teddy said. "He's only asking two hundred dollars. What do you think?"

"I think if you want to keep borrowing your mother's car, you should buy it. Why stick yourself with another heap?"

"You're absolutely right. But I think I'm going to buy it anyway."

Willy almost blurted out, "Why don't you just go out and get a new car," but remained silent.

Last year, Teddy had turned twenty-five. As just about everyone in Beacon knew, he had collected the inheritance that his father had left him, which was then over eighty thousand dollars. Even considering that he probably wasn't earning a lot yet as a lawyer, and perhaps there were student loans to repay, he should have had enough to buy himself a decent car. But, Willy thought, it was none of his business what Teddy did with his money.

Teddy would also inherit everything that Ed Smith had left in trust for Janine. A court proceeding to declare Janine legally dead would be necessary. Recently, walking into Zep's, Willy heard a couple of local barflies, no doubt eminent legal scholars on the side, arguing how long someone had to be missing to be declared legally dead. One of the men insisted that it was seven years. When everyone noticed Willy, the conversation had abruptly switched to football. At that moment, Willy made a vow that he would be nowhere near Beacon when the inevitable court hearing took place.

The rain was beginning to abate as Willy pulled up to the Smith house on West Willow Street. He turned to Teddy and said, "I think I'm going to California. I want to talk with Brian William Hull."

Teddy was silent a moment, then quietly responded, "What good will it do?"

"Maybe something he says will end all this uncertainty. He's facing all those murder indictments. What does he have to lose? Maybe if I just talk reasonably with him . . ."

"Talk reasonably with a psychotic?"

"What do I have to lose?"

Teddy nodded, then a look of such sadness crossed his face that Willy regretted having spoken.

Willy turned away and noticed that Amanda had come to her front door. A few months earlier, he and Amanda had met on Main Street.

"I came across some old photos of you and Janine," Amanda had said. "I made up some duplicates for you. Drop by any time and pick them up."

"Thanks, Amanda, I will," Willy had replied.

His and Amanda's relationship had mellowed in the last few years. After returning from Arizona, Willy had gone to see her. She had asked if he would like anything of Janine's as a keepsake. He wanted to ask for the beige cashmere sweater that Janine often wore which had belonged to her father. But with visions of himself getting drunk and weepingly putting on the sweater, Willy settled on a small pen and ink sketch drawn by Janine. Amanda had given him the framed drawing and, as he left, hugged him. That any sign of affection might pass between them would have been unimaginable before Janine disappeared. Still, seeing one another always seemed to be painful for both of them.

Since Teddy would be there to act as a buffer, Willy decided to go into the house and pick up the duplicate photos. Amanda greeted Willy with self-conscious cordiality. Without being asked, she went to the den and brought back the snapshots which were wrapped impeccably and tied with a slender pink ribbon. Then, as if embarrassed by her own kindness, she turned to Teddy.

"When are you going to get yourself a decent car? This is silly. I don't mind lending you mine, but you really need a new one of your own."

"Actually, I'm thinking of getting another car."

"Good, it's about time," Amanda replied. "What kind?"

Teddy hesitated and said, "A vintage automobile."

Amanda shook her head. "I really don't understand this newfound thriftiness of yours. You have responsibilities now. You have clients depending on you. What are they to do if you can't make it to court because your car broke down?"

"Don't worry. No one's going to wind up in the electric chair." Teddy stopped, as he realized what he had said. They all looked embarrassed.

Willy left a few minutes later. The next day he flew to California to talk with Brian William Hull.

Brian William Hull entered the cubicle and sat down. He wore a blue prison jumpsuit, had a cast on his right hand, and looked, Willy thought, strangely unimpressive. Hull was of average height and had a soft flabby body, a weak chin, thinning sandy hair, and dull brown eyes. Nondescript. He did not look monstrous, like a man who had ravaged and desecrated eight other human beings. One of the guards had told Willy that Hull had been wearing a VIRGINIA BEACH IS FOR LOVERS T-shirt when apprehended.

Willy had talked briefly on the phone with Hull once already. The previous day, he had telephoned the Fresno County Jail from Beacon to see if it would be possible to have an interview with Hull. A few minutes and three bureaucrats later, Willy was shocked to discover that he was actually speaking with Hull himself. It seemed bizarre, then outrageous, that a man accused of slaughtering all those women would be allowed to talk freely on the phone. He remembered once when Janine was sixteen and had come home an hour past her curfew, Amanda had not allowed her to see Willy or accept any of his phone calls for a week.

On the telephone, Hull had been cagey. When asked if he might have any idea what had become of Janine Smith, Hull had answered, "What are you, crazy? You think I don't know this phone is bugged?"

That the phone might be tapped had never crossed Willy's mind. He asked if Hull would be willing to talk with him about Janine in person.

"Hey, I'm not going anywhere. And I'm receiving all callers."

During his one brief phone call with Hull, Willy had felt very little emotion. He had not allowed himself to connect that innocuous voice with unspeakable horrors directed against Janine. Now, sitting across a glass partition from Hull and seeing the snide grin on his bland face, Willy felt a murderous rage building up inside himself. A vision of smashing through the inch-thick glass and using the shards on that leering face flashed through Willy's mind, but he forced himself to greet Hull with a neutral nod.

Hull picked up the phone on his side of the glass partition. Willy waited a moment, until sure of his emotions, before picking up his phone. "My name is Willy Buchanan. I'd like to talk with you about Janine Smith."

"Go ahead. Talk."

Willy held up a photo of Janine and placed it against the glass. "Do you recognize her?" Willy asked evenly.

Hull shook his head in disgust and said, "You think I'm a fucking imbecile?"

"I'm not with the police. Janine was my fiancée." He held up another picture of the two of them together.

Hull studied the second photograph a long time. "What was going on? A party?"

The snapshot had been taken at Teddy's college graduation party. "Yes."

Hull looked at Willy inquisitively, his expression urging him to continue.

"Janine's brother had just graduated. The picture was taken in their backyard."

"And they had a barbecue? Beer and soda pop in a big wash bucket filled with ice?"

"Yes."

"What kind of food did you grill?"

Willy considered the monster across the glass from him. He seemed sincerely interested in the party. And more than that, Willy got the feeling Hull was giving some greater meaning to it. "They grilled chicken and steaks."

"And she had chicken, didn't she?"

Janine had had a steak at the party. "Yes, she did," Willy said.

"That's your jacket she's wearing, isn't it? She was cold and you offered it to her."

Janine was wearing Teddy's jacket; it had been the first thing she had grabbed from the hall closet. "Yes."

"I've never seen your girlfriend."

"She was in New Orleans three years ago at Mardi Gras. So were you."

"And so was Al Hirt. I didn't see her."

Willy experienced a rush of hope, but then he heard, "I've never seen any of those women."

"The police found Francine Heer's ring in your van. She was from New Orleans."

Hull shrugged, "Yeah, so?"

"The police have a lot of evidence against you. For a lot of different murders."

"They're wrong."

Willy nodded. Hull obviously wasn't going to come right out and admit anything. Willy hadn't really expected him to do so.

"If you had to guess, what would you think happened to Janine? Not that you did anything, but maybe someone else did. What do you imagine someone else did to her?"

Hull smirked, and Willy steeled himself to hear something depraved. After a moment, though, Hull said, "They freed her from getting married to an asswipe like you. That should be worth a commendation."

Willy waited until he felt his anger subside. "I know you can't admit committing any crimes. But there's just you and me here now. You don't have to say anything. Nothing can be used against you in court."

Hull gave Willy a condescending look.

"If you know anything about Janine Smith's disappearance, close your eyes."

A hint of a smile crossed Hull's face. He stared at Willy for a long time, then swiveled around in his chair so that Willy saw the back of his head. Moments later, he turned back to Willy, wearing a sneering grin.

"Always glad to help."

As Willy placed the phone back in it's cradle, Hull began to laugh silently behind the partition.

This was a long shot, Willy told himself. It had been unrealistic to expect Hull to free him of his tormenting uncertainty.

Willy stood and left the jail. As he walked out into the dusk, he felt a sense of relief. Hull had not confessed to Janine's killing; he had not revealed the shallow grave where her remains were buried.

There was still hope.

PART SIX

1983

ONE

COOL AIR SWEPT OVER Willy's naked body as he opened the refrigerator in Karen's apartment. He took a carton of orange juice, drank from it, then closed the door. On the stove was some coffee that Karen had made before going to work. Willy poured himself a cup. He had a mild hangover, which surprised him, since he had only had five or six beers the night before. He and Karen and Patty Chisolm, who had introduced them, had gone to the Village Vanguard to see Oscar Peterson perform. Sipping the coffee, Willy felt his headache begin to ease. "I'm getting to be a lightweight," he told himself.

He had often heard the term *drifted into trouble*. It seemed to Willy that he had done the opposite—without any conscious effort, he had drifted away from trouble. He had not done any drugs in years—the last time he had even smoked a joint was probably at Teddy Smith's bachelor party, a while back. Before the last few days, he had not had a drink in a month. There had been no barroom brawls for a long time, and no fists punched through walls in fits of inexplicable rage.

Finishing the coffee, Willy rummaged through Karen's kitchen drawer for the train schedule he had left behind on his last visit. A train was leaving for Beacon at 10:14. If he took a shower now and managed to flag down a taxi without having to wait too long, he would just make it to Grand Central Station.

The bathroom was filled with Karen's cosmetic disarray—she had been running late this morning because they had been up half the night. Willy could still smell the fruity aroma of Karen's shampoo. It contained papaya, which Willy always found odd. Why, if you wanted to clean your hair, would you slather on the essence of a sweet sticky fruit? Nutrients? Then, why not a shampoo with steak added to it? Or pork and beans?

His last girlfriend, Solange, had used the same brand of shampoo. He had also met Solange through Patty Chisolm. "She's right up your alley," Patty had told him only half-jokingly. "Solange is in the country on a visa; she can only stay a year." And indeed, Willy had gone out haphazardly with Solange for about a year. They had had fun, but neither one of them shed any tears at the airport when she flew back to France.

Last night at the Village Vanguard, when Karen went off to the bathroom, Patty had said, "I knew you guys would hit it off." Willy supposed they had. He and Karen had met at a party in Patty's Tribeca apartment three months ago. Willy had come down to the city from a house he was renovating in Westchester County; Karen worked with Patty at the Metropolitan Museum of Art. Entering the party, Willy had immediately noticed Karen's jet-black hair. It was cut short with bangs and was reminiscent of the silent movie star, Louise Brooks, who had recently come back into vogue on account of a profile in *The New Yorker*.

Though he knew it was foolish, he couldn't stop staring at Karen's hair and thinking of the description of the woman who had used Janine's stolen credit card. Willy had Patty introduce them. "Karen, this is Willy, an old friend from my home town. He fixes houses."

They had made conversation for a few moments until Willy, out of the blue, asked if Karen had ever been in Taos. Or the Southwest. Or New Orleans. Karen, it turned out, had never been west of Pittsburgh. She had only had her hair cut short within the last year.

"So you're a handyman? You fix leaky faucets and windows that won't open?"

"You could say that."

The house in Westchester was the eleventh he had owned. Fixing up Bigtop's house in Beacon had been a revelation: Willy knew he had found his occupation in life. Seeing the house transformed had filled Willy with a satisfaction he had not felt for a long time. When he went to sell the house—he was eager to start another one—he had been expecting to lose money. Instead, purely by luck, through no foresight or business acumen on his part, Willy had doubled his investment.

Real estate prices had spiraled upward all across the Northeast, but the increase was even more pronounced in Beacon, even though the city remained outwardly the same homely, vaguely moribund place.

When Willy was growing up, almost everyone's job was in the area. Now, however, because of the exorbitant prices for homes in Putnam and Westchester Counties to the south, people who worked in New York City were moving into the Beacon area. That, coupled with the expansion of IBM in Dutchess County, had driven up the cost of homes in Beacon.

With the money from the sale of Bigtop's house, Willy bought a drafty, dilapidated Victorian with a breathtaking view of the Hudson. He spent six months remodeling and restoring the place to its former glory. Again, his mentor, Carl, would berate him for retiling a shower to its original condition instead of installing a prefabricated fiberglass stall, and would cry out, pained and indignant, when Willy lavished time, money, and labor on seemingly minor detail. And again, when it came time to sell, Willy made more money than he deserved.

Of all the remaining properties Willy bought, only one was located in Beacon. In order to do the kind of work he most enjoyed, he would have to buy houses in upper-middle class and wealthy enclaves in Westchester and Connecticut. And so Willy began a sort of nomadic existence. He would buy a house, forty or fifty miles from Beacon, and live in it while he renovated. Often, it was little more than camping out. Willy would haul in a cot, work clothes, tools. He built a frame covered with plexiglass and used it to shield his cot from grit, plaster dust, paint. That shrouded cot was his bedroom, often for months at a time. At first, he kept his apartment in Beacon, then bought his own place there, and would come up occasionally on weekends, or when he had to wait for subcontractors or between houses.

When he went to Patty Chisholm's party and met Karen, he was remodeling and living in a house just outside Scarsdale. Their relationship did not get off to a promising start—what with Willy harboring suspicions that Karen might be implicated in murder and fraud. Willy had even asked her what she was doing in the spring of 1973. It happened that she was studying in Florence. Luckily, Karen had misinterpreted Willy's insane suspicion as interest, and the following night they had gone out to dinner.

They had been seeing one another since. Every other week or so, Willy would come down to Manhattan and stay with Karen. With the house in Westchester nearly completed, he had just spent four days in the city. Now Willy wanted a little time in Beacon. He had not been home in over two months.

Willy flagged down a cab outside Karen's apartment on Twelfth Street near Fifth and made it to Grand Central with a few minutes to spare. Only a handful of passengers were in the train's car. At this time of the morning most travelers were headed into the city, not away from it.

Willy arrived in Beacon two hours later. His truck was still in Scarsdale: he had taken a train down to see Karen instead of driving because of the impossible parking situation in the city. The mile walk in the summer's heat to his place on Main Street would help sweat out the last remnants of his hangover.

Hundreds of cars were parked by the train station and up the road over the railroad bridge. When Willy was a boy, only twenty or thirty cars would have been parked here. Most of the cars belonged to commuters who made the two-hour trip down to Manhattan every morning. One of the cars probably belonged to the man who had bought Bigtop's house from him.

The house in Scarsdale was almost ready to be put up for sale. When a renovation was nearly finished, Willy always felt a restlessness and something of a letdown. This discontent certainly wasn't for monetary reasons—on the last house he sold in Greenwich, Connecticut, Willy made over three hundred thousand dollars. On the house in Scarsdale, he would probably make more. These prices for homes were incredible, and that people could afford them was a marvel. Willy was even more amazed that, by his own modest standards, he was successful, rich even. Although he had always sought to make a living, he had never aspired or even cared about earning all that money. It had just happened, as had so many other things in his life.

Willy turned into the building he owned on Main Street. He peered into Teddy Smith's office, which was on the ground floor. Teddy was not in; he was probably at lunch. Climbing the stairs to his second-floor apartment, Willy entered the huge loft room.

Buying this building had been something of a fluke. Five years ago, Willy had been renting Mrs. Tolessi's two-car garage and using it as storage for building materials and tools. One Saturday morning, Mrs. Tolessi informed Willy that she was selling her house, so he would have to find another storage space. Later that day, as he was drinking a cup of coffee at Carl's Sundries Store, Teddy Smith sat down beside him at the counter and began complaining about his landlord. The heating in Teddy's office had broken down for the third time that month, but the building's owner was the cheapest asshole in the world and wouldn't fix it.

"Carl, I didn't know you were Teddy's landlord," Willy said.

"He's lucky I'm not. I would have raised his rent." Carl turned to Teddy. "What are you complaining about, winter's almost over?"

"Yeah, and so is my lease. Only five more months."

"Really? Then where are you going?"

"Look at his avaricious little eyes light up," Teddy said. "Not to one of your firetraps, that's for sure."

Carl laughed and pointed to Willy. "You should get him to buy a building and fix it up and rent you an office. I could just see it now. It would have stained-glass windows. Willy would put in a bowling alley for you. And a sunken tub. Your mug would be on the cover of *Architectural Digest*."

"Don't listen to him, he's still pissed off that I made money on Bigtop's house."

"You don't know how lucky you were. You should be in rags right now, holding a tin cup."

"Hey, last week you were telling everybody that I was your protégé."

"Yeah, well I've changed my mind. You're not greedy enough to be my protégé."

Willy left Carl's. Driving down Main Street, he had stopped to allow an old woman to take a third stab at parallel parking when he glanced at the vacant building. It had once housed a plumbing supply business, but had lain empty and decaying for years. He must have passed by it hundreds of times without really taking notice—Main Street had dozens of vacant buildings whose former occupants had gone out of business or moved out of town to shopping malls. When the old woman finally parked her DeSoto three feet from the curb, Willy pulled over.

Peeking through a gap in the soaped-up window, he saw a large open space in the interior. In the rear of the building were two garage bays where delivery vans used to be parked. Willy reckoned this area had to be bigger than Mrs. Tolessi's garage.

Laughing to himself, he wrote down the phone number from the faded FOR SALE sign, then raced back to Carl's. Teddy was still at the counter, reading the sports pages.

"Do you want to buy a building with me?"

"No," Teddy replied. He gave Carl a taunting grin. "But I might rent from you."

"Jesus," Carl muttered. "I've created a Frankenstein."

As it turned out, Willy could have put bowling lanes in the building's upstairs space. It was this second-floor loft that finally convinced him to go though with his spur-of-the-moment scheme and actually buy the building. The loft had originally been used in the 1930s as the Lodge Hall for either the Odd Fellows or the Red Men, the owner forgot which, and then as a warehouse area for the plumbing supply business. Willy had had no other intention in the beginning than to find a storage space for himself, but the moment he saw the loft with all its possibilities, he knew he was going to make himself a home there.

The building's owner did not even make a pretense of bargaining. Tired of paying taxes on a vacant property, he asked for a ridiculously low price. "Just take the goddamn thing off my hands."

Willy agreed immediately. "On one condition. If Carl asks, tell him I haggled you down. Otherwise, he'll never speak to me again."

Even Carl, who insisted on inspecting the place, was impressed. The structure of the building was in fairly good shape; water, gas, and waste lines still went upstairs to where the Lodge had had a kitchen area and bathrooms. "You live upstairs, you rent downstairs to Teddy, and you got the back room and garage for storage. Just don't put in any sunken tubs."

Willy put in a shower walled with glass block instead. "You're up to your old goddamn tricks, aren't you?" Carl cried. Willy exposed and sandblasted the brick wall, installed skylights, laid down hard-wood floors, and put marble counter tops in the kitchen. "This is Beacon, it isn't Soho," Carl despaired.

As Teddy watched the remodeling of the new office space, he fretted that he wouldn't be able to afford it. Willy assured him that the rent would be the same as in his old office. Teddy had still been uneasy, "Willy, I don't want you to get extravagant because of . . . Janine. You don't owe me anything extra because she was my sister."

"I can afford to make the place look good because I'm doing most of the work myself. I'm not going to make any money on this, but I'm not going to lose any either. I'm getting what I want. This is not about Janine."

But they both knew that, in some fundamental way, it was about Janine.

Teddy moved into his new office the week before his old lease expired. He and Willy would see each other when Willy was in town, and they would often go out for lunch, or for a drink. Willy was an usher in Teddy's wedding when he married his girlfriend, Becky, and he got drunk with Teddy when he was divorced two years later. Teddy handled the closings of all Willy's properties in New York State for free, and in return, Willy built a deck onto the back of the house Teddy finally bought.

That house was purchased shortly after Janine was declared legally dead. Teddy also bought a new Jeep Cherokee. As he had promised himself, Willy was not in Beacon when the petition to declare Janine legally dead was heard.

Amanda had called Willy shortly before the hearing. "This is just a formality. If it wasn't for the trust fund, we wouldn't be doing this. It doesn't mean that we've given up hope."

"I understand."

"I just wanted to let you know. You won't have to make a deposition or anything. I . . ." Amanda's voice broke.

"Thanks for calling. I appreciate it."

For months after that call, he had stayed away from Beacon. He later learned from his mother that Janine was declared legally dead seven years and two weeks after she disappeared. Amanda and Howard brought the petition before the court; Teddy, perhaps feeling it inappropriate to participate since he was going to gain financially, had nothing to do with the petition. That, however, did not stop all the usual smug Beacon gossip about Teddy's new house and car.

Willy felt no resentment that Teddy had gained from Janine's being declared dead. They had never spoken of the court proceeding, but then they rarely talked about Janine.

After opening all the windows to air out his apartment, Willy straightened up a bit, then went out to run on the Asylum Road. When he returned, he noticed Teddy's office door was unlocked.

Willy went inside and stood in the reception area. Teddy's secretary, Bridget, was nowhere in sight. He heard someone moving in Teddy's office. "Teddy, it's Willy, I'm back in town."

Teddy's voice called out, "Yeah, I'm back here."

Willy strolled across the wide planks that he had refinished, and entered Teddy's office. Then he stopped as though struck.

The shock that Willy felt must have shown in his expression. A wan smile crossed Teddy's pale, emaciated face. He wore an old Beacon High baseball cap, but it did not disguise that he had lost most of his hair.

"How have you been?" Willy asked in confusion, and then immediately regretted saying it.

Teddy shrugged and again gave a smile. "I've got leukemia."

TWO

IT WAS A PERSISTENT CASE of the flu, Teddy thought. When he couldn't seem to shake it, he had gone to the doctor. Tests had been performed. Still, Teddy was not worried. He was at home, forcing himself to drink plenty of fluids, trying to cure himself when his doctor called and said maybe Teddy should go to Vassar Brothers Hospital in Poughkeepsie for some more tests. It was then that Teddy remembered his father going into the same hospital for tests.

Teddy remained in the hospital for almost a month. He had acute myelocytic leukemia, the same disease that had killed his father. He had undergone a grueling induction course of chemotherapy; so far the treatment wasn't helping.

Willy sat across from Teddy, unable to speak.

"I'm more or less closing down my practice. At least for now. Fred Krause will probably take over most of my cases."

"I hadn't heard," Willy said at last in a voice that sounded hollow.

"Not too many people know. Not yet." Teddy gave the desk a distracted stare.

They were quiet, then Teddy continued, "I gave Bridget her severance pay yesterday. And I guess I'm giving you my notice, now."

"Teddy, I don't care about the fucking rent. Just . . . stay here. Things may work out."

Teddy shrugged. "I know you don't care about the rent." He smiled. "You would have let me stay here for free, wouldn't you? But it's not the money. I've got plenty of that."

They talked for a few minutes more. Teddy seemed resigned, or perhaps he was in denial. Everything Willy heard himself say, every blithe affirmation, sounded false, grotesque, pitying, patronizing: "When you're feeling better," and "So you can get your strength back," and "Next year."

After a while, Teddy stood and glanced about the office. His gaze had a finality, and Willy realized with a shock that Teddy would not be coming back to the office ever again. They went out the front door together, then Teddy walked around the corner and was gone.

The mower rattled in Willy's hands. The swath of mown grass grew as he moved back and forth across the lawn in front of Teddy's house. Since hearing of Teddy's illness, Willy had been coming back to Beacon more often, and this was the third time he had cut the lawn.

This afternoon, Teddy would be returning from the hospital after having undergone yet another week of chemotherapy at Highland Hospital. He would have a week or two off until the next course. The chemotherapy left Teddy so weak and susceptible to infection that only family members had been allowed to visit, and even Amanda and Howard had been required to don surgical masks and gowns.

Willy finished the front lawn, then the back. He was trimming the grass around the flower beds that lay beneath the expansive front porch when Amanda's new Lincoln Continental pulled to the curb. Teddy got out of the passenger's side.

All of Teddy's hair was gone now; he wore a blue bandanna wrapped around his head. He had lost even more weight and appeared weakened by his latest therapy, but he walked steadily up the front walk.

"Hey, Willy."

"How are you feeling?"

"Not bad."

Amanda plodded along a few paces behind, looking troubled and preoccupied. She said hello and followed Teddy up the front steps.

Later, she came out of the house with a Coke for Willy. "You look hot."

Willy remembered that those were the same words Janine had called to him in front of the Beacon Federal Bank so many years ago. He took the icy bottle from Amanda.

"Thanks. How's Teddy?"

Amanda sighed, and for a moment Willy thought she might cry. "He's going to Mexico."

"What?"

"Mexico. Tijuana. He's going to a Laetrile clinic."

Willy was astonished. "You tried to talk him out of it?"

"Of course! Lord knows what those quacks will do to him."

"Jesus. Laetrile? He can't believe in that, can he?"

Amanda shrugged hopelessly and shook her head.

"I thought he had come to terms with . . . He didn't seem that desperate."

Amanda glanced away, then said, "I don't think I've ever asked you for a favor, but I'm going to now. Try and talk to Teddy. Maybe he'll listen to you. He only has a little time left. He should spend it with the people who love him. Not in some . . ."

"I'll talk with him."

Willy was in the backyard when he heard Amanda drive away. He finished trimming a border and walked up to the deck. His knock rattled the screen of the French doors.

"Come on in," Teddy called out.

Teddy's house was sparsely but expensively furnished. On the walls were original photographs by Walker Evans, Alfred Steiglitz, Diane Arbus, which he had started to collect about the time he had inherited Janine's share of their trust fund. Teddy was lying on the couch, and even though it was a warm summer day, he wore a sweatshirt that looked too large on his shrunken body and a blanket draped over his lap.

"I hear you're going to Mexico."

"And my mother has asked you to try and talk me out of it."

Willy nodded.

"It's funny how things work out. Did you ever think you'd be trying to talk me into doing something my mother wanted?"

Willy laughed and said, "Never in a million years. But your mother and I get along now. I guess we've all changed."

"So, tell her that you argued with me for hours, but I was adamant."

"Okay . . . Laetrile, huh?"

"What do I have to lose?"

Willy almost said, "Time," but kept still. He turned and saw two photographs that he had not noticed before. "Are those new?"

"Yes, I bought them a few months ago."

The pictures were dissimilar, yet seemed to be of a piece. One image, probably by Penn or Avedon, was of a nude woman who was staring into the camera. Her beauty, the photo's composition and lighting were perfect. The other picture, which was undoubtedly by Diane Arbus, showed a disturbed woman who was also staring directly at the camera. Though the disturbed woman looked nothing like the nude fashion model, something in the power of their gaze was remarkably alike.

226

"It's strange how things work out," Teddy said. Then, in a different tone of voice, he asked, "Is Andy still dealing drugs?"

"I guess so. He was the last I heard."

"Does he have pot?"

"Probably. He's a fucking mess, though. I saw him a few months ago at Zep's, and he was all strung out. He's drinking 151 rum, he can barely hit his mouth with the glass, his eyes are about to roll up into his head. And all the time he's telling me how he's clean now. Then he wanted to borrow fifty bucks."

"So he might rip me off?"

"I wouldn't put it past him. How much pot do you want?"

"I don't know. A couple of ounces?"

"Okay."

Willy was surprised, twenty minutes later, to find out that an ounce of marijuana now cost a hundred dollars. He gave Andy Brascia two hundred dollars and headed back to Teddy's house. Teddy hadn't suddenly felt an urge to relive his pothead youth, Willy knew. The marijuana's purpose was medicinal: it would help offset the nausea of the chemotherapy. Willy hoped that meant he would reconsider going to Tijuana.

When Teddy didn't answer the knock on his open French doors, Willy entered. Teddy was motionless on the couch, and for a moment, Willy thought he was dead. Then he saw the motion of his breathing. Willy dropped the baggie full of grass on the coffee table in front of Teddy and quietly left.

"You couldn't talk him out of it?" Amanda asked with a hint of accusation in her voice.

"I tried, but he was adamant. Though at one point, I thought he had reconsidered. When did he leave?"

"This morning."

"Well, maybe this trip won't be as bad as we think. It shows that he's still fighting," Willy said, though he didn't believe it.

"He's going to get sicker, he's going to need real medical help, not those charlatans."

"Maybe, he'll come back soon."

Teddy came back after only a week. Willy had just finished doing the yard work at Teddy's house and was driving down the street when a limousine approached and passed him. In his rearview mirror, he saw it stop in front of Teddy's. Driving around the block, Willy pulled in front of the parked limousine.

Teddy was on the front porch, handing the limo's driver some money.

"Thank you very much, sir," the driver said with seeming sincerity, which meant that Teddy had probably overtipped as he usually did. The driver nodded to Willy as he walked back to the limousine.

Teddy noticed Willy and called to him from the front door. "Come on in."

Inside the house, Teddy's bag stood next to the coffee table. The two ounces of marijuana still lay on the table where Willy had left it.

"I'm back," Teddy said from the couch.

"You took a limo up from New York? You should have called. I would have picked you up at the airport."

"I was intending to take the shuttle bus, but one had just left and the next shuttle wasn't for three hours. I felt exhausted, and the limousine service was right there. So, I figured what the hell."

On the handle of the overnight bag, Willy could see the Pan Am baggage claim stickers. LAX—JFK was written on its cover. Willy said, "You flew into Los Angeles?"

"Yeah, I got a cheaper fare. And I wanted to see a little of Southern California."

Willy tried to imagine what it had been like for Teddy as he went down the coast. Had he thought that he would never see the Pacific Ocean again? That he would never go to Tahiti, or Africa, or the Grand Canyon? Had he seen the squalid streets of Tijuana and realized that he didn't want to die there? Did he realize that, if he had to die, he wanted to die at home?

Willy could tell that Teddy was fatigued, so after a few minutes he left. Back at his apartment, he telephoned Amanda, who already knew that Teddy was back.

The next day, Teddy went back into the hospital for more chemotherapy.

Three months after that, he died.

THREE

"POOR AMANDA," Willy heard the elderly woman say. "First her husband, and then her daughter, and now her son."

Willy walked past the woman and toward the kitchen. It seemed strange to be at a party in the Smith house and not be talking with either Janine or Teddy. Amanda was by the counter, pouring herself a cup of coffee from a large percolator that one of the neighbors had brought over. As Willy threw some ice cubes into his plastic glass, Amanda came over and patted his arm comfortingly, before going to see to her guests.

Back in the living room, Patty Chisolm, who had come up from New York City for the funeral, was chatting with Kim Mooney, Earache Kehler, and Terry Pritchard. Nearby, Kim's daughter and Earache's son were trying to fish a maraschino cherry out of a glass of Seven-Up.

The funeral had been at St. John's Church, the burial at St. Joachim's Cemetery. After the graveside service, the undertaker had announced that all were invited to the Smith house.

Patty and Kim were chuckling as Willy rejoined them. Kim said, "We were just talking about Patty's acting career."

"*Arsenic and Old Lace*. I remember it," Willy remarked. Then echoing Janine's long ago comment, he added, "I remember your makeup. It looked like somebody poured a bag of flour over your head."

"I think Richler wanted to. I kept forgetting my lines. But Teddy would cover for me. He was so sweet. He'd try to whisper my lines to me, and then finally he'd have to ad-lib something like, 'Auntie, don't you want to offer the gentlemen some elderberry wine?' God, it was terrible."

"Well," Kim said, "it was supposed to be a comedy. And you certainly made me laugh. I went to see the play twice, just for your performance. And it wasn't like you forgot the same lines both nights. You varied the moments when you stood like an imbecile with your mouth open. You had me hanging on your every word, trying to guess when you'd screw up next. That's real star power."

They all told stories about Teddy, and then reminisced about growing up. Across the room, Willy could hear laughter and the racket of slightly tipsy conversations that grew louder as the afternoon wore on. More than one person noted that it was a party Teddy would have enjoyed.

Later, Willy stepped out onto the patio for some air, and when he turned he spied Howard leaning alone against the railing.

"Taking a break, too?" Howard asked.

"Yeah."

"It's extraordinary, isn't it? It's a Tuesday afternoon, the house is filled with people joking and getting mildly drunk. They should all be at work, or home, or two hundred miles away. And here they are. You travel just two or three blocks away, and somebody is gardening, or watching a soap opera, or working on a car. It's just another ordinary day to them."

Willy nodded, unsure what to say. He had known Howard for over fifteen years, and this was the first time he had seen him drunk.

"Teddy died upstairs, did you know that? The house where he grew up. There was no sense in him being in a cold impersonal hospital. Or even in his own house. It was his idea to come back here after the last chemo. He wanted to come home."

"I figured that is why he didn't spend much time in Tijuana." Willy suddenly recalled his own time wandering around the Southwestern desert and in Phoenix. "It must have been lonely for him there."

Howard waved his hand dismissively. "He was never really serious about Laetrile. I know he didn't have much faith in it. He wasn't intending to stay—he booked his return trip, for Christsakes. But, you get desperate. Who can blame him? What must it be like? Here he is only thirty-three years old, and the doctors tell him, 'Get all your affairs in order. In six months, you're going to be dead.' "

"Amanda asked me to talk him out of going. So, I started to bring up the subject—"

"And he said, 'I know my mother is putting you up to this.' "

Howard laughed. "Yeah, he told me the same thing. And we both told Amanda that we had tried to reason with him."

Willy smiled.

Howard looked out across the back yard. "I was forty-three when I married Amanda, and she was forty. It was my first marriage. I had always wanted to have kids of my own, I wanted a family, but given our ages, I figured that was a part of life I would never have. There was Teddy and Janine, but Teddy was already fifteen years old, and he didn't need me as a father. And Janine . . . she was so close to her Dad, and his death affected her so, that it would have been nearly impossible for her not to resent me. And I suppose she had good reason, I don't blame her.

"But Teddy . . . let me into the family. He accepted me, but it wasn't just being gracious. He permitted me to take on this role which was more for my benefit than his."

They heard a knock, and Willy saw Amanda at the patio door, waving for Howard to come inside. Howard returned her wave in assent, then heaved himself from the railing.

"He was a good son. And he was a good brother," Howard said, then went inside to join Amanda.

The first guests left as the shadows outside grew longer. Kim's daughter started to fuss, and Earache's son, as if taking a cue from her, also began to whine, and within minutes, everyone was gone, leaving Howard and Amanda alone in the large empty house.

FOUR

WILLY HAD ONCE READ about the nature of creativity and inspiration. The article recounted how mathematicians, physicists, and composers made breakthroughs. A mathematician might ponder a theorem for months, years. Or he or she might have considered it years ago and not consciously thought about it again. Then, while seemingly occupied with something totally unrelated—waiting for a light to turn green, or opening a bottle of port—the long-sought proof would spring into consciousness, complete. Or an apple might fall from a tree, and one aspect of the universe would be revealed.

Later, Willy wondered if some similar process had not occurred to him.

The paint bubbled behind the trail of the heat gun. Willy ran the putty knife across the face of the pantry door which lay on saw horses, and six layers of paint came up in a long strip, revealing the wood that had been covered for decades.

He focused the heat gun back at the bottom of the door. While working, he had been thinking of Teddy, his illness, his death. Howard's conversation on the patio at the party after Teddy's funeral came back to him. "He wasn't intending to stay—he had already booked his return trip, for Christsakes . . ." and "Here he is only thirty-three years old, and the doctors tell him, 'Get all your affairs in order.' "

Willy stopped the putty knife in midmotion. Teddy had booked his return trip. From Los Angeles, now that Willy thought about it, not Tijuana or San Diego.

The acrid odor of smoke penetrated his musing. Willy looked down and saw that he had scorched the pantry door. Turning off the heat gun, he sat down on the floor, stunned.

With just a few months to live, knowing he was dying, Teddy had gone to Los Angeles. He had bought a round-trip ticket, planning to return not after the Laetrile worked, or failed to cure him, but in seven days.

The fare was cheaper, Teddy had given as one reason for flying to Los Angeles. With every day precious to him, exhausted and sick, would Teddy have chosen to fly into L.A., cognizant that he would have to go to the further effort and expense of renting a car or taking a bus to Mexico? For a savings of perhaps a hundred dollars, would he have prolonged his fatiguing journey by hours? On his return trip, he had taken a limousine up from New York City rather than wait for the next shuttle bus. The limousine must have cost a few hundred dollars.

Another reason for flying to Los Angeles, Teddy had claimed, was that he wanted to see Southern California. At that time, though, just maneuvering from one room to another had taxed his strength. Would he really expect to enjoy Disneyland, or find pleasure driving in the urban sprawl of the West Coast?

Willy went to the phone. Moments later, a Pan Am operator quoted him the fares to Los Angeles and San Diego. The difference was ten dollars.

Ten dollars. Willy made sure that the heat gun was unplugged. Then, he locked up the house and drove to Beacon.

Willy paced back and forth across the large open space of his apartment, one flight above where Teddy had had his office. When Willy had urged him to keep the office until he got better, Teddy had replied, "It's not the money. I've got plenty of that."

Driving up from Scarsdale, Willy had barely been able to concentrate on the road. Teddy had plenty of money. He made a good living as a lawyer. And he had inherited his share, and then Janine's share, of the trust fund their father had left them. While not a spendthrift, he had, except for one period of his life, been free with his money. He wore good clothes, he ate well. All of his personal belongings were of the highest quality. He traveled, he collected original photographs. He owned a nice home and drove a new car. It was often a struggle when going out with Teddy to keep him from picking up the tab. Even in college and law school, Teddy had indulged himself, going to Europe one summer, and heading to Florida every spring break. Was it conceivable that he would endure significant hardship in order to save ten dollars?

The only time Teddy had ever seemed strapped for cash was when he had first started to practice law. After working for Fred Krause for a year, Teddy had struck out on his own. He probably didn't make much money the first few years, and what he did earn was probably put right back into the business. So it was understandable that he had made do with his beat-up, unreliable Volkswagen and a barely-furnished studio apartment.

It was also at this time, however, that he inherited his share of the trust fund. Even if some of the fund had been used to pay for his schooling, he still should have received over fifty thousand dollars. Yet, he had continued to live in uncharacteristic frugality. Even Amanda had noted it and had been puzzled by his unwillingness to buy a new car when his old one kept breaking down.

Willy suddenly became conscious of his pacing back and forth. "What am I doing?" he thought. "I'm behaving like a crazy man." His suspicions were absurd, irrational. Like countless other desperate, sick people, Teddy had sought out quacks for a cure. He had been momentarily gullible, or in a state of denial. Perhaps he had not acted consistently, but how could Willy know exactly Teddy's state of mind? Couldn't all of his actions be reasonably explained?

In despair, couldn't Teddy have indeed given Laetrile a try? Even though he didn't believe in it, couldn't he have thought that a long shot was better than none at all?

And certainly it was plausible that Teddy had overestimated his strength and capabilities. So that he may have truly desired to tour California before undergoing Laetrile treatment.

Willy stopped pacing and forced himself to sit. Teddy had been one of his best friends. And Janine's brother. In the face of some innocent, easily explained facts, wasn't he inventing a conspiracy? Had he lost his reason?

Teddy had asked Willy to get him marijuana. It had remained on his coffee table while he went to California, but wasn't it acquired to alleviate the effects of the chemotherapy? With the expectation that he would be back in Beacon shortly and that the chemotherapy would continue as planned?

He was letting his imagination run riot. Janine had died. Teddy had died. And now his mind was embracing farfetched shadowy theories rather than deal with those painful facts.

234

Willy stood and began pacing the room again. Like the demented moron that he was, he told himself.

Yet he could not control his thoughts. Against his will, Willy could not stop thinking over and over again of one reason why Teddy would travel to Los Angeles when he was dying.

FIVE

It was a little past noon; the overhead sun burned away shadows. Willy drove his truck up the driveway of Teddy's house and got out. His actions were not going to be clandestine. Everything was going to seem right out in the open.

A realtor's FOR SALE sign was pitched on the front flower bed. Mrs. Kleinman looked out her kitchen window and waved. She had seen Willy doing the yard work before, so she wouldn't be surprised that he was here again. He returned her wave and glanced at the lawn; it actually did need cutting. Though he hadn't planned on it, Willy decided to mow the grass. It would only take a few minutes. He wouldn't bother with the flower beds or any of the trimming.

The mower roared, and Willy pushed it across the yard. If Amanda should drop by, she would just assume he was doing another favor.

When the grass was done, Willy went to the back of the house and checked the windows on the ground floor. They were all locked and had additional slot locks that were engaged and could not be forced without conspicuous damage. A sheet of glass rested in the front of his truck. If necessary, Willy would break one of the window panes in the kitchen door and let himself into the house that way. He would repair the broken glass immediately, but that would be messy and time-consuming. With luck, he would be able to enter the house another way.

In the garage, Willy grabbed Teddy's extension ladder and brought it to the side of the house. Since the second-story windows on this side had no easy access, Teddy might not have locked them. The aluminum ladder clanged as he extended it. Willy whistled a tune loudly, hoping to convey that everything he was doing was aboveboard. The back bedroom's side window was locked. He climbed down the ladder and moved it to the pebble-glass window of the bathroom. Wouldn't that window have been opened and closed repeatedly to allow steam from showers to dissipate?

Willy scaled up the rungs. With a screwdriver, he bent back the latch that kept the screen in place and gave the window a shove. It slid open.

Leaning into the bathroom, he moved forward on his hands like a boy in the wheelbarrow race at a picnic, clambering over the vanity onto the tile floor. He went downstairs and out of the house. Still whistling cheerfully, he fixed the screen, then lowered the ladder and returned it to the garage. Back in Teddy's kitchen, he locked the door behind him.

The house was stuffy, but everything appeared undisturbed. Amanda had not yet gone through the place, setting aside piles of clothes for the Salvation Army and emptying drawers, as Willy had feared.

He was behaving in a crazed, obsessive manner, Willy knew. In order to satisfy wild farfetched suspicions, he had just committed a felony. He was guilty of breaking and entering. He was guilty of much more than that—monomania, dementia.

Willy roamed throughout the house, not quite sure of what he was seeking. Most of Teddy's important papers were in a metal file cabinet in the spare bedroom he used as an office. Other papers, receipts, and cancelled checks were in a kitchen drawer. The suitcase in the upstairs linen closet provided old airline tickets and itineraries.

It was not Willy's proudest moment. He was invading the privacy of a dead friend, pawing through the remnants of his too-short life. Flipping through a box of photos, he came across a picture of Teddy and his ex-wife, Becky. They were both naked, save for party hats, and sat on either side of a birthday cake with a large 29 on top. The picture had obviously been intended only for themselves—they would have been mortified that anyone else had seen this silly corny moment—and Willy felt ashamed of himself for having intruded, but he was not going to let this discomfort, or anything else, deter him.

Surrounded by papers, Willy sat in the living room and pored over financial statements, checks, bills. He discovered that the taxes for Teddy's house were two thousand dollars, that in April of 1979, he charged $117.87 to his American Express account, that every year he donated money to the Williams College Alumni Association, the

American Cancer Society, and UNICEF. He also uncovered more than charitable contributions.

Willy had been wrong about Teddy's income. According to income tax returns, Teddy had netted nineteen thousand dollars in the first year of his law practice. While not a princely sum, it was certainly enough money in 1976 for a single man in Beacon to lead a comfortable life. And given that he had inherited the $83,147.33 in his trust fund the previous year, there would have been no reason to scrimp and save. Yet, Teddy had. He had made do with his decrepit Volkswagen until it no longer ran, and then he had bought Andy Brascia's car which was in almost as bad a shape. Why?

Teddy's income had increased every year, and with it, his spending. He had bought a slightly better used car in 1978. There was no sign of the money from his trust fund. Since Teddy did not spend this money on himself, Willy had assumed that he had invested it. Yet he showed no income from interest on those year's tax returns.

In 1980, Teddy had inherited the additional sum of $105,344, Janine's share of the trust fund plus accrued interest. Where this money had gone was evident. That year, Teddy made the down payment on his house, purchased art and furniture, invested in an expensive computer system at work. He bought a new Jeep Cherokee for cash. He had put the rest into a mutual fund and declared the dividends on his subsequent tax returns—but what had happened to the first sum he had inherited?

Willy searched through bank statements, credit card bills, cancelled checks. Everything seemed in order. Then in the metal file cabinet, he came across part of the answer. In a folder with a lot of miscellaneous papers, he found the receipt stub of a cashier's check from May, 1976. The check had been made out to cash for the sum of eighty-three thousand dollars.

The lurid word *blackmail* bubbled up into Willy's mind. That was incredible, he told himself, the stuff of movies. What had Teddy done with the eighty-three thousand dollars? Who had received it?

In the pocket of a suitcase, Willy found an envelope from a Poughkeepsie travel agency which contained an itinerary. In addition to his most recent visit, Teddy had also flown to Los Angeles a year ago. He had stayed a week.

Searching through the credit card statements, Willy found no record that Teddy had rented a car or stayed at a hotel on either trip. He did find a credit card charge, however, that aroused his interest. Midway through the week Teddy was supposed to be in Tijuana undergoing

Laetrile treatment, he had charged forty-one dollars to a Los Angeles drugstore.

Willy tore the paper clip from the neat pile of telephone bills and leafed through them. In the last year, only one call had been made to Los Angeles. Hurrying to the phone, Willy tapped out this number twice before realizing that Teddy's line had been disconnected.

After scrutinizing every paper he could find, he returned them to their original spots, all except the phone bill with the Los Angeles number, which went into his pocket. Willy had just finished putting away the suitcases in the upstairs linen closet when he heard a car pull into the driveway. He peeked out the hall window. Amanda was getting out of her car and giving his truck a bemused glance.

Willy raced down the stairs. Amanda was heading for the back. His first instinct was to flee out the front door, but, she had already seen his pickup, which was blocked by her Lincoln. What was he to do— run down the street like a thief? He forced himself to go into the kitchen to meet her.

Through a part in the curtains, Willy observed Amanda as she went to the deck, lifted a flower pot, and took something from beneath it. She had not seen him yet.

Though he had not thought out his actions, he opened the cabinet below the sink and wormed his way beneath it so that he faced the pipe and his legs rested on the kitchen floor. He heard the back door open.

"Willy?" Amanda's voice called out.

"Yeah," His reply sounded muffled. Willy pushed himself from beneath the sink and lay propped up on his elbows on the floor.

Amanda had a slightly indignant expression and held a single key in her hand. "How did you get in here?"

"The key beneath the flower pot. I was mowing the lawn, and I remembered Teddy saying that the sink leaked."

Her indignation melted away. "You already mowed the lawn?"

He rose to his feet. "Yes." Aware that the absence of any tools belied his foolish posturing, Willy nevertheless turned on the faucet and made a show of inspecting the pipe beneath. "I think I've fixed it."

"Willy . . . thank you," she said softly. "I appreciate what you've done. Teddy did too, very much. But, you don't have to keep at it."

"I know."

"We're selling the house. As soon as probate is over. There's already been an offer. We'll just let whoever buys it deal with the lawn and everything else."

Willy nodded.

"You've been great, Willy. You've gone out of your way to be kind and helpful; it's meant so much. But, maybe we should all get on with our lives."

She smiled gently. He tried to return her smile.

"I guess I have trouble letting go," Willy said, and realized it was the truth.

"We're sorry," the recorded voice said, "You have reached a number that has been disconnected or is no longer in service. If you feel you have reached this recording in error, please check the number and try your call again."

Willy looked down at Teddy's telephone bill as the message began to repeat. It was a 213 area code; Teddy had been on the phone for thirty-two minutes eleven months ago.

There was an 800 number to call for billing questions. He dialed the number and was connected with a long-distance operator. "Hi, my name is Teddy Smith," Willy said. "I was looking through my old telephone bills and came across an unfamiliar number I don't think I called." He read off Teddy's number and the number in Los Angeles, then was put on hold.

"It can't be this easy," Willy murmured aloud. It wasn't. The operator came back on the line.

"I'm sorry, but that number is unlisted. We're not allowed to give out any information with unlisted numbers."

"But it's now disconnected. Can't you tell me who it was listed to previously? After all, according to my bill, I called the number."

"I'm sorry, sir, but we're not allowed to give out any information. If you think that you were billed in error, I can have the charge credited to your account."

"That's okay. Thank you."

Willy tried two other operators at the 800 number and received the same response. Teddy's telephone bill lay on the counter in front of him. A ten-digit number might change his life forever, he thought. Then he wondered at his sanity. Why Teddy had called Los Angeles could be explained in any number of reasonable ways. Couldn't the call have been made to an art gallery that had a Imogene Cunningham photograph Teddy wanted to buy? Or he could have been chatting with an old friend from college, or listening to the account of a witness who had seen a client's traffic accident.

Somewhere, someone would be able to glance at that number and nonchalantly give Willy a name, an address. And then?

* * *

Emil Deshayes wheeled himself from the bedroom, which had formerly been his dining room, to the front door. Willy Buchanan was standing uneasily on the front porch. Earlier, when he had called and asked if he could come by, Willy had also seemed anxious.

"Come on in," Emil said and twirled his wheelchair around so Willy could enter.

Emil no longer had a hip socket on his right side.

Twenty-six months ago, Emil had gone to K-Mart, instead of an auto parts store, because oil was six cents cheaper there. If he hadn't wanted to save a measly twenty-four cents on his car's tune-up, he would be walking around today, doing the polka up and down his stairs if he felt like it. If he hadn't sped through a yellow light, or if he hadn't stopped to leaf through a copy of *Road and Track*, he would be prancing around nicely.

In the K-Mart, as he ambled from the magazine rack toward the automotive section, he heard a loud snap. Turning with mild curiosity toward the sound, he saw a large shelving unit piled high with merchandise, slowly collapsing in on itself and toward him. The image of falling dominoes had crossed his mind right before the impact. One of the shelves, which was propelled by the weight of the entire unit, jammed into his hip. He felt an excruciating pain; the force of the blow took his legs out from under him and sent him spinning in the air. His shoulder hit the floor first, and then his head, knocking him out. He regained consciousness in an ambulance, but was knocked out again, this time with anesthesia, a day later when he underwent the first of his operations.

The hip socket was shattered, the surgeon told him. They had had to do bone grafts, but everything looked fine, and he should be up on his feet in five, six months. Everything, however, had not been fine. The bone grafts did not take, and two other surgeries were performed. The bone became infected. And then again. Finally, they had to remove his hip entirely and replace it with a plastic hip. That too became infected.

As a last resort, the plastic hip was removed. The doctors decided that they would make absolutely certain that his infection was gone before performing another hip replacement. Which meant that, now, the bone in his right leg was not attached to anything.

It wasn't much of a war story. No high-speed car chases, or facing down perpetrators in dark alleys. *How did you get hurt?* people would ask. And he would have to reply that he had been attacked by a shelving unit at K-Mart.

Of course, he had not worked since the accident. Ron Antone had retired as chief of police the previous year and, as Emil had expected, Sam Pittman was named the new chief. Emil, bed-ridden, unable to walk, had not taken over as detective for Sam. Two promotions that he should have received had gone to others. As of now, he was still a member of the Beacon Police Department, but that status could very well change. One thing was certain. He was not going to be chief of police before he turned forty. The doctors had told him that even if all medical procedures went as planned, something which had not happened yet, he would not be walking for at least another year. That was a best case scenario. The last time he talked with Sam, retirement with a disability pension was brought up. Sam told Emil to think about it.

A lawsuit was pending. The K-Mart lawyers had agreed to pay all of his medical bills as well as a small stipend, so he had not had to remortgage his home. His lawyer, Fred Krause, assured Emil he would be getting a sizable settlement.

"And you deserve it, Emil," Fred Krause had said. "There's your physical pain and suffering, with the potential for medical problems for the rest of your life. You've suffered a disability. Mental anguish. Plus, loss of earnings, loss of career advancement. Loss of conjugality."

"What's that?" Emil had asked.

"The loss of the ability to have marital relations, sexual relations, with a spouse due to injuries. You don't have to be married, by the way. I mean, it's not only married men who have the expectation to have sexual relationships."

Emil had felt himself redden. His accident had not altered his sex life one iota. It was true that he had not had sex since his hip had been shattered. Chances were though, he would not have had sex in those two years even if in good health, at least if the two years previous to his injury were any kind of gauge.

"I mean, there's been a Sexual Revolution," Fred Krause had continued. "For young guys like you, getting laid isn't dependent on marriage."

Emil had grinned stupidly. The Sexual Revolution had had about as much impact on his love life as the French Revolution.

Willy followed Emil into the living room and sat down on the couch.

Emil knew his visit wasn't to wish him a speedy recovery. "You mentioned on the phone you had a favor to ask?"

"You're still a police officer, aren't you?"

"Yes, just barely, but yes."

"Would you be able to divorce yourself from your duties as a cop?"

"I don't know. Why don't you just tell me what you'd like me to do?"

242

"Would you be able to trace an unlisted phone number for me? Or tell me how to go about doing it on my own?"

It wasn't much of a favor, except in Willy's mind. And apparently for Willy, it was of major importance. Could it be about Janine Smith? Could she really be alive?

"Do you have a lead about Janine?"

Willy stared at him silently.

"Is this a local phone number?" Emil asked.

"No. It's an unlisted number in Los Angeles that was disconnected sometime in the last year."

"It wouldn't be very hard for me to find out who the number belonged to. The Los Angeles Police would have a full listing of all phone numbers. If I called them, they would give it to me. I might be able to get the number right away, but there is a chance that they would insist on sending the information to me care of the Beacon Police. Now, Lonnie Kroll and Sam Pittman might wonder what I was up to."

"You don't know anyone in the phone company?"

"No, I don't. There are official procedures about gathering information from the phone company. A lot of times, a court order is necessary. For something like this, it's usually easiest just to go directly through local police agencies or the FBI."

Willy nodded unhappily.

Emil said, "If you want, I'll make a call to Los Angeles right now. If we're lucky, you'll have the information you want in a few minutes. But if I have to go through channels, Lonnie and Sam might have some questions. I'll make up some story, but you never know what might happen."

Willy sighed and swore under his breath.

"There is another possibility. It's probable that your number is listed in a *Polk* or *Haines* reverse directory."

"What are they?"

"Phone directories that are listed according to number. Some are listed according to street address. The numerical directory lists phone numbers in order from the lowest to the highest. Even if a number is unlisted in the regular phone directory, most of them are in the *Polk*. So you might get lucky."

"Are they just for police departments?"

"No. They're mainly used for business. Telephone sales, bill collectors. A large library would have them. Around here, you might have to go to the Poughkeepsie library, maybe even New York City, but you can find them. If need be, you could always send away to the company and buy one."

Willy sat silently, staring off in the distance. Excitement and anticipation flashed in his eyes, but Emil also saw fear.

Standing up, Willy thanked Emil and left.

Half an hour later, after phoning six different towns and cities, Willy drove sixty miles to the main branch of the New York City Public Library on Forty-Second Street.

PART SEVEN

1983

ONE

She called herself Alison Lunsgaard. She had found the name in a cemetery—the real Alison had died in 1953 at the age of eight months. Our Beloved Daughter, Called to Heaven had been etched in the marble of the tiny tombstone.

Janine wrote down *Alison Lunsgaard* on the homemade application that the elderly woman, Mrs. Anglim, gave her. The name flowed easily from the pen and seemed natural after all these years. Indeed, Janine thought of herself as Alison most of the time, even in most of her dreams. The good ones anyway. In the nightmares, when she saw Spencer Lyle plunging the slashing, hacking knife into Susie's chest repeatedly, the dreams so real that she could almost smell the blood and the decay of the bayou, and could hear the animal noises and the grisly sucking sound as the knife was withdrawn from Susie's breast, in those dreams she thought of herself as Janine. But those nightmares, however, as well as the involuntary daytime memories of that night, had become less and less frequent.

The elderly woman looked at the application. "Alison. That's a pretty name."

"Thank you."

"Lunsgaard. Is that Norwegian?"

"Danish," Janine said, though she wasn't sure. She had once said her family name was Danish when a former co-worker, a fellow waitress, had asked. This nice older woman renting out her guest house and the waitress who, stoned on Quaaludes, had spent most of her time dropping plates and mixing up orders would probably never meet and compare stories. Still, Janine knew that her precarious existence depended on her being consistent. And so for both women, and for anyone else who might ask, her family had originally come from Denmark.

Janine had become Alison in 1975 after two years on the run and shortly after arriving in California. Exhausted, lonely, despairing, she had gone to the cemetery to look for a new identity. The sad little tombstone had an angel on it. Janine had repeated the name to herself. She liked the sound of Alison Lunsgaard, it would be appropriate for her fair blond appearance, and their birth dates were only six months apart. Before leaving the graveyard, she had surprised herself by uttering a short prayer for the baby's soul.

In order to obtain a copy of a birth certificate in Los Angeles County, a name, date and city of birth, and parents' names, including the mother's maiden name were necessary. Janine had gone to the Hollywood Public Library on Ivar Avenue one rainy afternoon and pored over microfilm copies of the *Los Angeles Times*. She had not been able to find any birth announcement for Alison, but four days after her death, a paid obituary for the "beloved daughter of Hilmer and Mary Trahane Lunsgaard" had appeared.

Along with a money order, Janine sent in the request for a duplicate birth certificate to be mailed to the post office box she had rented in Hollywood. Every day for two weeks, she would approach the post office with trepidation, certain that Postal Inspectors or police officers would slap handcuffs on her the moment she opened her mailbox. Of course, nothing had happened on the day she saw the official-looking envelope in her slot. From that moment, she had become Alison.

With the birth certificate, Janine was able to apply for a social security card. She prepared a detailed scenario—her parents were wealthy, and then her fiancé had not wanted her to work—for the inevitable day when a federal government worker called to ask why she had waited until the age of twenty-three to get a social security number. No one, of course, had inquired. Her crisp new card had arrived in the mail without incident.

Then, the most nerve-racking of all, she had gone to the Department of Motor Vehicles and applied for a driver's license. Just as when she was a teenager, Janine had to take the driving test, but her fear and anxiety had nothing to do with three-point-turns or parallel parking. She was so pale and apprehensive during the test in the rented driving school car, that the DMV instructor dropped his impassive manner and encouraged and praised her driving performance. He did not arrest her, or call her a liar and a fraud.

"If I should rent to you," Mrs. Anglim said, "I would want first and last month, plus a security deposit."

"That would be fine. I really love this place."

Though the rooms were spacious, sunny, charming, those were not the qualities that attracted Janine. The guest house was hidden. Coming up the canyon road in response to Mrs. Anglim's advertisement, Janine had driven by the main house twice even though she had been given explicit directions. Mrs. Anglim's stucco home was concealed behind bougainvillaea, eucalyptus, and a thick hedge of bamboo. Even walking up the drive when she finally found her way, Janine had not been able to see the guest house, which was located behind the main house and on a lower tier. It was a little cottage in a glen—the description sounded like a fairy tale and made her feel safe. No one from her past life would happen to walk by this house. Unlike apartment complexes, there would be no constant coming and going of tenants and visitors, any one of whom might one day cry out, "Hey, I know you. You're Janine Smith."

"It is lovely, isn't it?" Mrs Anglim said. "When my husband was alive, we just used it for guests, and he liked to paint out here after he retired. But now . . ."

"It's exactly what I'm looking for. I can give you a check right now, or if you'd rather, I'll call back."

She laughed in confusion. "I'm not really sure what I'm supposed to do. This is the first time I've ever rented out the little house."

"Well, you should probably take my application and a few others, then decide which is the best."

Mrs. Anglim nodded and said, "Why go to the bother? I was hoping that a nice young woman would live here, and you look to be just that person."

Janine wrote out the check. As she took it, Mrs. Anglim noticed the jagged scar on Janine's palm. "Ooh. That must have hurt."

"I fell through a window," Janine said, instead of telling Mrs. Anglim the truth. She did not say that ten years ago, in a bayou outside of New Orleans, Spencer Lyle had tried to kill her, and that she had brought up her hand to ward off the blow of the eight-inch Henckels chef's knife.

Janine screamed and put up her hand. She felt the searing pain as the blade cut into the meaty part of her palm.

"You fucking cunt."

Spencer Lyle grabbed the front of her sweater and jerked her toward him. The knife was raised again, and Janine knew that he was going to kill her. Shrieking, she lashed out and felt her finger, almost against her will, jab into the wet softness of Spencer's eye. He howled in pain, and Janine was certain that she had assured her death, but miraculously he loosened his grip. Breaking free, she ran blindly into the dark.

She ran over the soft ground and through the undergrowth, her lungs burning. Crashing through thick brush, she hit a low branch and was knocked to the ground. The sound of her own heavy breathing seemed to roar throughout the bayou.

Janine lay there afraid to move. Her hand was bleeding badly. Then she heard him.

Spencer was smashing wildly through the thicket, looking for her. She forced herself to stop crying. If he found her, he would kill her. The crashing sounds grew louder until they were almost on top of her. Turning her head away, she closed her eyes and silently repeated, "Please God, no. Please God, no."

"Shit," she heard Spencer mutter, then the footsteps headed away from her.

Janine dared not move. After a while, his yelling echoed in the distance. "I'm not going to hurt you. Come on out." Later, she heard, "I know who you are. Janine Ann Smith. You live on West Willow Street. Beacon, New York." Spencer was back at Susie's car, going through Janine's purse. "I can find you any time I want. Come on out. I'm not going to hurt you."

Though she didn't believe what he said, Janine nearly went to him. Then she heard, "You fucking bitch. If you go to the cops, I'll kill you. I know where you fucking live. I know who you are. I swear to God I'll kill you."

The door to Susie's car slammed. Janine heard it start and drive down the dirt road. In shock, she sat up, took off her sweater, and pressed it to her bleeding hand. A while later, Susie's car raced back down the dirt road. Headlights slashed paths of light across the bayou, then Spencer drove away for the second time.

Janine remained hidden, shivering from the cold and fear. Horror and nausea came on her in waves. Susie was dead, she was *really* dead. This incomprehensible madness, this hideous nightmare had happened. The image of the knife hacking away at Susie's breast assaulted her, and she leaned to her side and was violently ill.

Later, she drew back the yellow sweater from her hand and saw that the ugly red gash had stopped bleeding. Throwing the bloody sweater away, she climbed up onto the dirt road.

She started to walk, numb and in shock, and only by chance went in the right direction. It was so dark, and there was so little traffic that Janine didn't notice the paved road until she was almost on top of it.

Hiding on the side of the highway, Janine watched as the first few cars drove by. With every set of headlights in the distance, she tried to build up her courage to get up and flag the car down, or at least stick out her thumb, but she couldn't bring herself to stand in the glare of the lights. The cars whizzed by.

At last, she just stepped onto the pavement and began to walk. Janine heard someone driving up behind her. Fighting back an urge to flee, she continued down the road. A pickup truck raced past her. Two more cars sped by as she strode down the blacktop. She had no idea why she was walking or to where. Then a car slowed behind her.

Janine turned in fright. From the car's boxy outline, she could tell it was a station wagon, not Spencer come back to kill her. Headlights illuminated her in their ghostly beam, revealing her torn, dirty, blood-stained dress, her wild hair, her muddy feet. The station wagon, which leaned at a strange angle, pulled up beside her, and a power window was lowered.

"Y'all okay?"

By the eerie blue light of the radio, Janine could just make out this man's gross features. He was immense; his body seemed to engulf the steering wheel, and his obesity was the cause of the car's listing. He had an overly trimmed beard and was dressed bizarrely, but his voice was gentle and reassuring.

"Darlin', you okay?" the man asked.

"No," Janine said.

The man turned on the dome light of the station wagon. Janine saw that the strange clothes were actually a mixture of Mardi Gras costume and everyday dress. He was still wearing extravagant rhinestone ear-rings. "Can I give you a lift?"

"Yes," she said and got into the car.

She could smell that he had been drinking and that he wore too much cologne. "You look like you've had some trouble. You want me to drive you to a hospital?"

"No!" Janine cried more sharply than she had intended.

"Okay," he said in a placating voice, then added, "Where would you like me to take you?"

"I don't know." Janine turned her head away and softly began to cry.

"Well, why don't I just drive a ways."

They drove in silence for a while, then he said, "Is it because you don't have insurance or no money? Is that why you don't want to go to a hospital?"

"No."

After a few miles, the man slowed the car and stopped before the entrance to the interstate highway. Janine must have looked panic-stricken, because he held up his hand in a pacifying motion.

"I'm getting on here. I'm headed to Texas."

"Can't you take me with you?" Janine felt terrified at the prospect of going back out into the night. Chaos lay out there. She just wanted to put herself into the care of this person, to float along in this warm, soft seat.

"To Texas?"

"Yes."

He looked confused. Light from a street lamp glared down, and Janine noticed that he had mascara smudges around his sad eyes. "It's a few hundred miles. You need to get looked after. I can see you shivering from over here." He studied her a moment, "Don't you have any belongings or clothes?"

"Please." Her tone was pleading, but she didn't care. Just hours ago, she would never have thought to impose on a stranger's kindness. Now, she knew she would beg, she would cry.

Still confused, he nodded. His arm swung toward her, and Janine gasped and shrank back. He froze, then slowly reached into the rear seat and handed her an enormous toggle coat. "Here, wrap yourself up in this."

The car pulled forward and drove onto the interstate. Staring straight ahead, he softly asked, "What's your name?"

"Patty Chisolm," replied Janine, and it was at this moment she realized she wasn't going back.

His name was Chrisbo Gavry, and much later Janine was to think that if he hadn't picked her up, things probably would have turned out differently.

"My real name is Chris, but when I was little, the movie, *Dumbo*, came out. Well, my aunt and Momma and everyone said that my tubby little self looked just like that baby elephant, so they started to call me Chrisbo. That's how I got my name. And it just stuck. Lord! Imagine naming someone after a baby elephant. No wonder I turned out the way I did."

Day was beginning to break and outside a sign welcoming them to

Texas appeared to flash by. Chrisbo had been listening to a talk show on the radio, but he turned the dial until he came to an easy-listening station. Janine sensed that he had tuned in Mantovani for her sake, hoping that the music would soothe her. He would speak occasionally, innocuous comments about himself, how he had enjoyed Mardi Gras, and happened to be out in the bayou in the middle of nowhere because he had given a ride to a friend, actually someone he had just met who wasn't really a friend, who had probably just hung around with Chrisbo for free drinks. This friend had his good qualities, though, even if he did use people a bit.

Janine listened more to his kindly, solicitous tone than to his actual words. She tried to fill herself with the rhythm of the moving car, the warm air from the heater caressing her, the dull scenery outside. If she could concentrate on all these unimportant details, perhaps soon she would be able to think of nothing at all.

But then Chrisbo asked, "What happened to you?" He quickly added, "If you don't want to talk about it, just . . ."

"My fiancé beat me up. We got into a fight. He'll kill me if he finds me," she lied.

"That's a bad wound on your hand."

"He cut me," she said, startled by her trashy, melodramatic voice. Her words reminded Janine of Willy, and she was filled with shame.

Later, Chrisbo steered the station wagon off of the interstate. The town Janine found herself in was small, flat, boring. A rusty water tower rose above forlorn-looking buildings.

They pulled into a drive-in restaurant that had once been part of a franchise but was now called Tina's and Phil's. Chrisbo drove up to a window, and a middle-aged woman with lacquered gray hair slid back the glass.

" 'Morning. You look like you had yourself a time in New Orleans."

Chrisbo smiled broadly and waggled the rhinestone earrings with his fingers. "Absolutely wicked."

"What can I get you?"

"How about sausage and eggs, biscuits and gravy, and pancakes and bacon?"

Janine thought he was ordering for her as well and was about to protest, when Chrisbo turned and asked, "What would you like?"

"Nothing, thanks."

"It's my treat. Come on, you should eat something."

"I really couldn't." She felt the woman's inquisitive stare from the drive-in window and wanted to pull the toggle coat up over her head and hide.

Chrisbo ordered a few sweet rolls, "just in case."

While they waited for the food, Chrisbo took off the earrings and said, "Back to reality." When the waitress handed out the breakfasts in foil-wrapped containers, she never took her eyes off Janine.

Without asking, Chrisbo drove down a side street, turned on another, and pulled up in front of a small, one-story, white clapboard house which rested on cinder block pilings. Janine suddenly realized she would have to get out of the car. She had not allowed herself to consider what would happen next. She had no money, and wasn't sure where she was or what she would do. Desperately, Janine hoped he would ask her into his house. Surely, if he knew that she had nowhere else to go, that she wouldn't get in his way, that she wouldn't—

He opened the car door and heaved himself out. Janine trembled and momentarily considered locking the door behind him and just staying in the car. Forever. She peeled away the toggle coat and got out.

Standing in the open, he appeared to be even larger—four hundred, perhaps five hundred pounds. His belly hung to midthigh and with every little movement, his body seem to shimmy independently, as if separate warring creatures resided beneath his clothes. He started for the house, but when he stopped and turned back to her, his stomach followed a beat later and continued further in its arc than the rest of his body.

"Thanks for the ride. And everything." Janine resisted the impulse to plead with him.

Chrisbo hesitated a moment before saying, "You want me to look at your hand? I've got a first-aid kit and bandages . . . I've got an extra bedroom if you need that for a day or two."

Overwhelmed with gratitude, yet also abashed, she nodded, feeling the tears trickle down her cheeks.

Inside the house, Chrisbo cleaned the gash in her palm with peroxide over the bathroom sink. The cut began to bleed again, and Chrisbo wanted to take her to the hospital, but finally it stopped. She sat on the edge of the tub and let him wrap bandages and tape around her hand. Chrisbo went to the medicine cabinet and glanced at her nervously.

"I've got some pills that might help you sleep. Some Valium."

Janine thought she might cry again. She had never before felt such a craving for any drug. "Yes, please."

He handed her the brown plastic vial. Janine opened the cap and a dozen, blue 10 mg Valium spilled out into her hand next to the bandage. She greedily took one, then knowing she was abusing his generosity, afraid that he might think her grasping, out of control, selfish, but unable to care or stop herself, took another.

She went into the small, second bedroom with its frilly white bed-clothes, and getting up once in the night to take two more Valium, slept fitfully for the next twenty hours.

When she awoke, the horrifying, impossible facts had not changed. Janine rose from bed and pulled on her soiled dress. Chrisbo was just getting ready to go to work. Halfheartedly, she told him that she probably should be leaving.

"Do you have anyplace to go?"

Shaking her head, Janine suddenly realized that her fate, possibly her life, depended on this stranger's compassion.

Chrisbo looked at her shyly and said. "Well, why don't you stay a few more days."

Before leaving for work, Chrisbo changed the bandage on her hand and gave her the bottle of Valium. Then, he waddled out of the front door, leaving a complete stranger, a woman he had picked up, bleeding and disheveled on the side of the road, alone in his house.

Janine sat on a satin-covered, ornate Victorian sofa, holding onto the bottle of Valium. Though she didn't take any, she felt reassured just having them. The house was a curious mixture of the run-down and the piss-elegant. It was crammed with knickknacks, gilt, ormolu, doilies, tassels, heavy, red-velvet drapes, which Janine assumed were the fur-nishings of a fussy, old lady, things left over from his mother perhaps. But later, Chrisbo boasted that most of the decoration was his own. Dust, however, lay thick on the tables, lint covered the threadbare carpet, the kitchen sink was filled with dirty dishes. Idly, she toyed with the fantasy of never leaving this house.

She found a bucket and rubber gloves beneath the kitchen sink. Hoping to repay Chrisbo for his kindness, and with the timorous, servile wish to prolong her stay by making herself useful, Janine scrubbed the kitchen floor, washed the dishes, vacuumed, dusted. Though her hand throbbed, and the bandage became soaked and started to seep blood, she continued working. Not until late afternoon, when she was nearly done cleaning the bathroom mirror, did Janine think of Susie.

She screamed.

Janine stayed with Chrisbo for six weeks. The first night, when he came back from his job as a telephone dispatcher, she had prepared a supper and a story to explain what had happened to her.

For dinner she roasted a chicken she found defrosting in the refriger-ator and made large bowls of mashed potatoes and string beans. Even considering his enormous size, she thought there was far too much food, and plenty would be left over. Chrisbo, however, looked at everything in the oven and quickly mixed up a huge pan of corn bread.

As they dined, Janine sensed he was accustomed to eating alone and that her presence at the table made him uncomfortably aware of his own gluttony. Terrified of offending him, Janine spooned food onto his plate like a grandmother at Thanksgiving, urging him to have a bit more, hoping to create the pretense that his hoggish gorging was just a polite response to her entreaties.

He gobbled down everything, except for Janine's small portion, which was less than she had planned on eating. When Chrisbo was finishing the last of the chicken and corn bread, Janine saw his sheepish, uneasy expression return. She quickly asked what was for dessert, and he happily took out a quart of butter pecan ice cream and scooped the better part of it into a soup bowl for himself.

All through the meal, no mention was made of what had brought Janine to be wandering—bleeding, alone, in just a light dress, with no money—on a dark road in the middle of nowhere. No mention was made of her knife wound, her sobbing, or her behavior, which must have seemed demented.

As he devoured the ice cream, she said, "I suppose you're wondering how it came to pass that you have a stranger in your house?"

She was running away from a violent, jealous fiancé, Janine told him. After months of abuse—being dragged around by her hair and punched, jealous rages, beatings—she had finally tried to call off the engagement. This had provoked an insane fury, and he had tried to stab her. "He's obsessed with me. If I go back, he really will kill me. I'm certain of it."

"What about your folks?"

"My father died a few years ago. He was all the family I had."

He nodded sympathetically. "My Momma died five years ago. I still miss her."

"I had to get away. If it wasn't for you, I don't know what would have happened."

"But what about . . . everything? Your clothes, your belongings, your job?"

"We had moved into an apartment together. I didn't have much, but what I did have is still there. It doesn't matter. I would have died."

"Wouldn't the police help? Couldn't you get a court order or something?"

"The police can't watch you twenty-four hours a day."

He nodded solemnly. Janine didn't know if he truly believed anything she said, but her lies seemed to satisfy him.

Janine insisted on cleaning up. When she came back into the living room, Chrisbo was dressed in a caftan that resembled a tent. Two glasses and a bottle of whiskey rested on the ornate gilt-edged table beside his sagging overstuffed chair.

They spent the night, as apparently Chrisbo spent all of his nights, drinking and watching television. He liked to watch old movies, or glitzy variety and talk shows, and was entranced by the costumes. A buxom television star was on the Merv Griffin show wearing an atrocious, spangly gown, and Chrisbo gasped and exclaimed, "Isn't that the most gorgeous thing you have ever in your whole life seen?" Janine was unsure if he meant the dress or the actress until he added cattily, "You would look much better in it than she does."

Slowly, Janine became less cautious with him, less desperately eager to please. And with time, Chrisbo revealed much about his own sad and lonely life in this dreary Texas town.

"I am such an oddity here. I guess I probably would be a freak just about anywhere. It's not just because I'm so fat. For most of the folks around here, my mind, my personality, my desires are all a lot stranger than my physical appearance."

His father had left before he was born, and he had been exceptionally close with his mother. Chrisbo's childhood had been lonely. He had weighed one hundred and fifty pounds before he was ten. "In the ninth grade, I couldn't fit in a regular desk. I had to sit alone at a table in the back of the room. Being a three-hundred-pound, thirteen-year-old sissy in a Texas town, you get used to being alone."

Chrisbo wanted to know everything about Janine; what her life had been like growing up. "You must have been popular. You must have had more boyfriends than you knew what to do with." Yet his questions had a plaintive quality, and Janine sensed that he wanted to hear tales of an adolescence that was the opposite of his own. So she obliged him, hoping to repay his generosity in any way she could.

At first, Janine was guarded about what she told him. She nearly let slip a mention of her brother, Teddy, though earlier she had claimed to have no family. And she had to be careful that the landscape of the small town on the New Jersey shore where she purported to come from did not acquire Beacon's mountains and river. Janine did tell him of proms she had never attended, and detailed descriptions of gowns and corsages she had never worn to them. "I just know you were a cheerleader," Chrisbo remarked, so she became one. She dated the quarterback of the football team, which in fact she had done, but the only similarity between Eric Boyd and this fantasy dreamboat was their physical beauty. It was like telling a child a bedtime story: the tale grew, Chrisbo came to know it better than Janine, and it fulfilled a need in both of them.

Though she felt that every moment she spent in the safe cocoon of Chrisbo's house was an imposition, he asked if she would like to stay on longer. "I'd love to have you," he urged. "I enjoy your company."

Janine couldn't believe that anyone would find her good company. She felt zombielike, as if she were in some weird anesthetized state in which all but the most primal emotions of terror and survival had been expunged.

Chrisbo went to work every day, but Janine did not leave the house for the first four days. On the fifth morning, she woke up with the familiar heavy, bloated sensations of the onset of her period. After looking through Chrisbo's medicine cabinet to no avail, she realized she would have to leave the house and go to a drugstore.

Janine sat down on the edge of the tub, humiliated. She had no money, just one dress; she was unable to take care of even the most basic of her needs without the help of a man who, although kind, she felt compelled to deceive.

While cleaning the house, Janine had noticed a small glass piggy bank half filled with change—"pin money" Chrisbo would probably call it. The only opening in the piggy bank was the wide slot on its back. Shaking the bank upside down like a sneaky child, she rattled nickels and dimes onto the counter top. Momentarily, Janine thought of using a butter knife to jiggle the coins though the slot, but quickly repressed the image of a knife plunging into a body. When enough change had dropped out, she wrote an IOU for two dollars and stuck it in the slot.

The few people she met on the drab Main Street of the town all seemed to give her suspicious glances. In the drugstore, she felt as self-conscious as she had at thirteen.

On the way back from the drugstore, Janine spotted a HELP WANTED sign behind the plate glass front of a Dairy Queen. Impulsively, she went to the sliding screen Order Here window.

"Hi," said the man with long sideburns and slicked-back hair.

"Do you still have a job available?"

The man gave her a puzzled look. "Uh . . . yeah. Do you live around here?"

"Yes."

"You do? Jeez, I thought I knew everyone in town."

"I'm staying with my cousin. Chrisbo Gavry."

"Oh," the man replied coolly.

"So is the job still available?"

"Well, yeah. You have any experience?"

"I've worked as a waitress."

He hesitated, then said, "Let me get you an application."

Janine sat at a pink metal picnic table that was smeared with syrupy red stains and filled out the application. Every line was a challenge. What was her name? Patty Chisolm? Where did she live, what was her phone number? Not only did she not know what street Chrisbo lived on, but she didn't even know the name of this town. For social security number, she put down the first three digits of her own, then made up the rest. She also made up three waitressing jobs in imaginary restaurants in Pittsburgh, Pennsylvania, a city where she had never been. The application was only half filled when she returned to the order window.

The man perused the form. "You didn't put down any address."

"I forgot Chrisbo's address. Just put care of him."

"Same with the telephone?" he asked dubiously.

"Yes."

He gave the application a suspicious stare. "Okay, I'll put you on file."

That night, Janine told Chrisbo about applying for the job at Dairy Queen.

"Did you talk with Wesley?"

"I don't know."

"A sleazy-looking guy with a rat face?"

"He wasn't that bad. I told him you were my cousin."

"Your cousin?" he beamed proudly. "I wish we were cousins. But unless you said you were adopted, or my family stole you out of some cradle, no one in this town is going to believe it."

"You don't mind I told him that?"

"Not at all, but it's not going to do you any good. He hates my guts. You can kiss that job goodbye."

The next day, however, Wesley called and said she could come to work that afternoon if she wanted.

Wearing her only dress, Janine went to the Dairy Queen. Wesley handed her a polyester uniform that was two sizes too large, told her to change in the storeroom, then showed her how to work the cash register and the ice cream machine.

While Wesley worked the grill, Janine made ice cream cones, handed out Buster Bars, poured Cokes. Every time she went to the register, Wesley would crane around to make sure she rang up the correct amount. Twice, he came over from the grill and insisted that

Janine had undercharged the customer. Twice, Janine calmly displayed her order book and added up the figures in front of him. When a gangly boy ordered a banana split, Wesley took over and made it because he wasn't sure if she could "handle it yet."

Apparently, Wesley was sufficiently pleased with her work, because at closing time, he gave her another polyester uniform and told her to come to work the next day. By the end of the week, Wesley began leaving her alone in the Dairy Queen for most of her shift.

The Friday after she began working, Wesley handed Janine her first paycheck. "You know, you never even asked me what your salary would be."

"Is it more than minimum wage?"

"Well, no."

"Then why ask?"

She cashed the check in the register and bought a gargantuan butterscotch sundae to bring home to Chrisbo.

The job at Dairy Queen was so simple that it quickly became routine. After just four weeks, however, Wesley came up to her holding an envelope. "Patty, I just got a letter from Social Security. There's a problem with your number."

Janine put on a puzzled frown. "How can that be?"

"I don't know." He handed her the form.

She glanced at the made-up social security number which she would not have been able to remember, then said, "They've transposed the last four digits. It should be 7238, not 7328."

"Well, fill it in the way it's supposed to be."

She changed the bogus number and handed the form back to Wesley. Though she thought of fleeing that night, she forced herself to continue on at the Dairy Queen for one more paycheck, figuring that the discrepancy of the numbers would not be noted for that long.

On the morning of her last payday, she told Wesley a family emergency had arisen; she would have to quit her job. Wesley's resigned frown said that Janine wasn't the first flaky helper to quit, nor would she be the last. He kept careful watch whenever she went to the cash register and made sure to count the day's take before allowing her to cash her check. As usual, she bought a butterscotch sundae to bring home to Chrisbo.

He was already dressed in a caftan and sipping on a beer when Janine arrived. She put the sundae in the freezer, then came back to the living room. Chrisbo was staring at her warily.

"You don't have your uniform on."

"No, I quit. I . . . I have to go."

Chrisbo nodded. "The minute I saw you in your dress, I knew you'd be leaving."

"I wish I could stay. I really do. But something came up."

"What?"

"I can't tell you."

"Is it your fiancé? I know the sheriff here. I can make sure he—"

"It has nothing to do with that."

He nodded again. "When are you leaving?"

"I checked at the bus station. There's a bus at seven-forty."

Chrisbo looked startled, then softly said, "I'll miss you."

It only took a few minutes to gather up her toiletries and the two changes of clothing she had bought at the Five and Dime and put them in a paper grocery bag.

Chrisbo's brave smile contrasted with his sad glistening eyes. Janine walked up behind where he sat on the huge, battered, reinforced chair and put her arms around his neck. She pressed her cheek to his.

"I've thanked you before, but it's never been enough. You are the kindest, the most generous. . . I'll remember you for the rest of my life."

She kissed his cheek.

"I wish you could stay."

"I know." She stroked his hair, "Good-bye."

Janine picked up the grocery bag and walked out the door.

As she marched the ten blocks to the bus station through the dark night, Janine tried to keep her fear at bay. How would she survive? Where would she go? She owned three sets of clothing, and had only managed to save ninety-seven dollars.

In addition to the cashier, an elderly couple and a young man in an army uniform were waiting for the bus to Houston. Janine bought a ticket. It cost eight dollars, leaving her with less than ninety dollars with which to find a place to stay, to eat, to live. Panic swept over her.

She waited on a bench off by herself. A pay phone stood across the grimy depot. She stared at it, and the dull, black metal box seemed to beckon to her. Though she would look away, her gaze kept returning to the phone.

Taking a ten-dollar bill from her pocket—she didn't even have a purse or a wallet—she went to the cashier and asked for five dollars in change. The pay phone seemed foreboding, yet also her salvation, as she approached it.

After putting in the additional two dollars and forty cents, she could hear the tone of a phone ringing, and then Willy's voice came on the line. "Hello."

His voice was so familiar, so comforting. She imagined going to him, being held in his arms. "Hello?" Willy's voice called to her again. She almost spoke, but then hung up the phone.

Willy had sounded the same. She could almost see him standing in the kitchen, *their* kitchen. It would be warm there. Secure. Home.

Janine dialed the number again, and deposited quarter after quarter in the slot. She had just enough change. Again, she heard the sweet sound of Willy's voice. "Hello."

Though she knew it was foolish, she closed her eyes and hoped he would start talking to her. "Hello," Willy repeated hesitantly. He had been hurt so much by her, she had caused him so much pain and heartache. She replaced the receiver in its cradle and leaned her forehead against the cold, coarse metal of the pay phone.

Later, Janine went back to the cashier and had her change five more dollars into coins. Although the cashier was sitting idle at her window, she appeared put out by Janine's presumptuous request that she do her job and perform the weighty, oppressive task of counting out change.

Janine went back and forth to the pay phone three times before finally making the call. The operator came on again, demanding two dollars and forty cents more. With each ringing sound of a coin dropping down the slot, Janine felt an increasing despair. She knew she would not be able to bring herself to speak.

Willy's voice carried across the thousand miles. "Hello."

There was a pause, and Janine heard static, not his voice speaking softly to her. And then she heard, "Janine?"

She pressed down the cradle; she didn't think Willy had heard her gasp.

Janine made one last call. Just when she was about to hang up, the familiar voice came on the line and said, "Hello."

"Teddy, this is Janine," she said.

TWO

JANINE MOVED INTO Mrs. Anglim's guest house the day after writing the check. Two guys in her apartment building were in a band and had a cube van which they used to haul their equipment. She paid them fifty dollars each to help her move. In less than an hour, her studio apartment was empty, and her plain, functional furniture loaded onto the truck which the musicians had defaced with shakily spray-painted quotes from William Burroughs and Henry Miller as well as bright yellow happy faces.

One of the musicians—the first time Janine had ever spoken to either of them was when she had asked if they would be interested in making a little extra money—dropped a lamp that shattered on the sidewalk. Chagrined, he glanced up from the broken porcelain and said, "I'll pay for that. You can take it out of my fifty bucks."

"Okay, now I only owe you $49.90."

She had not allowed herself to buy nice things. If she had to flee in the middle of the night, Janine would not miss the Formica kitchen table, the particle-board bookcase, the thrift-store rocking chair.

When they had brought out the last container, Janine stood in the drywall box that had been her home for a year and a half. It was as if she had never been here. No trace of her remained. None of her neighbors, from whom she had kept herself aloof, would miss her.

Living in the large, impersonal apartment building had been a mistake. Indeed, she had felt so exposed, so uneasy there, instead of anonymous as she had hoped, that she had given notice at the beginning of the month even before discovering Mrs. Anglim's guest house. People were always moving in and out, tenants and visitors constantly teemed about the apartments. Just going out her front door, down the elevator, past the pool, and through the vestibule had seemed like running a gantlet.

A few months ago, as she was leaving for her job as an attendant in a nursing home, a man had given her obvious and curious stares before finally speaking up.

"You look just like someone I went to school with."

Janine had studied the man's face, panic-stricken, trying to recognize him as someone from Colgate or Beacon High. Then the man had added, "You didn't go to McCluer High School by any chance, did you?"

"No."

"God, you look just like my friend."

He had continued to chat, and though Janine surmised that the man was trying to pick her up, and there probably wasn't any friend who looked just like her, she bolted out of the elevator the moment the doors opened, leaving him in midsentence.

Janine locked the front door to the apartment and dropped off the key with the superintendent. Then, as she had done so many other times in the last ten years, she simply walked away.

After Janine left Chrisbo's little town, she went to Houston. On the bus trip there, she kept recalling the long-distance phone conversation with Teddy. He had been shocked to hear her voice, and then relieved and jubilant. "Janine! My God, you're alive. Everybody's been . . . I was so afraid."

Teddy's joy was short-lived. Janine had had to argue and plead and finally scream hysterically before Teddy promised not to tell anyone else that he had heard from her. It was the harshest conversation they had ever had, but he had reluctantly agreed.

"Is Susie with you?" Teddy had asked.

"Susie is dead."

"Janine, Jesus Christ! What is going on?"

It was not until much later that she was able to tell him.

The bus arrived in Houston a little after midnight. Leaving the station, two different pimps accosted her. Outside, hoping to get away from the frightening and squalid neighborhood, she hopped on the first local city bus that stopped. Janine got off at a safe-looking area and began roaming the streets until she came upon a hospital. Nervously, she entered. No one questioned her or demanded that she leave, so she spent the rest of the night in the bustling emergency waiting room and even managed a light nap in a plastic molded chair. At dawn, she forced herself to leave and roved the streets again. Finally, she got on another city bus. Sitting directly behind the driver, she gazed out the streaked windows at unfamiliar streets, feeling hopeless, desolate, and more alone than she had ever been before.

By chance, the bus drove by Rice University and Janine got off at that stop. Wandering through the campus, she followed some students into the Student Center and discovered a small alcove with chairs and couches. She lay down on one and slept for a few hours.

After she awoke, Janine made her way to the student housing office. Listings for apartments and roommates were posted on a bulletin board, though most of the notices looked to have been there since the previous autumn. All but four of the listings were either too expensive, too restrictive—*lease, references*—or simply out of the question—*Hi! Are you looking for someone to share an apartment??? Are you looking for a friend, someone to share confidences with as well as expenses* . . . What she sought was a rooming house. Spartan, cell-like rooms, presided over by an elderly landlady who asked only that the weekly rent be paid on time. Did such places still exist? Borrowing a pen from a muscular jock in a too tight T-shirt, she jotted down the only phone numbers that couldn't be excluded out of hand.

Two of the rooms were already rented, Janine found out, and no one answered at the third number she called. The fourth listing, which had only stated ROOM FOR RENT and a phone number, was still available. A woman with an indefinable accent gave her the address over the phone.

The athletic student from whom she had borrowed the pen told her how to find the address, the muscles of his arm rippling ostentatiously as he pointed in the direction of alien streets and landmarks.

Then, in about fifteen minutes, her life fell into place. On the streets outside the campus, she went past stores, bars, restaurants. One shop's plate glass window displayed the word LOANS in gold letters. Janine trudged past the store for fifty yards before it registered that the place was a pawn shop. She turned and headed back.

The pawnbroker, a large, florid man, examined the engagement ring that Willy had given her, and said, "Three hundred dollars." It was that simple. Janine filled in Patty Chisolm's name on the ticket and gave a post office box at Rice University as her address. She left the pawnbroker's with the three hundred dollars, a fourth of what Willy had spent on the ring, and for the first time since leaving Chrisbo's, she thought she might survive on her own.

The rooming house was actually a single family home with an extra bedroom in the attic. A middle-aged woman dressed in a sari answered the door and offered to show her the room with what seemed an air of apology.

Indian music played in the back, and the smell of curry permeated the house as the landlady led her up two flights of stairs to the attic. Janine could understand why the room was still available. It was tiny, containing a metal frame foldaway bed covered with a worn chenille bedspread, a scarred table, and a Naugahyde chair. There were two doors, the entrance and a closet, neither of which could be opened fully without hitting a piece of furniture. Janine would have to share a bathroom with the woman's family on the floor below. During the humid sweltering heat of the summer, this attic bedroom would be unbearable.

"How much?"

"I am asking fifteen dollars," replied the landlady in a singsong voice.

"A week?"

"Oh, yes." The landlady surveyed the room, seeking to find some feature to extol. Finally, she added with not much conviction, "I wash the bedding every week."

"How soon could I move in?"

"Immediately," the landlady said, giving the paper bag containing all Janine's possessions a suspicious look.

After handing over fifteen dollars, and making up a previous address and next of kin for Patty Chisolm, Janine found herself with a place to stay. The landlady, Mrs. Nanji, went downstairs and came back with a set of keys. As Mrs. Nanji left with an uneasy backward glance, Janine locked the door, shutting out the rest of the world.

She would no longer have to roam the streets! She would not sleep in waiting rooms, or on couches, or have to seek warmth and safety at night. Janine lay down on the bed and covered herself with the chenille bedspread. She was safe here. Though it was less than twenty-four hours since she had left Chrisbo's, that time had been agonizing, lonesome, oppressive. Not knowing what she would do, where she would stay, had overwhelmed her with dread.

But, now . . . If she allowed herself five dollars a day for food—surely she could survive on that amount, possibly even less—she could get by on . . . fifty dollars a week including her rent. Janine had over three hundred and eighty dollars, enough to last seven or eight weeks, even if she didn't find a job.

She drifted off to sleep in this room of her own.

Janine didn't get a job for almost a month. The first few weeks in Mrs. Nanji's, she slept eighteen, nineteen hours a day. She would lose herself in sleep, in its deep narcotic peace. Wrapped in the cocoon of the bedclothes, she would be borne along into a soothing enveloping tranquility, and then, if she was lucky, nothingness. Only with a determined effort could she wrench herself awake. In those first waking moments, she would luxuriate in the comfort and calm of her bed, until the awareness of where she was and why overtook her, casting a pall of fear and pain.

She only had the horrible dream—Spencer Lyle hacking at Susie, the knife mutilating her body—twice, and both times she woke up gasping and in tears. Then, she would lie very still, stifling her sobs in the pillow, so that her cries would not carry downstairs.

Weeks went by before Janine began to leave her room for more than the minutes it took to pick up something to eat. She would meander around the Rice University campus, drawn to the familiarity and routines of college life. One afternoon she spent in the library, perusing old magazines from the 1930s and 1940s, just as she had done at Colgate in her last months there. Back then, school had represented drudgery and the frittering away of life, and the irony was not lost on her that a campus had now become her refuge.

One morning, waking early, at nine o'clock, rather than at her customary one or two in the afternoon, Janine left Mrs. Nanji's and spent the entire day looking for a job. The following day she did the same. At first, she was battered with hopelessness, as one after another store owner and restaurant manager told her that no jobs were available, but after a while just the task of trying to find work became curiously soothing. She had an occupation, even if it was only the search for a job. Order was being imposed on the anarchy of her life. Her life was continuing on.

On the fourth day of her search, she found a job. In her first interview of the morning, Janine was momentarily taken aback when the manager of a Mexican restaurant said, "Well, as a matter of fact, we are hiring. You've had waitressing experience?"

"Yes, lots."

"Okay, I'll give you a try tomorrow during lunch. If it works out, we'll set up a schedule for you."

The next day, Janine managed to keep her thumb out of the soup, she didn't spill enchiladas into anyone's lap, and probably what was most important of all, the manager approved of how her legs looked in the short skirt all the waitresses—there were no waiters—had to wear. As Janine was counting her tips—she had made two weeks' rent—the manager came up to her.

"So, how many shifts would you like to work?"

"How many do you have?"

That turned out to be every day but Mondays. Whenever any of the other waitresses, most of whom were students at Rice or the University of Houston, wanted to take off, Janine would work a double shift and fill in for them as well. Despite buying some new clothes, shoes, a purse, a wallet, and a cheap suitcase, the cache of ten- and twenty-dollar bills in her dresser drawer continued to grow. She went to the pawnshop and redeemed her diamond engagement ring. Though Willy was in her thoughts as she slipped it back onto her finger, Janine also wanted the security of having this nest egg worth hundreds of dollars always on her, something to fall back on should she have to flee again.

On Mondays, her one day off, she would sleep for fifteen, sixteen, seventeen hours. Then she would go to the library at Rice University and read magazines, or take long, rambling, exhausting walks. A few times, she spent the afternoon at the movies, but only when convinced that something completely innocuous was playing, a picture with no violence, no romance, no sex, no love.

Though some of the other waitresses at first asked Janine to join them after work when they went out to bars, or shopping, or dancing, Janine always declined and the invitations soon stopped. Once, the restaurant manager intimated that he might like to take Janine out for dinner, but he quickly retreated, stammering, when he saw the look of agitation and panic on her face.

She worked long hours, she ate, she slept. A bizarre existence, a limbo. Just as accident victims or people drowning were said to feel removed from what was happening to them, so Janine felt as if she were not quite living this life, but was disengaged from it somehow.

Though Janine knew that a problem would eventually arise from her made-up social security number, as at the Dairy Queen, nothing had happened yet. She continued through her motions of delivering hot plates crammed with rice, beans, burritos, tostadas.

At her weakest moments, when she didn't think she could keep on, she would call Teddy from a pay phone, her purse heavy with coins. Hearing his voice filled her with both happiness and such feelings of loss that she never was able to get through their conversation without crying. It was during one of these phone calls that she let slip where she was living.

"Houston?" Teddy mused aloud. "Dennis McFadden lives in Houston. He's getting his Master's at Rice."

Dennis McFadden was two years older than Janine and had gone to Beacon High. They had been in Glee Club together. He would recognize her in an instant, should he come into the restaurant or catch sight of her on the campus. It was amazing that they had not already bumped into one another at the library, or at Rice, or during one of Janine's long walks.

Janine had raced back to her room from the pay phone, nervously scanning the street for any sign of Dennis McFadden. The next day, whenever the restaurant's door opened, Janine anxiously spun around and stared at whoever strolled in. At the end of her shift, as she approached a table with bowls of salsa, she saw a rear view of the same tight curly hair, the exact stocky, broad-shouldered slouch, the familiar big ears of Dennis McFadden. Just as she was about to make her escape through the kitchen, the man turned to her. Janine gasped, and the startled man who was not Dennis McFadden asked for a glass of water.

She forced herself to work the rest of that day and the next, which was payday. When she received her check, she told the manager she would not be back.

Janine returned to her room at Mrs. Nanji's and slept the better part of three days. Then she packed her cheap new suitcase and left.

From Houston she went to Fort Worth where she worked at the counter of a doughnut shop. She drifted aimlessly through small towns in Texas and Oklahoma, and then made her way to Albuquerque. In Tucson, she nearly ran out of money, and one desperate night stood outside a bar featuring topless dancers—Twenty Pretty Girls and One Ugly One—holding a want ad that promised earnings of seven hundred dollars a week, but did not enter. Instead, she had managed to land a job working in the greenhouse of a nursery.

The jobs she found never seemed to last. Constantly, she worried about her made-up social security numbers. Temporary filing jobs turned out to be just that. The doughnut shop was frequented by cops during Janine's graveyard shift, and every time she had seen a blue uniform coming up to the counter, every time a policeman had tried to strike up a conversation with her, or flirtingly told her they would see her the next day, she had wanted to run away. After three weeks, she quit.

The Immigration and Naturalization Service had raided the plant nursery near Tucson. The agents had glanced at her fair blond features and had raced around her trying to cut off the escape of the Mexican workers. She had picked up her purse and walked away.

Finally, she had arrived in Los Angeles and had become Alison Lunsgaard. She first lived near Hollywood, but was filled with apprehension whenever she left her studio apartment. Hollywood Boulevard was filled with tourists. Any one of those people wearing souvenir sweatshirts from Disneyland or Universal Studios might be from Beacon. Any one of those cute, young women who posted their eight-by-ten glossies on the walls of the coffee shop where she worked might have been in Mr. Richler's drama class at Beacon High. She moved to a building in Echo Park with barred windows and security doors and quit waitressing. Nearby was the huge temple built by Aimee Semple McPherson, another woman who had disappeared.

Though she had thought of Los Angeles as just another stop on her flight, she stayed. She circumscribed her life to the narrow parameters of work and wherever she happened to live at the moment. She moved often. Something was always wrong with where she lived. The building was too small; the neighborhood was too fashionable; a man who looked just like Spencer Lyle from a distance lived in the next block; the superintendent was creepy and she was positive he had gone through her apartment while she was away.

In crowds, Janine often was frightened that someone from her past would spot her. In her seven years of living in Los Angeles, she had never gone to the beach. Nor had she ever been to a museum, concert, or shopping mall.

So even though people from her past might be drawn to this large city in which she lived, her existence had become so narrow, so far removed from the fashionable, or even the ordinary, so divorced from what others thought of as Californian—the beaches, Hollywood and Beverly Hills and the West Side, the entertainment and aerospace industries, other people—it was as if she was living in the most remote of regions.

THREE

At Mrs. Anglim's, Janine and the musicians unloaded the cube van and carried the furniture around the main house, down a winding brick path to the guest house. As she came back for yet another load, she overheard the musicians talking in the rear of the truck.

"So Blondie has just got this little twin bed."

"And it looks like she hasn't taken the training wheels off it yet. Shoot, that thing would only be good for limbering-up exercises. Not the full-fledged nasty."

"Well, get your ass over here and help me with it."

"That little love cloud, you can handle it yourself."

"I got something here for you to handle."

A moment later, the musicians bounded out of the truck, carrying the mattress. As they headed toward the house, one of them said. "The love cloud, floating along toward the love palace."

Janine did not have sex for almost three years.

Though more lonely than she had ever been those first few years, Janine did not seek out companionship. She kept to herself, and when co-workers or neighbors made overtures of friendship, she quietly rebuffed them.

When she had been in Los Angeles for a year, Teddy came out to see her, the first of what was to become annual visits. He brought with him a cashier's check for eighty-three thousand dollars.

"What's this?" Janine had exclaimed.

"That's the money from my trust fund. It's yours, now."

"I can't take this."

"Look at the way you're living. This place is a dump. What do you earn, four dollars an hour? What if you lose your job? Janine, I'm afraid for you. If you won't come back, then at least the money will help."

"But, it's your money. Daddy gave it to you."

"He gave it to both of us. This is just a loan. You can repay me in two years, when you get your own inheritance."

"I'm not going back. I won't be able to claim it."

"Then, I'll inherit your share. It's part of Dad's will."

"I can't take all your money."

"You don't have a choice. Either you take it, or I'm calling Mom and telling her everything."

That was the only disagreement they had. Teddy's visit was a week's respite from the bleak existence her life had become. Being called by her real name, talking for hours, going to movies, laughing, eating a meal with someone else, underscored how far she had really fled. When it was time for him to leave, the loneliness she felt was overpowering. She drove him to the airport, then stood in the terminal watching the lights of his airplane growing fainter and fainter until they disappeared.

From the airport, she drove aimlessly. She couldn't bear to go home to her empty apartment yet. Finally in West Hollywood, before heading home, she stopped at a market. Coming out of the store and putting the groceries into the trunk of her car, she observed three couples about her age ambling down the sidewalk. They were laughing; one of the women had her arm around her boyfriend. They had probably been to a party, or a play, or a concert, or perhaps they had just come from a long leisurely meal. Janine could picture them passing forks containing bites of their appetizers across the table to one another and drinking a little too much wine. It was Saturday night, she suddenly realized, date night. She felt cheated out of all the simple pleasures that others took for granted.

The group of friends headed down the sidewalk and went into a bar called the Raincheck Room. Music from a jukebox and the noise of a crowd echoed across the night, then died as the door closed. Janine slammed shut the trunk of her car, and instead of driving away, she found herself following those happy people.

It was smoky and crowded inside. Janine sat at the bar and ordered a white wine. Two men beside her were ridiculing all the commercial hoopla involved in the Bicentennial celebration. The stool on her other side was empty, but not for long. A man with meticulously groomed,

272

fleshy good looks sat down beside her and immediately started his campaign to pick her up.

No, Janine told him, she wasn't ready for another drink yet; no, she had never been in this place before; no, she didn't want to take a stroll outside and smoke a joint; no, she wasn't an actress. After a few minutes, she excused herself and went into a side room with three pinball machines.

The group of people she had followed into the bar surrounded two of the games. A man in his late twenties with thinning brown hair stood intently over the third machine. Janine watched the ball ricochetting and the lights flashing for a moment, then put her quarter on the glass top. When his ball had finished, he glanced up at Janine, and a disconcerted look crossed the bland round features of his face. He was intimidated by her and by her looks; it had happened to her before.

He tilted on the last ball, then stepped back to let her play and nearly knocked over the waitress.

"I didn't mean to drive you away," Janine remarked. "We can both play."

He nodded in confusion, and his hand shook when he inserted his quarter into the slot.

By their third game, he had calmed down slightly. His name was Ross, and he was a substitute teacher. After his initial nervousness, he played single-mindedly and took a comical pride in beating her in the second game. He was aware of his absurdity, however.

"You'll have to excuse me for getting carried away. But, you have to understand, pinball is the biggest thing in my life."

She had another glass of wine. It was the first time since leaving Chrisbo's house that she had allowed herself to drink, and the wine made her light-headed. When they left the game room for the bar and he offered to buy her a drink, she switched to Scotch, her hazy reasoning being that since she didn't like the taste of it, she would just nurse the drink for the rest of the night. A quarter hour later, however, she paid for another Scotch for herself and a beer for Ross.

He made her laugh. He would recount incidents in his life that cast him in an embarrassing, unflattering light, stories which invariably ended with him getting beat up, or shoved naked out of the boy's locker room, or told what a douchebag he was by just about every woman he ever met. For all his anecdotes, though, he kept trying to find out about Janine. What did she do? Where did she live? Was it possible that she didn't have a boyfriend?

When he asked where she originally came from, Janine said, "Are you familiar with upstate New York?" and felt a dangerous thrill.

"No, not really."

"Well, I'm from a small town you never heard of. Actually, it's not a town, it's the smallest city in New York State."

"What's the name of it?"

"Beacon." She could feel her heart pound as she said the forbidden word.

"I never heard of it."

"Not too many people have."

What had possessed her to tell him, she wondered? She felt an unsettling desire to say, "My name isn't really Alison. It's Janine Smith." But then he started to tell her about the time he was in a disco with his cousin, and earlier, getting ready for his big night out, he had put handfuls of baby powder all over his body, and he was ashamed to say, especially around his crotch, and then he had gone to the men's room and forgot to pull up his zipper, and when he came out of the men's room, little white clouds of powder had puffed from his crotch with every step as he walked across the deserted dance floor.

Before she knew it, a bright light went on. It was last call. They left the bar.

Outside on the sidewalk, Janine noticed that she was a bit unsteady on her feet. "I can't drive home. I'm too high." She stared up the street. "You see a cab anywhere?"

Though she knew that taxis didn't really cruise the streets looking for fares in Los Angeles as they did elsewhere, she gazed up and down Santa Monica Boulevard for a few minutes. Finally, she said, "I'll just go back inside and call a cab."

"This isn't a proposition, but I live two blocks away. You could stay over until you're sober."

She thought of her cold, empty apartment. "Okay."

They started down the sidewalk. At the corner, she stood and waited for the crosswalk light to flash green before crossing the street, even though no other cars were in sight. Ross thought this compliance was a charming quirk of her personality. She didn't tell him that she never jaywalked, or littered, or drove over the speed limit, or did anything at all that might bring her—a fraud—to the attention of the police.

Ross's apartment was sparsely furnished. An unframed, slick-paper poster of Big Sur was scotch-taped to the wall. At least it wasn't a model in a bikini holding a power drill, or a football player, she mused.

Nervously, he began to take sheets from a closet. "You can sleep on the couch, or I'll sleep out here and you can have the bedroom. Or we can both sleep in the bedroom."

Janine nodded, then walked into the bedroom, unbuttoning her blouse as she went. She kicked off her shoes, wriggled out of her jeans, and got into bed in her underwear.

The lights went out in the living room, and she heard Ross tossing on the couch. Relieved and a bit disappointed, she lay in bed. She wasn't sure what she wanted to happen.

Janine had developed a way to help herself fall asleep. She imagined it was raining, the wind howling, and she was caught out in the storm. Then she always saw herself coming in from the gale, wrapping herself dry in a huge towel, and bundling up in a warm comfortable bed. At home. Not the house she grew up in on West Willow Street, but rather the apartment that she and Willy had fixed up right before she left. Janine could picture the large mattress on the floor, the little lamp with a rosy shade, the—

Footsteps came from the living room, and Ross stood in the doorway. He was wearing just white briefs and looked faintly ridiculous. "This is strange, and I don't want to alarm you," he stammered. "But when we went to bed, it was sort of unresolved. I mean, did you want me to come in here with you, or do you just want to sleep? Am I supposed to . . . well not supposed to . . . but should I make a pass? This is really confusing. And I don't want to pressure you."

Janine looked at the anxious figure in the doorway, then pulled back the bed covers. She could never return to Willy. "You can sleep with me if you like."

Ross smiled shyly and said, "That's what women find irresistible in me. My savoir faire. My self-assured confidence."

The sex was awful. Ross was nervous, jerky, unsure of himself. And she was just as bad. Her body refused to respond in any way to him. Janine could tell he wanted her to guide him through this . . . procedure. When it was over in a few minutes, Janine felt only sadness.

Hoping that he wouldn't sense how wretched the experience had been for her, and suspecting he was probably even more disappointed and depressed, she snuggled up to him and laid her head on his bony chest. He would try to be amusing now, Janine thought, and she told herself to laugh at whatever he said.

"It's usually about this time that most of the women I've been with have thrown up."

Janine laughed.

He continued to talk for a while, then, thankfully, he fell asleep. She lay awake in bed for the next four hours, getting up once and going into the bathroom to cry.

At daybreak, she eased out of bed and started to dress. Ross stirred and awoke. He propped himself up and watched, enthralled, as she slipped into her underwear, then he made a show of giving himself a pinch. "God, I still can't believe it. I can't believe you're here. This had to be the most amazing night of my life."

That it might be true depressed Janine even further. She smiled, and said, "I have to be going. I have to be at work in a little while." The lie seemed even more obvious to her since it was Sunday morning.

He watched her dress in rapt admiration. "I don't know if you're exactly thrilled with the prospect, but I'd love to see you again."

She nodded stupidly, searching for the right thing to say. Ross smiled sheepishly and raced from the bed to the dresser. His body seemed even scrawnier in the daylight. He was scribbling his name and number on a piece of paper.

"Here, if you ever get bored, or want to play pinball, or play anything, give me a call."

From his expression, Janine could tell that he knew she wouldn't phone.

Ross offered to walk her to her car, but she declined rather too quickly, so he went with her to the front door, and standing naked in the hallway, kissed her good-bye.

A month later, she made herself go to another bar and pick up another man. It was even worse than her night with Ross, who at least had been nice, and amusing in his insecure way, and quickly satisfied. The man she met the second night was good-looking, smart, and, unfortunately, considered himself a consummate lover. She had had to endure his sexual ministrations, his earnest attention to every little part of her for what seemed like hours. He made it clear that something was obviously wrong with her the next dawn as she left. Janine had to agree with him.

After that, she remained celibate.

The musicians thanked her for the money, then made their way back up the path and disappeared. As Janine was unloading a box of kitchen utensils, Mrs. Anglim knocked on the open door, holding a potted lily as a housewarming present.

"I just wanted to give you this and welcome you."

Such a long time had elapsed since someone other than Teddy had given her a gift. "It's beautiful. Thank you so much."

"I hope you're going to enjoy living here."

"I really think I will."

When she was finished unpacking, she sat in the sunny living room. At her other apartments, she had kept the blinds drawn most of the time, hiding herself, in her paranoia, from prying eyes. Gazing out the

French doors past a small brick patio, she could see a garden splashed with color. Perhaps she would buy a table and chair for outside. She could picture herself eating breakfast, drinking coffee out there in the morning, listening to the birds, the sun warming her. Perhaps there was a way to begin life again.

A month later, Janine was sitting on the patio, eating breakfast at her new wicker table when the phone rang. It was a collect call from Teddy Smith, the operator said. Janine was not alarmed; she had instructed Teddy to call collect or from a pay phone, so no record of his calls would be on his telephone bill.

"I'm coming out to visit you."

"When?"

"This Friday."

Janine had not heard the despair in his voice. "You are absolutely going to love my new place." She was giddy with excitement.

When Teddy came shuffling out of the landing gate at the Pan Am terminal, however, Janine wanted to scream in rage and grief. The moment she saw him, the horrifying words, *acute myelocytic leukemia*, thrust themselves back into the deepest part of her and crushed her.

FOUR

JANINE OPENED THE FREEZER door and grabbed the ice cube tray. Just enough ice remained to fill the glass. Near the tray was some frozen salmon. She had gone to a good fish market to buy the salmon; it was one of Teddy's favorites. But he had had no appetite for the fish or any food, and so finally she was forced to put it in the freezer, along with all the other delicacies she had planned to cook with him.

The kitchen in Mrs. Anglim's guest house was small and galleylike, but fully equipped. Janine had imagined herself in here with Teddy, preparing complicated, delicious meals. Teddy had become a surprisingly good chef, especially considering he had never been made to do anything in the kitchen when they were growing up. On his earlier visits, they would spend countless hours shopping for fresh ingredients, cooking, and then lingering over lobster ravioli, or grilled rosemary chicken, or bouillabaisse. Teddy's stays were the only time she took such interest in how she ate; it was the only time she shared her meals with someone else.

On this last visit, Teddy had not been able to eat anything beyond morsels of the blandest food. He was often sick. Janine had envisioned both of them sitting on the patio of the little house, but Teddy was always cold, even with the two sweaters he wore in the eighty-degree July heat.

She did not find out about Teddy's death until three days after he died. After his visit that they both knew would be his last, Janine would call him every few days at home or on the private phone in his hospital room. Twice, Teddy had answered and said, "I'm sorry, you have a wrong number," which meant that someone else was with him. They would only talk for a few minutes, but Janine could sense the course of Teddy's disease from their conversations. The last few times, Teddy had been heavily sedated, and she could barely understand him. Then there was no word of him. No one answered Teddy's home phone. Finally, using a low raspy voice, and prepared to hang up if she recognized the name or voice of the other person on the line, Janine dared to call the Patient Information operator at Highland Hospital. The operator, a woman with a New York City accent, told Janine that Teddy had been discharged. It was this same operator who, one week later, said, "I'm sorry, but Mr. Smith died at home a few days ago."

She had not been with Teddy when he needed her most.

Janine poured some tea over the ice and cut a lemon—the first of the season—from the tree in Mrs. Anglim's backyard that would bear fruit all winter long.

Teddy was her brother, he had been in her life from the very moment she was born, and when he was sick, when he was dying, she had not helped or comforted him.

He had died one Tuesday morning, and Janine did not know it. Unaware, she had gone to work as on any other day. That night, as he lay in his coffin, she had eaten a sandwich and watched the news on television.

Janine made herself think of something else. Gazing out the French doors, she saw pink, purple, and white impatiens in Mrs. Anglim's garden. She sipped her iced tea and tried to make her mind a blank. Lying down on the couch, she hoped sleep would come.

Just as she was drifting off, someone rapped on the front door.

Willy scanned up and down the directory in the apartment building's vestibule. Alison Lunsgaard was not listed, but several of the door buzzers had blanks where the names should be. Perhaps she lived in one of those apartments. Willy pushed the button labeled SUPER, then opened the security door when he heard the blaring noise.

A concrete courtyard and a pool lay before him. The Super's apartment was around the corner from the lobby. A matronly woman wearing a purple sweatsuit was waiting at the open screen door. "Hi, can I help you?"

"I'm looking for Alison Lunsgaard. Does she still live here?"

"No, she doesn't. She moved a few months ago."

Though Willy had expected as much, still he was disappointed. "Do you know where she moved?"

"No, I don't. She didn't leave a forwarding address."

"Would any of her neighbors know?"

"I couldn't tell you, and I can't have you disturbing people."

Willy nodded. He momentarily thought of offering this woman a twenty-dollar bill, as in a private eye movie, but instead thanked her and left.

Outside the building, he leaned against his illegally-parked rental car. Towering palm trees and apartment buildings lined the street. He had come this far; he would find Alison Lunsgaard. If necessary, he would hire a detective to track her down. And then . . . probably a mystified woman would answer her front door and tell Willy that sure she knew Teddy Smith, they had dated in college.

Willy wondered yet again if he had lost his mind.

Less than twenty-four hours ago, Willy had driven into New York City to the Public Library. He had waited in line at the reference desk for the *Polk* Directories for Los Angeles County, certain that this lunatic expedition and all his preposterous hopes would be in vain. Then he saw the telephone number on the page, and beside it the name and address of Alison Lunsgaard.

From a pay phone in the library, he called Directory Assistance for Los Angeles and discovered that no Alison Lunsgaard was listed. He dialed the old number again to make sure it was still disconnected. Then he phoned American Airlines and booked a seat on the next available flight to L.A., which was seven o'clock the next morning.

Although Karen's apartment was only blocks away, he decided to get a room at a motel in Queens near the airport. He would feel strange spending the night with Karen when . . . Willy forced himself to continue the thought. When he would be seeing Janine soon. It was insane, this hope, insane and pitiful. He had contrived this fantasy because Teddy Smith had made a phone call and taken a trip? It's pathetic, Willy thought. Janine was dead. Why was he not able to accept that?

Willy had gone directly from the library to the motel, where he spent a fitful night, then had flown thousands of miles to arrive in Los Angeles with just his demented hopes. He had rented a car and managed to wend his way though the confusing grid of freeways and streets to the pink stucco apartment building that now stood before him.

Surely, Willy thought, he should be able to find where Alison Luns-gaard currently lived without going to the extreme of hiring a detective. Where would be the most obvious place to find a new address?

At the post office three blocks from the pink stucco apartment building, Willy found out Alison Lunsgaard's forwarding address. He had to go through a charade of making out a postcard to her old place, then the postal clerk *sold* him the new address for a dollar. It seemed absurd, but there on the card was a street name and a number.

For two hours, Willy drove around getting hopelessly lost. Finally, he honked at a taxi waiting at a red light and made a deal with the startled cabby to pay for the fare—twenty dollars up front—if he would let Willy follow him in his rental car to the address.

Halfway up a narrow canyon road, the taxi pulled over. The cab driver pointed at a house hidden behind foliage, then turned his taxi around and drove away.

Birds were chirping and the air was still. It was as if he were in the country, not a major city. Beacon seemed less rustic. Willy walked up the driveway and the brick path to the front door of the house. He could feel his heart pounding as he rang the bell.

The front door opened the few inches that a security chain allowed, and instead of Janine's radiant face, Willy saw a small elegant old woman peering out at him.

Willy wanted to laugh; he deserved the bitter disappointment he felt. It is all so pointless, he thought. He had been such an utter fool, pinning his hopes, his whole being, on this quest, wasting his money on the motel room in Queens last night, and the plane ticket, and the rental car, and strangely, what galled most of all, his dementedly optimistic dollar at the post office and the twenty dollars to the cabbie.

"I'm sorry to disturb you. I was looking for Alison Lunsgaard."

The old woman stared curiously, then said, "Alison lives in the back."

His emotions soared again with a heady and absurd optimism.

"Just go down and around the house. You'll see it. It's the guest house."

Willy marched down the walk, hope mixing with self-ridicule. No doubt this was just an ironic little pause, he thought. The gods would be laughing at him when he spoke with Alison and she turned out to be even older than the woman in the house.

He went up to the door of the guest house and knocked.

Janine opened the door, and there in front of her stood Willy. Dazed, incredulous joy crossed his face. But he must have seen something in her expression, because his joy gave way to bewilderment, confusion, and anguish.

"Janine?"

She saw him start to reach out for her, then stop himself. That Willy was uncertain, that he sought some sort of permission from her, that he was afraid she would not want his touch broke her heart. She wanted to hold him, to tell him so much, but instead she stepped back to allow him to come into the room. "Yes, it's really me."

The door opened and he saw Janine. Though he had been yearning for this day for so long, the sight of her stunned him.

Then he saw fear in her eyes. And something else. Shame? How could she not feel as ecstatic as he did?

"Janine?"

She did not cry out in happiness or rush to him. Her hair was cut short, blunt; she was still so beautiful. And she was watching him warily, and in pain. He wanted to reach out and caress her face, but couldn't.

"Yes, it's really me."

Willy entered the guest house, dazed. "Are you in any danger?" he asked, though he knew the answer.

Janine closed her eyes and shook her head as a tear escaped down her cheek.

Amber light of late afternoon softened the room and gave it a prettiness that seemed to mock Willy. No one was lurking in the shadows. Janine was not in dire straits. She was living her life in comfort without him.

Against reason, Willy had clung to the hope that Janine might still be alive, but he had never allowed himself to consider beyond that. Just as he had not be able to accept that she might be dead, so too had he been unable to acknowledge the implications of her being alive. Teddy had known about it: he had called her on the phone and visited. But Janine had kept herself from Willy.

He contemplated the tears on Janine's cheeks. His one last hope lay in those tears. Willy thought of all the miles he had traveled, the years he had spent looking for her. He would have done anything to find her, and now she was just five feet away. Willy stepped toward Janine. Slowly, tentatively, he reached out. If she should draw back, his world would end. He could feel the softness of her cheek and the wetness of her tears. Their bodies came together, Janine's face buried into his neck, and then came the great release as her arms encircled him. They clung to one another.

* * *

Later, Willy asked, "Why?"

Janine sat in a window seat and stared at him with ineffable grief. Then she told Willy what had happened in New Orleans all those years ago.

PART EIGHT

1973

ONE

On their way back to the apartment, Janine, Susie, and Spencer smoked a joint. Though Mardi Gras was officially supposed to end at midnight, which was just a half hour away, the streets of the Quarter were still crowded and rowdy.

Spencer was between Susie and Janine as they shuffled up the sidewalk, passing the joint back and forth. The grass got Janine very stoned, and for a few moments she wondered if it was just marijuana in the joint, or if there wasn't some other drug as well. She felt great, though, so what did it matter? The fiery tip of the joint illuminated Spencer's face; he was absolutely beautiful. Taking the joint, Susie cupped his hand in both of hers and leaned into him. Susie was going to spend the night with him, Janine thought. He was so incredibly sexy, who could blame her? Still, Janine felt a twinge of jealousy, which she tried to repress. Smiling, Spencer passed the joint to Janine, and his teeth against his tanned flawless skin seemed luminous, they were so white. Taking the joint back, he held her arm steady and Janine felt stirred by his touch.

They came to Susie's building. Climbing the stairs to the apartment, Janine saw Spencer's hand rest lightly on Susie's shoulder. As they rose, his hand slowly descended down her back to her ass. Susie smiled sexily. They both looked so erotic to Janine: Susie so voluptuous in the clinging costume, and Spencer, tall, handsome, sensual. In just a little while, Janine thought, the two of them would be in bed together.

Susie unlocked the door and entered the apartment. With a courtly manner, Spencer stood aside and ushered Janine into the apartment, his hand at her arm. She shivered, startled at how excited his touch made her.

As Susie rattled around in the kitchen, Janine sat down on the couch. Ambling around the room, Spencer picked up picture frames, books. Then he went to the couch and sat a space away from Janine. He turned to her and said, "Make yourself at home. Is there anything I can get you?"

Carrying three bottles of beer, Susie came in from the kitchen. With a nudge of her knee, she scooted Spencer over on the couch so that he was seated between them. She knelt beside him, her legs curled beneath her, and when she handed them both a beer, Janine saw Susie's breast rub against his arm.

"It's Mardi Gras," Susie said softly.

They talked for a few moments. Janine noticed that Susie was still pressed against Spencer. Momentarily, she thought to excuse herself so that they could be alone, but, where would she go? Her bed was on this couch, and certainly if they wanted to go into the bedroom, no one was stopping them. And there was something else. She wanted to stay here with Spencer. And with Susie.

Susie's fingers were making little circles in Spencer's hair. He closed his eyes, like a cat being petted. Glancing past him, Susie looked at Janine, and with her gaze never leaving Janine's face, she kissed Spencer. He barely smiled, then he too turned and looked intently at Janine. His hand slowly came up and lightly caressed Janine's cheek.

She could feel her heart racing. Overwhelming desire mingled with fear. The back of Spencer's hand slowly stroked her breast, and Janine heard herself give a longing sigh. But then he turned back to Susie and kissed her. It was as though something had been wrenched from Janine. She saw Susie straddle across Spencer's lap and gather his head to her bosom. Then as one they turned toward Janine. Susie smiled gently and said again, "It's Mardi Gras."

Tentatively, Susie leaned toward Janine. Susie's lips came to hers, and they kissed. It seemed so familiar, so erotic, yet so foreign as well. She was startled and made afraid at her body's fervid response. They kissed again, and she felt Spencer's lips on the back of her neck. Something inside her seemed to melt. Then they were all on the floor. Hands—whose?—were touching her everywhere, and she just let everything go.

Afterward, Spencer got up and strutted into the bathroom. In bed, Janine and Susie heard the sound of running water from the shower.

Janine gazed upward and saw the blush on the cheek of one of the plaster cherubs on the ceiling—the memento of a previous night's passion. She wondered if her life had changed irrevocably.

"Had you ever thought what it might be like to sleep with me?" Susie asked.

"I once had a dream involving you," Janine ventured. "It was . . . erotic. And confusing."

"And now you're really confused, aren't you?"

Janine nodded.

"You look like you're about to cry." Susie leaned over on her side, and gently stroked Janine's hair. "This was just a fling for you. Don't beat yourself up. These are confusing times. You've just had your obligatory affair with another woman. This isn't what you're about, but even if it is, what's so wrong about it?"

"I'm supposed to get married in a month. And I've just cheated on Willy with not one but two different people. And one of them is another woman." Janine thought about Willy and their upcoming marriage. Could she still marry him after what she had done? "Maybe I should beat myself up."

"What about? Giving yourself and other people pleasure?" Susie stroked Janine's hair again. "Supposedly, there are real old laws still on Louisiana's law books stating you can't get a divorce for anything you've done on Mardi Gras day. It may be apocryphal, but it's not a bad idea.

"Just tell yourself that you've done what people have always done at Carnival. You've given into pleasure. It's a pagan ritual. You're allowed to do things you would never in a million years do otherwise."

Janine nodded uncertainly. She absently noted that the shower's water had stopped.

Susie said, "Cheer up." She hugged Janine, and the unaccustomed feel of Susie's naked body next to her own was both a comfort and a dilemma.

The bathroom door opened, and Spencer came back into the bedroom. He regarded Susie embracing Janine and seemed hostile, resentful. "I'm not interrupting anything, am I?"

He was wearing Susie's foulard-print robe. As he approached the bed, he untied the silk belt and let the robe fall open in the front. Grabbing the back of Janine's head, he drew her toward him and said, "Get me hard."

The brutality, the naked hostility of his words appalled and shocked Janine. Despite herself, she thought, "Willy would never do anything so mean, or so rough," and then she felt profound shame. Not wanting to, she began to comply.

Susie must have sensed Janine's discomfort, because she said to Spencer, "Play nice," then gently moved Janine aside and pulled him onto the bed. The robe came off, and Janine saw Susie take the belt, circle it around the back of his neck, and draw him toward her.

But something had changed. His manner was different, disturbing. Spencer took hold of one end of the silk belt and looped it around Susie's neck. He kissed her throat just below where the belt dug into her flesh, and said, "Have you ever been tied up?"

"Yes, I have."

They studied one another; both seemed to be challenging the other to go further. Susie said, "You can tie me up, if you let me tie you up afterward." Spencer gave a taunting smile and nodded.

"There are some scarves in the top dresser drawer."

Spencer strode to the dresser. When he returned to the bed, he began to flutter the silky scarves on the inside of Susie's legs. Janine saw Susie shiver as the silky material lightly flicked up her body and then her arm until it reached her wrist which lay beside the rung of the brass headboard. He cinched her wrist to the rung with a complicated knot, then handed the other scarf to Janine.

Janine had become increasingly uneasy as she watched Spencer tie the knot. When he gave her the other scarf, she had nearly refused it. The sudden, scary change that had occurred troubled her. She didn't want to go along with what was happening, but the expression on Susie's face stopped any protests. It was a look of unabashed arousal. Janine tied Susie's other wrist to the headboard.

Spencer turned to Janine and kissed her, and then drew them both down toward Susie. He guided Janine's lips to Susie's breast, and thrust himself between Susie's legs. Taking hold of the two ends of the silk belt that encircled Susie's neck, he slowly began to pull. Panic flashed on Susie's face, and Spencer stopped the pressure. He gave her an inquisitive glance.

Susie hesitated, then turned to Janine. Fear had given way to excitement. She appeared to be seeking assurance, or some sort of consent to go ahead. "I can trust you," she said to Janine. "You hold one end."

Spencer took one end of the long silk belt, brought it through the rungs of the headboard with a fetishistic precision, and wrapped it around Janine's hand several times. He bound the other end to his own hand in the same manner. Then he pulled.

The pressure on the belt increased, and she almost let go, but Susie called out, "Tighter." Janine pulled on the belt.

Everything constricted in Janine's mind and centered on the tension she applied to the belt. Sensations collided within her: shame, dread, concern, feelings of debasement, and though she hated herself for it, arousal. Later, she would not know how long she held the belt—seconds, minutes?

Susie's face glistened with sweat, and then it began to turn red. Her back arched in response to Spencer's movements, and her body slowly crept up the bed, pulled by the force of the belt and driven forward by Spencer's thrusts, until her head rested between two of the wide rungs of the headboard. She let out a little moan, which alarmed Janine, but then she repeated hoarsely, "Tighter!"

Janine felt the belt tighten on Spencer's end. She couldn't bring herself to increase her pressure, but she did not let up. For a long time, it was as though she was withdrawn from everything that was happening in this room, but then a sickening fear enveloped her. She did not want any of this to continue. She turned to look at Spencer. Surely, he too must be afraid; surely, he too would want to stop. But his face was rapt, and he seemed oblivious to everything except his own pleasure. Then, Janine saw his arm. The muscles bulged; his hand, its circulation cut off, was nearly purple from the exertion of pulling.

She let go of her end of the belt and yelled, "No!"

Though she no longer pulled on the belt, the pressure did not subside. Because of the loop around Susie's neck, Spencer's grip was enough to choke her. Janine yelled again and grabbed at Spencer's arm. He stared at her, uncomprehending and then infuriated—but he rolled off of Susie.

A wave of relief came over Janine. Everything had seemed to go out of control. Susie wouldn't mind that Janine had made them stop. But then Janine noticed that Susie had not moved. "Susie?"

Something was horribly wrong. Susie was motionless; her face was a terrifying blue, her eyes stared vacantly. Janine set to the belt which dug deep into Susie's neck. Though neither one of them held the belt, it was wrapped on itself and was still taut.

"Oh my God!"

Janine clawed at the noose around Susie's neck. Spencer stirred, then pushed Janine away so roughly that she crashed off the bed onto the floor. Pulling Susie's head free of the headboard, he unwound the belt.

"She's not breathing," he cried out, stunned and terrified. Panicking, he slapped at Susie's face and pushed down on her chest in an attempt to revive her. He tried to give mouth-to-mouth resuscitation, though he didn't appear to know how. A moment later, he put his head to her chest. "Her heart's not beating."

Janine shook her head violently. This could not be happening. Susie had to be alive; there had to be some mistake. In shock, she watched as he pushed down on Susie's chest again in a futile attempt to get her heart to beat. Janine rushed to the bed and as Spencer desperately continued his efforts, she put her mouth to Susie's. The inert, lifeless touch of Susie's flesh filled her with disgust and terror, but she exhaled deeply, trying to blow life into Susie's lungs.

It was too late.

Nothing seemed real. When she tried to talk, she couldn't quite connect to the meaning of the words. She heard Spencer say, "We've got to call someone. An ambulance. Or the police." So Janine got up from the floor by the bed where she had sunk, dazed, and went to the phone although it was far too late for medical help, or for help of any kind. Dialing the operator, she noticed her nakedness, and that filled her with a sense of shame that she realized was bizarre, absurd. Before the operator could come on the line, Spencer hurried over and pushed down on the cradle to disconnect the call. "Wait a minute. Let's think this out," he ranted.

She didn't understand his actions, or his anger, but handed him the receiver acceptingly. What seemed most important now was to cover herself. That they were both still naked was appalling to her. Janine began to put on the clothes she had worn that day. "What are we going to do?" she heard Spencer say.

Janine looked down at Susie's body, and unaccountably, anger flared up inside her. Why had Susie gone along? She had told Janine that she trusted her, but she had also said, "Tighter." Susie was to blame. And Spencer, it had been his idea. Janine turned from the body, craving flight, escape, but where could she run? The police would come; everyone would find out. How could she tell Willy, and her mother? She thought of her dead father. He would have been shocked, disgusted, and ashamed of her.

"Man, we got to do something," Spencer said. He paced the room, angrily staring at Susie's body, then at Janine. "We've got to make it look like an accident or something. Or let's just get rid of her. We don't know anything about her."

Suddenly, a way out of this nightmare, a way to be rid of this great darkness flashed in her mind. Innumerable times over the next ten years, she would wonder what had caused her to think of this repulsive, horrific escape, but she would always have the knowledge that it had been her idea, and no one else's. She said, "We'll say someone else did it. Out in the bayou. They'll blame it on the killer of the other woman."

"What the hell are you talking about?"

"A woman was found murdered. In the bayou. We read about it this morning in the paper."

A glimmering of hope mingled with the panic on Spencer's face. "Where's the paper?"

With Spencer following behind, Janine dashed into the living room and ripped through the newspaper. She saw the story with its headlines of barhopping and the map of nightclubs. "See. She had been at a lot of bars. So was Susie."

Spencer took the *Times-Picayune*. Janine marveled that he was capable of reading, that the words would make sense. Susie was in the other room, dead. It was not possible. His eyes darted up from the paper, then he read the story again.

"Jesus, she was even strangled," Spencer said. "You could report her missing tomorrow. You could tell the police that she left with some guy and that you came back here alone. No, with me. But Susie wasn't here with us. And you don't know my name. I'll disappear."

An image of Willy came to her mind, unbidden. "But you didn't spend the night."

They went over the story Janine would tell. Susie had met someone at Linny's. But Janine had barely spoken to him, she was too engrossed in dancing and talking with Spencer. All she knew about Spencer was his first name, not his last. They had all left together, but outside the club, Susie and this stranger had decided to keep on partying. Spencer and Janine had gone back to the apartment.

"But we didn't have sex," Janine said.

"Okay, but I stayed about an hour or two and we talked."

"And Susie never came back here."

"No . . . How would you have gotten into the apartment? Do you have a key?"

"Yes, Susie gave me an extra set."

"The police should never be able to track me down. But if they do, we're going to have to tell the same story."

Janine nodded. Everything was happening too quickly and in a surreal way. It wasn't possible that they were having this discussion.

"What did the guy look like?" Spencer asked.

"He was tall?"

"We've got to be able to agree on this, in case I'm ever questioned." He sat pensively, then said, "Think of someone famous when you give the description. They may even have an artist make up a sketch. That way, if I'm ever asked, I can give the exact same description."

"Who?"

As Spencer pondered the question, Janine suggested, "Bruce Dern?"

"No. He always plays psychos . . . Elliott Gould, you know who he is? The guy in M*A*S*H?"

"With or without his mustache? Sometimes he has a beard."

"Exactly like he looked in M*A*S*H. Bushy hair, a Fu Manchu mustache."

It was mind-boggling. They were talking about movie stars. Typecasting. Hairstyles. They had just killed Susie Conover, and they were discussing M*A*S*H.

Spencer read the story in the newspaper again, then got up and went into the kitchen. Janine saw him opening drawers frantically, but then he stopped in midmotion. On a countertop by the stove was a block knife rack. Spencer withdrew a chef's knife with a long blade. Janine gasped and shook her head.

"The paper said she had been stabbed," Spencer replied to her unspoken objection.

As in a dream, Janine followed Spencer back into the bedroom. Susie was still on the bed, her eyes staring vacantly, her face a lifeless grimace. The silk belt was still draped loosely around her neck. Janine turned away and was about to flee from the room when Spencer grabbed her arm and propelled her forward.

"We've got to do this."

Janine couldn't breathe, then she thought she might be sick. Spencer took her face in his hand. "Don't freak out on me. She's dead. What happens now doesn't make any difference to her."

He waved the sheet that lay bundled by Susie's feet and it softly spread on the floor beside the bed. Then seizing an arm and a leg, Spencer yanked Susie's body from the bed onto the sheet and wrapped it around her like a shroud.

"Get me the car keys."

Janine ran from the bedroom, from the grisly sight of what they had done. Susie's keys were on a table beside her purse. "I've got them," Janine called out. She did not want to go back into the bedroom ever again.

Spencer came into the living room. "Where's the car?"

Susie parked her car in the courtyard of a slave quarter house, a half block away. Spencer swung open the gate and went inside. Alone on the sidewalk, Janine heard the engine start. She fought off an urge to run away—far away—and never return. The car backed out of the courtyard, and Janine thought, "He'll never be able to catch me if I just run now." Then she got into the Pinto after she reclosed the gate.

Spencer parked by a fire hydrant in front of the apartment. No lights were on in any of the nearby buildings. As Spencer unlocked the door to the apartment, Janine again felt an urge to flee. She hesitated in the threshold until Spencer shoved her inside. He had to grab her hand and force her into the bedroom as well.

Janine stood by the door as Spencer went to the body. "Take her feet," he called, but Janine could only stand and watch in horror. She began to cry soundlessly. He flashed a look of anger and disgust, then bent down and began to struggle with the body. On his second try, and after screaming at Janine, he was able to hoist the shrouded corpse over his shoulder.

"Go down and open the trunk of the car. Tell me when it's safe to carry her out," Spencer panted.

Janine stood frozen by the bedroom door.

"Do it!" screamed Spencer. Janine hurried to obey.

The street was still deserted. Janine could barely see through her tears to put the key in the trunk's lock. At last, the latch sprang open. She thought about getting into the car and simply driving away. Instead, she scanned the street once more, then went to the front door. Spencer was standing in the dark hallway, the ghastly load over his shoulder.

"I don't see anyone."

Spencer tottered from the doorway to the car. With a grunt, he bent over and eased Susie's body into the trunk. The sheeted body disappeared as he slammed the trunk down.

Back in the apartment, they began to clean up. Spencer would order her to change the sheets, or wipe down the floor, and Janine at first was affronted that he would order her about so, but her absurd outrage was immediately replaced with revulsion and shock. Susie was dead, Janine was responsible for her death. What did anything else matter?

Wearing rubber cleaning gloves, Spencer wiped down everything in the apartment. Janine heard him mutter to himself, "Was I in the kitchen?" and moments later, he was rubbing at the refrigerator and cabinet doors with his cloth. As they left the spotless apartment an hour later, Janine toted her own purse as well as Susie's, and Spencer carried a grocery bag containing the costume Susie had worn, a sheet and pillow cases that had been on the bed, and the eight-inch Henckels chef knife.

Though illegally parked, the car had not been ticketed. Spencer opened the car door for Janine and glared threateningly until she got in.

He checked the trunk to be sure it was locked before getting behind the wheel. They drove off.

Neither one of them knew their way around New Orleans, but after a while, they found themselves heading away from the city. A few stragglers from the day's festivities could occasionally be seen lurching down the shadowy sidewalks. Janine was assaulted by varying, often contradictory, emotions—numbness, shock, hysteria, calm, rage. Constant was the feeling of unreality, as though she was in a nightmare. Driving past a major street, she spied a man in a ghoulish, disarrayed costume coming out of darkened doorway like a hellish jack-in-the-box.

Near the outskirts of the city, Spencer hit the steering wheel with his fist, furious. "Shit. The gas tank's on empty. We're going to have to stop and fill up." He spat out the words as though it were Janine's fault.

That he could be angry, or feel any emotion about something so inconsequential astounded Janine. An empty gas tank? They were in a nightmare. Susie was dead. And in the trunk of the car. This was incomprehensible.

Janine barely took notice as Spencer steered into a sprawling gas station that was bathed in a ghostly white light. The car stopped at one of the islands, and a tall man came to Spencer's window.

"Fill it up," she heard Spencer say, as if from afar.

"Regular?" the man asked.

Spencer nodded, and the man hurried to the pump. Light shone though the wispy outline of his large Afro, giving it the appearance of an aura. He hooked up the nozzle to the gas tank, then rushed to another car on the opposite side of the island. Janine watched his actions, but they all appeared so irrational. Susie Conover was in the trunk of the car; this man had been just inches away from her body. She was dead.

The gas station attendant returned to the back of the Pinto. A few more cents rolled on the dial of the pump. Janine could hear the man replacing the gas cap.

Spencer was searching through his wallet. "All I have are fifties and hundreds. Shit." He glanced at her and said, "Do you have any money?"

The attendant's midsection came into view at Spencer's side window as Janine took the wallet from her purse.

"Five dollars and forty cents," the man called out.

Only three one-dollar bills were left in Janine's wallet—her traveler's checks were in the suitcase back at the apartment. She took out her credit card and handed it past Spencer to the man. She saw his large hand take the card, then he raced to a stand on the cement island.

"Are you out of your fucking mind?" Spencer hissed when the attendant was out of range. His face clouded over with barely suppressed rage.

Janine had had enough. She turned and opened the door latch.

Spencer reached over quickly and closed the door. With a quick, short jab, he punched her cheek. Janine was shocked—she had never been struck by a man in her life—and then terrified. With his face inches from hers, he whispered, "Act right, or I'm going to hurt you."

The gas station attendant came back and handed a clipboard with the credit card and slip to Spencer, who passed it to Janine with a steely glare. Then Spencer faced forward and stared out the windshield.

Janine took the pen from the clipboard and momentarily thought of stabbing it into the vein she saw throbbing in Spencer's neck. Instead, with a shaking hand, she scrawled her name on the credit card receipt. Again, she considered opening the car door and just walking away, but she handed the clipboard back to Spencer. As the gas station attendant raced to the cashier, Spencer started the car.

He drove in silence for a few moments, then said, "Why do you think I didn't want to use a fifty-dollar bill? Because, that asshole back there might remember it. So what do you do? You use a fucking credit card. You know there's going to be an investigation. How are you going to explain that you bought gas for your friend's car when she was already dead?" He glared at her. "You stupid twat. If your friend was supposed to be kidnapped out to the bayou, what are you doing along for the ride? Buying gas for the killer?"

Miles down the road, when the lights of the city had given way to the misty dark of the bayou, Spencer murmured to himself, "They're going to trace that credit card."

They drove into the darkness. After a while, Spencer suddenly stamped on the brakes, and the car screeched to a stop. He backed the Pinto on the deserted highway, then turned onto the barely discernible dirt road which he had driven past. The Pinto bumped down the dirt road for a quarter mile and stopped. Spencer climbed out of the car, turned to Janine, and stared at her until she got out.

The low constant din of insects, birds, small animals—chaotic and primeval—resounded in the thick damp air. Spencer went to the back of the Pinto, and Janine heard the trunk being opened.

"Give me a hand."

Janine could not bring herself to look toward the rear of the car.

"Get back here!" Spencer ordered angrily.

"This is a mistake. We can't go through with it."

Spencer glowered, slowly walking toward her. Janine backed away, but he grabbed her hair and dragged her toward the trunk of the car. Janine could hear herself screaming, then she saw Susie's shrouded body.

"This was your idea. You're in this as much as me." He let go of her hair. "Now give me a fucking hand."

"I can't do this. I—" Janine felt a stinging sensation, her head snapped to the side, and she realized that he had just slapped her.

"Take her feet," Spencer demanded. Janine bent over and took hold of the sheet that wrapped Susie.

As they lifted, Susie's body twisted out of the sheet and toppled, her face banging into the hard-packed dirt road with a dull thud. She lay there twisted, one arm pinned beneath her body and her buttocks jutting upward. Her position appeared so indecently vulnerable that Janine started to take the sheet and cover Susie, but Spencer snatched hold of the corpse's shoulders and dragged it twenty yards through the mud to the edge of the water. He untied the silk belt from her neck.

Clambering back up onto the dirt road, Spencer took the sheet from Janine's hand. He placed it and the belt in the trunk of the Pinto, where he retrieved the knife taken from Susie's kitchen.

Everything seemed far away, and she thought she would faint.

"Oh my God, no!" Janine uttered, just before Spencer without saying a word grabbed her hair again and yanked her back to the body. The shadowy, primordial bayou swung wildly in her vision. Falling off balance, she landed on top of Susie's corpse. Janine screamed and scrambled away from the body.

Spencer knelt beside Susie and tentatively raised the knife. "No," Janine yelled, "We can't do this."

Spencer stared at Janine with a sickened, fearful expression. He tried to stab down at Susie's corpse, but seemingly could not bring himself to do it.

"No! Let's bring her back. It's not to late. It was an accident. We can't do this."

Spencer turned to Janine, furious. "This was your fucking idea. It wasn't mine. She's dead. It doesn't matter to her anymore what we do." He rushed to where Janine lay. She tried to flee, but Spencer grabbed her hair once again and dragged Janine back to Susie's body.

Janine was crying uncontrollably. Susie's lifeless body, with its hideous spread position and distorted face, was inches from her. And then she saw the glinting knife approach, and she tried to run, but Spencer clamped his hand over hers. He forced Janine's hand to join with his other hand, so that they both grasped the hilt of the knife.

"This was your idea," he said.

She felt her hand raise. In a sickening second, their hands and the knife plunged downward into Susie's flesh. And again. A gash was cut open on Susie's chest, and blood slowly seeped from it. Spencer let go of the knife.

Janine held the knife in her hand. She momentarily thought of slashing at Spencer with it. A drop of Susie's blood dropped from the blade and splattered on the bare skin of Janine's leg.

"Stab her," Spencer said in a low voice.

She wanted to throw the knife far into the swamp. And she wanted to run to a place where neither Spencer nor anyone else could ever find her.

"You killed her," Spencer said in an unemotional tone, "You've already stabbed her. You have to do it. We're both in this."

"No."

"She's dead. That isn't her anymore."

Janine shook her head.

"Do it."

Janine lifted the knife. She just wanted everything to end. In one sudden burst, she plunged the knife into Susie. The blade hit bone, then sank deep into the flesh. Janine gagged, but withdrew the knife. It made a sucking sound. Dropping it, she crawled away from the body.

For a long time, Spencer studied Janine. Then, he went over to Susie. He picked up the knife and jabbed it with a fury into Susie's torso. The blade cut again.

"Stop it! Stop it!" Janine screamed. She looked for something to throw at Spencer, a stone, a branch, anything to make him stop. Her hand filled with earth, dried leaves, grass, and she threw it all toward Spencer, but everything scattered in the air and fluttered impotently to the ground yards short of him.

Spencer stabbed Susie repeatedly, the knife hacking away flesh. She could hear the gruesome sucking sound as the knife withdrew. Blood oozed onto the lifeless chest. Susie's body seemed animated by the force of the blows, but the grotesque expression on her face—ugly and unnatural—remained constant. Janine's screams, surrogates for Susie's own, pierced the night.

Still, Spencer hacked away. With revulsion, Janine saw that one of Susie's breast had been nearly sliced away. Nausea swept over her. "Stop it!"

Then he stopped. Spencer stared at Janine listlessly.

"I'm telling," Janine heard herself say. The words had come from somewhere in her distant past and sounded childish, bratty, and so inappropriate. *I'm telling.* It's what one said about a broken vase, or stolen candy. Not about this . . . evil.

"It was your idea, remember?" Spencer yelled. "You killed her. And you stabbed her, too."

All Janine could do was shake her head.

"You will go to the police, won't you? And even if you don't, they'll find out about that fucking credit card."

Spencer stood up. He still held the knife. Then he rushed toward her.

Janine sprang to her feet. The knife seemed to loom gigantically in her vision and she thought he was going to kill her too. Screaming, she put her hand up to ward off the inevitable blow and felt the knife cut into the meaty part of her palm. Before he could stab her again, she jabbed her finger into his eye and ran into the darkness of the bayou.

Hours later, she was in Chrisbo Gavry's car, speeding away from the horror, and traveling into a different life.

PART NINE

1983

ONE

As JANINE SPOKE OF Susie Conover's death and all that had happened in the ten ensuing years, long shadows filled the room and gave way to twilight. Neither she nor Willy turned on the lamp. When Willy, hurt and confused, asked, Janine tried to explain why she had fled.

What she had done was unforgivable, Janine said. How could she face Willy? How could she tell Susie's parents or Amanda? The image of her dead father had haunted her. He would have been so ashamed of her, crushed. By disappearing, couldn't she shield his memory? Couldn't she stop the ghoulish stories in the tabloids and the scandal? And she had been terrified of Spencer Lyle, convinced that if she did come forward, he would try to kill her again.

"It was nothing I thought out. If Chrisbo had not come along when he did, if vanishing had not fallen into place so easily, I might have turned myself in. But . . ." Janine glared at him. "Susie died because of me. She died! Willy, can you begin to imagine what that means?"

Janine was responsible for Susie's death, the squalid, obscene way it had happened and the abominable, evil details of the cover-up. In her cowardice and panic, she had thrown her friend's body into a fetid ditch, had desecrated her corpse.

Later, when Teddy had tried to convince Janine to return, he argued that she was not guilty of murder, as she had initially thought; her crime had been involuntary manslaughter, and quite possibly not even that. But Teddy had not been there on that monstrous night. Janine knew what she was guilty of, it didn't matter what the legal definition.

As they sat across from each other in the dusk, Willy listened to Janine, heard the pain, self-loathing, and disgust. He wanted to hold her in his arms and comfort her. Yet, he also felt such rage that he was afraid to be near her.

At last, Janine finished her story and fell silent. Willy had an impulse to scream that she had devastated ten years of their lives, that she had needlessly caused him such suffering, that she had betrayed and cheated and lied and destroyed. She was a murderer, a slut; she had killed her best friend, she had fucked other people. Why?

Yet, he also wanted to cry. He wanted to bury his face in her bosom and just let all the pain be released—but most of all, he felt an urge to hold her.

Just the sight of Janine startled him. She was really alive. It was astounding that she was here with him. Then the fear that she might disappear again, this time forever, swept over him.

Not trusting himself to say anything else, and knowing that of all of his thoughts, this was the truest, Willy said, "I love you."

Janine heard Willy say that he loved her. While she had told her story, she had seen the resentment, the torment, the humiliation, the abject loss and pain in his eyes. How could he possibly still love her?

"You hate me as well, don't you? For what I did to you, and us."

"You could have come to me," Willy tried to keep the recrimination from his voice and failed. "Why did you leave me?"

"I couldn't . . . face you. . . . I didn't leave you, Willy, I left myself, my life."

Willy was looking at her expectantly. She knew what he wanted her to say. She couldn't say it.

Willy stayed the night. He and Janine lay in the narrow twin bed, fully clothed. Neither one of them dared do more than just hold one another, terrified that their connection was as fragile and breakable as their embrace, and afraid of the irrevocable disasters that might befall them if they did more. Yet Willy permitted himself hope, and Janine gave herself up to a forgetfulness that allowed her to feel comfort at his touch. The few hours of sleep they managed was light, interrupted by the slightest shift or movement, and when either would awaken in the night, they would seek out reassurance in the sound of breathing or in the feel of the other's warmth.

In the morning, Janine asked Willy to leave. She saw the aggrieved, perplexed hurt in his eyes, like that of a child who has been unjustly punished. Janine started to say she needed more time, but the words sounded hollow even to her. Hadn't she just had ten years to herself?

"I have to sort everything out."

"Janine, how can I just leave? How can I pretend you don't exist?"

"Haven't you been listening to me? I'm not the person you used to know."

At first Willy tried to convince Janine she was wrong. "We can still have a life together. We were meant to have a life together." He soon fell into a helpless silence, as he saw her withdraw. Instinctively, he knew his argument would not touch her despair and guilt.

"What are you going to do about me?" Janine asked.

Willy wondered if he should go to Amanda and tell her that Janine was alive. Should he go to the police as well and tell them everything? It would bring an end to this nightmare. Perhaps, deep down, Janine hoped he would so that she could finally stop living her shadowy existence and resume her life, but he said, "I'll do whatever you want me to."

She looked at him in anguish and murmured, "I have to decide this. Alone."

Her words were like a blow. He stood. "The last ten years of my life were not a mistake. I'll do anything for you. And I'll do anything so that we can live our lives together. But I can't make you forgive yourself, and I can't make you love me."

Dumbfounded at what he was doing, Willy went to the French doors.

"Don't send me away. Tell me to stay."

Janine shook her head and said, "I can't." She saw him flinch.

"I'll wait for you until you tell me not to," Willy said, and then he went out the doors and disappeared.

TWO

When Emil wheeled himself to the front door and saw Willy Buchanan standing on the porch, he knew. Something in Willy's expression told him much more than Willy ever would himself. Emil almost said, "You've found her," but instead invited Willy into the house.

"Thanks for dropping by." Emil had called Willy earlier in the morning and asked him to come to the house.

Willy entered the living room and glanced at "All My Children" on the television with mild curiosity. Embarrassed at having this guilty pleasure found out, Emil turned off the soap opera.

Sitting down on the couch, he stared warily at Emil. Finally, Willy said, "What can I do for you?"

"I'm more interested in what I can do for you."

Willy remained silent.

Emil said, "How was Los Angeles?"

Again there was a long pause. Willy showed no emotion. At last, he said, "What makes you think I was in Los Angeles?"

"I called American Airlines. You took Flight 241 to Los Angeles on November First. You returned to New York the next day."

American Airlines had been the third airline Emil had phoned. Willy's last, agitated visit had aroused Emil's curiosity. For days afterward, Emil had wondered if the unlisted Los Angeles phone number had anything to do with Janine's disappearance. He had unsuccessfully tried calling Willy at his apartment and at the house being renovated in Westchester County. On a hunch, claiming to be working on a case for the Beacon Police Department, he had tried the airlines and found out that Willy had indeed flown to Los Angeles. Had that unlisted phone number panned out?

"You said something about being of help?" Willy had neither given an explanation for why he had flown to L.A., nor denied it, nor taken offense that Emil had pried into his private affairs.

"The last time you were here, you asked me if I could separate myself from my duties as a police officer. I don't think I gave you a response then. Well, my answer is yes. I can put my responsibilities as a cop aside."

Willy shrugged noncommittally.

"When I was younger, I used to daydream about helping . . . people in trouble." Emil could never tell Willy his overblown melodramatic fantasies about saving Janine from danger. "When I became a cop, I thought that maybe my work would make a difference to . . . someone, anyone. That something I would do would transform another person's life for the better. Well, that never happened.

"When Janine disappeared, I was hoping that . . . ." Emil's voice trailed away. Finally, not meeting Willy's gaze, he added, "If there is anything I can do, it will just be between you and me."

As Willy studied Emil, he suddenly recalled what the detective in New Orleans had mentioned ten years ago. Huey Oliver had said, "I know that Emil feels a personal stake in this case, him and Janine being such close friends and all."

The four days since Willy had returned from seeing Janine had been unbearable. An oppressive grief engulfed him. Twice he had made plane reservations for flights to Los Angeles and twice had cancelled them. He knew that he could not force Janine to lay aside her shame, nor could he reason with her sorrow and repentance. He sensed that if he acted rashly, or even decisively, he might drive her away again, possibly forever. So, he had done nothing.

In those days, however, he had also desperately sought some other way that would allow them to be together. What if he sold everything and he too disappeared? Would she allow him to join her life then, if she knew her secrets would remain hidden? What if he found Spencer Lyle? Could he do something that would convince Janine that he was no longer a threat to her? But what would he do? Beat Spencer senseless? Put a gun to his head? Kill him? Or could he somehow learn something that might make a difference to Janine?

For four days he had done nothing, and he thought it had probably been the wisest course. Now, though, he considered Emil sitting in the wheelchair in front of him. Willy knew that he should just get up and leave Emil's house. Instead, he said, "There's someone I want you to track down. He may have a record. He's about six-two, has blue eyes, a scar on his chin, a tattoo of a star and a crescent moon on his arm. His name might be Spencer Lyle."

Emil tried not to let his excitement show. By the description, it was obvious for whom Willy was searching. Somehow Willy knew more about the suspect—the tattoo, the name. Emil was about to ask Willy all the questions that raced through his mind, but did not get a chance. For Willy stood up, and without saying another word, left.

The biggest difficulty Emil encountered in tracking down Spencer Lyle was having to hobble up the front steps of the Beacon Police Station on his crutches. He had waited two days until he knew that Sam Pittman would not be working, and that Lonnie Kroll would be filling in for him. Lonnie's greeting had been as sincerely hearty as it was gauche: "Emil, it's good to see you. It's too bad about you being crippled. How are you feeling?"

"I'm getting by."

"Just couldn't stay away, huh?"

"No, I was getting a little buggy just watching TV all day. I got to thinking that I might go over some old unsolved cases. It would give me something to do."

Emil had prepared a lie about wanting to check on a two-year-old drugstore break-in, but Lonnie just shrugged. "Sure, no problem."

Lonnie had gone back into his cubicle after chatting a few minutes, and Emil had gone into the computer room. He patched into the FBI-maintained National Crime Information Computer, requesting a suspect search for a male Caucasian with the description Willy had given and the possible name Spencer Lyle. Within two hours, the search had produced the name of Justin Spencer Skiles.

Emil handed Willy the jacket containing Justin Spencer Skiles's criminal file. "Here's who you were looking for. You had everything but the name, and that was one of his aliases. Justin Spencer Skiles. Six foot two. Blue eyes, scar on chin. Tattoo of crescent moon and star on upper right arm—that, and the AKA, were the last pieces of the puzzle that helped make the computer match. He was arrested in 1976 and then in 1977 for assault and battery on his wife, but both charges were later dropped. In 1978, he got popped for selling five kilos of marijuana to an undercover cop in Aspen, Colorado. He must have copped a plea, because he only did two and a half years. Two years ago, he was shot and killed in a hotel room in Laredo, Texas, an apparent drug deal gone bad."

Willy leafed through the file. A handsome face with a scar above its chin stared up from a mug shot. This man had tied a belt around Susie Conover's neck, had plunged a knife furiously into her chest. He had punched Janine, dragged her around by the hair, tried to kill her. Ten years ago, in Susie's bedroom, he had let his hand run down Janine's body and . . .

Willy quickly turned to the next page in the file and saw a copy of Justin Spencer Skiles's fingerprint card. Attached to the card with scotch tape was a blow-up of another fingerprint. Willy looked at Emil inquisitively.

"That's the latent print that was found in the trunk of Susie Conover's car. I'm not an expert, but if you look at the print of Skiles's left index finger and that latent, you'll see it's a match. This is the guy we were looking for."

Willy nodded. He had known that Emil would figure out who Spencer Lyle was.

Emil shrugged. "I hope it's of use." Though he had performed no valiant deed, he wondered if he had at last been of help to Janine.

"So do I," replied Willy.

Willy picked up the phone and dialed. When Skiles had been killed, the next-of-kin notified had been his ex-wife, Carole Urbaniak, of Houston, Texas. The phone number next to her name in the case file was probably no longer in service; still what did he have to lose? A woman's voice answered after three rings. "Hello."

"May I speak to Carole Urbaniak, please."

"I'm Carole."

Willy had been expecting all sorts of obstacles to tracking down Skile's ex-wife—the number had been disconnected, Carole Urbaniak had moved—and he was taken aback that it had been this easy. "Hello. My name is Willy Buchanan. I'm calling about your former husband, Justin Spencer Skiles."

There was a pause, then Willy heard, "I'm sorry, but Spencer died a few years ago."

"I know. I'd like to talk with you about him."

"Yeah, well, what do you want to know?"

"This is a bit delicate. Maybe it would be better if I met with you in person."

"Something delicate involving Spencer? That's a good one. Listen, whatever you're going to ask, you can ask over the phone. I probably won't answer your questions, anyhow."

"Ten years ago, did you have short black hair with bangs?"

"Who is this?"

"Willy Buchanan. You don't know me. I was once engaged to a woman named Janine Smith."

There was a longer pause.

"Maybe, it would be better if I flew down and saw you in person," Willy finally said.

"Fly down? Where are you calling from?"

"New York."

"And you want to fly down to Houston to talk to me about my hairstyle?"

"Among other things."

After a few moments, Carole Urbaniak asked, "How much does a round-trip plane ticket cost from New York?"

"I don't know. Three hundred dollars? Four hundred? I can be in Houston tomorrow."

"That seems like a waste of money. You might come down here and I wouldn't be able to tell you anything."

"I'll take that chance."

"Yeah?"

"Yeah. I think if we met in person, I'd be able to convince you that you have nothing to fear from me. I'm not looking to cause trouble. I just want information."

Carole Urbaniak was quiet again. Willy said, "Just say that you'll meet with me. That's all I ask."

"The plane ticket costs three hundred dollars? I tell you what. I'll talk with you, as much as I can, anyway. If you like what you hear, send me the three hundred bucks."

"I'll send you a check today."

"Okay," she said. "In answer to your question, I had short black hair with bangs ten years ago."

"Maybe I can make this easier for you. I know a bit about you. I know that you and Spencer used Janine Smith's credit card all across the Southwest in 1973. You tried to buy some bracelets in Taos, and the store clerk confiscated the card."

"Yeah right. The card was in Janine Smith's name. I remember it."

Willy was amazed that this woman would admit committing a felony to a stranger over the phone. There was a statute of limitations for crimes. Was she exempt from prosecution because of the time elapsed, and if she were, would she be aware of that immunity? Then, Willy was surprised further when he heard Carole Urbaniak say, "I know a little about you, too. You're Willy. You wanted to buy a house and fix it up."

Willy wondered how she could possibly know anything about him. Then he had a vision of Janine and Spencer lying in bed, intimately talking about him. Had Janine lied about the extent of her involvement with Spencer? Was he more than just the terrifying stranger she had claimed? Then, Carole Urbaniak said, "I read the diary in Janine Smith's purse. She wrote about you. A lot."

"Yeah?" Willy just barely kept himself from asking for all the details.

"It sounded like she loved you. It also read like she was confused."

"Do you still have the diary?"

"No. We threw away the purse and wallet and everything after the credit card was taken," she said. "How did you find out Spencer's identity?"

"It's not really important."

"No, I guess not. Well you know he's dead. What more do you really have to know? Why are we having this conversation?"

"I'm not sure. For ten years, I've lived with this . . . uncertainty. It's time for everything just to end."

"Well for me, it all ended a long time ago."

"How much do you know about what happened in New Orleans?"

"About the woman dying? I probably know most of it—but, not at first. Spencer neglected to tell me what had happened until years later, after we were married, when he got really drunk one night. What happened in New Orleans had nothing to do with me. At the time I was scamming the card, I just thought it was stolen. We had run up stolen credit cards before, so it was no big deal."

"But why did he use the stolen credit card? If you were caught with it, wouldn't that link you to the death of Susie Conover?"

"You'd have to have known Spencer. He was a lot of things, but brilliant wasn't one of them. He was a criminal, a thief. He was always hustling, always looking for an angle. Spencer could be so charming he could get anything from you. But he did wind up in prison, didn't he? You know many guys like that who you'd call smart?

"Of course, he thought he was really wily. When he finally told me everything that had happened, years later, I started to scream at him. After all, he had gotten me involved in this murder, or accessory after the fact, or whatever it was. But he told me he had it finessed, that it was a no-lose situation. A no-lose situation! God! That was Spencer.

"When he was driving away from dumping the body, and getting rid of Janine Smith, he had her wallet and the credit card. He was going to use it for a day or two, then ditch it, figuring it would take that long for the card to make the hot sheet. You see, he assumed Janine Smith was going to go to the police. So he thought, 'Hell, if I'm going to be hanged for a penny, I might as well be hanged for a pound. What's a credit card beef if they get me for the death of the woman and dumping her body like that?'

"But then, when he got to Houston and dumped the car, he found out that the New Orleans woman had been reported missing, and that the police weren't aware she was dead."

"How did he know that?"

"He told me he went to the newsstand at the airport that carried newspapers from all over and picked up the New Orleans paper. After a few days, he saw a story about two women having disappeared. That was a green light to Spencer. An invitation to really run that card up."

"But wasn't he afraid that if he got caught with Janine's credit card, it would tie him to the killing, or at least he would be questioned about the disappearances?"

"Well, if you expected to be caught, you wouldn't use the card at all, would you? How were we going to get caught? We'd use it for a week or so and dump it. No one had reported it stolen, right? We scammed stolen cards all the time and never got caught. Spencer used to call them crime sprees, and we took them like other people took vacations. It was a lot easier back then, but it's not that hard to do even now. And besides, Spencer wasn't this criminal genius. I mean he certainly fucked up plenty, didn't he? Jesus, look how he died."

"Why did he go to New York and break into Janine's house?"

"Well, I guess he thought he could intimidate her, like an incentive to keep her mouth shut. He was sure that the family was shielding her, so that the police wouldn't find her. The break-in was supposed to convince her to stay hidden. It was another no-lose situation according to Spencer. He could break in, let her know that he was around, that he could testify against her just as easily as she could testify against him, and as a special added attraction, he'd steal all of her jewelry, because the family would be afraid to go to the police. He was such an asshole."

"The family did go to the police."

"Well, that's not a surprise. Most of Spencer's schemes blew up in his face."

"Wasn't trying to kill Janine enough intimidation?"

"Oh that . . . Spencer told me that he wasn't trying to kill her, he only wanted to scare her and that he cut her by accident."

"It was an accident?"

"So he said. But he once broke two of my ribs, and another time he knocked me out with a hammer and put me in the hospital. They were accidents too, according to Spencer."

Willy told her Janine's version of the attack in the bayou. Carole Urbaniak was quiet for a few moments, and when she replied her voice was tinged with sadness. "That sounds like it's closer to the truth."

Neither one of them spoke. Finally, Willy asked, "Do you still have short black hair?"

"No, it's long, and sort of auburn. I've gained some weight and probably don't look much like I did then. Why?"

"I was just wondering."

"You have anything else you want to know?"

"No, I guess not."

"So, you'll send the money?"

"Yeah, let me get your address."

Carole Urbaniak gave it to him, then added, "I know we agreed to three hundred dollars, but do you think you might make it four hundred instead? You did say that a plane ticket might cost that much."

"I'll make the check out for four hundred."

"Thanks. I wouldn't ask except I've had some tough times these last few years. You know how it can get."

"Yes," Willy said, "I do."

Willy gathered all the information about Justin Spencer Skiles and put it into a manila envelope, along with a short note: *I thought you would want to know. Maybe it will make a difference. I love you.*

From Beacon's slate-roofed, mortar and stone post office, he mailed the envelope addressed to Alison Lunsgaard in Los Angeles. By the time it reached California, Janine had already gone to the airport and taken a flight.

THREE

Driving into town again after ten years, the first thing Janine noticed was that the Casino was no longer atop Mount Beacon. She never did know why it was called the Casino. As far as she knew, gambling had never taken place in the large, stucco building that stood looking down on the city. Big band dances had been held there in the 1930s and 1940s, and she seemed to remember that Teddy may have gone to a rock and roll dance when he was around thirteen, but besides those few dances, she didn't think it had been used for any other purpose since she had been alive. The "World's Steepest Incline Railroad" which use to climb straight up Mount Beacon was also missing, the victim of a fire. Its tracks as well as the ski trails of a lodge that had gone out of business still scarred the face of the mountain.

Main Street was busy. Janine stopped at a red light and saw a bunch of teenagers hanging out in front of the Yankee Clipper diner. It seemed odd that she didn't recognize any of the kids. They were all strangers. The girls wore dungarees and high top sneakers and had elaborate hair. Two of the girls, probably best friends, had pierced their ears identically with six or seven studs arcing upward. A few of the boys proudly wore blue and gold Beacon High jackets with varsity letters, a style that had been hopelessly square and hokey in Janine's hippie high school days. Janine stared at the kids, trying to discover the youngest brother or the oldest daughter of someone she had gone to school with in their faces. One boy noticed Janine staring at them and returned her gaze with, she realized in surprise, one of sexual interest. The light turned green.

She drove by the Beacon Federal Bank where once on a hot summer's day, Willy had tossed aside his tools and had gone with her to Sylvan Lake. Further down Main Street, she and Teddy had once lain in the street at dawn, the only people in the world. Then closer to home, she passed the spot where Willy had asked her to marry him on a snowy Christmas night.

As she came to West Willow Street she slowed the car as if to park, but then forced herself to drive on. If she stopped now, she would never continue those few hundred yards to home.

The house she grew up in looked the same. She parked the car across the street and got out. It was then that she noticed the woman, partially hidden by the evergreen bush, raking leaves. It was her mother.

Janine stood, riveted by the sight of her mother, unable to move. Amanda shuffled backwards, raking leaves from under the bush into a larger pile. She had aged. The lines of her jaw had blurred, and the figure, of which she had been so proud, had softened.

Janine crossed the street. As she began to climb the slate steps to the front yard, her mother turned and gazed at her. A look of fright and shock crossed Amanda's face; Janine was afraid that she might faint, or worse. Just by being here, Janine thought, I can cause even more injury than I have already.

"Janine?"

"It's me, Mom. It's really me."

Janine stood on the last step, afraid to go further. She felt the tears on her cheek.

Amanda dropped the rake and rushed to her daughter. "Oh my God. Janine!" Janine saw the look of startled joy on her face and felt Amanda's arms wrap around her. "Janine."

She let herself drift in her mother's embrace. "I'm so sorry," she said, "I'm so sorry."

"Shh, shh, baby you're home." Amanda held her tight and stroked her hair. "You're home."